I0609008

The
Wild Ways
of Tim O'Reilly

(Second Edition)

a novel by
John Roland Hughes

Allswell Publishing Company
TACOMA, WASHINGTON

Cover design by Nikolett Mérész
Author's photo by Jared Retter

John Roland Hughes/ The Wild Ways of Tim O'Reilly—2nd edition
ISBN 978-0-9907357-2-4 Paperback
ISBN 978-0-9907357-3-1 Hardback

In memory of many excellent flying friends and acquaintances, of whom not all were as lucky as I

"Wild ways in the world our worthy knight rides . . . "

Sir Gawain and the Green Knight,
translated by Marie Borroff

1

MONEY HANDLES AND TRUE LOVE

He was flying high now. High in spirit, that is. Physically, however, he was right down where he had to be, a couple feet off the ground.

A rare, wide grin creased the young man's gaunt and darkly-stubbled cheeks. As seldom as such smiles had appeared for the past couple years, they had been lighting up that somber face much more often and much less tentatively since his recent escape. It was as if he'd just proved a great lie of the old saying, "You can't run away from your troubles."

Run he had, and at the end of this amazingly easy first day of his new life as a throttle jockey on the seasonal circuit, there seemed to be a promise of nothing but a whole lot more carefree running, completely free of all the hassles that had gotten him down so badly back home. But he had to knock off the daydreaming now and focus on his work.

He scanned the end of the field where he'd have to choose to fly under or over the power lines. He couldn't see any surprises in his way—no road sign, old fence post, or any other obstruction hiding in the weeds that could make a disaster of this fine first day.

Great as it's been, though, he reminded himself, daydreaming again despite his intention, *we're still way too slow.* That had been the only downer of the day. That and having to team spray in the first place. But seconds later, as his lead pilot's sprayer up ahead passed beneath the roadside electric wires and tipped into a low turn, Tim realized that he should actually be thankful for Dave's caution, and he thought, *A lot better than the opposite extreme.*

He reflexively ducked as he took his turn passing beneath the wires. He snapped the money handle shut, and he sneaked a look at the second hand of his wristwatch. Then he began to concentrate on carefully spacing his turn to match Dave's. It was crucial to keep just the right spacing between the two airplanes to avoid making a mess of the next formation turn at the other end of the field. He carefully regulated the banking of his plane accordingly.

Earlier, Tim had agonized that he'd be under so much pressure to hurry that he'd get rattled and make some crazy mistake, the worst of which would be to break an airplane. He'd heard plenty in flight school about how frantic some of these big surprise runs could be. "Plagues," one ancient storyteller who hung around the airport back in the Delta had called the worst ones, and this outbreak sure did have all the signs of being one of those.

The first sign of its severity had burst upon Tim barely twenty-four hours earlier when he'd been abruptly hustled out of that Mississippi flight school a week and a half before graduation and sent rushing north through the night. Catfish, the man who ran the school and tried to find all his graduates their first flying jobs, had told Tim that he had little left to learn that wouldn't come with actual work experience. He had made Tim accept a partial refund.

"Teacher's pet," Tim's fellow duster student and nemesis, Smartass Robinson, had sneered, acting like a little boy, and for the first time in weeks, Tim hadn't felt like popping him. For some unknown reason, the puke had singled out Tim as the primary target for his needling on the very first day of the program. After Robinson had kept at it for a few days, Tim, struggling to contain the hair-trigger temper that he'd been cursed with the past couple years, had silently nicknamed him "Smartass." It helped. It took some of the edge off his temper to be able to privately and somewhat humorously think such foolishness as, *There she spouts again; good old faithful Smartass Robinson.* But Tim was able to take Smartass's final dig with far more humor than usual. The dude had suddenly seemed so ridiculously juvenile that Tim had inadvertently laughed out loud and then had given him a truly friendly, light jab on the shoulder.

All that really mattered at that point was, wonder of wonders— even though Smartass and the others would have to wait—he, Tim, was heading out for the real thing. However, he wasn't completely happy about it. Happy enough to be giddy about it, but not completely happy. It made him nervous. He wasn't so sure that he really deserved so much of Catfish's confidence. He would have felt more comfortable hanging back to wait for the scheduled graduation date. Then he would have been off in mid-April to a seat somewhere for a calmer, regular wheat season. But it hadn't taken much for Catfish to overcome his protests, hustling him on his way, telling him, "Hurry, now. Man says he needs another pilot *yesterday.*"

So Tim hadn't even considered getting some sleep first. Besides, he was so wired about going down the road so soon and so nervous about whether or not he'd measure up that he wouldn't have been able to sleep anyway.

The second indication of the intensity of the situation up there in Oklahoma had come a couple hours after he'd arrived in the dark the next morning. He'd set the alarm for 4:45 before he'd gone to sleep in the Dog's front seat, but he'd been awakened a bit before 4:30 instead by the sounds of tires—numerous vehicles' tires—crunching across the icy gravel parking lot and the voices of men calling out to each other as they'd trooped into the office that ran down one side of Will Walker's huge metal hangar.

More powerful lights had flashed on to boost the illumination of the all-night security fixtures, brightly flooding the concrete apron immediately before the hangar bay and far across the parking and loading areas beyond that. Even as Tim, shivering with cold, had scrambled out of his old junker and headed for the office, other cars and pickups were arriving, and ground crews were sliding open the massive, screeching hangar doors so they could shove the planes outside.

Tim had entered the warm and noisy office to find the owner of the operation, Mr. Walker, talking animatedly to a man wearing a stockman's hat who looked like he was probably a farmer. Tim assumed it was Will Walker who stood within the office area enclosed by a long counter, since there was a plaque bearing that name on a large desk immediately behind him. He certainly was a distinguished-looking old gentleman, wearing khaki trousers, along with a brown wool vest over a crisp white long-sleeved shirt. The next desk past Mr. Walker's on the same side of the counter that divided most of the long room was vacant, but beyond that in front of a third desk stood a middle-aged man who was apparently briefing pilots and swampers for the day's work. Tim could see that the apparent scheduler on one side of the counter and a couple men on the other side were huddled over a large map. A dozen or so other men stood in a curved line behind those two. As Tim had waited to tell Mr. Walker that he was the guy Catfish had sent to help out, he'd overheard a couple boisterous men entering the office say that individual pilots and entire outfits were piling in from all over the Midwest to halt the devastation.

Later, adding to the tension out on the job whenever Tim and his lead pilot, Dave, were briefly on the ground to load up and, less often, to refuel, Tim would hear the nurse-rig truck's Citizens' Band radio blaring constant hurry-up chatter between home base at the municipal airport near town and the crews that were working off regular landing strips and improvised ones for many miles around.

It took only a couple minutes for Ken, the loader man, to fill each Pawnee's hopper full with 150 gallons of goop, and that didn't allow the older pilot time to climb out of his plane and get on the CB to yak about the latest change in the work schedule, but Ken would relay messages and hastily-scribbled field maps he'd made on yellow legal-tablet paper to Dave. Only during refueling would Dave and Tim get out of their airplanes, mainly to stand on their wing roots to jam a nozzle into the gas tank filler neck up toward the plane's nose and hand it back down as soon as it clicked off. However, "the old man," as Tim perceived Dave, would also hop down off the wing and step out of sight behind his Pawnee during each refueling to take a quick whiz.

The closest thing to a real rest break they'd had all day had been when they'd scarfed a couple sandwiches and gulped some coffee shortly after noon during one of those refueling pit stops. Since there were no radios in their planes, the two pilots had spoken little to each other since they'd left the muny just before dawn, but they started getting to know each other a little better as they sat out of the late-winter cold in the loader truck's cab and hurriedly ate while Ken did the refueling. There was no other warm place to duck into where they were. To avoid wasting time ferrying loads all the way from the municipal airport, most crews were using farm roads, farm landing strips, and pastures as close as possible to the fields they were spraying.

Adding to the pressure to hurry, they'd been flying since dawn in the increasingly dark and foreboding shadows of black-bellied clouds that now blotted out every trace of blue sky, validating the forecast of an approaching storm. Should that storm stall after it hit, rain or wind could shut them down for days. Yet, with Dave acting as a buffer against all that pressure to hurry, notwithstanding the talk Tim had heard about how wild "plague flying" could be, his first day as a paid pilot had actually turned out to be too easy.

He marveled at the irony of his earlier fear that he'd be pushed too hard for his limited experience. Despite the urgency, Dave was *still* going to what Tim considered ridiculous pains to keep a rookie pilot safe.

Come on, old man, Tim thought, as he had more than a few times already that afternoon, but wryly grinning about it now. He had timed the previous turn, and it had taken them 26 seconds from spray off to spray on. That would have been quick enough for a beginner if his sprayer had been heavily loaded, since the airspeed at which an airplane goes into an aerodynamic stall increases with increased weight, but the large hopper filling most of the space between the Pawnee's cockpit and the engine firewall was nearly empty now. Tim had told Dave during their very first pit stop in the morning and again at lunch that he'd be fine tightening up the turns, yet the veteran ag pilot had just smiled and drawled both times, as if he'd rehearsed it, "We gonna do it gradual, son. You take and bust your can, and we'll lose a whole bunch more time."

Dave had gone on to increase the pace through the turns so excruciatingly slowly that, from time to time, it had made Tim squirm in his seat and shout out loud in mock protest. Sometimes, mimicking Catfish's good-natured shouts back in the Delta about some excessively timid student's turns, Tim would holler, "Ain't nobody gonna make no money lollygaggin' way up yonder in the dadgum *sky*." But the truth was, the more he thought about it, Tim much preferred being held back rather than being pushed to the limits of his meager experience.

He'd started getting the feel of grossly-loaded airplanes a mere four and a half weeks earlier. That 1967-model Piper Pawnee's small inline motor put out only 235 horsepower, which isn't much for tugging along an airframe, a pilot, and more than a half-ton payload, all supported by nothing more substantial than mere air.

Tim was widely grinning again. Although it was very frustrating to have to dog it so, the pace had not only kept him from goofing but had given him time to keep his spacing from Dave exactly right and to fine-tune his spray pressure to the proverbial gnat's ass of precision. He was sure that he and Dave, notwithstanding their "lollygagging," had done some very nice, straight, evenly-distributed work.

They plowed on through another pair of restrained turns, and Tim once again had to pay closer attention to keep the spacing between the two planes just right, but once he was back down on the crop and could relax for a few seconds again, he began to wonder what might have happened if he'd been paired to fly doubles with some hotshot who had no concern at all for a beginner's limitations. Some highly experienced hotshot of a Smartass. Some puke who flew as hard as he could, slamming his plane through turns that matched the quickest of the other sprayers that Tim could see working nearby, even with a beginner floundering behind.

Tim thought he might have gotten so distracted flying with such a creep as to stupidly ram open the emergency dump handle instead of the money handle, which one student practicing with water had done back in Mississippi. Or, shame above all shames, he might have even stalled out trying to turn too tightly with a heavy load for his level of experience and destroyed an airplane. Better to die if that happened than live to bear the shame.

He then thought how he might have completely lost his cool flying doubles with some smartass like that and flipped into one of his rages. He'd gotten crazy enough over the past couple years that he could see himself leaping out of his Pawnee during reloading and lighting into the jerk physically. That sure wouldn't have produced a very good recommendation when it was time to head on down the road for the regular wheat season.

That temper of his was one of the main reasons he'd set out to fly the circuit in the first place. He hadn't always been so hot-tempered, and it had gotten so bad some months earlier that, along with some other problems, it finally caused him to bail out of college and flee LA, desperately hoping that repeated, radical changes of scene and activity would, as he put it, "help me get my head back together." If it hadn't been for the way he'd been freaking out, he might have been able to handle his two other big problems, which were the plummeting grades in his business classes and, even worse, being dumped by Jen. If it hadn't been for his temper, he might have managed to concentrate and get back to accomplishing what he'd set out to do originally. All his life, except for occasional kid fantasies about being a race car driver or a professional basketball player, he'd wanted only to get a degree in business and, like his dad, become a respectable Los Angeles businessman. He might have held on to Jen, too. Although they hadn't been formally engaged, they had begun to discuss whether they really wanted to wait until after they graduated. But those rages he'd fly into from time to time spooked not only Jen, who really hadn't seen the worst of them, but Tim, himself. Jen was concerned about them; he was hammered with fear and shame by them.

He'd come home from 'Nam with quite a chip on his shoulder, alright, and he still couldn't figure out why. According to his own opinion of himself, it couldn't be that he was suffering from "battle fatigue," which Jen had seemed to insinuate. *No O'Reilly would sink to that,* he believed. Three generations of O'Reillys had served in wars, and his paternal grandfather and father had done so heroically. They never made much of it, but Tim, when he'd been a boy, had sneaked long looks at the medals they'd tucked away under handkerchiefs and underwear and stuff in the top drawers of their dressers. Besides, if it was battle fatigue (as PTSD was known back in the 60s), surely he would have freaked worse in 'Nam, not afterward. That was his opinion, anyway.

It wasn't that he was all that ripped up emotionally toward any situation or any person in particular, either—not even the enemy, especially not the low-level "gooks" in the field, and not even the ones who had killed his good buddy, Smitty. Sure, there'd been something like rage right after Smitty got it and in some other fire-fights, but the latter had almost always been a state he'd been able to work himself into more or less intentionally. It was after he'd come home when he'd flipped so crazily out of control, so crazily it had made him wonder whether he was actually going insane, sliding into one of those late-onset psychoses he'd read about in his freshman Introduction to Psychology course before 'Nam.

Now, mental illness didn't seem like the remotest possibility. The first change of scene from LA to the Mississippi Delta and the intensity of flight school there, first for his commercial license and then to learn ag flying, had begun to work wonders almost immediately.

His temper was still something of a problem, he knew, courtesy of the fact that dear old Smartass's goading had clearly pushed him in the general direction of the edge, but he hadn't actually freaked out since way back in October, that time when he and his old pal since childhood, Nick, had ridden their motorcycles up the coast to the '68 Monterey Grand Prix and he'd gotten mixed up in this bizarre bout of road rage. He did continue all the way through flight school to have what he called his 'Nam-mares, but they were considerably fewer than they had been back home. The replays of Smitty getting it were as rough as ever, yet he could realistically hope now that he'd eventually get some relief from that, too.

Once again, he momentarily curbed his habitual daydreaming as Dave's Pawnee, a two-year-old 1967 model nearly indistinguishable from Tim's new-looking '65, once again raced up to the electric power lines and shot on through the narrow space between those wires and the gravel surface of the farm road. The low-winged, closed-cockpit sprayer reared its long, pointed nose as soon as it was out from under the wires and, for a couple seconds, climbed up the leg of an imaginary inclined "P" to the base of the P's big belly fifty feet off the ground. Then it tipped into the first part of an old-fashioned duster turnaround. After holding that first part of the turn several seconds, Dave rolled the Pawnee back the other way and came all the way around to level the wings and dive back down the straight back of the P's entire length.

At that point, the two planes were converging nearly head-on. Tim was still spraying across the wheat toward Dave as Dave descended toward Tim. Dave was aiming his left wingtip at Tim's left wingtip, using that image to accurately space the next spray swath.

Tim yanked shut the chromed money handle just above the throttle quadrant with his left hand, once again ducked his helmeted head as the power lines flicked by several feet overhead, then simultaneously nudged back the control stick with his right hand and firewalled the throttle handle with the left. He sharply banked out of Dave's way, completed his P-shaped turn-around, and dove back under the wires to shove the money handle open and follow the other Pawnee across the glossy dark-green field.

Tim chuckled as he happened to glimpse the airspeed pointer settling so predictably on exactly 100. He'd become so giddily lighthearted over how precisely he'd matched Dave's turn that it just seemed extraordinarily cool for a Pawnee to behave as if it had a mind of its own about how fast it would go in straight-and-level flight, which was precisely 100 miles an hour. There was no need for him to jockey the throttle to maintain his spacing behind Dave's predictably 100-mile-an-hour Pawnee. He only had to ease the control stick forward until he could feel the solid resistance of ground effect, that cushion of air made palpable when the wheels got down to a couple feet above the wheat, and sit back to relax for a few seconds until they got to the opposite end of the field.

He wished for a moment, as he had a number of times already, that he could be flying one of Mr. Walker's more powerful, open-cockpit Stearman biplanes. Nevertheless, the Pawnee was a pleasure to fly. It was a very efficient little moneymaker back in those days—way back in those ancient times when hippies still roamed the country—before bigger, faster, new sprayers displaced the little Pipers.

Soon, Tim and Dave made their last pair of passes lengthwise over the field. Each pilot swung to different ends of the field to make a couple cleanup passes alongside the power lines. Dave, being in the lead, made a loose, natural turn to line up on the south side, and Tim made a tight turn to make a couple passes alongside the road on the north.

Since he no longer needed to match his flying with Dave's, Tim made a nearly vertical pull-up at the end of the first pass and held the Pawnee's nose high until the plane slowed to the verge of an aerodynamic stall. When the plane began to tremble, signaling that it was about to quit flying and start behaving like any old hunk of heavier-than-air junk, he slackened back pressure on the stick, pressed forward one of the rudder pedals, and watched that long, pointed Piper Pawnee nose smoothly slice back down through the vague horizon between darkening earth and sky.

He rounded out just above the wheat and kept on shoving the stick forward until the wheels ticked through the tops of the wheat stalks, sending delightful little tremors up the quivering landing gear into the combined brake-and-rudder pedals beneath his big Redwing-booted feet. He and his fellow students of agricultural flying had been taught to wheel-mark bare dirt a few feet beyond the edge of a crop, so it wasn't such a radical departure from common practice that clipping the wheat seemed dangerous, but it was fun.

Just then, something bright flashed low across the dimming evening scene a couple miles to the north. Tim turned his head to catch sight of what looked like a silvery World War II fighter plane. It was hightailing it for some destination to the west, somewhere nearby to judge by its low altitude. That was mildly interesting, since he was curious to know just what kind of plane it was, but he got too busy to think any more about it.

Unlike those who claim to receive warnings from God or to have some other power to sense the future, Tim had no idea that the silvery non-sprayer he'd just seen was the first manifestation of a profoundly fateful convergence already in progress. He simply forgot about the sighting for the time being, began a steep pull-up at the edge of the field, and reached down to lock the fan brake to stop the pump that pressurized the spray system. He happily—innocently—scanned the rapidly darkening scene for Dave, whom he'd rejoin in formation for the flight in the dark back to the muny.

* * *

The silvery fighter-like North American AT-6 had departed Stillwater, Oklahoma, less than an hour earlier. It had crossed the last of the rough, untilled country west of the college town when its pilot had slowly swiveled his fine, aristocratic head to note a few biplanes flying down low in the distance ahead. He'd pass well clear of them, since he was cruising just below the gloomy overcast hundreds of feet higher than those ag planes that were skimming the ground and flipping through their typical crop-duster gyrations way down low.

The blocky biplanes were much different than the low-wing sprayers being flown far out of sight to the west by Tim and Dave. These were much older, highly-modified, open-cockpit aircraft. Unlike Pawnees and most of the other new agricultural aircraft of that era—the CallAirs, Cessnas, Snows, and so on—these modified old Stearmans had upper and lower wings and a big, un-aerodynamic, wheel-shaped motor mounted flat side to the wind. There may have been a Grumman Ag Cat or two among them, but those modern agricultural planes also had upper and lower

12

wings and big round engines, making them less distinguishable at a distance. However, Lance wasn't paying close attention to the sprayers yet, and they all seemed the sort of agricultural aircraft that he was most used to seeing.

Normally, since it was only March and still very cold, Lance probably would have wondered right away what in the world they could be spraying so early in the year. However, he was too preoccupied with trying to come up with some scheme to make Lisa, his fiancée, forget about his big goof the previous Friday.

I should've given it a lot more thought before now, he groggily reflected.

Although it was late afternoon, Lance hadn't been awake for long, and he was suffering a low-grade headache. The previous night had been a long and beery one. He'd begun the evening with the intention of having no more than a couple as compensation for the teetotaling weekend to come at home. He and Kristy would have spent just an hour or two visiting with their college friends, and he would have been up bright and early to try to dream up something he could do to erase Lisa's memory of his miserable failure a week earlier. Instead, he and the other guys had ended up drinking and playing poker until dawn, long after Kristy and the other girls had given up and gone to bed.

Kristy had gotten up at sunrise, had driven him to his apartment, and, knowing he wanted to get home that afternoon but not why, had helped him to bed and lovingly set his alarm for two o'clock. He'd been in no shape to attend any of his Friday classes. Since Lance had bought the T-6, he'd been leaving his car back home, so Kristy had been providing much of his transportation around Stillwater. She had driven him out to the airport when he'd finally been ready to go.

That had been their intention the previous Friday, too. Kristy had taken him to his apartment after his last class so he could pack a few things before she drove him to the airport, but one thing had led to another. By the time he'd realized how late it was, it would have been impossible to fly home, pick Lisa up, and get to the preacher's house in town at a reasonable hour. He and Lisa were supposed to have had supper with the pastor and his wife, followed by the beginning of the premarital counseling that Lisa had insisted on. He had phoned in a panic to tell Lisa that he must have ptomaine poisoning or the flu.

Everything would have worked out fine, too, if she hadn't tried calling later on.

"Don't you lie to me, Lance Levenger!" she had shouted when he called her the next morning. "I talked to Alex, and—"

"Alex? How—"

"I remembered his last name. I do have a brain, you know. I even figured out how to dial information and ask for his number."

Lance was dumbfounded. He'd brought the guy home with him one time, introduced him to Lisa before they'd taken off with her brother to do their own guy thing, and she'd remembered not only his first name but his last. "You were *spying* on me?"

"I was worried about you. I wanted him to look in on you. I thought you might have been too sick to answer!"

"I *was* too sick to answer."

"Lance . . . " She heaved a great sigh before she continued. " . . . He said he'd just seen you having a hamburger. He didn't know about your lie. Ptomaine certainly does wonders for your appetite, doesn't it? *Then* where did you go?" She hadn't waited a second for an answer. *"After* you told me you were so very sick."

"Okay, okay. I didn't want to admit that I could be that absentminded. I was studying. At the—"

She hung up before he could finish, and the line was busy for almost an hour afterward. When her mother finally answered, she said that Lisa had left for Norman to spend the rest of the weekend visiting some former dorm mates.

Thank God Alex had sense enough not to tell her I was having that burger with Kristy!

Although he was sure that Lisa would never meet anyone else like him, she did stand up to him as no other female ever had. She was no pushover.

Beginning last Monday and continuing through yesterday, he'd called a couple times every day to try to talk to her, but she'd had her mother answer all the calls and had refused to come to the phone. At least Amanda McLean had been as nice as always. She had advised him to be patient. "I just wish you hadn't told her that big story about the ptomaine," she'd said each time he called. Then, at last, a couple hours ago, right after he'd stumbled out of bed, chased a few aspirin with a tall glass of icy, vodka-fortified orange juice, and called again, Lisa had relented and come to the phone.

"I know it was a terrible thing to lie to you that way, honey," he'd said, "but when I saw that I'd blown it, I just panicked. I mean, it was pathetic to forget something that important!"

He'd gone on to say that, once he'd made his stupid excuse, he had left his apartment to grab a burger before he got back to the books. He'd said he had thought he would just have to wait until morning to go home, since neither his airstrip nor the McLeans' was lighted.

"Oh, Lance . . . That's . . . But let's talk about now. We're holding off supper 'til after dark for some spray pilots. They're going to be staying in the old house for a couple weeks. I suppose you could join us. *If* you feel like it."

He certainly did. Somehow, he had to erase her memory of last Friday's fiasco. He wished he could dream up something completely new, something so stimulating that it would rid her mind forever of that little misstep.

I doubt you could ever come up with a better marriage than this one, he warned himself. And the thought caused him to slip right on into one of his favorite visions of his future. If he could keep from blowing it over some crazy goof like last Friday's, he was going to have an awesome life. Eventually, he'd be in control not only of the Levenger land but the McLeans' as well. And that wasn't all! So he dreamed on as he flew west beneath the sagging clouds.

Quite some time had passed since Lance had spotted the first spray planes when he became conscious of others he was passing over, and he did wonder at last why they were spraying in the icy chill of late winter. Since there was no way to find out at the moment, he quickly lost interest as he compared his boring, straight-and-level flight with the action those crop sprayers were getting down below. This flight home was the longest ever. Except for all those sprayers flitting about down there, the shadowed land was so drearily familiar. It was the same old checkerboard of live winter wheat, lifeless wheat stubble, and green pasture as far ahead and to either side as he could see. The gloomy overcast and his queasiness made it more repulsive to him than ever. He loved the wealth that such land produced, but he much preferred city life—not too-tame OKC, which was near, but Dallas, which he was able to enjoy only occasionally.

Having forgotten all about his need to come up with something to divert Lisa's attention from the previous week's fiasco, he considered climbing up through the overcast. That would take some concentration and help relieve the boredom. He wasn't officially rated to fly on instruments in the clouds, but he'd done it before. On the other hand, the air would probably be even more turbulent in the clouds and make his hangover worse. How he wished that he could have called this trip off!

For a couple weeks after he'd bought the T-6, the purely utilitarian, military cockpit view in the old fighter-trainer had pleased him very much, but he had much too active a mind to do nothing but sit and admire it now. If he had felt better, he might have done a stunt or two to kill the monotony. Instead, for want of anything better to do, he impulsively thought he could at least have a closer look at the sprayers. He fancied the way they were flipping around so close to the ground. He'd have to talk to Will Walker, the man who handled the Levengers' spraying, into letting him try one out some time.

As he descended, he watched one blocky biplane with a gray fuselage and bright yellow wings and tail dive toward a field almost directly ahead. When he saw the sprayer rear up steeply seconds later and snap into a sharp turnaround with its wings nearly perpendicular to the horizon, a dazzling smile suddenly brightened his exquisite face. Hangover and worries about Lisa instantly forgotten, he eased the control stick forward and increased power to 32 inches of manifold pressure and 2200 rpm. The 600-horsepower Pratt & Whitney radial engine roared, and the big constant-speed Hamilton Standard prop loudly rasped in response.

Lance turned a bit to the right to try to cross the sprayer's path just ahead of it, thinking, *I'll get right down in front of that fool and give him a little surprise!* He imagined how startled the man would be to suddenly see an AT-6 streaking by so low and near. Once the man recovered from his surprise, he'd have to admire what he'd seen.

Lance had bought the plane only a few weeks earlier, and he was still quite proud of it. It sure beat the little Stits Playboy his folks had bought him when he was seventeen and which he'd sold recently. This low-winged, aluminum-skinned airplane with the long Plexiglas canopy stretching all the way over the front and rear cockpits had been designed specifically to prepare military pilots to fly fighters, and it was built to withstand the G forces of simulated aerial combat. The old hunk of surplus had already provided him a hugely disproportionate measure of exciting noise and aerobatic fun for only a little over $3,000.

Of course three thousand wasn't quite pocket change for most young men back then, but Lance was no ordinary college student. He was sole heir to one of the larger wheat and cattle operations in northwestern Oklahoma.

As he held the T-6 in a power dive, it became clear that he wasn't going to get close enough to the sprayer in time to cross in front of it right down on the wheat. It was going to be too near the road and power lines which bordered that end of the field. He'd either have to break off his dive and circle to try to get into better position when the biplane turned around and was spraying back the other way or just go ahead and buzz it from outside the field and a bit higher.

He decided on the latter to save time. He wanted to make it to the McLeans' farm strip before dark. It was possible to land on the unlighted airstrip using the T-6's landing lights, but he'd rather not until he was more familiar with the new plane. He dove to an altitude about twice the height of the electric-power lines just across the road from the approaching biplane. The T-6 was cooking right along with its airspeed indicator needle hovering a bit under the red line at 200 miles an hour.

Lance thought it would be perfect to cross in front of the sprayer just as it was starting its pull-up to clear the power lines. However, as it turned out, the open-cockpit Stearman began to rear back a couple seconds or so before the T-6 got directly in front of it. It would be close, but Lance was pretty sure he'd be out of the way in time. If it did get too close, he'd simply flick right and zoom up and out of the way.

He flashed that dazzling smile once again as he watched the biplane's blunt, round nose pitch upward to clear the mass of roadside power lines. He was almost directly in front of the steeply climbing Stearman and looking right into the pilot's goggled face now. He was close enough to see the fool's mouth make a big O of surprise. Then, in a panic, the man jammed the Stearman's nose right back down to avoid a collision, and it plowed into that thick mass of black electric wires.

Lance pulled a tight, climbing turn and got partially turned around quickly enough to look back over his shoulder and see the snagged power lines that hadn't been cut stretching and stretching like slingshot rubbers. They were visibly slowing the sprayer as they stretched. Then, one after another, the lines began popping and whipping in all directions.

Lance didn't linger to observe the outcome. He slammed forward the prop and throttle levers and dove away at full power to closely hug the ground, where he'd be less visible until he was completely out of sight. As much as he'd originally wanted that other pilot to get an eyeful of the T-6, he now desperately hoped that neither that man nor anyone else who happened to be in the vicinity had gotten more than a blurry glimpse.

"There you've gone and done it again," he moaned. "That jackass will call the feds sure as heck."

Then, a minute later, he hopefully thought, *If he survived.*

A few seconds after that, he thought, *If he didn't, that's just what you need. Lose your license and be grounded the rest of your life.*

He could not let that happen. He would not let it happen. He made one of his characteristic mental scrambles for escaping consequences and quickly found comfort in the knowledge that, should the feds come calling, he could simply deny that he'd been as close as the man claimed. There was no law against flying low over vacant ground. Then, too, he hadn't noticed any houses nearby, so it was very unlikely that there had been any witnesses. It probably would be that nobody's word against the word of a Levenger.

Even so, he thought he'd better keep an eye on the news. If there was no report on the late news that a crop sprayer had died in a crash, maybe he should find out who that pilot was and have a little talk. He'd learned by previous experience that a lot could be forgiven for enough cash.

2

CONVERGENCE

As he flew on toward the McLeans' place, Lance was still thinking that he'd be willing to do almost anything to save his license. Having the means to rapidly escape the monotony of life so distant from what Lance regarded as "civilization" was going to be one of the most important facets of the beautiful life he'd been dreaming about making for himself. He'd been thinking a lot in the past few days about buying something much faster and cooler-looking than the T-6 before too long. A P-51 would be nice, but lots of people had those. There were other old war birds out there that were much more unique.

Since he'd be receiving not only a generous salary but a larger share of the farm's profits as well when he started working full-time, he might be able to swing it fairly soon. A possible complication was that he'd need to have a nice home built somewhere on the farm in the near future, too, but he might scrape together enough for both anyway. Lisa had said they could stay in her folks' older original home for a few years, but he hated the thought of living in that little house down in a hole below the new house and facing a huge, ugly shop building. Also, depending on whether he could marry Lisa and get her pregnant in time, he might have to postpone going right to work full-time after graduation and taking on any large debt. Lacking dependents, he'd have to return to Stillwater for graduate school to avoid being drafted. He'd already applied in case he needed to exercise that option, and he had no doubt that he'd be accepted.

Lisa had approved his graduate-school idea, saying it would be fine whether they were married by fall or not. She'd said that, if they were married by then, she'd probably take some classes no matter what her father said about supposed "Commie" profs and war-protesting "long hairs." The presence of Lisa on campus, of course, would interfere in his relationship with Kristy.

How he loved just looking at that girl! Like his mother, Kristy was petite but really quite shapely. Like his mother also, her olive skin was fine-textured and free of blemishes. He disliked Lisa's coarser, freckled skin.

If he did end up in grad school, though, there was still a chance that he could get Lisa to give in eventually, whether it be in marriage or not. With luck, he would get her pregnant in time to beat the draft, and not have to do grad school.

As much as he wanted to get right to work creating his envisioned farming empire, though, he would not regard graduate school as a waste of time if he had to do it to avoid the military. He was sure there were things he could still learn to help him leverage the two farms into something far more magnificent than a simple combination of two farms.

It seemed perfectly realistic to hope that he could ease his father into early retirement in ten years. Later, when he had a competent management team in place, he could finally move to Dallas. He'd still be close enough to keep an eye on business if he had a very fast airplane.

But that's out if you lose your license, he reminded himself. *If you scrape through this one okay, you do have to be more careful.*

He'd learned a long time ago that life was much better when he kept himself in check and stayed more or less within society's bounds, but there were times when he simply couldn't help acting before he'd had a chance to think. He'd have to keep a tighter rein on himself if he was going to achieve the life he was planning. However, his usual optimism boomed back into play after a few minutes, and the fear of losing his license began to fade away.

Now he was sure that the crop duster's attention must have been fully occupied with those power lines ahead of him as the T-6 had swept in from the side. Even if the fool had survived, the biplane's upper wing probably would have kept the T-6 completely out of that pilot's sight until he'd raised the nose to clear the lines. He probably registered nothing more than a vague flash of the other airplane before he dove back into all that wire.

With that, the last of his anxiety melted away, and his thoughts returned to his problem about last Friday. All of a sudden, he knew what would get Lisa's mind off his little story about being sick. Since she was so adamantly one of those not-before-we're-married types, he'd never bothered very hard to test her resolve, but he could really turn up the heat later on tonight. She'd have to drive him home because it would be too difficult to try to land in the dark on the airstrip near his house. Surely, she'd resist him, but he'd make a point of stoking her passion far beyond where they'd ever been before. If she didn't give in, it still might erase her memory of Friday.

Heck, it might even get her interested in having the wedding sooner after all. Like June. Maybe late May right after graduation. And if I get really got lucky she'll end up pregnant before then!

As he daydreamed on, he flew past the lake where her brother had drowned. If that hadn't happened, he might have never even thought about dating Lisa. He'd known them both all his life, for they were next-door neighbors, but he'd thought of Lisa as nothing more than Billy's bothersome little sister, since she'd always been so determined to be such a very good girl. There'd always been lots of other, prettier girls who didn't take their religion so seriously. Billy would bring her along on some of their tamer adventures, such as playing indoor games when the weather was foul, tearing around on the horses or the farm bikes and three-wheelers, water-skiing, or flying somewhere in their daddy's six-seater, but Lance had just put up with it to please Billy.

Lisa hadn't come waterskiing that day, and neither had Billy's fiancée. It had been just Billy, Lance, and CR, a younger hired man who Lance regarded as having uses that fully compensated for his slovenly appearance and manners.

"He's down," he recalled CR saying. The runt had said it so calmly that Lance hadn't bothered to get the boat turned around in any great hurry. He hadn't even looked back until CR, who was in a rear-facing seat behind him, said, "He still ain't got up."

Then, seeing Billy face-down in the water, Lance had gunned the boat around as fast as it would go. As soon as he'd gotten the boat stopped, he had leaped into the water to try to save him. Billy's death had been a huge loss for Lance. Billy had been his life-long partner in some wildly entertaining escapades.

All of that group, including Lisa whenever she'd come skiing, used to like sweeping in close to the shore, as the sense of speed was heightened by the proximity of rocks and brush blurring by. This time, Billy's skis had hit a nearly invisible, waterlogged raft of scrap lumber, flipping him headfirst into the rocky shallows.

After the funeral service, Lance had made himself go along with the crowd filing past Lisa and her folks to express sympathy. Lisa had clung to his hand too long, and to end it he'd said, "We can talk later," although what he really had in mind was to get away from all that whimpering. He'd managed to almost get past the last couple people who would say the same old thing—that they knew he and Billy had been so close—when Lisa had latched onto him again.

She'd carried on in the same vein as those other mindless nincompoops, saying what a big loss it must be for him. Of course it was. Billy had been a heck of a hoot. But he was gone, and that was that. Yet Lisa in her teary intensity did get him to pay closer attention to her than usual, and he noticed that she was more attractive than he'd ever realized. It also occurred to him for the first time how very much they had to offer each other, their farms being right next to each other. He'd gone over to their place the very next day and every day after that for a week to join the McLeans in their mourning. After a while, he'd asked Lisa to go to supper in Enid with him, and they had started dating regularly soon after that.

He flew on, thinking again about his plan for later that night. It wasn't long until the trees around the McLeans' home on the knoll began to appear in the dusk, and Lance aimed more directly toward them.

* * *

Meanwhile, Tim spotted Dave's Pawnee and fell into position a plane length behind and a wingspan off to one side. Dave had turned on his navigation lights, and Tim activated his. They were going to need them to keep track of each other in the dark before they could make it all the way to town.

Tim sighed with contentment. Except for the pace through the turns, it had been an excellent day, and it would be so very nice to completely relax and sleep in a bed. There had to be far more comfortable lodging, he was sure, than his crappy old Dodge. He and Dave made their formation landing in the dark, shoved the Pawnees into the huge old hangar among the Stearmans, and went into the office.

"Dave! Tim!" Will Walker called out as they squeezed past a clot of men Tim didn't recall having seen early that morning. He did recognize other men farther inside as fellow employees and surmised that these near the boss must be customers. "I need to talk to you all," the owner of Will Walker's Flyers went on. Right after I finish with Todd here. We're planning how we can line up some of his fields with his neighbor's and make better time."

The men Tim recognized as fellow employees lounged in old

wood chairs or stood in line on the opposite side of the long counter from the space occupied nearest the door by Mr. Walker, then
one desk beyond the boss, a thin little woman with a tall beehive
hairdo, and near the end of the counter, Olen, the scheduler. The
woman sat whipping her beehive back and forth as she vigorously nodded to whoever she had on the phone. Olen was bent over
his big maps and work orders to give each of the men waiting in
line the following morning's assignments and the rough maps he
was rapidly sketching on a yellow legal pad.

The door into the office opened again, and here came Johnny
Crash, bringing another big smile to Tim's face. It had been a huge
surprise to see the man again, although the veteran duster had
made it clear that he'd always been a goin'-down-the-road breed
of pilot. If Tim hadn't happened to meet Johnny Crash back home
in California and get clued in on seasonal flying, he never would
have come up with the idea to take off on an adventure like this.

Johnny Crash really did look a lot like the famous singer, but he
seemed to be a lot bigger. He made a very impressive figure with
his raven-black hair and a rugged face weather-battered from flying open-cockpit airplanes. He was probably only a couple inches
shorter than Tim, who was six four. The Crasher, as Dave also
called him, apparently hadn't warmed up enough yet from his
winter's day in an open cockpit to take off his bulky, fleece-lined,
World War II flying coat. Unlike Tim and Dave, Johnny had been
assigned a Stearman, and the temperature outside wasn't much
warmer than freezing. Nevertheless, despite that reminder of how
much warmer it was by being protected from icy prop-blast by the
Pawnee's enclosed cockpit, Tim's viewpoint was that the veteran
gypsy pilot had lucked out. Mr. Walker's modified biplanes were
almost twice as powerful as his Pawnees and hauled seventy more
gallons of payload.

"Mr. Will wants to talk to us," Dave told Johnny, referring to
Will Walker the Southern way, using "Mister" followed by a

man's first name. "Soon's he's done with that farmer."

"How'd the boy do?"

"He done good. Ain't no flies on *him*."

Tim fairly thrummed with elation. It was as if he was some stringed instrument and Dave had just strummed a magical chord.

"They're done," Johnny said, nodding toward the young man who was turning away from Walker to rejoin the other farmers.

The three hired pilots hurried over, and the weary-looking, silky-white-haired owner of the operation said, "What with all these other pilots and outfits flocking in, I couldn't find you boys a place in town to stay." But he smiled and went on to say, "When I told it to a friend of mine, he said you all can stay in the old house at his place. It's way out yonder on the other side of town. Extry twenty-minute drive in the dark before and after a day of flying ain't the best deal, but it's better than having you all crammed up together in that spare room like the two of you were last night or . . . " He paused to turn from Dave and Johnny to cast a baleful look at Tim before he continued, " . . . or sleeping in a car."

"Fine with me," Dave said. "I ain't all that peculiar."

Tim knew by then, having heard such nonsensical talk before dawn as he and the two old dusting friends had gotten ready to fly, that Dave and Johnny amused themselves by doing their dumb-ol'-country-boy routines. But whenever Dave had hurriedly clued Tim in on one important matter or another during their refueling, he'd spoken more normally.

"I expect he'll want me to return the favor," said Mr. Will. "Like maybe getting to the rest of his wheat quicker than humanly possible."

"Sounds reasonable to *me*," Dave commented. His cherubic face crinkled as he cocked his head and mischievously eyed Mr. Will.

Tim appreciated Dave's lighthearted mood after so many hours of flying. It was confirmation that Dave hadn't praised him just for encouragement but really had enjoyed a fairly productive day.

"Truth is," Mr. Will said, "Ned McLean don't need a bigger hammer to make me pay attention. Man farms a *bunch* of wheat."

"McLean?" Johnny said. "I done some work on his place for a while this morning."

"Good. Then you know where it's at. Come to think of it, with you all being right there on the spot, maybe that drive ain't necessary after all. I bet Ned would be happy to let us park them airplanes right there at his home strip. Between him and his neighbors, I'm sure we can keep the three of you boys busy right there, and there wouldn't be any point driving back and forth. You two might remember from that run you were on back . . . Was that five years ago?"

"Six," Dave said. It was '63. Same year as JFK got it. First summer I didn't spray Texas cotton and went up to Idyhoe to spray."

"Idaho?" Tim said. "What—"

"Anyhow," Will Walker went on, "Ned McLean's next to my biggest customer. Maybe you remember that big old Levenger farm right to the south? McLean's got 18 sections, and Josh Levenger's got 21. Just the two of 'em got enough . . . But never mind that. Ned says go right on up to the house. They're holding supper for you all. Says come as you are so nobody faints from hunger."

* * *

Not much later, the three spray pilots were standing in the spacious foyer of the McLeans' newer home on the knoll above the older, smaller one. Beefy, reddish-haired Ned McLean was grinning and saying to Johnny Crash, "That's not your real name, is it?"

"Barnes. John Barnes. But nobody's called me that for years."

Mrs. McLean, Lisa McLean, and Lance had accompanied Ned to the door to greet the ag pilots, and Tim subtly eyed the younger pair, who were about his age. The guy was as handsome as any leading man Tim had ever seen, and he had seen a few in person, having

28

grown up just down the street from Hollywood. This dude dressed the part, too. It was abundantly clear that he hadn't bought his duds just anywhere. Tim wondered what he did for a living. He was sure it was a big-city calling, whatever it was. The girl was attractive, too, but not to the same degree as the guy. She looked a lot like her somewhat heavier, older, but also attractive mother. Both females had the most wonderfully thick and curly golden hair.

"This is my wife, Amanda," Ned McLean went on, "and that's my daughter, Lisa, and her fiancé, Lance Levenger. Johnny, if you would introduce the others . . . "

"Well, this here's Dave Cooper, and thatun's Tim O'Reilly."

When Tim shook Lance's hand, he couldn't help but notice how slender and fine it was, compared with his own hairy monstrosity. His own big hands reminded Tim of overgrown tarantulas. They had been pretty good at handling a basketball, though.

"Go on in," McLean said, "Dining room's to the left."

"That's a right nice old T-6 Texan you got parked out there," Dave commented, looking at Ned McLean as they turned toward the dining room.

"Oh, 'tain't mine. It's Lance's."

Tim eyed that young man with all the more interest as they went on down the hallway. They'd all ridden out from the airport to the farm in Johnny's pickup, missed the first turn into the farmstead, and come in past the near end of the private airstrip, where they'd seen the parked AT-6 and two other airplanes, a big six-seater Cessna Super Skywagon and a little yellow Piper Cub. Tim, too, had presumed that all three belonged to the farmer.

They filed past a kitchen wafting wonderfully tantalizing fragrances and entered a spacious dining room that reminded Tim of pictures of the interiors of ancient European castles. His folks' home in Santa Monica was certainly no hovel, but it didn't have a dining room even remotely as impressive as this one. A fire of oversize logs crackled in a massive stonework fireplace, and eight stout chairs surrounded a grand table. It all looked very masculine, compared with the formal living room he'd glimpsed from the entry. The chairs proved to be as heavy as they appeared when Tim pulled one out to sit on while mother and daughter began bustling back and forth between kitchen and dining room to set out two huge bowls of mashed potatoes, two tureens of brown gravy, a hefty platter supporting a sizzling rack of prime rib, two baskets of hot rolls, and two big bowls of steaming vegetables, one of peas, the other of green beans.

Tim liked the way Lance gently touched the back of Lisa's hand as she set a basket of steaming rolls before him, and he said, "I've sure missed the McLeans' cooking. That'll be one of the truly great things about being home again this summer."

Tim also noticed how quickly Lance got to his feet to seat Lisa when she and her mother were ready. Everyone else, including Tim, was a bit slower in doing so. Since Tim had taken a place nearest Mrs. McLean, who sat at the opposite end of the long table from her husband, he moved the heavy chair for her. These people's old-fashioned manners, including Dave's and Johnny's, reminded Tim of his dad, who never failed to seat Tim's mom, no matter how casual the meal might be or who might be present to witness it.

"This is *McLean* beef," Ned McLean said as he began to carve the prime rib. "None better. I guarantee it. Fed out half grass, half grain. So tell us where you all are from."

Johnny Crash and Dave told about East Texas, and when Tim said where he was from, Lisa exclaimed, "California? I hope I get to see California before too long. Did you live by the sea?"

"The beach is a couple miles from where I grew up."

"It must be beautiful."

"We could go there on our honeymoon," Lance said.

"Oh, no. France first. California some other time."

"We could fly there in the T-6 if we went to California."

"*France,* Lance." She laughed at the coincidental rhyme, and so did he. He reached out to hold her hand and gazed at her fondly.

Tim gazed at her, too. She seemed so nice that it made him wonder whether he was ready to risk dating again. It had been almost six months since Jen had dumped him. He'd been so busy with his training the past three months that he hadn't missed female companionship at all. Now, however, thinking what a wonderful couple Lance and Lisa made, a sort of empty sensation momentarily swelled up inside of him.

"But them's your Cessna and Cub in the T-hangars, aren't they?" Johnny asked, looking at Ned McLean.

"Yep."

"Man, this here's flyin' *country,*" Dave remarked.

"We both fly," Lance said, inclining his head in both Lisa's and her dad's direction but looking down at Lisa, making Tim wonder whether she could be the one he'd meant. "Say, I'll trade one of you boys a ride in that T-6 if I can fly one of your sprayers!"

Tim grinned at that, thinking, *This dude's something else!*

The two older hired pilots solemnly shook their heads.

"Why not? I've done a little spraying before."

"Lance!" Ned McLean exclaimed. "Now, I have heard you tell some tall ones, but—"

"Well, we kept it quiet, of course," the dashing young man glibly replied, dismissively waving a graceful hand. "After all, I've only got a private license. I'm sure there's some law against it, but one of Will's other pilots let me do a little spraying on our place one time."

He's a farmer? Tim thought. *More likely, son of a farmer. Went on to something else.* Being a big-city boy, Tim was still getting used to the idea that American farmers didn't all live below the poverty line.

"Actually, 'tain't against the law," said Dave. "You was perfectly within your rights to do some sprayin'. So long as it was your own prop'ty."

"Well, there you go!" said Lance. "I didn't think one of those boys would do anything illegal!" He looked around at all of them, beaming his dazzling smile.

What? Tim thought. *You did think it was illegal, but you did not think it was illegal?* Normally, stretching the truth put Tim off, and Lance's comments had been so obviously contradictory. The O'Reilly family code had very little tolerance for lies. Yet, Tim could not judge Lance so harshly. Without being fully aware of it, he'd already taken a strong liking to the guy. Lance's cheerful, carefree ways were very appealing, which might have been amplified by Tim's own determination to get back to being more cheerful and carefree himself. He went on to assume that Lance must have been joking. Lance looked much too cool to be anything but first class, what with his gallant manners, his erect bearing, those classy casual clothes.

As soon as they finished eating, Lance scooted back his chair and stood, saying, "Well, you boys fly that T-6 of mine anytime you want." He turned to Lisa, held her chair to pull it back, and said, "Shall we, honey?" Then he spoke once again to the working pilots: "If you boys want to fly it while I'm here, I'll leave it home this time and take my car back to school."

Just a poor, starving college kid! Tim thought ironically.

"Lance," McLean said sternly, "they need to be killing them dad-gum greenbugs. They aren't here to play airplane."

"I know. I mean whenever they aren't busy."

"Well," he went on, "it has been nice meeting you all. I need to be getting on home now. I've been staying up too late every night studying. If Lisa will drive me . . . "

* * *

"Why don't you pull in at that old house site?" Lance said a few minutes later, kissing Lisa on the cheek. He was sitting right beside her in her old Ford Falcon. "Let's talk some more about setting a date this summer."

She drove right on by the weedy driveway that led into the abandoned farmstead and said, "The way you've been acting, I'm thinking maybe it shouldn't even be late summer now."

"Come on, honey. I thought you forgave me. Stop the car and back up. Let's talk." He scooted closer to her side and stroked the back of her neck.

"We can talk at your house," she said. "Or tomorrow if you're so very tired." She took her right hand off the steering wheel to gently elbow him. "Stop that."

"Tell the truth, I had a little necking in mind, too."

She stiffened and leaned away from him, saying, "Lance, something tells me we shouldn't get started."

"You *say* you forgive, but you haven't forgiven me in your heart."

"This has nothing to do with forgiveness. I'm just not going to let you try to mess with my emotions right now."

"Let's elope! Tonight! We don't need a big, fancy wedding!"

"After that story you told last week, you expect me to jump the gun just like that? Is it really because you were studying so hard that you forgot? I do want to believe you. Why do you have to tell all those stories?"

He laughed and said, "I don't know. They just pop out of my mouth sometimes. I don't mean anything by them."

"Will you do that always?"

"Of course not. I'm sure I'll be like Pa, and you know how he is."

"Yes, I do. You're like him in some ways already. He's so smart. And he helps so many people. I'm sure we don't know all the good he's done. But I wonder if he's ever lied to anyone the way you have."

"Did you like how I offered those pilots a chance to fly my airplane? You have to admit I'm generous. Just like Pa."

"Yes, I did like that. You really can be wonderful at times. Other times, though . . . " But Lance was no longer listening.

He might as well have been trying to hug the steering wheel, she was so rigid. He'd have to dream up something for the following day. He just wanted to get home now, turn on the tube, and relax as he waited for the news. He had to know whether there was news about a sprayer crashing out there east of the lake.

3
THE NEW GUY

The following morning, Saturday, Tim and Dave took off from the muny at the first hint of sunlight, as they had the day before. Olen had lined them out with their day's work before the others, since the Pawnees, unlike the Stearmans, had electrical systems to power navigation lights, which are those small lights, one on each wingtip and one on the tail, that made the planes visible to other aircraft in the dark. On their takeoff run, all Tim had to do was to maintain a consistent distance from the only two lights on Dave's plane that he could see from his position diagonally behind and slightly to the left, which were the small white light on the tail and the small red light on the left wingtip. Neither pilot bothered using the much brighter landing and departure lights because a row of runway lights to either side on the ground kept them heading straight in the right direction.

Some minutes later, when he could see more clearly, Tim noticed that the overcast, which had shaded the countryside the day before, had sagged lower. The wind was kicking up, too. He wondered how long they'd be able to work until they got blown out.

Soon, Dave led him on by the landmark abandoned schoolhouse at a lonely intersection of the two farm roads they'd be using as landing strips. The north-south road was gray gravel, and the one running east and west was rutted brown dirt. The dilapidated little clapboard box of a single-room schoolhouse stood a couple miles away from the nearest dwelling.

Ken was parking the loading rig in the schoolyard. He should have been ready to start pumping loads into the sprayers by now.

Dave made a couple passes alongside the power lines that closely flanked both roads, and Tim knew he was checking for guy wires, cross wires, road signs, and other hazards, and he did the same. Such things might seem obvious from a car or truck dinking along at fifty or sixty miles an hour, especially since there's no danger that road-bound vehicles would strike any one of them, but such obstructions are much more difficult to detect from above at a hundred miles an hour. However, these two roads were so little traveled that there weren't any signs at or near the intersection, and there didn't seem to be any other hazards.

Dave led him on in to land, and Tim watched the lead plane crab on down between the power lines along either side of the road with its nose cocked sideways into the quartering wind. It was a pretty tight fit, and the crosswind made it seem all the more so, but Tim welcomed the challenge. He'd done it before at school and much of the day before, though in less wind. He landed smoothly and taxied over the culvert into the schoolyard to join Dave in helping Ken get set up.

"Sorry I'm late," the young swamper said. "Big lash-up at the loading dock this morning. We're gonna get slowed down some later on, too. Boss man called to say some outfit he's got coming in from Colorado will be working off our rig."

"Cain't be helped, times like these," Dave said. "We'll do what we can."

The two pilots started pulling the long, thick loading hose off the racks welded to the trailer's big water-supply tank while Ken pulled a couple five-gallon containers of parathion off the truck bed and lugged them over to the mixing tank on the back end of the trailer. The pilots got the hoses hooked up in a hurry only to hear Ken say, "Pump's froze." He gave another futile tug on the pump's starter cord to show them. "Won't budge. Got to wait 'til it thaws out."

"No way," Dave muttered. "This ain't no time to set around waiting. We'll go borrow some kind of torch. That house off to the east. Blow torch—"

"Exhaust," Tim said. "Slide the loader-hose nozzle over the truck's tailpipe." The bulky aluminum nozzle was more than big enough.

"Dang!" Dave said. "Let's try that!"

Having slid the nozzle over the idling truck's puttering exhaust pipe, they stood by to see whether routing the hot exhaust into the frozen impellers was going to work. After a few seconds, Dave impatiently asked, "Have you seen what we're killing, Tim?"

"In pictures."

"Come on. It'll take a minute to melt that ice."

They strode through the schoolyard weeds to the edge of the wheat. Dave squatted and parted the dense mass of shin-high, grassy blades, and Tim knelt to peer into it.

"Good grief!" he exclaimed. The wheat was swarming with tiny aphids.

"You got it, bub. A *lot* of grief for them farmers. Gonna cost a bunch to kill. Plus, their yield's dropping by the hour. You wouldn't think such itty-bitty critters could do so much harm, but they'll suck tons of production out of a man's wheat."

They were, indeed, incredibly small creatures for all the trouble they were causing. They were a few shades lighter than the color of a canned pea but very much smaller. None was quite the size of a single small letter of normal book print, but there were so many scurrying up and down slender stalks that they were very obvious. The sight reminded Tim of views from aloft of rush-hour traffic on LA freeways.

"Remember reading about the big famines they used to have?" Dave asked. "With a name like O'Reilly, you must've paid attention in school about the Irish potato famine. A lot of people used to die in situations like this. Did you know the Irish potato, AKA Idyho potato, was developed to resist the blight that caused that Irish famine? Yep—"

"Pump's loose!" Ken shouted.

"Will that parathion freeze in the booms?" Tim asked as they hurried to their planes.

"Naw, it ain't that cold. I doubt it'll freeze that quick."

When the planes were loaded and ready for takeoff, Dave turned the tail of his Pawnee away from Tim's airplane and the loading rig, ran up the engine so the little wind-driven pump fan mounted on the belly would spin and pressurize the spray system, and let loose a quick burst of spray so they'd know for sure that the liquid hadn't frozen in the booms. Then he swung the nose around and gunned his Pawnee down the road.

Tim rather grumpily followed. It had begun to irk him again that he still had to fly behind another pilot. It had to be costing Will Walker quite a lot in lost productivity. For one thing, there was the time lost waiting for two planes to be loaded, instead of one. Tim quickly estimated that if it took a couple minutes to pump 150 gallons into each plane, and if they sprayed, say, two loads an hour for a 12-hour flying day, that would be almost 50 minutes of lost flying time. There'd also be the time lost waiting for each other to refuel. If they lost a couple hours a day, and if a single plane could spray 300 acres an hour, flying doubles could cost Mr. Walker $600 a day gross. Tim was sure they were team flying because he was a beginner. He'd seen some of the boss's older planes, which were easily identifiable with bright-yellow sunbursts overlaying a green background on the tops and bottoms of the wings, spraying alone. And having a beginner fly a much newer plane, one specifically engineered to be an agricultural aircraft, was no compliment; a Pawnee's simply a lot easier for a novice to land on a narrow, improvised airstrip.

Although it nettled Tim to have to keep on tagging along that way, he was aware of team flying's advantages, too. For one thing, it made having flaggers on the ground less important. Automatic flaggers, the mechanisms that drop weighted tissue-paper streamers into the field to mark each swath, were just coming into vogue. It was more common for farmers to pay people on the ground to pace off the swaths and wave flags to guide the sprayers, although many didn't bother.

A lone pilot without the guidance of human or mechanical flaggers had to keep sharp watch on every pass for some distinctive weed clump, fence post or anything else that enabled him to space his swath widths accurately. An old pro of a lead pilot would make certain that a beginner was laying down the spray where it should be.

Didn't Catfish tell him I was good at all that stuff? Guess I'll just have to show 'em.

Some time later, during their first refueling, the two expected airplanes showed up to share the loading rig. They were dark-blue open-cockpit Stearmans.

"Lookie," Dave said, coming over to the base of the wing on which Tim stood, monitoring the gas nozzle jammed into the fuel tank. Dave inclined his head toward the nearest of the Stearmans that had stopped out of the way in front of the school to give the Pawnees room to maneuver, and Tim paid more attention to the great bear of a man perched high on cushions in the Stearman's cockpit the way some pilots do for straight-over-the-nose visibility. He had on a thickly quilted brown jacket and an old-fashioned leather helmet with goggles still drawn down over his eyes. "Bear matin' a dragonfly."

Tim laughed. It did look comical, all right. Tim was glad that Catfish had taught his students how to sit down low and lean to the side to see around the bulky, upslanting nose of a Stearman duster. As tall as Tim was, he would look foolish if he sat that high when his time came to realize his dream and work a Stearman. But Catfish's method had nothing to do with caring how a pilot looked; sitting lower kept a pilot's head from being batted around as badly by prop blast. That was especially desirable in a true duster of an open-cockpit airplane. True dusters lacked wind-shields. A windshield creates a greater partial vacuum than the open cockpit alone and sucks an extra helping of dust onto the pilot.

"Good night!" Dave exclaimed some moments after Tim had turned to pay more attention to his nearly full gas tank. "Bear's got one of them custom cockpit heaters!"

Tim looked back in time to see the giant hoisting a dark-brown bottle in one gloved hand, his leather-helmeted and goggled head tilted back, taking a long swig of liquid fire. As the day progressed, Tim would occasionally think of that and shake his head in wonder. A couple times, he caught sight of the bear riding his dragonfly nearby, and it was a relief to see him making such smooth, quick wingover turns. The dude was no alky comedian when it came to flying an airplane.

* * *

To most people, Lisa's faded Ford Falcon would have looked out of place parked in front of such a fine home. Any vehicle on the order of that older economy car would have fit in better over at the hired men's houses and trailer a half mile west. But Lisa didn't give it a thought as she flung open the creaking driver's door, hopped out, and hurried up to the entrance, tossing back her head and casually shaking out her thick golden hair.

Her clothing, though casual, was much more presentable than her old car. She was wearing jeans, but the quality of her quilted, waist-cut ski jacket of pearl gray and her soft black Western-style boots strongly suggested that this country girl was a cut well above average. So did her bright, alert facial expression.

The maid opened the door and smiled with obvious delight. "Good morning!" she said, quickly stepping aside. "Hurry in out of that wind! It's *cold*." She hastened to shut the door as soon as Lisa entered. "How *are* you?"

"Just fine, Millie." She gave the plump little woman a quick hug. "Is Lance still in the house?"

"Far as I know. Let me call." The middle-aged woman turned to the foyer's intercom and said, "Lance, Miz Lisa's here." She cocked her head to listen for a reply.

"Is Mrs. Levenger up?" Lisa asked.

"Yes, she's feeling pretty good today. She's in the parlor."

"I'll be out in a minute," Lance's voice replied.

"Nice to see you, Millie." Lisa gave the maid she'd known almost her entire life a loving touch on the arm and turned toward the living room. As she passed Joshua Levenger's office door a bit farther into the foyer, she looked in and paused, saying, "Good morning, Mr. Levenger!"

He was already on his feet, apparently having been alerted by the intercom. "Good morning! Isn't it time you called me Josh?"

She stepped inside the neat, finely furnished room and gave him a quick one-armed hug, saying, "It does sound too formal now, doesn't it? But I don't think I could ever call you by your first name. We'll have to come up with something better."

"To tell you the truth, it makes me cringe when some youngster calls me Josh. Things are changing fast. But that's different. You're grown up now, and you're practically family."

She glanced at the large open ledger and papers on his desk. "I'm sure you're busy. I'll go on in and say hi to Mrs. Levenger."

"This aphis outbreak does have me hopping more than usual this time of year. Thank God for the better years."

"Amen." She couldn't help taking a last, quick glance around the office. It was as neat and dignified in appearance as its occupant, who was dressed in wool slacks, a sportshirt, and a vest. Her own father preferred faded Jeans and a plain, strictly utilitarian office in a corner of his cavernous shop building.

"Will you be able to have a bite with us after your ride?" Mr. Levenger asked.

"Yes, I'd love to."

"Be sure someone lets Millie know."

"I will." She went on into the parlor.

"Lisa!" Mrs. Levenger happily cried out, raising her arms for a hug but remaining seated. "Lance said you two are going to exercise the Arabians! I almost feel well enough to do it myself, but not quite."

"I love riding your horses," Lisa trilled, making an effort to sound happier at the sight of the ill woman than she really was, and she leaned over to gently give her a little hug. She knew that this woman she loved so was able to look and sound as well as she did only because she had the inner strength and discipline to pull it off. "But it's going to cost you. Mr. Levenger said you'll have to feed me."

"I'll have Mil—"

"Hi, Lisa," Lance said, entering behind her. He wore gleaming, intricately tooled Western boots and a rust-colored wool shirt tucked into a neat pair of faded jeans. He bore a thick wool chocolate-colored stockman's coat in the crook of his left arm and a wide-brimmed pale Stetson stockman's hat in the right. "Sorry. I think I interrupted."

"I was just saying I'd have Millie fix something special for Lisa," his mother said. "Run along now. Those horses will be very happy to get out!"

They were indeed. They quivered, stamped their hooves, and huffed little clouds of vapor out of their rubbery nostrils as Lance and Lisa put the Western saddles and bridles on them. Once the two riders were astride their eager mounts, they had to vigorously rein them in to keep them from running on the asphalt drive just outside the paddock. But there was soggy, bare earth on down the drive at the edge of a wheat field, where the two let them break into a canter toward the dirt road that branched north from Lance's airstrip not far ahead. There were a truck and trailer on the strip, both bearing the Walker Aviation logo, and several biplanes could be seen spraying here and there in the distance.

Lisa slowed her mare to a trot, swept a glance from left to right out toward the horizon, and said, "Look at those airplanes. They're everywhere. Daddy says the wheat's just crawling with greenbugs."

"That's farming," Lance said, edging his mount close alongside hers. "It's always one thing or another. And it doesn't bother me a bit. We do what we can and trust the outcome to God."

"Oh, I like that! I do love you, Lance!"

"Race you!" He gave a couple of chirps with his thin lips as he loosened the reins, and his mount instantly leaped forward. He was feeling more chipper than ever, having just realized that morning that he still hadn't heard a thing about a crop duster crashing. He thought, *You lead a charmed life, Lance Levenger. God really is watching out for you.*

Soon both sleek dark animals, ropy muscles rippling their gleaming hides, heads cocked downward, were running flat out and side by side. But, gradually, Lisa's mount inched ahead. A minute later, its streaming tail was just ahead of the other horse's nose. Lisa stood a bit higher in the stirrups and sassily shook her tightly-jeaned behind at her rival.

With that, Lance lashed his mount's muscular neck with the ends of the reins, left and right and left and right, over and over again. Wishing he wore spurs, he slammed the heels of his boots against the creature's hard belly. Nevertheless, Lisa's horse kept edging ahead.

After a few more minutes, Lisa began slowing her mount. She rose a little higher off the saddle and firmly reined the beast back to an impatient prance. "I win!" she cried out when Lance came alongside.

"Your *horse* won," he replied, tightly checking his twisting, jerking gelding to keep it more or less in place.

"Horse and rider," Lisa insisted.

Smart aleck, Lance thought. *I really don't like that tone.*

"Another mile or so?" she asked. "But take it easy for a while so we can talk?"

He curtly nodded and thought, *But maybe that attitude will come in handy. Genetic potential. Competitive. Smart. Strong. Our oldest boy will learn to run this outfit fast, and I can retire without a worry in Dallas while I'm young enough to enjoy it.*

"Easter vacation's coming up," Lisa commented as they jounced along. "We can see each other every day."

"It'll be fantastic," he said, smiling and vigorously nodding. But her comment about vacation had him thinking of Kristy. He was going to miss her if he didn't go to graduate school the following year.

So lovely, he thought. *But stupid. At least Lisa isn't that!*

"Lance?"

"Yes?" He'd missed something.

"I said maybe we could play cards or dominoes with your ma after we eat."

"Yes. And while we're doing that, we should set a wedding date. How about right after I graduate?"

"Oh, Lance. You know it can't be that soon."

"Why not, sweetheart?"

"Lance, I've told you before. For one thing, I'm sure Mama needs more time than that to plan everything."

"Two months?"

"That's not long at all, considering everything that has to be done."

"Come on!"

"Like making sure the date will work for the bridesmaids and flower girl, like time to have the dresses made, once we've decided what we want, like—"

"I hate to put it off so long."

"So do I, Lance, but we will have a lifetime together."

"We don't want to visit France in the winter!"

"Spring would be nice. Spring of next year. What's that old song?"

"*Lisa!*"

"Race you back!" She wheeled the mare, tapped its sides with the heels of her boots, and away it sprang like a tightly-coiled spring suddenly released.

This time, however, Lance's Arabian overtook it. For a moment, he felt triumphant. But then he subsequently thought, *She's not trying to beat me. This is a sop! Very clever, Lisa!* He gritted his teeth and lashed the horse in a fury. However, when he reined in the trembling horse as he approached the paddock gate, he composed himself, thinking, *I'm not done with you yet, woman.*

He gallantly lifted down Lisa's saddle for her, saying, "Let me help with that, my love." After he'd set it on its stand in the tack room and Lisa entered to put away the blanket and bridle, he cast an arm around her waist and nuzzled the side of her neck, saying, "I'm so thankful that you like Mother's horses. They won't miss her nearly so badly when she's gone."

Lisa frowned and cocked her head in apparent puzzlement, and he feared he'd said something to offend her. He wondered whether she was thinking he was trying to manipulate her by reminding her that his mother's illness was terminal.

"Please consider this summer," he said, pressing on nevertheless, as if his mother might die sooner than they'd been led to expect.

"Before harvest is definitely too soon."

"Then later. Late August. It'll be a wonderful time for Paris and the Riviera."

She just stared at him thoughtfully, which Lance took as a good sign.

"We'll look at a calendar when we go in," he said. "We'll pick a definite date."

"Oh, Lance. I don't think yet. But let's get a move on. It's chilly out here."

Needing no more encouragement than the indecisive sound of her "I don't think," Lance hurried away to get a calendar while Lisa joined his parents in the informal dining nook beside the kitchen.

"Here we go!" he said a couple minutes later. He leaned between the two women, and he held the calendar before them. "August 22 would be perfect. Mother?"

"I think I might like that," said his mother. "What do you think, Josh?"

"Yes, that would a good time. We'll be done planting."

Lisa glanced out the window she was facing and said, "Look who's back."

"Well! It's about time!" Lance's father said, watching the older pickup Lance had given CR go by on the crossroad to the north, heading toward CR's parents' trailer near the small houses where the other permanent workers lived. "We need him on a spray rig right *now*. I don't like the work that other boy we hired is doing."

I have missed the little turd, Lance thought.

At first, he'd only been doing his father's bidding by having anything to do with the scruffy little kid who, along with his parents, had moved onto the farm with his parents some years earlier. Lance had learned very early in life how generous his folks could be if he made a strong effort to please them. His father had said it would be nice for him to invite the younger boy to Sunday school and church, and that was what Lance had done. Soon the mostly middle-class adults in their church were complimenting him for being so nice to that poor little boy, and Lance still gloried in the attention he got from continuing to be seen with the runt, along with the added benefit of CR's adulation. CR's barroom brawls were quite an entertainment, too. The little cripple had a thing about picking on big men, and he really was quite a scrapper.

"I'll call down there and have him take over that rig as soon as he can," Lance's father said. "That other boy can help clean up the shop. Would you excuse me?"

Lance got to his feet, too, saying, "And me? For just a minute?" He'd just conceived an idea of how he'd like to announce the wedding date. He'd use another line to call information and see whether he could locate a flight service in Oklahoma City that might help.

* * *

Tim and Dave were using the McLean home strip, and the bear and his partner had gone off to spray somewhere else, when a stranger in another Pawnee showed up. Tim and Dave were loading up for another sortie, despite the increasing wind that would have shut them down hours earlier in normal circumstances.

Tim looked at his loader man and raised his chin, wordlessly asking Ken, *Who's this?*

Ken shrugged. Apparently nobody at base had given him any warning of any other planes coming out to share the strip with them.

Tim watched the stranger let the Pawnee's tail wheel down from a fast taxi at the last minute to get past Dave's plane up ahead and go on by his own wingtip pretty rapidly, too. Seeing that his hopper was still less than half full, knowing that he still had a minute, Tim unbuckled his seatbelt and shoulder harness to hitch around and watch the stranger turn and stop behind him. The short, slight stranger crawled out the side window onto the wing and yanked off his motorcycle helmet, revealing a much more youthful face than Tim had expected. The kid seemed too young to be a commercial pilot.

He had very unusual hair. His tight cap of woolly hair looked white at first, making him look almost angelic, but Tim then realized that it was an extremely pale shade of blond.

Probably some lost ferry pilot, Tim guessed. He grinned, thinking, *Kid delivering planes to build up hours for a commercial. Going to ask us where he is, I'll bet.*

The youngster raised the lid of the chemical hopper in front of the cockpit and hauled out a stuffed military sea bag.

Hey, looks like he's staying.

Tim watched the stranger hustle his bag over to the elevated cement loading platform and tip it upright into a space among all the drums, boxes and cans of farm chemicals, then come jogging over to him.

"Tim?" he asked, and when Tim nodded in surprise, he said, "I'm Jeremy. I'll be joining you out here."

That could be good news, Tim thought as the kid stepped aside for a moment to give Ken room to unhook the loader hose and drag it out of the way. At his age, he had to be a rookie, too. *They'll probably put him with Dave, and I can do some real flying for a change.*

When the woolly-haired youngster stepped back to the side of the cockpit, Tim reached down to shake hands and said, "Welcome."

"Mr. Walker says you and me will be team flying."

Damn! Tim managed to keep a poker face as he silently cursed his luck. He doubted very much that such a young guy could make things go half as smoothly as Dave could. If the kid wasn't a teen-ager, he must have been one very recently.

The little dude handed up a legal-tablet page of scribbled directions to a half dozen or so crudely mapped wheat fields and said, "Olen says tell Dave to keep on with what you two were doing. You and me'll do this stuff. He says you're familiar with the country out here, so you'll fly lead."

Tim's eyes snapped wide with surprise at the implied compliment, but he calmly asked, "You've flown doubles before?"

"Yeah, a little."

"Okay. I'll spray out this load with Dave while you go put your stuff in the house."

"I'll take it in later. Mr. Walker says we need to get on these fields right now. He says we need to get things moving out here."

"Right! Like we've been sitting around playing with our toes!" But Tim was already studying the crude maps and the scribbled instructions, and he said, "How 'bout giving Dave the word."

Not many minutes later, the two young pilots were airborne and heading off across the checkered green-and-beige plains in formation. Tim wryly chuckled over his former confidence that he didn't need anyone to lead him around. He was getting pretty tense about picking out landmarks that would guide him to the first of the new fields. There wasn't a whole lot to go by in that vast, open expanse. Here and there was an occasional creek, a few trees, a farmstead, or maybe a corral, but not much else. The most basic means of navigating to a field was the orderly network of roads, generally one road every mile north and south and one road every mile east and west. If a plane was heading in one of those four directions, it was easy to count the roads, but heading at a significant angle across the network, which Tim was doing just then, made it more difficult.

He spotted Dave's Pawnee working a field a couple miles away. His jaw dropped at the sight, for the old slowpoke was just snapping through his turns, flipping first one way then the other as rapidly as any of the tightest-turning agricultural aircraft he'd ever seen.

Flying on, during the moments when he wasn't completely focused on finding his way, Tim tried to psych himself up for the patience he was sure he'd need to hack through the work with the kid. Soon, he spotted a landmark corral by a lone tree, which corresponded to the sketched map, and he knew he was on the right course and getting near the field he was looking for. He was looking for a nearly square thirty-two acres, and it eventually came into view. Tim sighed with relief. He was positive that it was the right field. It had been nice when he'd been able to leave it up to Dave to keep them from spraying the wrong fields.

He banked to line up, crabbing at quite an angle into the wind, on the downwind side of the field. There were no power lines there—just some brush that ran alongside a meandering creek—so there was no need to circle the field to check things out before they started spraying. He dove on down and thought, *Here's hoping the kid knows what he's doing.* In the first turn and for some time, without realizing just how cautious he was being, he led the newcomer every bit as slowly as Dave had led him. Nearly an hour later, however, as they sprayed a second field with the same load, he was chortling, "Lucked out again!" The kid was sharp, and they'd gone on to comfortably exceed the Dave-Tim turn times. However, his good luck did not include a diminishing wind. By the time their hoppers were empty, it was clear that they were going to have to quit for the day.

As they flew back toward the McLeans', Tim fished a small spiral notebook out of his jacket pocket to roughly tally the day's acres sprayed. Yesterday's tally had been a huge surprise, and he was wondering what it would be today if they kept on spraying in such a wind. The day before, he had personally sprayed almost nine hundred acres. The math was simple: At a dollar per acre, his plane had grossed Will Walker nine hundred dollars. While he was at it, he went on to estimate how much he'd earned in pilot pay: Since a pilot was paid a fourth of the gross, rounding 900 down to 800 and dividing by four, Tim figured he'd earned a little more than a couple hundred dollars.

That was big money at the time, considering that the minimum wage was a buck sixty and the average yearly income was less than ten grand. It didn't seem likely to Tim that he'd earn anywhere near that much often. He didn't try to think of reasons to support that thought. He'd made up his mind when he'd headed for flight school that he'd be satisfied with whatever he could earn flying the seasonal circuit here and there. Money had nothing to do with why he'd decided to go flying. It had just seemed like something sufficiently intense to get his mind off everything else.

And it is working, he thought. He nodded. *It really is.*

He and Jeremy landed, and the other two ag pilots, Dave and Johnny, helped shove their Pawnees backwards between some pieces of heavy farm machinery in the adjacent equipment yard and tie them down with stout manila rope.

When they walked up past the shop, Ned McLean glimpsed them from his office window in the near corner of the building and hurried outside to hail them. "Damn!" he said. "You absolutely sure you all got to quit? Our ground rigs are still at it."

Johnny Crash said, "The wind'll be blowing that Par-thon all the way to Texas if we don't, Ned. Them ground rigs don't have wingtip vortices to swirl that spray up where the wind can catch it."

"Well, I guess there's no help for it. Come on up to the house after you clean up or whatnot. We'll trade a few stories and have coffee while Amanda fixes something nice and hot for you all."

"We still got our sack lunches," Dave protested.

"Save 'em for tomorrow. Or toss 'em. Who's this?"

Tim introduced Jeremy, and McLean said, "Well, the more, the merrier, far as I'm concerned. I'd like to see the air plumb thick with bug bombers!"

4

FRIENDS

"There's an extry bed in Tim's room," Dave said as they tramped into the older house.

Tim suddenly felt a flutter of panic, and he disgustedly thought, *Tighten up, O'Reilly! You up to that craziness again?*

"I think I'd better sleep on the couch," Jeremy replied. "I snore like anything."

"Oh, go on," Dave said. "We can stuff some cotton in Tim's ears."

"Or he could wear that fancy brain bucket of his with all the fancy padding," Johnny added. (Although Dave had taken to wearing a simple sixties-style Bell motorcycle helmet, his old friend Johnny still used a flying helmet of thin leather. Tim, taking Catfish's advice, had bought a shiny new state-of-the-art Cal-Mil crash helmet with lots of padding over the ears.)

Tim was still distracted by his weird reaction to the prospect of sharing the room, and he didn't respond to Johnny's kidding. He was thinking how this little flutter of panic was how he'd felt when he'd first shared his hootch with the new guy in 'Nam after Smitty and again when he'd entered the barracks on his way home and again when he was being discharged at Treasure Island. He'd been fine being crammed into closely-packed barracks with other guys in boot camp, and there'd been no problem with it for quite some time in Vietnam.

Crazily, only later had something gone haywire in his brain about that, and here it was again. Freaking over some loud noise was understandable, but not this thing about sleeping in the same room with other guys.

"Tim don't mind," Dave was saying.

Tim forced an indifferent shrug in affirmation, thinking, *High time you knocked that crap off, O'Reilly.*

"He doesn't look all that thrilled about it," Jeremy said with a careless grin. He gave Tim a friendly punch on the shoulder.

"Nah, you're welcome to share the room," Tim said. "I've bunked with other guys. I'm used to it. I haven't been a civilian *that* long."

"Hey, no kidding? I've been out a little over a year, myself. What branch?"

"Marine Corps," Tim replied, masking his surprise that the tender-looking little guy had to be much nearer his own age than he'd thought.

"Waddaya know? Junior branch of the outfit I was in!" Jeremy laughed and gave Tim a friendly shove on the shoulder.

"*Navy?*" Tim said, looking disgusted, kidding despite the dude's constant touching. The kid didn't seem to have a clue he should maintain a more manly distance. "You're a *squid?*"

"A *reservist* squid at that," The kid laughed. "I'm so ashamed!" Then he said more seriously, "Hey, I really do think I'd drive you nuts. The deck apes I bunked with said I vibrated the bulkheads when I hit my stride."

"Whatever," Tim said with another shrug. "Suit yourself."

"Oh, go 'haid on and use that bedroom," Dave urged. "If it's still blowing, us old folks will be up early watching the TV while you young 'uns is sleepin' like babies. You don't want to be on that settee with us *old* bones rattling around in here."

" 'Cept for Tim," Johnny said. "He'll prob'ly be up with his nose stuck in some book."

"That might just be so," Dave said. "How late did you stay up doing that last night, Tim? Don't you need sleep?"

"Blame it on my mom," Tim replied. "Twice a week after school and Saturday mornings, off we'd go to the library. She made me a reader for sure. It's a right bad habit fer shore, but I cain't git shut of it."

The part about his mother was the truth. The main library in Santa Monica was a short walk from the house. He'd continued to enjoy the quiet and restful place long after his mother had stopped taking him there. All alone, taking periodic breaks from outdoor play with his friends when he'd been in junior high, he'd retreat there to enjoy the restful silence and the resources that would enable him to explore whatever mystery happened to be on his mind. Later, he and his steady in high school had enjoyed studying there together. And if he wasn't reading in some library, he'd be filling his solitary moments elsewhere, poring over some book or magazine wherever he happened to be. It was especially important to read in bed just before sleep. A day didn't feel quite complete if he didn't end it with at least a few minutes of reading.

"Well," Jeremy said, turning to Tim, "if you're really sure . . . "

Tim shrugged, telling himself, *You just have to shake it. Same as that other crap that made you crazy.*

"Come on," he said to the kid. "I'll move my stuff out of the way."

They went into the small bedroom, and Tim moved a few clothes off Jeremy's bed. "I don't have anything in the bottom three drawers," he said, waving toward the single chest of drawers.

"What's this about?" Jeremy asked, looking toward the little cardboard reminder on the lamp table beside Tim's bed. "Assess first?" he asked. "Don't just react?"

"Oh . . . Yeah." Tim wished he'd stuffed that thing in a drawer. "A habit I was getting into. I made it so I wouldn't forget."

"Hey," Jeremy said, "There's times it pays to react and *not* think.

Like crop dusting. Like, 'Hmm . . . Wonder where that wire came from? Oh, dear. Shall I turn away?' Or when the bad guys' guns have your ship bracketed. Hit the damn deck! No sitting around and assessing first then."

"Yeah, true." Tim didn't really want to get into it. "How long you been spraying, anyway?"

"I started last summer. Over in Ohio. Operator I flew for's the one who sent me and the Pawnee to help out here. But I want to find me a spring seat someplace different. Then maybe I'll go back next summer and play junior fill-in pilot again if I can't find something better. I'd rather knock around some first, though."

"Yeah, that's my trip, too," Tim said. He laughed and took a paperback copy of Jack Kerouac's *On the Road* off the top of the chest of drawers to show Jeremy. He turned the cover toward him and said, "I'm studying up on it so I get it right."

"Hey! We should go down the road *together*."

"I don't think so."

"Why not?"

"Well . . . " Tim turned away to put the book back on the chest of drawers, right beside his treasured copy of Bertrand Russell's *History of Western Philosophy* that he'd brought along on the trip from California. He tried to think of an adequate answer and said after a few seconds, "Well, for one thing, it's gotta be twice as hard for two to find a seat in the same place."

* * *

A little after they'd enjoyed a hot lunch of chicken and dumplings, the three older men were still trading flying stories, and the two young men were raptly listening when Lance and Lisa showed up.

"Hey, how's everybody doing?" Lance said as he entered the dining room. He looked and sounded excited. "Since you all aren't in any hurry to fly that AT-6 of mine," he went on, "I'll use it. I need to go talk to somebody about some things I want done to it. But I'll be back in a few hours. You can fly it then if you want. And tonight I want you all to come on over to my place. We'll put the billiards table to use."

"That sure would be nice," Johnny Crash replied, "but me and Dave promised some other old suitcase-bum friends of ours we'd meet 'em for supper at The Conestoga and get caught up." He turned to Tim and Jeremy, saying, "You two are welcome to come along."

"I will," Jeremy said. "Maybe I can get a lead on the spring season somewhere."

"Tim?"

He had thought earlier how nice it would to just relax. He'd imagined how he would have sat with the others in the old house as they chatted and watched TV, but whenever his close attention wasn't demanded, he would have read. Now he wasn't sure what he wanted to do. He'd like very much to spend an evening with Lance and Lisa, but meeting those other veteran circuit flyers would be very interesting and, just as Jeremy had said, he might even hear of someone who'd be needing a driver up in North Dakota or thereabout.

"I . . . Oh, I didn't introduce you. This is Jeremy. Jeremy, Lance Levenger."

"Pleased to meet you," Lance said, giving Jeremy's hand a quick shake and turning immediately back to Tim. "So, I'll be expecting you. Around seven?"

"We could play some Ping-Pong before you go," Lisa said, tugging at Lance's arm. "We haven't played for weeks."

"No, I really do have to take care of something. You all go ahead and play if you want."

McLean got to his feet, saying, "Well, that was a good visit, but I suppose I'd better get back to work. I sure do like having you all out here."

"Feeling's mutual," said Johnny Crash, and the other working pilots nodded.

"If any of you men know how to pray," McLean said, "we need a lot of prayer about this storm. If it don't blow on through . . . "

"Don't you worry," Dave said. "I'll be praying hard."

Ned and Lance went on toward the front door, and the crop dusters trailed along behind but paused at the kitchen to thank Mrs. McLean for the hot meal.

"We have a Ping-Pong table downstairs," Lisa told them. "You're welcome to play. Help pass the time."

Jeremy nodded enthusiastically and said, "Sure! You play, too, Lisa."

"Oh, I'm . . . "

"Go ahead, sweetie," her mother said. "There's not much left to do here."

"Well . . . But you know, I really would like to."

"I like Ping-Pong," Johnny Crash commented.

They all followed Lisa down the interior stairs into the basement.

"Seein's there's two old dogs out of five," Dave drawled, "how 'bout Mr. Crash and me team up with one of y'all young 'uns? We'll duck in and out whenever we get winded."

Tacitly agreeing, Lisa said, "I'll spin a paddle to see who you get. Okay?"

"Go 'haid."

She spun a paddle on the table, and the handle pointed closer to Jeremy than anyone else. So it was Johnny, Dave and Jeremy versus Lisa and Tim.

"You go first," Dave said to Johnny. "You're the one got me into this."

"How 'bout we just warm up a little and take it easy?" Johnny suggested, stepping into position beside Jeremy on one end of the table while Tim and Lisa took the opposite end. "It's been a while."

As they played, they heard Lance running up the T-6 to check the magnetos and cycle the constant-speed prop. Then they heard it go to full power and max RPMs for takeoff.

At the end of two games following the warm-ups, the two teams were tied.

"Championship game now," Dave said. "I want to get cleaned up to go into town before too much longer."

Despite all Johnny Crash's energetic lunging and paddle swiping, Dave turned out to be on the winning side.

"I'm going to wash up," he said, "but we cain't all get in that bathroom at once."

"I'll be happy to set for a while," Johnny said. "I don't mind you hoggin' that bathroom one bit."

The three young people agreed to play on for a while, and Jeremy insisted that Lisa and Tim play first. He took a seat on the short, plain bench beside the downstairs door that led outside and watched for a couple of minutes. Then he got up and said he needed to iron a shirt and a pair of pants to wear to The Conestoga.

"I'll iron them for you," Lisa said.

"No, I'll do it. But thanks, Lisa. That's really nice of you."

"Daddy says we should do your laundry for you. You won't have much time when the weather's better."

"Well, I have time now. Thanks again."

"One more game?" she asked Tim.

"What's the point? I'm no Ping-Pong player."

"I wouldn't be if I didn't get so much practice. I make Daddy play me almost every evening."

They were playing their second game when someone knocked on the door. Lisa went to the door, opened it, and gave a start, saying, "Oh!"

"Sorry," a young man with a long ponytail and long sideburns said. "I would've rung at the main door, but I saw movement down here through the window. We're broke down up the road a ways."

Tim joined Lisa at the door and eyed the young guy, a hippie, judging by his hair, the rolled red bandanna tied around his forehead, and heavy leather sandals over his bare feet despite the frigid temperature. "What's the trouble?" Tim asked.

"No idea. Like it just quit."

"Let's have a look. Maybe I can figure it out."

"You could use one of our trucks, Tim," Lisa said. "You could tow it right into the shop."

"Wow," the stranger said, "That would be out of sight!"

"Do you live around here?" Lisa asked.

"We're from Colorado. Like we're on our way to Tulsa. We got off the highway to get gas."

"We?"

"Yeah. Me and my old lady and our little girl."

"Oh, my! It's too *cold* for them to be sitting out there. I'll bring them down here while Tim and you look at that car."

"It's okay. They got blankets and stuff. We're moving. We got everything with us."

"I won't hear of it. No telling how long it'll be. You go with Tim, and I'll follow in my car."

The guy's transportation was a ratty old International pickup with a small trailer hitched to it. The trailer was piled high with their belongings, which were covered with an old tarp and lashed down with rope. The guy's wife looked like a teen-ager, and their little girl might have been a year or two old. Lisa took the mother and daughter to the farm, and Tim and the stranger started checking the engine.

"There's your problem," Tim called out as he held a spark-plug wire close to the plug and had the guy engage the starter. "Your generator's shot, man."

The young fellow looked very troubled, and Tim guessed it had to do with money.

"We'll see if there's an auto-parts store in town," Tim said. "If not or if they don't have the right generator, we can go to Enid. It's no big deal to slap on a new generator."

"This mechanic dude I know said I wouldn't have any trouble."

"Ah, you never know. These things happen."

They managed to find the right generator in Enid, and when Neil was paying for the reconditioned generator, Tim peeked over his shoulder. He didn't want to ask how much money the young guy had and take a chance that he might not get an honest reply. As far as he could tell, it looked like he had a ten and a one after he'd removed the twenty.

"Got a job in Tulsa?" Tim asked as they drove away.

"Yeah. That's why we're moving."

"Friends there?"

"Family. My uncle and some cousins."

They rode along in silence for several minutes before Neil pulled a little bag and some roll-your-own papers out of his jacket pocket. "I'm feeling pretty uptight, man," he said. "Mind if I smoke?"

"Yes!" Tim snapped. "Put it away." He, too, had smoked some pot after he'd been in 'Nam a while. It came with the contagious cynicism that had swept through the platoon. But he'd stopped after Smitty had kept after him.

"Sorry. It kind of, like, calms you down. You know?"

"It gives me bad memories."

"No kidding? Like . . . "

"Like Vietnam," Tim said a little less severely. "If you can dig it."

"I can, man. I'm real sorry now that I know where you're coming from."

He put it away and said no more. He began to have trouble staying awake. It had been the same on the way to Enid. His head would sharply tip forward, then, jerk when he caught himself. Tim had told him to just relax and sleep, but the guy had continued to fight it.

"I don't think you should drive all that way tonight," Tim said as they approached town.

"I can handle it."

"When did you set out, anyway?"

"Early this morning."

"Does your wife drive?"

"She doesn't have a license yet, but she can."

"Then you should get a room for the night."

"I can make it."

When a fairly decent-looking motel came into sight, Tim pulled in.

"What are you doing?"

"Getting you a motel room. You shouldn't go on. Especially in this weather. Hear that thunder?"

"Oh, man. I can't let you do that."

"I'll give you my address. You can pay me back once you've got your feet on the ground."

"No way."

"Yes. Way."

Tim paid for the room and drove on.

They swapped generators right out there on the road in the gusting wind and the sound of thunder getting louder. It didn't take long.

Tim got a scrap of paper and a pen out of the old Dodge's glove compartment, scribbled his name and his parents' address, and said, "Here. This is my folks' address." Then he handed over the several bills he still had in his wallet.

The other pilots had already left for town by the time Tim returned to the house where they were all staying. It was too late to get cleaned up, drive all the way to The Conestoga, and make it back out to Lance's by seven. It would be nice to just take a hot bath and continue reading *On the Road* over one of the sack lunches they'd put in the refrigerator. When it was time, he'd drive on over to Lance's.

He had started filling the bathtub, relishing the thought of soaking in steaming-hot water after his exposure to the icy wind, when the doorbell rang. He turned off the water and went to the door. It was Lisa. Her car was out front, and Tim could see Lance sitting in the passenger's seat. The windshield wipers were clacking, and tiny raindrops glinted in her hair.

"Hi. Lance and I are on the way to his place now. Why don't you come along with us and have supper there?"

"I need to get cleaned up. I'll be down later."

"You sure?"

"Yeah."

"Well, suit yourself." She began to turn, but she hesitated.

"Tim," she said, "I just have to say how much I love what you did." She reached out to place a hand on his forearm and give it a squeeze. "That was so generous of you. Neil told me about the motel and the money." She made a slight, quick move toward him, as if she were going to give him a hug, but she apparently changed her mind.

He was very glad of that. He would have felt more uncomfortable than ever—even if her fiancé hadn't been looking on.

"Not that big a deal," he mumbled, berating himself for not telling the hippie to keep his mouth shut about the money.

"Oh, I think it *was*." Her eyes were very large and moist. "A very big deal."

"Hey!" he said sharply, fearing that she was about to start crying. "He'll pay me back! He has my folks' address. It wasn't that much anyway."

"They had barely enough for gas when they set out. I know. I got her to tell me, and I gave her what I had on hand, too. Now they won't have to worry about any more emergencies."

"Yeah, well . . . We'll see you at seven."

"Okay. Be sure to come now." She stepped forward and gave

him a quick hug after all.

He darted a look at her car. Sure enough, Lance was watching.

"Oh," she said, seeing him staring toward Lance. "That little hug? I told Lance what you did. He understands. He knows it's a Christian hug."

* * *

Not much later, while Tim was having his simple evening meal as he read about Kerouac's adventures on the road, Lisa was telling the Levengers over their supper what he had done for the stranded travelers.

Lance reacted to it by sulkily thinking, *That boy sure has gone out of his way to impress my woman.* He dully gazed at Lisa as his parents cheerfully responded, and he thought, *Not that I'm all that worried. She's got more sense than to fall for some hired pilot. An ugly one at that.*

"Lance?"

"What's that, Lisa?" He'd drifted too far from the conversation.

"What's wrong?"

"What do you mean?"

"You look . . . well . . . You don't look very happy. Did you make your arrangements okay? Whatever they were?"

"Yes, I did."

"It's a secret?" She looked at the senior Levengers and winked.

"It's just about getting the right paint scheme on my T-6 is all."

"Why do I sense you're up to something more exciting than that?"

He smiled and shook his head to tell her that she was just imagining things, but he was thinking, *You'll see!*

Some minutes later, the doorbell rang, and Lance got up, saying, "It must be that sprayer pilot."

"*Tim,*" Lisa reminded him.

He went to the entry and assumed a great smile. He opened the door and brightly said, "Hey, buddy! Come on in out of the weather! Have you decided to let me fly your sprayer yet?"

Tim just laughed and shook his head.

"Hi, Tim," Lisa said, joining them. "Shall we?" She got between them and took each one by an arm.

That irritated Lance, of course. He'd prefer his wife to be much more reserved, especially with strangers. For a moment he thought he'd have a word with her about it later. However, considering that he couldn't take a chance crossing her after his goof the previous week, he reconsidered.

Lisa led them around the corner and a short way down the hallway to the stairs into the basement. As he emerged from the stairwell, Tim paused to sweep an appreciative look around the sprawling, immaculate room. A small kitchen set off from the rest of the room by a beautiful long bar lay directly before him, but most of the room stretched away to his left. A pool table stood nearest in that section. A luxurious arched couch faced an entertainment center beyond that. There was a large TV, a stereo-record player, and shelves full of record albums. A gleaming modernistic table with six matching chairs graced the far corner of the room opposite the entertainment center and couch.

"Nice!" Tim said. "That pool table sure is a beauty."

"Do you play?" Lisa asked.

"Not very well."

"What are we going to do with you?" she teased. She playfully punched Tim on the shoulder. "Poor boy! Can't play Ping-Pong, can't play pool? I guess we'll just have to teach you."

There she goes again! Lance thought. He'd never seen her act this way before. She'd never even been that familiar with *him* until they'd started dating.

* * *

The two senior pilots had gotten home before Tim, and Dave was quick to give him some news the moment he stepped through the door. "You missed something amazing, Tim!"

Obviously, it had something to do with Jeremy, since both Dave and Johnny Crash were eyeing the kid, wagging their heads in wonder.

"You are bunked up with the fastest, smoothest operator I ever saw in my life," Dave said. "I'm sure half of all them visiting pilots who eat at The Conestoga regular are after this one sweet-looking little gal that works there, and this boy steps right in and puts 'em all to shame."

They all looked at Jeremy, waiting for his response, but he merely shrugged and said, "I made a date. Guys do it all the time."

Jeremy's success with a girl didn't surprise Tim. He could easily imagine how females would think Jeremy had to be the cutest little thing they'd ever seen.

"With that storm banging around out there, y'all boys can sleep in tomorrow," Dave said, "but I'll be up early as usual. So will the crasher if he's the same's he's always been."

Johnny nodded.

"So, you two want breakfast early or late?"

"Early for me," Jeremy said.

"I reckon," Johnny kidded. "Gotta get all spiffed up to meet that gal."

"True. Might have another bath, too. Even though I already took one just a few weeks ago."

"What for? I doubt a boy your size could sweat a thimbleful in a whole Texas summertime."

"That's really offensive, Mr. Crash, but I guess I'll have to take it. Seeing how you're letting me use that nice pickup of yours tomorrow."

"You do owe me, all right."

"Not many would take a gal to church their first date," Dave said. "Good to see in these troubled times. Not all the young people have gone hog wild."

"She's the one who suggested it. I guess I look like I need saving bad."

"You look like a cotton-picking teddy bear," Johnny Crash said. "Watch out you don't end up married."

"What kind of church does she go to?" Dave wanted to know.

"Southern Baptist."

Dave made a sour face and turned to Tim, saying, "Tim? Sleeping in?"

"Nah, I might as well get up if everybody else is."

"Then four thirty it is. Same as any other day."

"Whoa!" Jeremy exclaimed. "I don't gotta be up *that* early. How 'bout six?"

5
AIRSHOW

Tim awoke to the jangling of his wind-up alarm clock. He raised himself up on one elbow only to fall back. He was exhausted. He'd been having another 'Nam-mare about Smitty. He could still hear the screaming. "Jesus! Jesus!" He wondered whether it would ever stop.

"Hey, partner!" Jeremy called out. "Rise and shine!"

Not a chance, Tim thought.

"You're still here!" Jeremy chortled. "I thought I would've driven you out to the living room. Or kicked me out."

If the kid had snored, Tim sure hadn't heard it, but he did wish he'd shut up now.

He felt a sudden yank on his big toe. He jerked his foot back and shouted, "Knock it off! Keep your damn hands to yourself!"

"Sorry! You sure are touchy, man."

"Who's touchy? What's *with* all that touching, anyway?" Tim was sitting upright now, all hope of getting some sound sleep obliterated.

"Well, it's not because I think you're cute. Just goofing around, man."

Tim swung his big feet on down to the floor, stood, and started getting into his jeans and a sweatshirt. He headed for the bathroom, but the door was closed. He went on to the kitchen, where Dave was using a fork to turn over the strips of bacon he was frying in a wide black skillet.

"Say, Tim?" said Dave. "Mind finding a station with some local weather on it? Praise the Lord, I do believe our prayers have been answered. Seems them thunder bumpers went right on through last night."

Tim went into the parlor and began twisting the selector knob, fading out the country music. He found a strong night signal coming from a station in Chicago, another in San Francisco and, of course, that great powerhouse down in Del Rio, Texas, which must have been the one Dave had been listening to. But the radio mostly crackled with low-key static, except for an occasional loud burst sparked by lightning somewhere. Finally, however, he heard an announcer identify a station located in Oklahoma City. OKC wasn't exactly in the neighborhood, but at least it should have the Oklahoma weather.

The voice introduced some singer named "Leapy Lee," and a goofy-sounding, high-pitched male voice started doing a dumb song about little arrows in some girl's hair. It sounded almost as bizarre as Tiny Tim's tiptoeing through the tulips. Tim, who had listened to very little country music before his escape from LA, shook his head and turned up the volume anyway so that Dave would be able to hear from the kitchen.

"Good night!" Dave immediately shouted. "They playing that thing again? *English* Western? Them English is invading all over! There's this here boy, and there's them Beatles . . . They ort-ter *spray* them dadblamed Beatles."

Tim, having largely recovered from his nightmare by then, grinned at Dave's nonsense and went to a side window that directly faced open wheat fields to the west, thinking that he sure was getting a great sampling of how different life can be in different parts of the same nation. First, it had been the Mississippi Delta, and now this. It was pretty much what he had wanted, lots of intense flying and knocking around to experience all the variety and get his mind off the bad stuff that had gotten him down.

Using the sleeve of his sweatshirt, he swiped away some window condensation and peered outside. It was raining, and the branch ends of a winter-bare bush quivered in the wind. Even if the storm had passed, he'd still have some reading time until the wind calmed.

"Beatles!" Dave shouted as Leapy sang on. "Leapies!"

That brought another small smile to Tim's haggard face. He went to the opposite side of the parlor and peeked through a window there. There were glimmers of retreating lightning in the distance—not the bright downward-flashing arrows of a near storm but the distant, quivering glowballs that reminded him of artillery bursts far away.

"What in the world are you hollering about?" Johnny Crash demanded of Dave as he entered the kitchen. "Something nibble on you last night? I'm sure you done brung it with you if it did."

It wasn't much later when Dave set out a big platter of scrambled eggs, liberally shot through with flecks of black pepper and the dark residue of fried-bacon grease. Then he brought a platter of bacon and toast that he'd kept warm in the oven.

"Lordy!" Johnny Crash exclaimed. "If we got to shovel our way through meals like this, we'll have to cut down our payloads!"

"Well, you ain't gonna be hauling no loads for a while yet," Dave commented. "You gonna be whining about the weather 'til that wind calms down."

"I'm afraid that's the truth. I'm here to make me some money, boys. You got alimony payments to make, Tim?"

"Never been married, actually."

"Yep," said Dave, "that's what I thought. You do look fresh and unsullied. You also look a whole lot smarter than us two."

Jeremy came in and joined them at the table.

"Mornin', lover boy," Johnny said to Jeremy, passing him the platter of bacon and toast.

"Good morning, sir. Good morning, Dave. Hey, this looks

great!"

"Thank ye. I do like to cook. Wait 'til you taste my biscuits."

As they ate and the two older men kept on kidding around, Jeremy started turning the conversation to seasonal flying, and the two older men began telling about the more exotic places where they'd worked. They had told about Egypt, Rhodesia, and Mexico when Tim remembered that Dave had mentioned Idaho. That didn't seem much like farming country to him. He pictured forests and mountains.

"Dave?" he said. "You say you flew in Idaho?"

"And that's where I'll be going again come June," Dave said. "Lord willing."

"Ah! Idaho *potatoes*," Tim said. "What was I thinking?"

"And lots of other crops, too. Like seed alfalfa. That seed alfalfa's what makes it night-spraying country."

"You spray at *night*?"

"Yep. Got to protect the pollinators. Seed growers got a lot of money tied up in bees."

"I guess they're in their hives at night."

"Bee boards. Not hives. Leafcutter bees, not honeybees. Spray right over the top of 'em while they're snoozing away, snug in their boards."

"At *night*."

"We do use lights, Tim."

"Of course. Still . . . "

Jeremy had gone to iron some clothes for his church date when the kitchen phone rang. Dave, who happened to be on his feet at the moment, answered, and he held the handset to one side to tell Tim and Johnny, "It's Miz McLean. Saw our lights on earlier. Wants to know if we'll go to church with them."

"Please tell her I said thank you," Johnny Crash replied, "but I need to make some long-distance calls. Ask her if she minds, so long's I charge them to my American Express."

"Tim?" Dave asked.

"I can't. I don't have any church clothes."

"Ma'am, Johnny Crash said to thank you, but he's got some calls to make. We both do, and we're wondering if we can use the phone down here and charge the time to our calling cards . . . " He listened for a moment to whatever she was saying, then commented, "Thank you. We appreciate it.

"You all might see Jeremy in church today if it's Southern Baptist . . . Oh, it's not . . . And Tim's worried about not having church clothes . . . But that's what I was thinking, too. Blue jeans and a new flying jacket do look nice on a young man . . . All right. We'll have him ready."

"Hey!" Tim said, and he was about to tell Dave to tell her he wasn't going. But it really wasn't that big a deal. An hour or so to see what church is like in rural Oklahoma might be interesting. The last time he'd been to church had been a long time ago back home in Santa Monica, an entirely different world. And jeans and a jacket probably would get him by in a small farming town.

He heard Dave say, "Me? Well, I thank you, ma'am, but . . . Well, I suppose I should. I normally do when it's not flying time . . . Yes, ma'am, I'll ask Johnny Crash one more time, too. Thank you. Two of us'll be ready for sure."

He set the hand piece back in the cradle and said, "They'll come by for us at ten after nine."

"Not for me, they ain't," said Johnny.

"I wish I had a nicer shirt at least," Tim said. "All I have are T-shirts and sweatshirts."

"You do travel light," Johnny said. "A cardboard box for such a potentially fine, young suitcase bum? But I've got a dress shirt that'll fit you. Maybe a little short in the sleeves, but plenty of room around the middle."

"You ought to come, too, Crasher," Dave said. "Give Jesus a chance."

"Uh-uh. Not me. I ain't going in that church. If you thought that lightning was wicked last night . . . "

* * *

Tim and Dave were waiting on the front porch when the blue Lincoln came rolling down through the rain from the big house. They'd been guessing at the altitude of the cloud ceiling, which had risen higher, smoothed out, and turned light gray. The car's left rear door swung partway open, and Dave gave Tim a little push. Tim ran, dove in, and scooted to the middle of the back seat to make room for Dave. He turned to say good morning to Lisa, but the sight of her nearly stopped his breath. She had such an incredibly sweet smile, and her golden mane, glittering even in the poor light from the opaque plastic dome in the ceiling, was simply too striking to not stir some emotion. No little arrows, but he felt he could understand how Leapie might have gotten carried away in his perceptions.

"Good morning, Tim, Dave," she said as Dave piled in and slammed the door. She shook their hands, and her breath smelled of Colgate.

When her eyes briefly met Tim's, he noticed that the irises were not completely blue. There were delicate rods of amber that radiated through them from the large, dark pupil. But she immediately dropped her eyes from his and looked away.

She and Lance are just perfect for each other, he thought. *Fine-looking people.*

Ned McLean gunned the big car around in a tight circle, went up the knoll past the new house, and turned south onto the paved road to town. "Now if this rain would just move on . . . " he said, not bothering to finish.

"It's on its way out," Dave said. "Our God does answer prayer."

The two older men then launched into a long discussion about the weather, the bugs, and the wheat crop. Soon Mrs. McLean craned her head back, and Lisa leaned forward to listen to a whispered tale about some woman in church who'd apparently lost her husband recently.

It was no business of his, and Tim drifted in and out of awareness of what they were saying. He was thinking that he should get to a library and learn something more about his options in establishing a seasonal spraying circuit. But Lisa looked so pretty that he had to keep on stealing glances at her, as well. He'd never dream of making a pass at someone's fiancée, of course. An O'Reilly just didn't do that sort of thing. But he did take pleasure in admiring her wholesome beauty. It made him wonder when he'd start dating again. Maybe when he went up to North Dakota to find a seat for the six-week spring season but maybe not until summer, wherever he went for the cotton spraying.

Whichever, it won't be for a while, he thought. *Could be I'll stay so busy I won't even notice.* He reminisced about being so busy day and night in flight school that he'd completely forgotten about Jen for days at a time. The loss, so very painful at first, no longer hurt very badly even now. His crop dusting adventure was turning out to be good medicine, all right.

Not even sure I ever want to get that close to anybody again anyway, he thought.

McLean pulled up to a nice-looking old church building of red brick with white wood trim and a white wood steeple. He stopped directly before the entrance to let them out, and they dashed in through the dwindling rain.

As Tim hurried into the foyer behind the others, a startling outburst of shrill, strange cries brought him to a halt. He darted looks among the clusters of people in suits and dresses, searching for the source of the disturbance. A young woman in a wheelchair arched her back and sharply threw her head up just as the harsh cry sounded again.

Mrs. McLean got between him and Dave, grabbed their arms,

and said, "I'd like you all to meet the preacher." She propelled them past the girl in the wheelchair and called out to the thin, young preacher wearing a snappy black suit and red tie. Thick horn-rimmed eyeglasses perched on a curved beak. "Pastor Glen, I'd like to introduce . . . "

They went through the formalities, and Mrs. McLean told about the crop dusters staying in the old house while Tim reflected that the preacher's smile looked as if it had been pasted on. The dude inclined his head close to Mrs. McLean's, and he nodded as she spoke, but the dark eyes behind the thick lenses were busily scanning the foyer.

The girl in the wheelchair continued to cry out, and Tim felt obligated to offer a few polite words to the preacher. As he did so haltingly, since the preacher kept glancing away and nodding greetings to others, Tim randomly checked faces among the crowd to see how they reacted to the girl's raucous disturbance. It had no visible effect on them at all. Apparently, they were well used to it. Tim didn't like the preacher, whose indifference to a visitor was pretty offensive, but the congregation's acceptance of the disruptive girl more than compensated for it.

"So you go on to young folks Sunday school with Lisa, Tim," Mrs. McLean said as the preacher abruptly left them. "Dave will come with us."

As he edged through the crowded foyer, heading toward Lisa, Tim felt a hard thump on one thigh. He looked down to see the crippled girl spasmodically swinging a clawed white hand at him again. He reflexively reached out to grasp it. She clenched his hand with surprising strength, and she began to squirm and huff, apparently trying to speak. As she struggled, he saw by her unfocused eyes that she was blind, too.

"Hiii!" she shrilled at last.

"Hi," he said, attempting to make the best of an uncomfortable situation. "How are you?"

"Fiiiine!"

"My name is Tim. What's yours?"

"Taaammy . . . Sue-hoo!"

"Nice to meet you."

"M-m-me, too!"

A very big smile now revealed ragged rows of teeth that looked like rotten old tree stumps.

"I'm new around here," Tim said, making conversation. "Do you come here often?"

"Y-yes! J-J-J-Je-Jesus lovvves me!"

Just then, someone else just out of his field of vision touched him, and he turned. It was Lisa. Her eyes were charged with emotion again, just as they had been the night before, and it flustered him. She said, "Time for Sunday school," then, "Good morning, Tammy Sue. We have to hurry on to Sunday school, Tam. Love you, sweetie."

"B-bye!"

Lisa slipped a hand to the inner side of Tim's elbow and gave him a little tug toward the hallway that led off to one side of the sanctuary. She left her hand there as she murmured, "That was good of you, Tim."

"What else could I do?" he said a little too sharply, knowing that she was going to make too much of it, just as she'd made too much about his helping the people with the broken-down pickup. "*She* latched onto *me*. That girl has a *grip*."

* * *

As they gathered in the McLeans' pew after Sunday school, an organ solo ended, and a plump, youngish woman with auburn hair slicked down to her shoulders took up a microphone and said, "Let's sing." She made a rising, palm-up motion with her free hand, and the congregation stood. Dave had opened a hymnal in advance, and he held it before Tim as the organ played the familiar prelude, and they all began to sing, "On a hill far away . . . " Dave was belting it out very noticeably with great enthusiasm, but Tim was able to imagine that he could hear his dad's strong and earnest but off-key voice. It was the one of the senior Tim O'Reilly's favorite hymns. As for Tim Junior, he sang very softly and self-consciously.

The song leader sounded professional. Her voice was husky. It was the sort of voice, Tim thought, that one might hear in the wee hours at some smoky nightclub. She had her pale face tilted back and her eyes closed. She delicately held the mike between the stubby thumb and the forefinger of her left hand, and the other little sausage-like fingers fanned delicately upward with the stubby pinkie on top. She momentarily held the open palm of her pale right hand beside her sleek round head and the bent elbow jutted out to the side. She began to repeatedly snap the forearm straight in line with her upper arm, causing the open palm to fly up high.

Tim glanced around. A middle-aged couple off to the right across the aisle were flinging their hands over their heads, too. He'd seen that sort of thing on TV as he'd flipped through the channels, but they'd never done such stuff in the restrained, upper-middle sort of mainline church that he'd attended back home in Santa Monica when he was a boy.

It startled Tim to see Lisa's free hand, the one not holding her hymnal, float upward, too. He was glad when it stopped to hover only a little higher than her shoulder. But both Dave's hands had flown all the way up to arm's length.

Tim hunched his head down between his shoulders. He would have made like a turtle and gone completely out of sight if it had been possible. He glanced around again, and he could see a few others in the congregation doing it, but most of the people behaved more like those in Tim's home church. This was one of those times that made him wish he was a foot shorter and wasn't so obvious, sticking way up there above most other people, stuck between two friends whose waving had to be attracting attention.

At last, after far too many hymns with that hand raising on either side to have Tim feeling anything but badly embarrassed, the thin young pastor with the thick, horn-rimmed glasses, now wearing vestments of the purest white over his black suit, strode forward to deliver the sermon. He leaned over the pulpit and rhetorically demanded, "What kind of man or woman lays down his life for another?"

Smitty's horrifically sacrificial death in 'Nam instantly sprang into Tim's mind, and he silently and cynically replied, *People like you, I'm sure.* But then he thought, *There you go again, O'Reilly. Knock it off. You don't know this man.*

That flash of anger and his guilt-ridden ruminations over it kept him from hearing much else of the sermon. His upbringing, not simply his parents' admonitions but their example, had been very effective in driving home the conviction that temper tantrums were not an acceptable element of what they called "the O'Reilly way."

He was daydreaming about their strong example when the sound of persistently droning airplanes dragged him back into the present. It sounded like there were two of them circling high above. One sounded a lot like a Stearman duster, and the other, like a lighter plane with a smaller motor. *Like a Pawnee?* Tim wondered.

He shot a look outside. The rain had stopped. But then he could see that the wind was still shaking the winter-bare trees out there.

The preacher's amplified voice was becoming very loud as the volume of the droning planes increased. He began to hesitate as he spoke. Judging by the man's grimaces and glances upward, Tim gathered that the noise was getting to him. He glanced at his watch and wondered why the guy didn't just wrap it up and stop. His watch showed the time to be very nearly noon anyway.

Instead, the bespectacled young man kept on urging his

audience to continue to strive to serve others through sacrificial living. By doing so, he said, they would experience a profound and enduring inner peace despite all the alarms of on-going assassinations and rioting and threat of annihilation by nuclear warfare. But the planes' infernal rasping and buzzing was causing the congregation to stir and murmur and stare inquisitively upward by then, and the preacher's face began to darkly glow and his voice to harshly blare.

The sound of the smaller plane droned off into the distance, and the preacher abruptly quit speaking, prayerfully pressed the palms of his hands together, and gazed upward. But the sound of the bigger plane alarmingly intensified, and the gangly fellow suddenly shouted into the microphone, "My God!"

Immediately, he seemed dumbfounded by his own strange outburst, and his eyes popped nearly as wide as the round frames of his glasses. His mouth flopped ajar. He rapidly shook his dark head, as if he might shake it free of whatever evil had possessed him to utter such vulgarity.

"*May* God," he now snarled, obviously correcting his slip of the tongue by putting extreme emphasis on the misspoken word. "*May* God," he repeated, "be with you." But it was doubtful that many among his flock had any idea of what he was saying by then.

Judging by the racket the noisier airplane was making now, it had commenced a loudly whining power dive toward them, and the people were about as distracted as a congregation could be. The airplane sounded something like an enormous industrial generator spinning out of control, spooling faster and faster, and the preacher yelled in hasty conclusion, "Go in peace!"

Brrrowww! The distinctive rasping roar of a big round engine swinging a long prop adjusted to flat pitch displaced the swelling whine as the plane went by close overhead.

Nearly everyone ducked. Women screamed. Men whooped. Tim and Dave whipped their heads around to stare wide-eyed at each other. The young woman in the wheelchair in the aisle at the back began to shriek. And some of the boys, apparently filled with joy by such a hellacious disruption, bolted into the aisles and raced for the doors to go see.

The young preacher took off, too, but, judging by the smoldering look on the fellow's face, it was neither with joy nor with any measure of the peace he'd just preached. His rich vestments of pure, glistening white flapped wide of his coal-black inner suit as he awkwardly sailed off the dais like some caricature of a comic-book superhero. The combination of momentum, gravity, and poor motor skills had their predictable effect, and down he went. Yet, an instant later, he was right back up and flailing onward.

Meanwhile, Lisa sat hunched over with her burning red face buried in the palms of her hands. Her mother nervously patted the mortified young woman's bowed back, and Ned McLean began to grate, "That . . . damn . . ."

As a tumult of excited chatter filled the so-called sanctuary— certainly no sanctuary from the mad world at that point—the louder airplane that had buzzed the church could be heard making a rudely blatting, climbing turn nearby. Its engine had to be at full power and its prop blades cocked almost all the way to their flattest possible pitch to create such an obscene din. Nothing at all could be heard now of the other, quieter plane.

Lisa lifted her head and heaved a ragged sigh. She lurched to her feet. So did they all, joining the jam-packed exodus surging up the aisles.

Some of the people, now that they'd recovered from their surprise and could assure one another that there was no cause for alarm after all, began making comments such as, "It's that Lance Levenger again," "Yep, same sound as when he was doing tricks a couple weeks ago," "Well, boys will be boys," and so on.

That was insane! Tim thought, trying to reconcile the two starkly conflicting impressions he now had of Lance. He scanned the throng in the opposite aisle and caught sight of Lance's parents, whom he'd met the night before. That elegant-looking couple bore their son's eccentric act with their heads held stoically high.

One man near them shouted, "He's a character, all right, but he's a likable young cuss." And a bent and severely wrinkled crone squawked in her more old-fashioned, Central Southern accent, "That boy's plumb wild, but he's got a right good heart!"

Tim was relieved. There hadn't been a single condemning remark. He wanted very much to go on liking and respecting Lance. He and Lance had gotten along well the night before, and he'd thought several times by now that it would be nice to swing on by after North Dakota and say hi to Lance and Lisa on his way to wherever, maybe Texas, in May or June and whenever else he could thereafter.

When he finally got outside, he could see that the offending plane was, indeed, Lance's new toy.

* * *

As Lance held the silvery low-winged aircraft in a steep climb, the tip of its altimeter needle gradually arced through 4,000, which indicated the altitude in feet above sea level. That put him about three thousand feet over the town. Another two thousand and he'd do a stunt to hold the attention of the congregation until the other airplane came back into view at a lower altitude. Originally Lance had wanted to do his aerobatics down there, too, but both the owner and the pilot of the other plane had balked. They had pointed out that it would put the hired plane and pilot at risk, and they had said they wouldn't go through with it unless Lance stayed clear.

Now, as the T-6 neared 5,000 feet, Lance peered into the distance to check on the location of the other airplane that had first circled above the church with him. It was getting close to time for the Citabria to turn around and start coming back within sight of the people he could see watching from the churchyard far below. He had only several minutes before they'd see the banner.

And how's this for a good sign? he thought, considering the weather. The wind was still blowing, but the gray cloud ceiling had lifted a bit higher than necessary, and the rain had stopped.

As soon as he leveled off, Lance tipped his silvery, low-winged plane into another power dive. When he'd gained sufficient speed, he pulled the nose up until it seemed to be just above the distant horizon, tilted the wings into the beginning of a slow roll, and simultaneously commenced a gradual turn to the left.

Lance was not a highly experienced aerobatic pilot, but he was having some modest success so far in making the top of the T-6's cylindrical engine cowling (as viewed from his seat in the front cockpit) almost seem to roll along the horizon. However, the maneuver he was attempting was a difficult one, and it frustrated him that he couldn't keep the nose from erratically rising a little above and sinking a little below the distant juncture of earth and sky, and the progress the plane was making toward completion of a full 360-degree turn with simultaneous slow rolls came increasingly in alternating little jerks and hesitations. He doubted that the slight imperfections so far were noticeable to more than a very few former military pilots down there, including Lisa's pa. But as the airspeed decreased, he began to fear that the T-6 might end up clumsily falling out of the rolling turn, and Lisa and everybody would clearly see that he'd goofed.

Better to stop now than blow it completely, he thought, hanging upside down in his snug web of military seat belt and shoulder harness straps. So he terminated the roll as soon as the plane had returned to a simple upright bank. He had made it almost three-fourths of the way through a complete 360-degree orbit, and he hoped that his audience wouldn't realize that he'd failed to make a complete one. He just held the left wing cocked about thirty degrees downward and continued the turn normally to look down on the blue-and-white high-winged Citabria that was making its approach from the west, towing the banner.

He glanced at his fancy pilot's watch. In just a few seconds, it would be exactly 12:07, the precise time he'd specified for the Citabria's initial flyby, and here it came. He was sure that most of the congregation had made it out to the parking lot now and could clearly see the long, fluttering banner that proclaimed,

LANCE–LISA WEDDING 8/22

He only wished that he'd thought of announcing the engagement this way, which would have been so much better. Or, better yet, he should have asked Lisa to marry him this way. Now, all of a sudden, his dramatic announcement of a mere wedding date seemed strangely overblown even to him. But he wasn't one to harbor thoughts of failure for long, and he brightened as he thought how, on the other hand, the plane he'd owned at the time of their engagement, his Stits Playboy, was so small and quiet. The T-6 was anything but that, and it was only one step along the way to much bigger and better things.

Once he and Lisa were man and wife, two of the biggest outfits in that part of the state would be on their way to becoming a single great entity. His own father, along with Lisa's, would be grooming him to become the head of the whole shebang.

* * *

"Did you come up with that idea, Lisa?" one of the younger men standing in the church parking lot teased, and when she protested that she'd had nothing to do with it, an older woman said, "Don't you worry, hun! We know you're just the one to tame that boy!"

Lance's dad glanced around, giving them feeble smiles of

appreciation, but Mrs. Levenger didn't look amused. It may have been because she simply felt too ill. Her husband's hand at her elbow was not always there these days for mere appearances but to hold her steady.

"Well," Levenger said to the McLeans, ignoring Lance's on-going demand for attention as he performed a Cuban eight, "now that we have a wedding date, we'd better get together soon and start planning."

Lisa gave another deep sigh and turned to trudge toward the family car, closely followed by her mother and, one after another, the three men. She didn't look up when the smaller, high-wing plane went by a second time with the banner. She climbed into the back seat and sat gazing downward as her mother stood beside her, patting her shoulder, and her fiancé buzzed the church one more time, roaring and rasping by just above the white wood cross atop the steeple, then, in a shallow climb out over the nearby open farmland, flipped the AT-6 into an old-fashioned victory roll and climbed away.

Mrs. McLean slipped onto the back seat beside Lisa, and the three men went to get in. Tim sat with the two women in back, and Dave sat up front with Ned McLean. Before he started the car, Ned hitched around and reached back to pat Lisa's knee and say, "Looks like he sprang that on you."

She gave a flurry of quick little nods.

"But you did agree on that date?"

She shook her head and managed to say, snuffling, "Not really. He mentioned it. His *folks* said it was fine. *I* didn't."

6
CLYDE ROBERT

A little later that Sunday afternoon, Ned McLean was telling Johnny, Dave, and Tim a Korean War flying yarn when his eyes suddenly bulged at something he saw out the dining room window to the south. Whatever he saw caused him to roar, "That damn kid!"

The heads of the three visiting crop dusters swung. They saw a yellow hardtop Corvette speeding up the paved north-south farm road toward the knoll on which the big house perched. It was drizzling again now, and the 'Vette came on so fast that it sprayed a rooster tail of glistening road moisture.

The car dipped into a swale about a quarter mile from the house then quickly popped back into view. Its engine started going, *wowww . . . wowww . . . wowww*, as the driver shifted down through the gears. It momentarily went out of view again behind the windowless east wall of rugged stonework and massive fireplace that once again contained a cozy, crackling fire.

McLean violently hitched around in his chair at the head of the long dining table to peer out the opposite picture window just behind him. It provided a view to the north of the immaculate front lawn and the wide gravel drive that curved up that side of the knoll to the house. Tim's, Dave's, and Johnny's heads whipped around to face that way, too.

The 'Vette had already gone into a four-wheel drift by the time it reappeared. It slid on down the wet blacktop but nosed gradually across it into the oncoming lane and toward the wide gravel entrance to the farm.

Tim was on his feet now to better view the spectacle. He was thinking, *That dude can drive!* He wondered whether it was the absent son that Mr. McLean had briefly, sadly, mentioned as being the intended occupant of the immaculate older house below the knoll.

The bright and shiny machine slid off the wet pavement onto the broad gravel entrance to the farmstead in a smooth arc. It turned more tightly once it was on the loose stuff at a lower speed, slewing at a sharp angle, and accelerated up the knoll toward the house.

"What in *hell* am I going to do with that boy?" McLean bellowed.

"Ned!" his wife said, glaring at him from around the end of the long wall that separated the dining room from the kitchen.

"Well . . . " he huffed. "Well . . . " But he gave it up and turned back to the window to mutely watch the gleaming yellow machine rocket up the north side of the knoll toward the house.

Tim wanted badly to have a car something like that some day. He hadn't always driven a junker. He'd sold a lot of stuff to help pay for flight school, including the cool car he'd had since high school. But he needed to get something better than the Dog soon. Of course it wouldn't be anything as nice as that new Corvette or, better suiting his own taste, a Porsche, but he definitely would not go looking for his next seat in a faded old Dodge sedan that sickly trailed a dark cloud of oil smoke.

The Corvette was cocked less radically sideways now, but its rear tires spewed gravel as they clawed for traction, and Tim couldn't help grinning and nodding his approval even though the gravel had to be nicking the undersides of the rear fenders. He wouldn't have wanted Mr. McLean to see such signs of approval, but the farmer's eyes were locked on the car as it gradually straightened and slid to a stop at the curbed edge of the lawn.

The driver's door swung open, and out scrambled Lance Levenger.

Tim grinned all the wider and thought, *This guy is just out of sight!* Lance had treated him grandly last night. He cut such a striking figure as he strode around the nose of the wetly gleaming, low-slung car in the rain. *Looks like an ad in* Esquire *or something*, Tim mused. *He's just the type to be driving a machine like that. No, actually, not. He really needs a Ferrari or something.*

Then the passenger door opened, and out lurched a scruffy little dude dressed in faded jeans, a motorcycle jacket, and black engineer boots, the kind with big chrome buckles made famous by Marlon Brando in *The Wild One.* This scrawny young guy with his stringy black hair tied back in a short ponytail and his pointed chin decorated with a sparse, untrimmed Fu Manchu goatee looked a lot wilder than Marlon Brando or any of that fictional biker gang. His arms were disproportionately long, and his hands were disproportionately large, reminding Tim of a monkey. He just stood there in the drizzling rain, slightly hunched with his long arms hanging down, grinning and nodding his cocked head at Lance, who briskly strode on toward the entrance.

"Good night," McLean muttered. "He brought that one along? But why should I be surprised?"

Lance made a curt gesture for his companion to follow, and the little cripple began hurriedly hop-skipping to catch up.

Lance wore a leather jacket, too, but its rich, creamed-coffee color and supple folds made a stark contrast to the one worn by his strange companion. The combination of Lance's erect, elegant bearing and his jacket's trim cut close to the waist reminded Tim of photos of bullfighters. He doubted that the color of Lance's sport shirt, revealed by a dramatically-high collar, perfectly matched that of the Corvette coincidentally, and he grinned again.

What a kick! Tim thought. *Never a dull moment around this character, I'll bet.*

He recalled Lance's repeated urgings to fly his AT-6 and

wondered whether they'd get around to that later on. But the improving weather made it look like they might go back to work instead.

Lance and his friend passed out of sight as they neared the front steps, and the three working pilots at the dining table glanced around at one another and shook their heads in wonder at all the drama. They sat silently, expectantly, now, Ned McLean's vintage war tale apparently forgotten, as they waited for the odd pair to enter.

"Oh, Lance!" Mrs. McLean's kindly voice soon called out from the kitchen on the other side of the wall from the dining room. "How *nice*. You brought CR along. We'll set another place."

"Oh, *yes*," her husband muttered. "*Nice*. Nice, my aching *foot*."

Tim sympathized with the man's irritation, but he was also impressed with his wife's cheerful acceptance of an uninvited guest—and such a rough-looking character at that. He couldn't imagine why Lance would be dragging such a misfit around unless the dude had something great going for him that compensated for his appearance.

He didn't seem to fit in at all, other than possibly belonging to the same species, and it wasn't because everybody else was all that dandied up. Mrs. McLean had told them they were going to wear "just comfortable clothes."

Tim heard Lisa's voice, a sharp, ironic edge to it, say, "Well, Clyde Robert. You made it back all safe and sound, I see."

"Go on into the dining room and get warm," her mother urged the newcomers. "They've got a fire going in there. But take this fresh dish towel and wipe that rain off yourselves first."

Seconds later, the two entered the dining room, and the three guest pilots got up from their chairs. McLean didn't bother. He kept his seat to gruffly introduce his future son-in-law's companion.

"This here's CR," he said, and the emaciated, pocked face of the young guy tilted down and turned slightly away. The creepy little dude stood so near now that Tim could see that both the dull black leather boots and jacket were severely scuffed, and he couldn't think of anything that would have made those marks other than falling off a bike. Along with that greasy black hair and thin goatee, he looked like a biker of the worst sort. "CR works for the Levengers when he isn't off drifting around the country."

"I should've had him dress up some," Lance said, "but I thought I'd bring him along at the last minute. I didn't want to be late."

Tim reached out to shake hands, and CR raised a rough, hard, grease-stained hand to passively accept a couple pumps. Tim got another good look at the grotesque paw as it went out to shake Dave's and Johnny's hands. The broad nails were thickly rimmed with black grease. Tim noticed, too, how CR hung his head as he shook hands with Johnny and Dave and how he mumbled, "Howdy," without making eye contact.

"Lance," McLean said, "I do wish you'd slow down a little. I've got some say in what you do if you're going to marry my daughter. Have you—"

"I'm sorry, sir! Sometimes I just don't think ahead." His fine hands flew about, expressively punctuating his penance. "I am making an effort to be more careful."

Tim noted that CR was giving Lance a snaggle-toothed grin now, as if Lance was making some joke. His head was tilted to one side again as he gazed up at Lance, and the uneven teeth revealed by the grin had the glossy, caramel appearance of residue from habitual tobacco chewing.

Lisa rushed in and began gathering another place setting out of the big old china cabinet at the far end of the room, and Tim ceased listening to Lance's chatter as he watched her. *Such a sweetheart!* he thought. *Her mom, too. They're so nice to this piece of bad news.*

Lisa's hair continued to fascinate him, as it had on the way to church and back. *Spun gold*, he thought. He'd read that somewhere, and that was exactly what it looked like with all its glittering highlights and springy-looking, shadowed whorls. Her figure was already full enough to make Tim think that she'd end up just a little on the slightly plump side like her mother, but he guessed that she would still, like her mother, continue to be a very lovely woman. She looked so wholesome in her bell-bottom jeans, spotless white Keds and long-sleeved blue-and-white striped jersey.

She went back into the kitchen and out of sight, and Tim tuned back in to what else was going on around him to hear some of what McLean was saying about, " . . . on the Levenger place. And so does CR when he's in these parts. Where have you been at *lately*, Clyde Robert?"

Fellow ramblin' man, Tim sardonically reflected. He was alluding to a Hank Williams song on an eight-track tape he'd listened to a number of times on the drive up from Mississippi.

"Texis," CR drawled.

"What doin'?"

Lisa scurried back in with a big bowl of steaming mashed potatoes. The men leaned aside to make room for her, and she set the bowl on a trivet.

CR's mumbled reply sounded like, "War brush'n ole barls," but Tim had been around such accents enough in the past few months to guess he probably meant, "Wire-brushing oil barrels," even though it seemed a strange way to make a living.

"Pa's happy as all get out that he's back," Lance said. "He's our best ground-rig driver."

"Careful now, Lance!" McLean sternly warned. "Watch your language!"

Tim didn't get it at first, but he did when McLean went on to say, "Let's not use them kind of words around these here airplane drivers!"

"Oh, we have done heard talk about ground sprayers before," Dave spryly retorted. "We are hardened to it. Some folks say it don't matter a'tall if the wheat gits all mashed down flat and the soil gits squshed down hard as rock by them big ol' tires."

Lance beamed one of his dazzling smiles in response, and it made Tim think once more what a perfect picture of a young aristocrat he made. He was just the sort to be an heir to all those miles of Levenger real estate. He wondered how many brothers and sisters he'd share it with. And that, in turn, made him momentarily think about Lisa's inheritance and her absent brother. But he was soon thinking how Santa Monica might have an area of ten square miles and how, combined, the Levenger and McLean farms would be somewhere around four times that size. He wondered whether that might be close to the size of all of LA County. Whatever, it was a heck of a big piece of ground.

He wryly recalled his former city-boy concept of what family farms must be like. Maybe he'd been unduly influenced when he'd read in a high school history book something about "forty acres and a mule," but whatever the reason, he'd presumed that was pretty much the story of American farming, less the mule and substitute a little tractor, of course, but do include a milk cow, some chickens, a few hogs, and so on to keep the family fed. He hadn't had any idea how large or small forty acres was back then, but he knew now that the sides of a forty-acre square were a quarter mile long and that many farms, such as these and some of those down in the Delta that Catfish had told his flight students about, occupied miles and miles of highly productive land.

"I'm thinking about getting a P-51," Lance said. "That'll get me where I want to go in a hurry. Or maybe a Hellcat."

"If you last that long," McLean grumbled. "That victory roll you did this morning was awful low."

"I know, I know. I don't know what made me do that. But when Lisa and I do aerobatics, we keep 'em way up high."

"Lisa's a flier, too?" Dave asked, his pale-blue eyes widening.

"She grew up flying our J-3," McLean said.

"And you, Miz McLean?" Johnny Crash asked Lisa's mom, who'd just returned from the kitchen, bearing a platter of smoking-hot, oven-broiled steaks.

"Oh, my, no. *Somebody* in this family needs to keep her feet on the ground."

Lisa set out two butter dishes, and she and her mother went to their places. The three crop dusters hurriedly got to their feet. Since her husband sat at the opposite end of the very long table, Tim moved to help seat Mrs. McLean, and Lance seated Lisa.

Johnny Crash nodded at CR and asked, "How 'bout you? Are you a flier?"

Instead of answering, CR just looked at Lance.

"He's comin' along," Lance drawled, suddenly sounding much more Southern. "This here boy's got talents you wouldn't believe. He's flown Ned's J-3 with me a few times. Ain't that right, Clyde Robert?"

The sallow-faced young man bobbed his head a couple more times and worshipfully gazed up at Lance again. He couldn't look directly at anyone else, but he sure could focus on his master.

"But I promise you, sir," Lance went on, speaking to his future father-in-law, "I *will* be more careful. For Lisa's sake. In plane *and* car. I'll save it all for the races. I've been thinking I should take the T-6 over to Reno and work off some of my energy racing. Same as the Corvette."

"You race that Corvette?" Tim eagerly asked while, at the same time, Ned McLean loudly groaned.

"Uh, not formally," Lance said, glancing disconcertedly at his future father-in-law. "Not yet." Immediately changing the subject, he said, "Clyde Robert here races motor sickles," pronouncing "motorcycles" the old Southern way.

"No kidding?" Tim said doubtfully, turning to CR. He could picture the guy tooling down the road on a chopper, but not racing on a designated track. "What do you ride, CR?"

"Say *whaaat*?" drawled CR, whose attention had apparently lapsed.

"What kind of bike?"

"Triumph."

"Hey, me, too." Tim's bad-biker image of CR shifted a bit. "What model?"

"TR-5."

"That's what *I've* got. Did have, actually. Had to sell it for crop-dusting school. I was going to race it someday, too. Dirt track?"

CR gave a couple nods.

"He don't just fiddle at it, either," Lance said. "You should see this man train. Not just ridin'. Works out with weights, too. Took some karate in Enid two winters and still practices. Says it all gives him an edge racin'. No, sir. CR's not somebody you might want to make light of."

Tim eyed the little guy and wondered whether Lance was exaggerating.

"Racing's how he tore up that leg of his," Lance said. "This boy's a charger. Heck of a mechanic, too. He's just aching to get into that T-6's motor."

"Well, shall we pray?" Mrs. McLean asked. "Ned?"

They all bowed their heads, and the beefy man commenced praying, "Dear God, we thank you for being so good to us. You know we always strive to live right, and you have rewarded us for it."

There was a small *clink*, and Tim peeked through his eyelashes to see Lisa absently fidgeting with the silverware at one side of her plate. He wondered whether it was a coincidence or whether she'd flinched at what her dad had said. He'd done enough Sunday school when he was young to be pretty sure that getting a big payoff in the here and now was not a Christian concept.

"So, please keep on watching over us, dear God," McLean was saying, "and watch over these here pilots while they do their work. And give us . . . well, victory, I guess . . . over them green-bugs before . . . Well, anyhow, keep Lance safe. He's done your will, too, Father in heaven, helping younger people the way he does and all that. And Clyde Robert here one of 'em. Light his way, too, and bless us all. Amen."

"*A*-men!" Dave echoed enthusiastically, putting a whole bunch of stress on the long "A" sound and nearly drowning out the murmured amens of the two women.

"Enjoy them steaks, men!" McLean said. "There ain't no equal. That's *McLean* beef."

"CR does a *lot* of stuff for excitement," Lance commented as they passed the steaks around. "The reason he went down to Texas was scuba diving. You should see the picture of this big fish he killed. You got that picture with you, CR?"

CR shook his head without replying. He was already cutting into a steak, wielding both steak knife and fork with blade and tines projecting straight down from the heels of his hands.

"That right?" Tim said, eyeing his own huge paws and thinking he'd probably judged this kid much too harshly. He'd thought once that he'd like to get scuba-certified some day himself. An acquaintance from high school days in Santa Monica had shown him how to use his diving rig toward the end of his senior year in high school, and it had been a blast. He did like the ocean, but his enjoyment of it, except for that one dive, had been confined to surfing.

"And how big was that fish?" Lance coaxed.

"Hunnert seventy-one pounds."

"What are they called again?"

"Groper."

Grouper, Tim thought. He was no fisherman, but he knew that much. He'd seen them in the diving magazines he'd occasionally leafed through.

"CR can do anything mechanical or physical," Lance said. "I tried to get him to take an engine-repair class this winter. But no, he just had to get down to the gulf. I do want him in our shop some day."

"Lance's protégé," Lisa commented dryly. "He's had him under his wing since . . . When was that?"

"I think it was probably around my first year in high school when they came," Lance said. "CR here must have been . . . What grade was it, CR?"

"Ah 'on't know," he said around a great wad of McLean beef.

"I'd guess he was still in grade school when you started bringing him to church," Lisa said.

This Lance is full of surprises, Tim thought as Dave went off on a tangent about how important church had been in his life. *Wild enough to buzz a church, but brings some misfit kid to Sunday school. And sharp enough for graduate school, too.* He eyed Lance with more respect and liking than ever. However, his attention soon shifted from Lance to Lisa.

Now he was thinking that Lance probably could have chosen a truly great beauty, instead of this modestly pretty young lady. That was in Lance's favor, too. Although Tim's one love after Vietnam was quite a looker, there'd been far more than her appearance that had caused him to fall in love with her. Having struggled so hard to refocus on his major in business on his return to the university, he hadn't been particularly interested in dating anyone for a while. He hadn't even noticed at first how attractive Jen was at their first encounter and casual chat in the university's cafeteria. It had dawned on him only when they'd parted. But far more important to him than Jen's beauty had been the way they'd so smoothly meshed in conversation. It had been as if they'd known each other for years.

Gradually, Tim tuned back in to the present conversation, and he heard Dave say, "Mr. Crash here's done flew a T-6 or two. Ain't that right, John?"

"Well, yes. I did. 'Harvards,' the Canucks called 'em."

"Canucks?" inquired McLean. "You?"

"That's right," Dave said. "As in Royal Canadian Air Farce. You wouldn't know it by his boyish looks, but this here Texan done went north to join up and get after them Jerries while the US of A was still dragging its feet—"

"Just the opposite of these days!" McLean growled. "They're goin' up there now to *avoid* doing the right thing. But go on, Dave. Sorry 'bout that."

"Well, as I was sayin', Mr. John E. Crash here was one bad, fire-spittin' Spitfire flyer!" He abruptly stopped, wide-eyed. Then, he laughed and said, "Now, don't *you* all try to say that. "Y'all might could hurt y'all's selves. But, as I was saying, our Mr. Crash done softened 'em up for slugs like me to come along later and . . . "

* * *

"Them draft-dodging, flag-burning long-hairs better steer clear of *my* part of the country," McLean was roaring some time later as they finished eating.

"Makes a man right sick to his stomach," Dave agreed.

"I won't have my Lisa here going back to college 'til they start putting them draft-dodgin' Commies behind bars!"

Tim watched as Lisa lowered her eyes. Her dad's comment had brought some pink to her oval face. He shot a look at her mother, who was seated on the far side of the long table from her husband. Her eyes were downcast, too. She kept making nervous smoothing motions with one hand across the snowy-white tablecloth that was already perfectly smooth.

"They don't give a hoot how many of our boys died to hold back them Commies," he roared. "I got friends I flew with they never did find over in Korea."

Tim wondered whether Ned McLean had flown off carriers. That had always seemed extremely tricky business to him. So he spoke up, asking, "What branch?"

"Air Force. Did you serve?"

"Marines."

"Vietnam?"

"Yes, sir."

"It must burn you up to see what's going on, too."

"No fun a'tall," Tim said, playing chameleon. He didn't want to get bogged down in some depressing discussion about Vietnam.

"Pilot, I suppose," McLean said.

"No, sir. Just a grunt." That was about as lengthy a statement as he'd ever uttered about his role in the war since he'd come home, and it was enough, as far as he was concerned.

"No 'just' to it!" McLean exclaimed.

"Well, I can't wait to have *my* chance," Lance chimed in. "I just wish there were more enemy aircraft to make it challenging. I mean, there's not much challenge in napalming people on the ground, is there?"

Lisa gave a start and looked at him with alarm. All the men, except for CR, gaped in shock at him. But Lance didn't look the least bit ashamed of what he'd said.

"I sure *hope* the war's still on when I finish graduate school," he said.

Tim cringed, but he was quick to excuse him. *I think he just gets carried away by his imagination.* He presumed he could rely on the gist of what he'd heard about Lance in church that morning: *The main thing is, his heart's in the right place.*

"Some say them draft-dodging hippies are the ones behind the cattle mutilations, too!" McLean commented, breaking the silence. "It ain't all that mysterious, the way the news makes it. They just tie cardboard on their feet so they don't leave tracks. Devil worshipers! That calf they found across the line in Colorado the other day? Didn't have a drop of blood left in it. Sexual organs gone. So were the lips. Devil worshipers. That's what."

"Cattle mutilations?" Tim asked.

"Good Lord! You haven't heard? It's been going on all over! You can read about this one in the *Gazette* a few days back. It's on the stack in my den. You take it when you all go."

"I done heard it's the gov'ment," Dave said. "Sometimes folks hear helicopters in the night, and they'll find another the next day. It's our people doing *coe-vert* experiments."

"Well, let 'em try this place," McLean threatened. "I'm ready. *Plenty* ready." He grimly nodded, thrust out his lower lip, and got a faraway look in his blue eyes. Other mature heads nodded in the sudden and profound absence of speech, and embers in the fireplace popped like gunshots.

Tim was pleased to note that he didn't react to gunshot-like sounds the way he'd been doing for a while not so long ago. Earlier, the popping of that fire might have sent him diving for cover. He felt very secure here among these kind strangers.

"Do you all want your pie now or later?" Amanda McLean asked.

The men glanced at one another.

"Dave?" Ned McLean asked.

"Well, not much later would be nice. It's starting to feel like nap-time. This kind of weather always makes me want to climb in bed."

"Let's have it in the family room," Ned McLean said.

When mother and daughter came into the family room and set out pie, coffee, and so on, Ned McLean was telling the others how he'd almost flown into a tree one day. "Dang coyote cut a dido, and I hauled that Cub around, poked the shotgun out of the window, and uh-oh! Here's this tree jumping out at me! Only tree in a mile! Wouldn't you know it?"

"Ned!" Lance dramatically exclaimed. "I hope you don't take any more chances like that!"

McLean's big reddish-haired head whipped around. He started to say something, for his mouth began to work, but he swallowed it.

"Lots of varmint shooting go on around here?" Johnny Crash

asked, obviously trying to ignore how Lance had caught his future father-in-law out.

"Lots," Lance replied. "I haven't tried it in the T-6 yet, but I will. Slide that canopy back, and it will be a heck of a lot easier than shooting out of a Cub. I'll have to be in a steep turn or that wing will block my view, though. Not a very wide arc from wing to prop in level flight."

"Be careful," Dave warned. "A Cub is a whole lot better at low-and-slow than a T-6. Slow that Texan down close to the ground and it might just slip right—"

"Lord save us from this madness," said Mrs. McLean. "If it's not cutting up with airplanes or cars, it's getting banged around by horses and cattle. I just hope you all are right with the Lord."

"Amen!" Dave enthused for the second time that afternoon.

"And you all be careful with that crop spraying," Lisa said. She happened to be standing beside Tim, and she grabbed him by one wrist and gave it a yank.

CR, noticing what Lisa was doing, nudged Lance and said, "Lookie."

Lance hissed so that only CR would hear, "I know. That no-'count's been messing with her ever since he got here."

Lisa let Tim go, saying, "We read from time to time how some sprayer wrecks."

CR whispered, bending near, "I hate that damn yankee sumvabitch! How 'bout I kick his ass for yuh?" He leaned back and fixed Lance with one of his sly grins and did something with his hazel eyes that made him look demented.

"There you go again," Lance quietly said, chuckling. CR's thing about big guys tickled him. The scrappy little farmhand's brawls were a major source of entertainment. "The bigger they are, the harder you want to make 'em fall. But you can forget about this one."

"What for?"

"I'd be in more trouble with Lisa than ever is what for."

"Well, you—"

Mrs. McLean joined them just then and said, "You be sure to have all you want, CR."

"What do you say, CR?" Lance prompted when the little farmhand failed to respond. "You should thank her, CR."

"Thankee, ma'am."

"That's my man." Lance patted him on the back, and said, grinning, "I'll have him civilized someday!"

"We're glad to have you, CR," Mrs. McLean assured him. "We'd love to see you in church again, too."

All the others had formed a line for dessert and coffee and were still chatting. On his way past them toward an easy chair, Lance paused to tell Dave and Johnny, "I'll be leaving for college, but the T-6 is here for you to use."

"I'll wait for you to come back," Johnny Crash replied. "I would like to give 'er a whirl, but I'd want you in it with me."

The others nodded that they felt the same way.

"If you insist, but I don't know why. I'll be back next weekend."

* * *

Dave was the first one out the door as they left, and he abruptly halted just outside the screen door and swung his head left and right. "Look at that! Wind's dropped a bit more!"

"Hey, good deal," Johnny Crash said, pushing on by him to have a look. "If this keeps up, we might get some work done before the day's over."

7

SKIING THE SICKLE

The weekend after the first storm, the two younger pilots were rudely awakened by the racket of what sounded like a wildly revving small motorcycle ripping by their bedroom. They had gotten up earlier before daylight, but it had been too windy for spraying, and they had gone right back to sleep. Now they groggily gazed at each other across the space between their narrow beds as the racket faded.

"Damn!" Jeremy yelled. "Here it comes again!" He scrambled out of bed and went to the window. "It's that Lance," he said.

Tim grinned and said, "Who else would it be?" He got up and began putting on his clothes. He made himself pause long enough to read his bedside reminder to think before reacting then followed Jeremy out of the room.

Johnny Crash had let Lance in, and the young heir boisterously called out to Tim and Jeremy, "Hey! I didn't mean to wake you!"

"Hi, there," Tim calmly replied, suddenly inspired to pretend that he hadn't noticed Lance's riotous arrival. "I didn't know we had company. How's it going, Lance?"

"Fine as I can be! Looks like you've been sleeping!"

"Never slept better."

"What'll it be, boys?" Dave said as they all went into the kitchen. "Eggs? Bacon? Ham? Hotcakes? All of it?"

"Not me, thanks," Lance said. *"I ate at breakfast time."*

"Whatever you want to make is fine with me," Jeremy said.

"Yeah, me, too," Tim agreed, thinking that whatever Dave fixed would be tasty. He didn't bother to say he and Jeremy could fix something, since Dave so obviously enjoyed doing it.

"Lisa told me you were ground-bound. I thought you might be bored and want to do something."

"Sure," Tim said. He had intended to spend a few more hours at the little local library or maybe even drive to the larger one in Enid. But goofing around with Lance sounded even better.

"Worst season for weather I've ever seen!" said Johnny Crash.

"No," Dave said, "it ain't neither, John. Have you done forgot the spring of '57? We like to never got a field sprayed."

"You expect me to remember over ten years ago?"

"Why, no, now that you mention it. You are getting along. Couple years from now I'll be saying, Remember the great green-bug run of '69 and staying at the McLeans' place? And you'll be saying, Greenbugs? McLeans? What are them?"

"What did you have in mind, Lance?" Tim asked as soon as there was a lull in the Dave–Johnny bantering.

"We can go fly that T-6 of mine later on, but let's mess around a little with the trail bikes and three-wheelers. I brought a few over on a trailer, and the McLeans have some we can use."

"Just happen to have all that handy?" Jeremy asked.

"Less trouble than horses and a lot cheaper than pickups for getting around the farm."

"Sounds like fun," Tim said.

"You?" Lance asked, looking at Jeremy.

"If you can put up with a beginner," Jeremy replied. "I never fooled much with bikes, and never a three-wheeler at all."

"And you?" Lance asked Dave and Johnny.

"No, thank ye," Dave said from where he stood at the stove. "I might like to fly that T-6, but y'all whippersnappers and maybe Mr.

Crash go on out there and snap y'all's whippers on them sickles. *Somebody* got to tend the thermostat 'til it warms up a little."

"I better stay and give Dave a hand," said Johnny. "We'll keep it nice 'n' warm for when you all get back. But we do need to make a quick run to town and get my airplane pretty quick. Need to have it out here and ready to go when this wind quits."

"He blew a jug yesterday," Tim explained to Lance.

"Jug?"

"Cylinder."

"You made an emergency landing?" Lance asked Johnny Crash.

"Naw, them ol' round engines just keep right on a-running. Flew it on into town so they would fix it."

"Keep on a-running if it ain't number five," Dave commented.

"Number five?" Jeremy asked.

"Master-rod cylinder," Dave explained. "If that 'un blows, down she goes! Hey, I *am* a born poet."

"Same with my T-6?" Lance asked. "Isn't that motor the same as mine?"

"Your'n is bigger, but it's purty much the same."

"Good reason to trade in my T-6 for a P-51 right now!" Lance kidded.

Dave laughed and said, "Your chances of having number five pop is about the same as gettin' rich playing poker with old John Crashomatic here."

"But they really blow that often?" Lance persisted.

"Now and then," Johnny Crash said. "Them ol' nine-eighty-fives is getting wore out. Now, your thirteen-forties like you got on that T-6, they ain't been used much in ag planes so far, though I'm sure the day is coming, so I'd imagine they ain't got the same amount of wear and tear."

"The Cat I fly in Idyhoe has a thirteen-forty," Dave said.

"The whole thing just pops off?" Lance asked. As soon as he'd bought the T-6, he'd taken the cowling off to study the engine with its nine big silvery cylinders that radiate outward from the central crankcase, so he had a good mental picture of what might have happened.

"Sometimes. But the ones I've heard of mostly is just the tops. That's how it was yesterday. They say a nine-eighty-five'll always keep on a-chuggin' along so long's it's just the top done blowed."

"So," Lance said, switching back to his original interest, "I'll call Lisa and tell her to meet us at the shop."

"Lisa?" Tim hadn't thought anything of her going horseback riding, which seemed a ladylike thing to do, but it surprised him that she might want to rip around on a bike or three-wheeler. "She's going, too?"

"Oh, yes," Lance said. "That gal does like playing around with those things. In fact, name any machine around here, and she'll drive the dickens out of it. We'll be in the shop when you all get done eating."

"How about CR?" Tim asked. "Is he in on it?" He'd like to see whether CR really was that good a rider. He wondered whether it was too windy for CR to be spraying with a tractor.

"He'll probably be along after a while. He's out spraying, but I told him to get this other boy to fill in for him for a little while. CR's just a hoot to ride with."

"Bringing his Triumph?"

"Not sure. Sometimes he'll fiddle around with a farm machine."

So, after Tim and Jeremy had finished eating and washed their dishes, they put on their sweatshirts and jackets and went right over to the shop. Lisa and Tim chose to ride the little Honda 90 trail bikes, and Lance and Jeremy selected the Honda three-wheelers.

"One more thing and we'll be ready," Lance said. He turned and jogged over to the pickup he'd used to tow a flatbed trailer with the three-wheelers and bikes. He leaned into the cab and emerged with a gun belt and a holster containing a pistol. "For coyotes," he said.

He wrapped the belt around his waist and was about to buckle it when he thought better of it. He held the rig out toward Tim and Jeremy, saying, "One of you is welcome to use it." He glanced at Lisa to be sure she'd noticed his generosity.

"No, thanks," Tim hastily replied.

"I wouldn't mind," Jeremy said. "I've got a .22 back home. What's that?"

"Forty-four Magnum."

A couple minutes later, with Lance in the lead, they tore away from the shop building and down a couple farm roads, heading west and south into Levenger country. After a while, they pulled up to a stock gate at the edge of a large pasture.

Lance hopped off his three-wheeler and held the gate open for the others. Lisa raced through, probably at full throttle, judging by the sound of the bike's tinny howling, and kept on going full-tilt through the lashing waves of high, wind-tossed grass. Jeremy went after her on his three-wheeler, and Tim followed at full throttle on his bike.

Tim grinned widely at the sight ahead of him. He was feeling great. He'd been sleeping more soundly lately. He'd experienced fewer nightmares, and he'd bummed some cotton for his ears from Johnny Crash to make sure he couldn't hear Jeremy's snoring. The little dude still pestered him too much about teaming up for North Dakota, but he didn't get on Tim's nerves the way he had at first. The kid's exceptionalism as a team-flying partner made up for whatever habits he had that made living so closely together less than perfect.

For someone who'd never been on a three-wheeler before, Jeremy was really moving along. Although Tim had his throttle wide open, he couldn't see that he'd gained a bit on either Jeremy or Lisa. He glanced back to check on Lance, who surely had his three-wheeler at full throttle also. And there he was, head hunched low between the handlebars, streamlining himself to reduce drag, doing his best to catch up, too.

Jeremy's head suddenly whipped right, and he peeled off in that direction. Tim caught sight of a coyote as it scampered over a little knoll, looking back over its shoulder with its tongue lolling back from the corner of its long jaws. Lance followed Jeremy, but Lisa was stopping.

Tim pulled up beside her. She had stopped near the edge of a small bluff.

"I was hoping we wouldn't see one," she said.

"It would be okay with me if they didn't shoot it," Tim said. "I always thought they'd be scrawny and mangy-looking in the wild. That's a nice-looking animal. We have coyotes back home, but I never got to see one except in a zoo."

"Coyotes? In . . . What's the name of that part of Los Angeles you're from?"

"Santa Monica when I lived with my mom and dad. Long Beach more recently. And yes, we do have coyotes in the foothills all around LA. They come down into the neighborhoods sometimes."

She scoffed and said, "Coyotes in a big California city!"

"It happens," he said.

"Oh, come on now! You're pulling my leg!"

"It happens!"

She peered at him, saying nothing. After more than a few seconds, it was obvious that she was studying him. It was starting to make him feel uncomfortably self-conscious.

"Sure hope CR brings his TR5," Tim said to break the silence. He put his little trail bike in gear and moved right up to the edge of the low bluff, pretending that he wanted a better look at the large, muddy depression below, but really wanting to get away from that appraising look. There was a black pond out there amid the cattle-trampled mud.

"He might bring it," Lisa said, riding up beside him. "We might as well go on down. No telling how long they'll torment that poor creature."

She turned to the north and took a worn cattle trail down to the mud. She stopped, looked up, and motioned for him to follow. "Watch out. It's right slick down here." She gunned the little knobby-tired bike and it went fishtailing away, kicking up black mud and commencing a left-hand circuit around the pond.

Tim laughed out loud at what seemed like a very unfeminine maneuver and her rare bit of Southern dialect. He rode on down to go slewing off through the mud after her. He did his best to catch up, but he didn't make any progress at all until they were halfway around the pond. She took the risk of giving him a long look back over her shoulder. Then she stood on the pegs, jutted out her rear end, and gave it a sassy shake. He didn't take it as anything sexually suggestive but simply as some competitive taunting, and he laughed again. He tried all the harder to catch up, but she kept her lead until they'd completed the first lap.

She purposely slowed to let him get beside her. "Come on!" she shouted, grinning impishly. "I'm tired of waiting for you!" She opened back up to full throttle, and he followed suit. Around and around the pond on the impromptu race track they went. She'd take the lead for a while then lose too much traction in a slide, and he'd overtake her. Then he'd mess up, and she'd be back in the lead. The bikes weren't very powerful, but the mud made racing quite a challenge. Finally, however, she was ready for a break and slowed to a stop where they'd begun.

She was looking back at him as he rode up, and all the rays in those intense light-blue eyes, almost gray, were throwing off minute sparks. She laughed and gave him a very mischievous look, and something in the vicinity of his heart went a little hot and achy for a moment—not that he was falling for her romantically, but he'd begun to like her far more strongly than he'd ever liked any other girl in a strictly platonic way. He sort of felt that way about his best old friend's wife back home, but not to the point that it stirred him as strongly as his growing affection for Lisa.

"Now *you* have freckles," she said. She came near enough that she was able to reach out and wipe onto a forefinger one of the globs of goo that her bike's rear tire had slung back at him. She held it for him to see and said, "Actually, more like really huge, gross *warts*." She laughed again, and he thought how much he liked the sound of her laughter. It was husky, which didn't seem to quite match her usual tone. But she quickly changed her mood and scraped a bigger glob of mud off her jacket to hold it near her nose, saying, *"Phew!"* She laughed.

Her mood instantly changed again. She looked intently into his eyes. He could tell she was thinking hard about something by a little frown that vertically furrowed the space between her fuzzy golden-caterpillar eyebrows. She said, "You like him a lot, don't you?"

"Who, Lance? Sure! He's amazing. I've never known anyone like him. He's really something else."

She was still intently peering into his eyes. After a few moments, she said, "Yes, he is. And so are you."

"I are what?" he joked self-consciously, mimicking Dave's and Johnny's fractured play-grammar.

"Something else. Different."

The obvious compliment made him squirm. He guessed she was thinking of how he'd helped that hippie, as though it had been some great sacrifice. However, he only made a self-conscious joke of it, saying, "You aren't the first to say I'm not quite right!"

Lisa gave a little smile before she said, "Seriously, Tim. You're becoming such a friend."

"Hey, you really know how to ride that bike," he said, embarrassed, hastily changing the subject.

"Why, thank you. Surprised that a gal can keep one upright? Heck, I'd probably make a good crop duster." She grinned at him mischievously. "You—"

She abruptly stopped talking, cocked her head, and looked up toward the brink of the bluff. "Here they come."

All he could hear was the muttering of their two idling bikes. He finally heard the first of the three-wheelers only seconds before it came soaring off the little bluff. It landed near the upper edge of the improvised racetrack not far from them. Lance immediately leaned hard right and gunned the machine to keep it from sliding down to the pond.

Tim went hot with anger, thinking, *It's one thing to risk your own neck . . .* He didn't like the way his body was reacting. He tried to stop thinking that Lance might have landed on them if they'd been out from the bluff a little farther. He shut his eyes and concentrated on calming himself.

Moments later, as Lance ripped on around the pond, Jeremy arrived more sanely. He cautiously nosed his three-wheeler onto one of the cow trails and over the edge. He shot Lisa and Tim a big grin and rode over to them.

"Hey, you won't believe what Lance did!" he said. "He rammed that old coyote right in the butt! It turned and wanted to fight him!"

Meanwhile, Lance had charged all the way around the pond and was going right by them with the throttle wide open and his three-wheelers' fat, knobby tires slinging up crud. Jeremy took off after him. Lisa and Tim mirrored each other's shrugs and sighs, then ripped away in pursuit.

They raced on for something less than a half hour, but it didn't take that much time for every one of them, except Lance, who kept his lead, to become grossly spattered with mud and, judging by the odor, churned into the mud by previous races, mementos from the cattle that drank from the murky stock pond.

After a while, Lance pulled up high on the banked track and stopped below the bluff. "I'm done," he said, reaching out to grab Lisa's hand when she and the others rode up to cluster around him. He looked at Jeremy and Tim and said, "Too bad you have to be moving on so soon. We could find all kinds of trouble to get into!"

Jeremy, who'd stopped next to Lance on the side opposite Lisa, put a hand on Lance's shoulder and said, "Plant some row crops that need spraying in the summer, and we *will* stay."

"This boy can shoot," Lance said. "He put a round right in the middle of that critter's head."

"Lucky I didn't have to shoot again. I would've flinched. I'm not used to shooting anything that kicks that hard."

"You come over to my place, and I'll show you my other guns. We'll go shooting. There's a lot we can do while I'm home for Easter. Right, Lisa?"

It seemed to Tim that she nodded rather absently, distracted by some other thought. Nevertheless, the sight of them side by side on their machines made Tim wish that he had a camera. It would be nice to have a photo to remember them by when he, too, went on down the road. It wouldn't be long. He'd definitely make an effort to swing back through Oklahoma in the future to see them.

"It's not quite the good city life around here, but we come up with a few things to do," Lance said. "We have a ski boat. Summers—" He abruptly halted and jerked a quick look at Lisa. Then he swung his attention back to Tim and Jeremy and took a different tack: "Which reminds me . . . Have you ever waterskied an airplane?"

"Constantly," Tim kidded, grinning, expecting another tall tale. He glanced at Lisa, thinking that she might clue him in with a humorous look that communicated, *Here we go again!* But she was just peering down at a clump of old, hardened cow pie, absently toeing it with the tip of her muddy boot.

"Hey, here comes CR," Lance said.

"He's on that motorcycle you're so interested in," Lisa said, looking at Tim. "You hear it?"

Tim shook his head. His hearing was pretty bad, thanks to Vietnam.

CR rode up to the brim of the sink, turned the Triumph broadside, and stopped to look down on them. He was wearing a greasy plastic-mesh cap turned backwards.

"CR!" Lance yelled. "A hundred bucks you don't have the guts to waterski that bike across the pond!"

CR cocked his head and stared at Lance without the slightest change of expression for a few seconds. Then he flatly gazed down toward the pond.

"Come on!" Lance yelled. "Why would it be any different than an airplane?"

CR kicked the Triumph into gear and gunned it back out of view. Then they heard it go full throttle.

"Hey!" Jeremy shouted. "No way!"

The TR-5 flew spectacularly off the rim of the muddy depression with CR standing on the pegs and his long black hair streaming out behind him. The engine went silent as he closed the throttle. Bike and rider sailed on and on through the air, making a gradual arc back to earth far out toward the pond, considerably farther than Lance had jumped the three-wheeler. Just before the bike landed, CR leaned sharply back to raise the front wheel, and the rear knobby touched down just before the front one. The motor, lacking a power-stealing muffler, screamed once more, and up sprayed a filmy black curtain of filthy mud.

The curtain of mud turned to water for a moment as the Triumph started across the pond with its rear tire spinning at full speed. CR was still standing on the pegs, but that didn't prevent the water from quickly rising to his waist while the bike submerged out of sight. Then CR mushed over onto his face into what had to be some very icy water.

Lance was laughing hysterically.

There was no flailing about for CR. He simply stood, turned, and began groping around in the black chest-deep water for his sunken machine. He cast a brief look up toward his audience, grinned, and slipped out of sight for a few seconds.

Lance's raucous laughter went on and on.

CR rose up, apparently dragging the sunken bike upright with him, but it still couldn't be seen. Struggling, he got the invisible motorcycle turned around and tried to push it back to the pond's edge. He went down twice in the effort.

Jeremy was the first to spring into action. He gunned his three-wheeler down to the edge of the pond, leaped off, and waded right in. The rest of them followed.

"Don't come in!" Jeremy yelled back at them. "We can handle it!"

So the three onlookers waited as Jeremy and CR, one on either side, hauled the Triumph out of the water.

"Look at them shivering!" Lisa wailed. "Lance, you—"

"Come on, CR!" Lance yelled, laughing. "Get on here behind me! Let's go get you some dry clothes!"

"What about the bike?" Jeremy asked, arms clasped about himself and teeth chattering.

"He can bring a pickup back for it," Lance said.

"I bet that motor is ruined!" Jeremy said.

"Not really. He can flush it out, and it'll be good as new. If it isn't, I'll get him a new one. We'll see you all at Lisa's in a bit. We'll go fly that AT-6."

Off the two rode. It was steep going up the one cattle trail that was wide enough for the three-wheeler, but CR clung like a monkey to Lance's back, and they were soon out of sight.

"You believe that?" Jeremy asked, shivering, getting back onto his three-wheeler. "Am I dreaming, or did that really happen?"

As Lisa put her bike in gear and Jeremy crawled onto his three-wheeler, she wearily commented, "CR would do anything for Lance."

8
A MATTER OF PERSPECTIVE

"Wind's straight down the strip," Lance said. He turned his head to look down at Lisa. They were holding hands as the group walked past the shop. "Perfect day for a solo."

Not me, Tim thought. The T-6 wasn't much different in horsepower and size than the four-fifty Stearman he'd flown in flight school, but he wouldn't feel comfortable flying it without Lance.

They stopped beside the military-surplus trainer, and Jeremy said, "Johnny Crash should go first. You know, kind of like a homecoming."

"No," Johnny drawled, "ladies first."

"You heard the man," Lance said. "Come on, honey."

"I don't need to fly today. I'll just watch."

"You're taking lessons?" Jeremy asked her.

"I've been working on my instrument rating lately," she replied, and Jeremy's eyes went wide with surprise.

"Come on," Lance said, tugging at her hand, and they went on.

"*Instrument* ticket," Jeremy exclaimed to the other ag pilots. "These people are something else!"

"Makes sense to me," Johnny Crash said. "I'm sure that Skywagon of her daddy's is loaded with instruments."

"Quite an airplane, alright," Dave said. "Go anywhere, anytime, weather or not."

Meanwhile, Lance had led her to the front of the plane, told her to go on ahead and climb into the front cockpit, and reached up to grab hold of a prop blade. But Jeremy rushed up beside him and said, "Go ahead. I'll pull it through for you."

"Why, thanks, buddy."

So Jeremy went through the laborious process of turning the prop through nine revolutions, one revolution for each of the nine cylinders to make certain that no oil had seeped into them.

"That prop's bigger than ol' Jeremy," Johnny Crash said, chuckling. "It's putting up quite a fight, too."

"That compression does make some resistance," Dave agreed.

"For little folk," Johnny wisecracked.

"Don't get ugly, John. But ain't he a fine boy?" He turned to Tim and said, "You, too, Tim. We got a right good crew staying out here."

"That's for sure," Johnny said. "How about us getting out of this wind?" He headed for the open north bay of the shop building, and the others followed.

Designed to admit a monstrous grain combine, that open bay would have admitted any of the airplanes out there with plenty of room to spare. But the wall of the building gave the pilots shelter from the wind while offering them a high, wide view to the north and the opportunity to poke their heads out into the cold wind if they wanted to look down the airstrip or off to the east. Farther inside the shop, a couple of McLean's men were working on the engine of a large tractor with an enclosed cab.

Lisa taxied the T-6 out of the farm-equipment yard toward a ten-foot-square cement pad that McLean used to do his airplanes' pre-flight run-ups to keep gravel from nicking the props. It was near the front of the shop, and the men in the shop had a clear view of it out of the wind. Lisa had left the plane's long canopy slid back, and she was leaning out one side of the cockpit then the other as she swung the plane's nose one way and the other in order to see where she was going.

"Gonna be some kind of family, her and Lance," Dave said. "Ain't that gal a sight with the propwash blowing her hair that way?"

"Completely out of sight," Jeremy said, putting a hand on Tim's shoulder but quickly jerking it away as Tim flinched. "Sorry," he said.

"It's okay," Tim quietly commented. He gave his head a shake and heaved a small sigh of resignation. *He really is okay*, he reflected. *Just too darn clingy.*

The four ag pilots stood just inside the shop bay and watched Lisa warm the T-6's engine at fast idle. Her canopy and the one over Lance behind her were closed against the icy wind now.

"Here she goes," Dave said.

The bulky aluminum trainer roared and began to accelerate away from them into the wind toward the west. The takeoff run remained perfectly straight. Fifty feet off the ground, the T-6's wheels receded into the undersides of the wings, and it began a gentle climbing turn to the north. In a couple minutes, it had come all the way around and was descending for a landing with its flaps and landing gear lowered.

"You think she's the one flying?" Tim asked.

"It's the gal, all right," said Dave. "He wouldn't have put her up front if it wasn't her."

The T-6 swept down before the large metal building, its landing gear and flaps lowered. The way Lisa sat hunched forward in the front cockpit, repeatedly cocking her head in swift little movements left and right, it did appear that she was the pilot in command. The wheels smoothly crunched onto the gravel a plane's length beyond the concrete run-up pad.

"Whooee!" Dave yelled. "That gal can fly!"

They all laughed and nodded.

The T-6 turned around in the wide spot at the far end of the strip and taxied back toward them. It passed the cement pad and swung around right in front of the shop. Lance crawled out of the rear cockpit, shot everybody a big grin, and hopped down from the trailing edge of the wing root. As soon as he was clear, Lisa eased in the power, and off she went to fly her fiancé's new airplane alone.

"I hope you don't expect *all* of us to solo that thing," Tim said to Lance.

"You're certainly welcome to. If it feels right after I check you out, do it. If not, maybe some other time. I don't even need to check Johnny out. Probably Dave, too."

"No, I'd just as soon you be in it," said Johnny Crash.

"Here she comes again," Dave said.

Lisa shot a couple touch-and-go landings and then a full-stop. The men immediately started taking turns, and Lance sat in the rear cockpit each time.

Tim and Jeremy had each argued about going last, so they'd flipped a coin, which decided that Jeremy would precede Tim.

Johnny Crash, once he'd gained plenty of altitude, started his trip down memory lane north of the farmstead with a sixteen-point slow roll, tipping the left wing downward a little over twenty degrees, hesitating, flicking it farther downward by the same amount again, and so on until the T-6 had gone inverted and slowly, tipping bit by bit after subsequent brief hesitations, returned to normal upright flight. Since the T-6 had a gravity-fed fuel system, the motor sputtered after it had been inverted for a while, and Johnny visibly compensated for the loss of power by letting the nose gradually drop to sustain flying speed. That initial stunt so clearly revealed the old vet's skill that it got the male onlookers gleefully hooting, and Tim glanced away to see that it had brought an absolutely beatific smile to Lisa's upturned, freckled face.

"Look at that old man fly," Dave hollered. "Smooth as if he'd kept right on flying them Texans all these years."

The former Spitfire flier zoomed on through several more advanced maneuvers, then steeply dove to roar downwind just above the airstrip and past the shop building to sweep smoothly upward and around to make a military-type turn to a landing.

Dave went up next to do a few similar "tricks," as he called them, and Jeremy took his turn after that. When the cherubic young sprayer returned, his oval face was flushed and beaming.

"Oh, yeah, man!" he shouted as he climbed out of the front cockpit and Tim jogged over to take his place. "I gotta do some more of that!"

"Did you land it?" Tim asked.

"Yeah! Nothing to it!"

While Tim was coupling the wide brown military lap strap and the two narrower shoulder-harness straps, Lance spoke into his mike, saying, "Cinch 'em up tight, buddy. You'll be hanging upside-down when you show me a slow roll."

"You'd better do one first. I'll follow you through on the controls to get the feel of it."

Lance agreed and told Tim where to find the landing gear and flaps controls. Then he said, "Okay, let's do it!"

"Hey, Lance?"

"Go ahead."

"I'm not used to retractable landing gear. Be sure to remind me, okay?"

"Of course. Relax and enjoy yourself."

The engine had been idling since Jeremy had flown, so all Tim had to do was glance at the gas gauge to make sure there was plenty of fuel, let down a bit of flaps for some extra lift, release the brakes, and ease the throttle forward. He added power cautiously at first, giving himself some extra time to get the feel of the airplane, but he quickly saw that there was nothing unusual about it. It wasn't any different than flying a Stearman, except that he'd closed the canopy and couldn't lean out the side to better see one edge of the strip.

"How about making a few low passes like we're spraying first?" Lance said over the radio's intercom frequency as they got airborne.

"If you say so."

Tim retracted landing gear and flaps when things felt solid, cranked a fairly steep turn, and dove right back down toward the big wheat field that was one section south of the McLeans' farmstead, off toward Lance's place. It occurred to him to be conservative about the airplane's height over the wheat, since the landing gear was retracted. There'd be nothing at all between the prop and the wheat. It was one thing to feel an airplane's tires ticking through the wheat tops and quite another, he was sure, to have the prop in it. At the south end of the field, he pulled up sharply and bent into the first part of the standard, old-fashioned, P-shaped duster turn. He took a little extra time in the turn, pulling enough g's to keep Lance from falling asleep but staying well clear of risking a low-altitude stall in a strange airplane.

He felt like a fighter pilot on a strafing run as he dove back toward the wheat with the aluminum-banded Plexiglas canopy curving over him, the big round cowling up front, and the pointy wingtips on either side. The noise also contributed to the illusion of fighter-aircraft speed, even though the trainer was doing only 170 in the dive.

"My turn," Lance said.

"It's yours."

Lance pulled up sharply and, as soon as he'd cleared the power lines, turned downwind. Then he flipped the plane back the opposite way, copying Tim's duster turn. He shaved the wires going back into the field as closely as any ag pilot and got down a little lower than Tim had.

"You're making me pucker," Tim said into his mike. "A little higher would be nice. You don't want to be chopping wheat with that prop."

"Roger."

Lance hauled back on the stick and climbed to three thousand feet. Then he entered a shallow dive to build up some extra air-speed and tilted the T-6 into a very slow roll, holding the nose on one point on the horizon.

Tim tightly gripped the underside of the seat with his left hand when they went inverted and hung from their seat belts. He knew that must be awfully amateurish, but he hung on anyway. He did, however, have enough self-control to keep his right hand lightly on the stick and his feet on the rudder pedals to feel what Lance was doing with them.

"Whee!" Lance said into his mike. "Now you."

It was surprisingly easy. Tim didn't try to think ahead of time how he should blend stick and rudder. It seemed too complicated to try to think his way through the maneuver. He just did it.

"How's that?" he asked afterward. He'd done it without Lance having to take over, but he knew it hadn't been perfect.

"Very good! You go ahead and use this airplane whenever you want!"

"Man, I don't know. That's—"

"It's nothing. You're all pros. *Use* it. Any of you. Okay?"

"I don't know. Maybe the others."

"Well, let's go back. I need to get home. Promised the folks."

Tim turned toward the McLeans' place.

"Look down there a quarter mile west of my house," Lance said. "See that north-south turn row? That's my strip. Someday I'll have it paved, and there'll be a hangar. I'll have something better than this old crate to put in it, too."

"Cool."

"You know, life can be such a matter of perspective. Down there on the ground, it looks like I've got a sizable piece of property, but up here I can see way far beyond my place. It's not so big after all."

"Riiight," Tim thought.

"Lisa likes to say not everything's as it seems," Lance chattered. "She's right about that. It's all a matter of perspective."

9

BUSTED ASS

One day not much later, Jeremy became a hero to people for many miles around. Then, only two days after that, having just cut such a wide swath of public affection by not only taking such a big risk but then by making self-effacing, embarrassed comments in the media interviews, the lovable young pilot sent everyone's emotions plunging. News of Jeremy's first deed quickly spread so far that it drew reporters, photographers and cameramen from Oklahoma City and Wichita.

The interviews disrupted the spraying, but Will Walker gave the media his enthusiastic approval and helped the reporters and photographers locate whatever road, pasture, or airstrip Jeremy and Tim were using as they moved about the countryside. The pressure to get all the wheat sprayed was easing off anyway, and Mr. Will happily told the two young pilots that the interviews made powerful publicity for his outfit. He assured Tim and Jeremy that he'd more than compensate their lost spraying income with bonuses when the run ended. "I can't buy that kind of advertising," he said. So the two young men stoically bore the interviews with minimal protest.

Tim was interviewed by a couple reporters about the part he'd played, but it was Jeremy who was far and away the hero of the story. And how it made that young man squirm! Jeremy shuffled his feet and ducked his head and mumbled such replies as, "Anybody would've done the same," and, "I had no idea it was gonna blow."

Jeremy's efforts to play down the heroism of the feat were useless, however, since his eyebrows and the front portion of his distinctive cap of woolly whitish hair were so noticeably singed. The photographers and cameramen made sure they captured that evidence of heroism to transmit to the public, and every reporter commented on it.

It began one morning as the two young pilots were flying off a road a few miles south of the Levengers' home. They were on their way to a wheat field with a couple fresh loads when Tim saw Jeremy suddenly peel off and dive away. Tim looked back in surprise, wondering what in the world was so important that Jeremy would slow their work. The fact that the season was winding down didn't mean that the remaining wheat-devouring pests didn't need to be zapped in a hurry. The weather was just too unpredictable, and not spraying a given field during one day of good weather might mean it wouldn't get sprayed for a few days.

Tim couldn't see what had caught Jeremy's attention at first, so he turned to follow and find out. Then he, too, spotted the wreck.

A semi-truck with a cattle trailer lay crookedly on its side, angled into the intersection of two farm roads. As he drew nearer, Tim caught sight of the little foreign pickup that the big truck, apparently as it was simultaneously swerving and tipping over, had plowed into. It looked like the pickup might have unexpectedly popped out in front of the semi, and the driver of the big rig had swung too late to avoid it.

Tim couldn't see anyone outside the wreckage and concluded, since there was still steam venting from the front of the big truck, that the accident had just happened. It looked like the occupants of both vehicles hadn't gotten out yet.

Jeremy made a power dive to the wreckage and a couple tight, low-level orbits around it. Then he turned out wide to line up on one of the intersecting roads. It was obvious to Tim then that Jeremy was going to try to land, and Tim circled his Pawnee a hundred feet or so higher, sizing things up.

The electric-power poles on one side and the telephone poles on the other side of both roads were close, since they weren't major roads. That alone made it look a little iffy for a landing. Then, too, Jeremy had the choice of landing on the one road that had some brush too close alongside it, which was the one he was lining up on, or landing on the other road that had a cut-bank alongside it that also would be perilously close to a wingtip. At least the brush would have some give to it.

Tim wished that Jeremy would hold off a minute and see whether people would start climbing out of the wrecks. However, lacking radio communications, all Tim could do was watch.

Seconds before Jeremy's Pawnee touched down, Tim saw a corpulent man in coveralls struggling to crawl out of the truck's upturned side window. He was moving fitfully, and he was not making much progress, but he didn't seem to be seriously injured. Tim couldn't see any sign of anyone in the little pickup, which was badly caved on the passenger's side. He fervently hoped that nobody had been sitting on that side.

Then Jeremy's Pawnee was on the ground, rolling out toward the wreck, and its left wingtip was clipping through the long strip of brush on that side. Tim could see the plane's nose veering in jerks as Jeremy fought to keep the brush from pulling him completely off the road. However, after a few seconds, he was free of the brush and tracking straight down the road.

Tim momentarily considered getting on down there to do whatever he could to help, but he decided, *Forget it. Just get to a phone.*

He flew straight to the Levengers' place, which was the nearest farm in sight. Instead of landing at the airstrip where Lance kept his AT-6, since he'd have a time-consuming run from there to the house or the shop, he pulled on full flaps to slow the plane and flew under the power lines on the main road, between the masonry columns and under the wrought-iron sign over the ranch entrance, and touched down at the beginning of the asphalt driveway.

He mashed down hard on the twin brake pedals to slow the heavily laden sprayer so that he could make the turn up the narrower paved loop directly in front of the house. The Pawnee lurched into the loop with its small tires squealing and came to a halt directly before the palatial home's entrance.

Mr. Levenger, who must have seen the plane from his office window, rushed out as Tim leaped to the ground and started running toward him, shouting, "Telephone! Gotta report an accident!"

"Come on!" Levenger ran ahead of Tim and yanked the door open. "I'll dial it!"

They dashed into the office.

As soon as he'd made the call, Tim ran back to the airplane, scrambled into the cockpit, and cranked up the engine. He gunned the Pawnee through the loop and simultaneously yanked up the side window and latched it. Once the plane's nose had swung almost all the way back down the straight stretch toward the road, he shoved the throttle forward to the stop and, as the sprayer slowly accelerated, used both hands to fit the four-piece seat belt and shoulder harness connections together. He looked left and right, prepared to abort the takeoff if a vehicle appeared on the roadway, but there was no traffic in sight.

If the plane had been empty, it would have gotten off the ground with plenty of driveway left. However, since it was loaded down with twelve hundred pounds of goop, he might just have to dump some of it to keep from running across the main road into the wheat. He remembered that he'd have to be ready to shove the stick forward should he hit the dump handle. Otherwise he might balloon into the iron arch over the entrance. But he finally felt the wheels break free of the pavement just shy of the entrance, and he was reflexively ducking the next moment as the farm sign and the power lines flicked by overhead.

He sighed with relief as he made a staggering, climbing turn southward. He would have hated to dump a part of the load. The wheat where much of it would have landed probably would have been condemned. Yet he had to get back to the scene of the wreck, for he'd promised to circle above it to clearly show the emergency responders exactly where it was. If anyone was critically injured, seconds lost hunting for the site could make the difference between life and death.

Once he had a couple power lines' altitude, Tim saw a lot more smoke now in the direction of the accident. He feared that someone could be burning alive.

Soon he could see that it was the small pickup that was burning. Seconds later he spotted Jeremy. He had his helmet off and was kneeling beside someone who was stretched out in the wheat thirty or forty yards from the blazing pickup. Nearby, also in the wheat, sat the big man he'd seen struggling to get out of the truck.

When Tim caught sight of the flashing emergency lights of the first ambulance, he flew south to make a low turn in front of them. Then he flew straight back to the wreck and kept circling until the medics got there.

* * *

The McLeans made a point of honoring Tim and Jeremy the following evening. Ned had walked down to the house the evening before to say in a very low-key way to all four pilots, who thought it would be nothing more than Ned's usual hospitality, "Come on up to the house for supper tomorrow."

When Lisa ushered them in, there at the inner base of the foyer stood the elder McLeans, the Levengers, Mr. Will and Normajean, his wife, and Ruthie, the waitress Jeremy was dating.

"Oh-oh," Jeremy groaned. The entire group was blocking his way, just standing there, smiling at him. "What are you *doing*?"

"What are we doing?" boomed Ned McLean's big, happy voice. "We just want you to know how proud we feel about what you did! That's what!" He gave Jeremy's puny shoulder a mighty swipe with one thick, freckled paw, knocking the little guy slightly sideways. "Not many would have done it. And you, too, Tim. Good, quick thinking and some real fine flying. Both of you."

"*Anybody* would've done it," Jeremy protested.

"Yes, so you keep on saying," Mr. Levenger commented. "Anybody might have done *some* of what you did, maybe, but not just anybody would have dived into the fire to get that woman out."

"That's the truth!" Dave said.

McLean said, "You're lucky to be alive, son. You're lucky that fire didn't do a lot worse than it did do to you!" He chuckled and said, "You are a sight!"

"It wasn't burning that *bad*," Jeremy mumbled. However, that obviously wasn't so, given that his whitish eyebrows and the front part of his wiry whitish hair had melted away.

"Oh, no! Maybe that car didn't blow up while you were dragging that woman away. Maybe she isn't being treated for burns after all!"

Normajean Walker piped up, "Praise God she'll be alright. But we're embarrassing the daylights out of the poor boy. We ought to ease up."

"All right," Ned McLean agreed. "Let's go on into the dining room. I truly doubt there's any better prime rib anywhere than this home-fed we're having tonight. And the ladies have gone all out, even more than usual, especially with dessert. You pilots will have to cart away what you can't finish this evening."

"You all go ahead on in," said Mrs. McLean. "Lisa and I will bring in the fixings."

"We'll help," said Normajean, and all the women—even Lance's ill mother, despite the other women's protests—headed for the kitchen.

"It was Lisa's idea to go in and fetch Ruthie," McLean said to Jeremy, nudging him with a thick elbow and mischievously grinning.

"You're getting close to the end of the spraying, aren't you?" Levenger asked Johnny Crash, who was standing by his side. "I know we just about have it licked at our place."

"Another few days and we'll be on our way. Them bugs have just about done had the course."

Over an hour later, they were still sitting at the dining table, chattering away, when Dave said, "Well, don't let me ruin the party, but an old man . . . "

"That makes two of us," Johnny Crash said, getting up. "I sure do thank you all."

McLean replied, "Well, it's awful little in the way of saying we appreciate what these two boys did. What you all did, too, getting rid of them bugs."

"That was a mighty powerful Christian act," said Mrs. McLean, gazing fondly at Jeremy.

"Amen!" Dave said.

They had all liked the diminutive, cheerful pilot very much before his heroic act, but now their affection had been multiplied. Despite Tim's reluctance to get too close, Jeremy had been kindling his affection, as well. It had been harder all the time for Tim to keep on being as gruff and dismissive as he had at first. Nevertheless, he wasn't about to take a chance of getting as close as Jeremy seemed to want. He liked having friends, but he wasn't going to get too close to anyone anymore.

For a couple seconds, he visualized how his old buddy Nick back home had started to give him a hug on his return from 'Nam. He could still hear Nick saying, after he, Tim, had jerked away, "Right. We wouldn't want to start feeling each other up or anything."

Just part of growing up, he'd defensively thought at the time. *There's a time when a guy has to grow up, act like a man.*

"It makes me quake to think how close you came to not being here," Mr. Will's wife said to Jeremy in a trembling voice near breaking.

The others, except for Tim and Jeremy, quietly and all at once began making brief comments extolling Jeremy's act of self-sacrifice, including Mr. Will's strongly voiced pronouncement, "Human nature just don't get no better than that."

As for Tim, he couldn't say anything for the lump in his throat. The praise was also bringing back memories of Smitty's sacrifice in Vietnam, how he'd fallen back without Tim realizing it at first, defending the rest of the platoon's retreat, how he'd been cut down in the clearing trying to make his own belated withdrawal.

* * *

After they'd left the McLeans' house, Tim and Jeremy were shucking down to their boxer shorts and T-shirts for bed. "So, how 'bout it?" Jeremy was saying. "We don't have more than a few days left here. I'll drop the Pawnee back in Ohio, then catch a bus to meet you somewhere. I'll pay my share of the gas."

Tim cynically laughed out loud, and he said, "Let's see. Thirty or thirty-five cents a gallon . . . " He rolled into bed, pulled up the covers, and reached for his latest book on the night table. "At ten miles a gallon, that's, say, three and a half bucks a hundred miles, so . . . thirty-five bucks per thousand miles? Is that right?"

"Beats the heck outta *me*. Nobody ever accused *me* of being intelligent."

Tim laughed more genuinely this time and said, "So you're saying I could save maybe ten or twenty bucks if you came along! Wow! What a deal! But why don't you confess it isn't a generous heart that prompts you to make such an amazing offer."

"Like what else?"

"Like I don't think you done got weaned right, boy. There's gotta be *some* reason for this excessive need for bonding."

"Company," Jeremy said, getting into bed. "Companionship. Friendship. What normal people do." His tone of voice and expression clearly indicated that he was kidding. He yanked the covers up to his chin. "You'll learn. You're a city boy. You didn't grow up lonely. I was a city boy, too. At first. Friends all over the place. Then my mom met this guy from the country, and we moved onto this place out in the middle of nowhere. Think about it. What would it be like out here if it was just you?"

"Quiet. Peaceful. I'd be able to read."

"Well, think about it. Seriously."

"About you moving to the country? I did. Poor you."

"About being going-down-the-road partners."

"I'll meditate on it as soon as we get nice and quiet. I'll get my face behind this book so I can concentrate without seeing you staring at me." He got behind his book and thought, *It wouldn't be okay even if there did happen to be a couple team-flying seats open at some outfit. This dude's just way too clingy.*

* * *

Then Jeremy made the news all over again. He and Tim were team-flying off the McLeans' home strip. They had started out with a little over a half day's work scheduled. The greenbug run was nearly over.

Should've brought a thermos of coffee, Tim happily mused, following Jeremy across an entire section of wheat, laying down swaths one full mile long. *I could just put my feet up and sip a cup.*

It seemed to be taking a very long time to get across the field. Suddenly wanting to know exactly how long that was, he began to do the math: *A hundred miles an hour, so 60 minutes divided by a hundred . . . gotta be six-tenths . . . uhh . . .* He was distracted as he passed beneath the massive cross-country power lines.

Thirty-six seconds? That quick?

Then he was pulling up to get over the regular, non-towered power lines that ran along the edge of the road. Had there had been room to get under those, too, he would have done so. However, there didn't seem to be quite enough space between the lines and the fence and clumps of brush beneath them. He quickly banked out of the way as Jeremy's Pawnee came diving back toward him.

Yeah, sounds right. Two miles a minute or 120 miles an hour would be half a minute. So 36 . . . yeah, that's it, alright.

It was a rare treat to get a mile-long field. This one was also a mile wide, a full section, 640 acres. It would take 160 swaths across it in all to finish. Yet the big field did present some difficulties.

Olen had told their swamper, Ken, to be sure to warn them that it was "a wire farm" with towered lines crossing at an angle. So, since Jeremy had said that he'd once sprayed a field strewn with big steel towers back in Ohio, Tim had told him to take the lead so he could see how it was done.

It was safer by far to fly under the gigantic steel-towered lines than it was to make such high pull-ups and dive-ins over them. Although the drooping, thick high-voltage lines crossing the field were plainly visible, the taut guy wires that stretched horizontally high above them were very hard to see against a gray- or blue-sky backdrop. Besides, flying beneath those massive, sagging electric-transmission lines accurately placed the insecticide where it should be, which was the main reason to fly under any wires. However, the two young pilots would have to make those high dives and steep pull-ups over the last tower and the rigid guy wires in the northeast corner of the section.

That was where the regular power lines and the power lines that sagged between the steel pylons converged. As Tim and Jeremy threaded the needle between towered lines running at an angle across the field and the lines on wood poles running straight beside the road, the eye of the needle got progressively smaller.

Eventually, it would be impossible to continue the under-over-and-over-under routine. So Tim and Jeremy had agreed ahead of time that whenever one of them thought it was getting too tight, he'd stop going under the big lines, and the other would start going over both the towered lines and the regular lines along the road, too.

Another challenge was trying to get the spray as close to the bases of the pylons as possible and still managing to stay parallel with the previous swaths. Jeremy had explained that one pass would be made head-on with a last-second, cross-controlled, flat skid away from the pylon, and another pass would be made by coming in at an angle, hitting the money handle when the wingtip was near the base of the pylon, and skidding back to complete the pass directly in line with the previous one.

They had agreed that Jeremy alone would demonstrate the skidding around the first tower while Tim watched from above. After that, they'd team-skid the other pylons with Jeremy flying lead for a change.

"All right!" Tim triumphantly yelled after he'd made his first skidding pass. "I like that! Superpilot stuff!"

The time finally came when, following Jeremy on another over-and-under to the south, Tim thought, *Okay, that's it. Over the top now, Germ.*

So, on the return pass, he saw Jeremy reach the approximate point where he'd need to start the first of their early climb-outs far back from the big lines and thought, *Okay, up you go. Watch those guy wires up there, dude.* But Jeremy's Pawnee remained a foot off the crop a second longer . . . and another . . .

Come on, man!

It was too late. Jeremy had no choice. He'd never make it over. He had to go under.

Too tight for me! Tim thought. He eased back on the stick and shoved in full throttle.

The rising long nose and the low wing off one side blanked out any further view of the other Pawnee—not that he was worried about Jeremy; it was tight down there, but he'd make it through. Tim kept easing back on the stick, gauging the pressure of the g-force pressing his butt down hard on the seat, tugging back hard enough to swirl backwash off the trailing edge of the wings to blow the insecticide down with extra force. Since there was very little wind, he dragged the spray all the way up to maybe thirty feet off the ground. Intently gauging his progress toward the slender, barely visible guy lines above the thick power lines, he snapped the spray handle shut and kept climbing. A moment or two later, he nodded his appreciation of the fact that he was going to clear the guy wires by some twenty feet. *Close enough!* Those nearly-invisible guy cables had him far more spooked than the cross-country power lines drooping below them.

Once he'd cleared the twin guys, Tim let the nose drop toward the horizon, eased into a gentle left turn, and began looking for his partner so he could get back in formation. Still not seeing him after a few seconds, he began to slowly rock the Pawnee left and right, tipping the wings steeply downward one direction then another so he could see better directly beneath him. Then he made a full turn, searching the sky everywhere.

No matter how far he kept swiveling his head back over one shoulder to the next, he just couldn't find him. Knowing that Jeremy had to be somewhere near made Tim edgy. If Jeremy didn't see him either and they weren't far apart, they risked running into each other. So he broke off the turn and flew on straight and level to the north to get clear of the danger. Once he was well clear he turned to scan all the airspace in a wide arc that included the entire wheat field.

Where the heck are you, knucklehead? He imagined how Jeremy could get directly behind him and remain hidden. *Are you playing with me, you little germ?*

He banked back to the left, and he banked to the right, turning his head as far back as he could to look behind. Then he happened to glimpse a small splotch of white in the dark-green wheat on the north side of the road they'd pulled up over.

Things went haywire in his gut. He gasped for breath.

Sure enough, flying near, he could see that it was a Pawnee, glossy white on deep-green. It was upside down just beyond the road from the field they'd been spraying. Its crumpled tail was pointed in the opposite direction he'd last seen Jeremy flying. The fuselage was sharply bent halfway back to the tail, and the tail was crushed. Jeremy apparently hadn't gotten out from under the towered lines in time to clear the ones that ran alongside the road. His sprayer's wheels had snagged the roadside wires, flipping him backward into the ground.

Tim banked away from the cross-country lines and flew on west forever, it seemed, giving himself enough space to land before he whipped a turn to line up on the road. He had his seat belt and shoulder harness unbuckled before the Pawnee skidded to a stop.

He yanked off the mixture control to kill the engine, piled out of the cockpit, and dashed into the wheat. He couldn't see the Pawnee's canopy, since the nose had settled into the wheat, so he couldn't see Jeremy, either. He feared he'd see the cockpit flattened.

Tearing around the inverted nose, he was greatly relieved to note that the tubular-steel cage just beneath the fiberglass exterior of the canopy had withstood the impact. By hitting the ground first, the fuselage had absorbed much of the energy. The wing was higher than the cockpit, and Tim dove to his hands and knees to scramble under it.

Now he could see Jeremy. The kid was suspended upside down. His eyes were open, still looking startled, and Tim thought he must be in shock.

It was surprisingly easy to move the window latch and swing open the large, horizontally-hinged window that also served as a hatch to climb into or out of the cockpit. Tim had expected it to be jammed. Since everything was upside down, the window didn't fall down beside the fuselage when he unlatched it. Instead he had to hold it up with one hand until he could keep it wedged open with his shoulder.

"Okay, Jer! Let me check, and then I'll get you out!"

He slowly moved his hand lightly up the back of Jeremy's neck, feeling for anything that would signify a break. Nothing. So far, so good. He wouldn't want to move him if there were any bones broken in a vital area. There was time. There was no smoke. He moved his hand all the way up the spine, sliding it between Jeremy's back and the seat back. Then it occurred to him that he might not be able to feel anything wrong even if Jeremy's spine was fractured. He wondered whether he should leave him hanging upside down 'til the medics got there and did their thing with braces and a stretcher.

"Won't hurt to stay right where you are, Jeremy! Hang on!" He scuttled backward.

Tim heard the rapid approach of a vehicle. He swung his head to peer out from beneath the wing to see the top of the cab of one of McLean's green farm pickups.

"All right!" he told Jeremy. "Help is here! I'm sure they have a radio!"

"Tim?" Lisa's voice cried out.

"Here!" But doubt suddenly flooded his mind. He scuttled back to get the pads of his fingers on Jeremy's wrist. He searched for a pulse.

Lisa was kneeling beside him now. He heard CB chatter in the pickup. Help was on the way.

He just couldn't find the kid's pulse. He kept shifting his fingers. Then he placed them against the side of Jeremy's neck.

"Tim?" Lisa's voice was thin, quavering.

Then the face of Elroy, the man in charge of the McLean farm shop, showed beneath the wing's edge. And there was Johnny Crash coming into view.

Still probing for a pulse, Tim looked back into Lisa's glittering blue eyes as they widened, reading his own.

"No!" she cried. Crawling forward, she shoved past Tim and reached for Jeremy's wrist. Soon, however, she settled back onto her heels and began to weep.

Tim felt as if he'd been shot up with some kind of mind-numbing dope.

"Here!" Elroy said, "Let me!" He crawled into the dim little cave beneath the wing and put a hand on Lisa's shoulder. "Let me by, Lisa."

He, too, probed for a pulse as Lisa trembled and wept, and Tim sat impassively staring. "He didn't make it," Elroy finally concluded. "Come on, honey."

She wouldn't be moved. She continued to kneel there, weeping, her face now buried in the cupped palms of her hands, mumbling a prayer.

Tim watched Johnny Crash turn and leave.

Belatedly, Tim crawled to Lisa. He put his hand on her back and absently stroked it over and over and over again. He heard Johnny Crash making contact with Mr. Will.

"We got a bad one out here."

"Go ahead."

"Jeremy's done busted his ass."

"He's a goner?"

"No doubt about it."

"All right. I'm on my way."

10

AND CLOSER STILL

Tim re-entered the living room from the kitchen, where he'd taken a phone call on the more private extension instead of interfering with the conversation, halting as it was, in the parlor. The others looked at him expectantly.

"Jeremy's step-dad," he said. "Got our number from Mr. Will."

It was evening, and Lance and Lisa had come down to the smaller house to visit with the three crop dusters. It had been a very subdued visit, although Lance had made a few attempts to get their minds off Jeremy by changing the subject. Lisa told how she had called the young waitress Jeremy had been dating and had invited her to come out, but Ruthie had declined.

"What did he say?" Lance asked Tim.

"Says Jeremy told him we were good friends. Says he's coming to take Jeremy home and wants to talk."

"Flying down, I suppose," Dave absently commented.

"Yes. He'll rent a car in OKC, come up here, and they'll fly back from there in a couple days."

"That's good," Lance said brightly. "Glad he's not hauling that boy home in the back of a pickup." He grinned. "It's still winter, but . . . "

Lisa's jaw dropped, and Dave, with his eyes flashing in anger, snapped, "That ain't funny, mister!"

"I'm sorry! That was stupid of me. I guess I was just trying to lighten things up."

Sometimes, Tim thought, turning now to gape at Lance, *it's like you haven't got a brain, man*. However, feeling sorry for Lance moments later and since nobody else was rushing to put an end to the uncomfortable situation, he calmly spoke up, saying the first thing that came to mind. "His dad thinks we were a lot closer than we really were."

"Maybe he needs to," Lisa snuffled. Tears were streaming down her freckled cheeks again. "It really helps to know someone was loved. You be sure to tell him how we all loved Jeremy."

"I will." A minute passed as Tim thought how thankful he was that he and Jeremy hadn't been close at all. "But, hey, I think I'd better turn in now. I'm wiped out."

"We'll see you all some time tomorrow," Lance said, standing. "Come on, honey."

As the two were about to pass by Tim, Lisa paused to place a hand on his arm and say, "I'm sure you're going to be a big comfort to him, Tim. I'm glad it's you."

Lance frowned.

"I'm sure that poor man's in terrible pain," Lisa said. "I thank God you're going to comfort him." She gave Tim a hug and turned to go.

After Lisa and Lance had walked a short way up the knoll toward the newer house, she halted and said, "Lance Levenger, how could you say such a thing? How could you be so insensitive?"

He stopped and said, "I can't tell you how sorry I am that I said that." He hung his head. "I forget that you all knew him so much better than I. Being away at school so much and all . . . "

They stood there mutely for a while, Lance with his head down and Lisa intently staring at him.

* * *

Lance was on his way back to Lisa's right after breakfast the following morning. She'd be busy getting ready for church, but he wanted to do whatever he could to repair the damage his gaffe the night before had done. He saw a ground rig spraying wheat a half mile west and north then spotted CR's motorcycle near it. He went on past the first farm road that would take him past the downwind, contaminated side of the wheat and made the next turn. He got out of the Corvette, waved his arms overhead, and began wading through the wheat toward the sprayer as CR hopped off the tractor and came to meet him.

"Hey, Clyde Robert."

"Hey."

"Want you to do something for me. That big spray plane boy you like so much is making a play for Lisa. I want you to keep an eye on him."

"Shoot, I'll *git* him for yuh."

"Git?" Then, after he realized what CR had meant, Lance said, "You're crazy!" He chuckled and shook his head in wonder. "You do mean *git*, don't you?"

"I do."

"No, no," Lance said, laughing hard now. "I don't want to see you hung by that scrawny little neck of yours. I need to keep you around—at least until I can find an adequate replacement. What would I do for entertainment if we lost you?"

For a moment, Lance fondly recalled the dozen or so men and boys he'd sicced CR on over the past few years. Those were just fistfights, of course, with little harm done. He looked at the scar over one of CR's eyebrows and chuckled.

"Listen, CR, I just want you to watch. I can get that boy fired if Lisa gets too cozy with him. I can have him sent packing in a minute."

"All right. But I shore would like to put some hurt on that damnyankee."

"Yankee? CR, he's . . . Never mind. But I tell you he'll hurt badly enough if I tell Walker to get rid of him. I want you to have a good look at what's going on, starting this evening. I'll leave some binoculars in your pickup before I head back to Stillwater. And I want you to keep it up every evening until he's gone. You know I'll make it worth your time."

"Well, you kin count on me. I'll git 'er done."

"All right. You need any more goodies for that pickup or something, there'll be some extra cash in that bank account of yours in the next few days."

"Yuh think she might be gettin' sweet on him?"

"I doubt that a whole lot. She'd have to be crazy." He paused and turned to gaze up toward the McLeans' place. "But people do act irrationally sometimes. We'll just make very sure it doesn't go that far." Lance turned and walked away.

That boy worships me, he thought, smiling and nodding as he waded back through the wheat toward the Corvette. *And not only for the favors, either. It's pure adoration!*

The favors included their occasional weekend jaunts to distant towns to do what couldn't be done close to home, such as messing around with gals they befriended in dance halls, getting drunk, and setting CR up for the brawls. Lance had also given him some of his things he'd gotten tired of, including the Triumph motorcycle, the nice old pickup, and a Weatherby rifle that Lance had dinged when he'd hurled it to the ground after he'd overshot a nice buck. It had all been easily worth it in Lance's estimation. Besides CR's entertainment value, including his gross manners, his ignorance, his penchant for ripping into big guys, and all the rest that Lance enjoyed relating to acquaintances in college, it was profoundly satisfying to have so much power over another person. He knew he had power over other people, as well, but none of them came close to matching CR's adoration.

I really am his God, he warmly reflected.

* * *

Not long after Lance had left for Stillwater, Tim was sitting on the middle front step of the older house. He was cautiously stroking the pale and bony chin of a sickly old farm cat. He was being very careful to not touch the repulsive creature with anything but the second joint of one index finger. At first he had resisted the cat's patient, hopeful gaze out of its one good eye and refused to touch it. The closed bad eye was runny, and the emaciated animal's dusty, matted fur was littered with bits of straw and other, unidentifiable crud. After a while, however, Tim had reached out the one finger.

"But that's it, cat," he insisted. "You're gross. I'm itching to wash my hands right now."

I do need to go in soon, he thought. It was getting too uncomfortable wearing just jeans and a sweatshirt without a jacket after sundown. Yet he wanted to be alone, and he didn't want to seek his solitude in the room that he and Jeremy had shared.

Maybe I'll go for a ride. Maybe even have a beer or two. Maybe ten. I don't . . .

He caught sight of distant movement out of the corner of an eye and looked up to see Lisa coming down the gravel drive from the big house on the knoll. She bore a familiar serving basket containing something bundled in a white dishcloth. Jeremy's death had been a severe blow to them all, but the two women kept the home-making part of the farm routine moving right along, just as Ned went about his work and the pilots went about theirs whenever the weather was right. Mrs. McLean and Lisa, except for the day of the crash, kept up their daily baking, pouring forth the usual abundance of treats. The baked goodies were always wrapped in spotless, bleached white dish towels and placed in serving baskets.

As Lisa drew nearer, giving him a subdued smile, Tim reflected on the mother's and daughter's insistence on cleaning the house as well while the pilots were out working. It seemed more or less fitting for them to be baking, just as they said they'd always done for the traveling wheat-harvest crews, but it did not seem right for them to be doing such menial work as sweeping, mopping, and dumping trash. Tim marveled at their humility, considering their obvious wealth and elevated standing in the community.

"Hi," Lisa murmured, drawing near. "May I put these in the oven?"

"Of course," he said, and he got to his feet.

"I'll turn it on real low. That should keep them warm enough 'til suppertime."

"Thanks. Thanks for everything you do for us."

He opened the screen door and then the solid one and leaned in. Johnny Crash and Dave were still slumped on the couch, stonily staring at the TV. They didn't even look up. "Lisa's brought more goodies for us," he said.

The two hurriedly got to their feet, mumbling their greetings.

Instead of remembering to go inside, Tim absentmindedly returned to his chilly seat on the hard wood step. He scooped up the cat and flopped it upside down on his lap. As he rubbed its grimy belly, he continued to reflect on what a sweetheart Lisa was. They'd become even closer after the accident.

Several minutes later, he heard the two doors bang shut behind him and soon felt Lisa's hand touch his shoulder. "Hi," she said once again. She briefly ran a hand back and forth across his upper back. Then she sat beside him. "How are you doing?"

She sat very near, one shoulder lightly touching his. He knew it was only to comfort a friend. She was no flirt. He was absolutely certain that she had no romantic interest in him, just as he had no romantic interest in her. But he'd begun to wonder whether he might have had such an interest if she and Lance hadn't been in love. Her sweetness did put a little ache in his heart at times.

"I'm fine," he replied.

Like no female friend I've ever had before, he reflected. Whenever he was conscious of it, how he was beginning to feel about Lisa now amazed him. It was nothing like the romantic love he'd had for Jen or the high school girlfriend he'd had back in California. He imagined that, if he'd had a sister, that's how he would have felt about her. The closest approximation of platonic love he'd ever had for a female was how he felt about his old friend Nick's wife back in LA, but that loyal affection didn't come close to how he now felt about Lisa.

"I'm okay," he emphasized, sighing. The truth was, he felt rotten, but what else could he say? Start gushing about how miserable he was and how he could have kept it from happening?

He hadn't been sitting out there alone in the dark for nothing. He'd been thinking that he really could have prevented the accident. Instead of worrying so much about getting the spray into that corner where the power lines converged, he should have knocked off going under the big wires well short of where it became an absolute necessity. Jeremy would have had to follow suit—if not immediately on his following pass, certainly on the one after. Once again, he wondered why Jeremy had decided to try to squeeze that last pass under and over. A sneeze would do it, Tim reflected. Any distraction at the wrong moment.

Lisa stirred against him, reawakening his awareness of her presence.

"I've seen people die before," he gruffly said. He was trying to communicate that he was pretty well hardened to death, that she needn't feel too sorry for him.

"Airplane spraying is dangerous."

"No, not that. Vietnam."

"Oh." She bowed her head. "You've been through a lot."

"Hey, lots had it worse than me!"

She flinched, which made him realize how sharply he'd spoken. What had him so uptight all of a sudden was that he could hear the dying all over again. It didn't sound anything like kids play-ing cops and robbers.

She lightly leaned against him once more, and he thought to ask, "How are *you*?"

"Not so well. He reminded me of my brother."

Tim felt her tremble and knew that she'd begun to cry.

He wondered again what was going on with her missing broth-er. Maybe there hadn't been a falling-out. He'd even imagined once that her brother might be in prison. But maybe he died. He didn't want to ask. He didn't want to risk intensifying hurtful memories.

"It still hurts," she sobbed. "I know he's in Heaven, but I miss him terribly."

Seeing that she was going to talk about it no matter what he said or didn't say, he asked, "What happened?"

She told him about the water-skiing and the accident the previ-ous summer.

"Twenty-two years old," she said. "He was so . . . " Her head was down, and she was slowly shaking it from side to side so that the golden whorls of thick hair gleamed even in that inferior light. "I just thank God he was a Christian. I do hope that Jeremy was born again. You, too."

Smitty used to bug him about that. Smitty had been the one person he'd ever known who really did seem to believe and tried to act in accordance with his belief. In some ways, although they'd been about the same age, Smitty had reminded Tim of his bright and morally straight father. But he'd come to doubt that his fa-ther really believed in a risen Christ. Not literally. If he had, he wouldn't have continued going to a church that did not literally believe that.

There had been a time when Tim had presumed that all church-goers believed, especially his parents. Then, when he was around twelve or thirteen, one of the very brainy kids had clued him in one day after Sunday School, telling him that only ignoramuses still believed in an afterlife in this age of science. So Tim, diligently trained by his mother to seek not merely entertainment but answers to his most pressing questions in libraries, naturally turned to the books to check.

"Tim?"

"Yes?"

"Born again. Are you?"

"I guess," he said defensively, shrugging.

"Guess? Tim, you would know for certain." She turned to look directly at him.

"I'm a Christian," he said.

She gazed at him for a few seconds before going on, saying, "You don't know much about the faith, do you? We're going to have to talk more about this. Soon."

She nodded emphatically, saying, "Billy was definitely born again. Yes, he was. He didn't just talk about it. He evidenced the fruit of the Spirit. You never would have met a kinder boy."

She grabbed hold of Tim's hand. Her grip was fierce.

"He was so good to everybody. You know boys who some would call no-'count? Well, he treated them the same as anybody. Rich or poor, smart or slow, it didn't matter. He lived his faith."

"Like Lance," Tim said. He was recalling Lance and CR and Lance's talk of church work with other youth.

Lisa stared at him for a while, saying nothing more, then turned to face the shop building across the gray gravel of the lighted farmyard.

At least Jeremy was having fun, Tim thought, not for the first time. *Same as her brother.* He nodded. It helped to know that. *They went out a hell of a lot better than Smitty.*

Tim struggled to move on to more pleasant thoughts about beginnings, rather than endings. He tried to think of all the reasons why Lisa and Lance were going to make such a fine couple. But he'd start down that path only to absently wander away from it seconds later.

His mind kept on stubbornly swinging back to that worst day of some extremely bad days in 'Nam. Smitty had taken such a very long time to get it over with. It was still in his ears now. Tim agonized over the knowledge that he could have put an immediate end to it.

There was no way anybody could have gotten to Smitty alive, much less dragged him out of that clearing. There were just too many gooks popping away at them from the cover of the brush and trees on the other side. But he could have ended his friend's suffering.

He briefly tried to escape the memory by another route, attempting to focus on the work he needed to get back to in the morning. But there just wasn't much to think about when it came to that. He had his maps of the fields and the couple other landing sites he'd use, and he had already figured out the mixes and load sizes for the various customers and fields.

He eyed the skeletal branches of the one winter-stripped shade tree at the edge of the small lawn to the left. The wind wasn't strong enough to move them yet, but the forecast was calling for more wind overnight. If he couldn't spray in the morning, he'd have to find something very active to do to avoid sitting around thinking about people dying. He couldn't imagine any book ridding his mind of that.

Maybe take Lance up on his offer. Go turn that T-6 inside out.

"I need to get out of here and do something if it blows tomorrow," he said to Lisa. "I'd go nuts just sitting around."

"That Bonnie and Clyde movie is back," Lisa said. "Over to Enid."

"Oh?" It didn't really interest him at all.

"I need to stop thinking about him, too, and I hear it's a good one. Do you know if it is?"

"What?"

"Oh, Tim. The movie. Have you seen it?"

"No." He wasn't interested.

Suddenly he realized that he still had that grungy cat in his lap. He gave a start and quickly set the nasty thing aside. He grimaced as he dusted off his palms, then, using the backs of his hands, brushed his Levi's where the frail thing had been sprawled.

"I've heard it's . . . well, there's a lot of shooting in it," Tim said.

"We could fly over tomorrow if it's windy and see something else. Take Daddy's Cessna. You, me, Johnny, and Dave."

He wondered for just a moment what Lance would think about him going to a movie with his fiancée and decided, *No, not a good idea.*

"Tim?"

"No, not me, thanks."

"Not that," she said. "I'm thinking something else. We've gotten to be pretty good friends, haven't we?"

"Yes."

Lisa leaned against him and quietly said, "Tim, when someone's truly born again of the Holy Spirit, a closer relationship is established, and I think the Spirit's been warning me. I don't know if I should say such a thing, but I'm so vexed about it! I really do need to talk to someone."

She eyed him steadily before she went on. "I guess you're the one. Lucky you, huh?" She stared at him as he fidgeted. "Seriously, you're so easy to talk to."

"Thanks."

"So, no more hemming and hawing. Like Lance and CR . . . " She stopped and gazed off into the distance. "I've made so many excuses about him." She paused again. "I've tried talking to Mama and Daddy about these things, but they head me off before I can get started.

"I've always had such mixed feelings. I was proud of Lance, the way he would stick up for CR, but some of it was so ugly.

CR like to beat one boy to death one time. No exaggeration. He put him in the hospital. And then he got in hot water about . . . well, this rumor or whatever it was. The point is, Lance stood up to everybody about CR. He said CR would change when he accepted Jesus. I was so proud of him when he talked that way. But rumors kept on bubbling up.

"I had to wonder, What's the truth? We don't really know that much about CR. He's here for a while, and then off he wanders again, and there's no way to know what he's up to. But that's not the hardest part. I've made so many excuses. It's not just CR I'm talking about." Again she paused, apparently very conflicted about what she was trying to communicate.

"The Holy Spirit's just turning my thoughts inside out lately. It seems He's clearly warning me now. Okay, I'm going to stop beating around the bush. I'm getting really, really—"

"Lisa?" It was her mother. She'd walked down to where she could see them from beside the low hedge that separated the side yards of the new house and the old.

"Hi, Ma."

"Hi, sweetie. Hi, Tim. Honey, I invited Thelma Clausen over. She called and sounded so sad, I told her she had to come. I told her we'd come get her. Would you do that for me?"

"Sure, Ma."

"We can't wait too long."

"All right."

She turned to Tim as her mother went back up the driveway and said, "Well, I need to hurry." Yet she lingered, eyeing him with her head tilted inquisitively. "Tim, after the greenbugs, is there any chance you'll stay on with Mr. Will?"

"Nope. Off I go again."

She gave him another long look before she said, "I'm going to miss you."

"Me, too."

"I've so taken to you as a friend."

"I do want to visit in the future. I need to set up a regular circuit. North first, as you know. Then maybe right back through here on my way to Texas cotton. Even if I decide on the Southeast, it wouldn't take me that far out of my way to stop by to see you and Lance."

"That would be nice," she said, but she still looked very unsettled.

He stood and put out a hand to help her up.

Then, with CR peering through Lance's binoculars at them from his hiding place in the dark, Lisa hugged Tim and said before she turned to walk away, "We'll have to talk again tomorrow."

* * *

CR called Lance a little later that evening. He laid it on pretty thick about Tim and Lisa "neckin' and all."

"That's it!" Lance reacted. "That boy's gone! You just continue keeping a close eye on them 'til he's out of there!"

Lance hung up, dialed long-distance information, and got the home phone number of the crop-dusting company's owner. "Will," Lance said as soon as Walker came to the phone, "this is Lance Levenger . . . Fine, thank you, sir. Say, I've got a little favor to ask . . . Thank you. I figured I could count on you. I'm sure you know that Ned McLean's daughter and I have been planning on getting married this summer . . . Yes, she is. I'm sorry to say that one of your pilots has gone a little too far with Lisa." He paused longer to listen this time and grinned.

"I knew you'd be concerned," he said. "I appreciate it. It just embarrasses the dickens out of me, sir. I tell Lisa to just ignore him, but she's too soft, too kind. She's a little too country to know how you have to handle a smooth-talking California . . . Yes, sir, that Tim O'Reilly."

He paused for a while longer, but he was frowning now.

"I thank you for wanting to help, Mr. Will," he went on. "But

I have to wonder if just talking to him will do any good. And it would get back to Lisa. She'd be embarrassed. I was hoping, since he isn't one of your regulars anyhow, that you might be able to tell him you no longer need his services . . .

"Is that so? Well, I do hate to cause you any difficulty after all these years of loyal service." He stuck out his tongue and crossed his eyes. "How many years have you done our flying?"

Lance nodded and made faces as Walker replied, and he said, "Well, I'll truly appreciate your helping us any way you can. I won't forget it."

* * *

"Say, Tim," said Johnny Crash, who'd happened to be nearest the phone when it rang after supper. "It's Mr. Will. He wants to talk to you."

Tim went over and took the phone, saying, "Tim here." He listened for a minute or so and said, "All right. I'll fly in first thing in the morning. I'll just put my things in the hopper and leave my car here. Someone can help me drive it in later."

The two older pilots looked at him expectantly as he hung up, and he said, "He wants me to work out of the muny 'til we're done. Says he'll put me up at his house."

11

SURPRISES FOR SUPERPILOT

Since Tim had been moved into town, he and Lisa never did have that talk about her vaguely-stated fears before his work in Oklahoma ended. A couple days later, he was spraying his last field of the greenbug run.

Feeling more and more elated as the time approached for him to break free onto the road again, he was really into this "Superpilot" thing. That was what he'd started silently calling himself, partly in jest, but also with some pride for having made it through one of the fabled "plagues" without making an ass of himself. Thanks to that and to the imminent continuation of his travels, his guilt over supposedly being responsible for Jeremy's accident had gradually sunk out of consciousness.

He was lightly brushing the Pawnee's wheels across the wheat, which enhanced the idea that he was getting to be an absolute ace with an airplane. He could feel the wheels ticking through the tops of the densely planted crop by the slight tremors transmitted through the landing gear and brake lines to the brake-and-rudder pedals beneath his feet. In his turns, he could also plainly see the perfectly spaced dark green stripes of previous passes that the tires had left in the silvery-gray film of morning dew that overlay the wheat. Running a plane's wheels through the tops of the plants was entertaining, of course, but it had also led Tim to the discovery that the twin tire lines in morning dew made spacing his swaths and keeping them perfectly parallel much easier.

After Jeremy had bought the farm, Will Walker had not paired Tim with anybody else. Therefore, Tim had to make do without a partner's wingtip to mark exactly where he should enter the field each time. Whenever a farmer didn't provide flaggers, and few around there did, a pilot usually had to strain to find other things to mark each swath, perhaps a particular clump of weeds, a telephone pole, a fence post, or whatever else happened to stand out somewhere in or near the field.

Although Catfish had taught his students the old trick of leaving short wheel marks in dirt off the end of a field, there wasn't such an opportunity on either end of that particular field. Automatic flaggers, devices that dropped a long streamer of tissue paper in the field at the pull of a trigger on the control stick, had been invented, but they weren't in use universally yet. GPS systems, of course, were way off in the distant future. But nothing could be better than these pairs of parallel dark-green stripes that ran all the way across this dew-frosted field.

Having little need now to concentrate so hard to find objects he could line up on and having no need to push his turns so hard to get done in a hurry, Tim had far more leisure than usual to think about other things, such as trying to figure out how much money he'd be getting from Mr. Will when he was done and how much he'd allow himself to spend on a new car. He hoped the boss could cut a check right away so he could start looking for a car that afternoon.

When he'd hurriedly calculated his pay while he'd been taking on a load some minutes earlier, he'd thought he'd made a mistake. So on the way to the field, and even as he'd sprayed, he'd held his little pocket notebook in his throttle hand and, using the tip of his tongue, turned the pages that noted the acreage of each field he'd sprayed since the first day on the job. While his right hand busily worked the control stick to keep the wheels on the wheat or to sustain a fairly tight turnaround at the end of a pass, his left hand held the small notebook up where he could keep glancing at the numbers and still keep an eye on where he was going. Whenever he needed to increase or decrease power or open or close the spray-valve handle with his left hand, he'd push or pull the throttle or spray handle with his left fist or the heel of his hand.

He didn't attempt to get a precise figure. He rounded off the numbers so he'd have a rough idea.

He was itching to know whether he'd been right the first time. If he had, he was owed a lot more money than he'd previously guessed. And that, of course, would mean that he could afford quite a bit better replacement for the Dog than he'd expected.

Before Jeremy crunched, Tim had been having too much fun with the flying and getting to know the various pilots and his new Oklahoma friends to give his earnings much thought. He'd taken a cash draw of 50 dollars each week, which was far more than enough for his share of the groceries, an occasional meal in town, and whatnot, and he had guessed that he'd earned an average of several times that much a week, considering all the no-fly weather. Then, having to deal with Jeremy's death, he'd been even less interested in the money.

He'd had a very casual attitude about crop-dusting pay from the beginning. It had been the extreme flying and the opportunity for frequent travel that had been his main interest all along, and whatever he'd earned, so long as it was enough to get by, he would have been satisfied. The only reason he'd gone to the trouble of buying a shirt-pocket notebook back in Mississippi was that Catfish had repeatedly told his students that was what they needed to do, just in case some operator didn't tally the pay correctly.

The first time he'd tried to get a better estimate that morning, he'd thought, *How'd you screw up simple addition that bad? Fifteen thousand, seven hundred acres? Almost 4,000 bucks? No way!*

There hadn't been time to go back through the book and add the fields up again while he'd still been on the ground. Dave had been coming in, and Tim hadn't wanted to be in his way.

Now, having completed a second mental-math tally, there was only a couple-hundred-acre difference from the previous figure.

Unbelievable! he thought. *But it's gotta be!*

Mr. Will charged a dollar an acre, not including the chemical, and the pilot got a fourth of that. It was very simple math.

It's right around four thou for sure!

That was quite a pile for a few weeks' work in those days.

I could buy a Porsche! A pretty decent one, too! That creepy old boyfriend of Jen's mom had said he'd paid $2,500 for his used Porsche. It had some dings, but Tim had driven it once, and it had been an okay car.

But be cool now. Your first priority is saving for college. No Porsche or anything like that maybe, but definitely something better than I thought!

His elation flowed into his feet and hands, and he pulled up into a soaring wingover turn at the end of that pass. The early morning March air was cool, offering lots of lift, the load was down to a mere few hundred pounds, and the very efficient wings of the little Pawnee did their part to enable him to bring off the glory turn beautifully. Up, up the Pawnee steeply soared to an altitude over a hundred feet; then, having slowed almost to stall speed with the chord of the wings nearly vertical to the horizon, over it swung to the left, nose sweeping steeply downward.

"All right, Superpilot!" he shouted, chortling. "Superpilot," the recent creation of his imagination, had amazing telekinetic powers and such an exquisite feel of the controls that he made airplanes do wondrous feats that the laws of physics deemed impossible. Seconds later, his toes sensed the faint vibrations of wheels lightly ticking through wheat once again, leaving another perfectly parallel set of stripes in the dew.

He had not made a single goof all season long. He had coped well with the pressure to keep things moving at a professional pace, and he was sure that he'd satisfied the panicky farmers as well as any beginner could have done under the circumstances. He was confident that he'd get a twenty-four-karat recommendation from Mr. Will for his next seat down the road.

He thought how glad he was that Mr. Will had called him into town to stay at his house, although he did miss seeing Lisa, her folks, and the two senior pilots as often. He and the boss got along very well. The gentlemanly old operator obviously enjoyed having Tim there, and his wife had to remind the noble, white-haired fellow to get to bed every night, despite the effects of his sleep deprivation and the pressures caused by the surprise off-season run. The experience had been very pleasant for Tim. Most importantly, Will Walker and his wife were very nice, conservative people, and the grandson who stayed with them was a good, sincere kid. Tim greatly enjoyed Mr. Will's eagerness to share his many entertaining crop-dusting memories.

Mr. Will said nothing to Tim of the real reason for moving him into town from the McLeans' place. He'd spoken of it as a purely logistical concern. But he did strongly resist Tim's occasional comments that he should go out to the McLeans' to visit his new friends out there, making up one excuse or another.

As Tim finished his last pass across the field and turned to spray a cleanup pass or two along the power lines on the west side, he toyed with the idea that even a used MG might do. MGs were fairly common, and he might find one for sale in Wichita. He took note of the power lines running from one pole to a small mobile home that was closely surrounded by the wheat, except where the weedy driveway led in from the farm road.

He eased on down, close beside the main power lines, excitedly repeating one of the popular sayings of the day, "All right! Get down!" Another cleanup pass or two, and he'd be done with

the Oklahoma spraying and ready for North Dakota! He wondered whether he could have a bumper sticker made that said,
"Get down, dusters!" He shoved the money handle forward and
reflected that an MG was hardly his dream car, but it was sporty
looking and would be fun to drive. It would have a sufficiently
stiff suspension to comfortably slide around some curves if he felt
like it.

Maybe in a year or two, with—

WHACK!

Right before his eyes, hung up on the hopper-lid clamps inches
ahead of the plastic windshield, was the black phone line he'd just
snagged. Prevented from contacting the vertical wire-cutter bar
just ahead of the windshield by hanging up on the clamps, the
line stretched much farther than Tim would have thought possible before it snapped.

Tim didn't see any point in turning off the spray. The damage
was done. He might as well finish the pass and keep on spraying until the hopper was empty. Of course, even as he processed
those thoughts, he was burning with shame.

Unlike the wires that supplied the trailer with electricity, the
phone line must have been too low to show against the pale sky
above the horizon, drooping down to blend with the background
of dark wheat that continued on past the other side of the dirt
driveway.

"Idiot!" he shouted. He finished the pass and made his pull-up
and turn. He could see that there was just enough chemical down
in the bottom of the translucent fiberglass hopper to make one
more cleanup pass one swath nearer the house and maybe two
more on the opposite end of the field. As he dropped back down
close to the wheat, he figured, *Might as well go under the again. No
phone line to worry about now!*

He wondered how much it was going to cost to string a new
line, and he thought, *I'll pay!*

As he rapidly neared the trailer again, a white-haired crone in a pink bathrobe and fluffy blue slippers came flying out the door and down the wood steps. She began jumping up and down, flinging her hands up high, as he ripped on by beneath the main power lines. It might have looked a lot like a scene in some old-timey hillbilly comic strip to some other onlooker if there had been one, but there wasn't a bit of humor in it for the mightily humbled "Superpilot."

* * *

Tim's new ride turned out to be a flawless white '57 Austin-Healey roadster. It was the full-size Healey, of course. He wouldn't have had one of the miniature ones. If he couldn't own a Porsche or a Jag in decent shape right off the bat while he put aside money for more college, a Healey would do just fine. He always had fancied those graceful lines and that long, long hood in front of the two-seat cockpit. In that way, it was a lot like the long-nosed Piper Pawnee he was flying.

After he got back to Mr. Will's house, he hurriedly said good-bye to the gentle, old-fashioned couple, put his things into the new car, and headed off to the McLeans' to say goodbye to everybody there. Mr. Will had made light of the wire strike, saying his insurance would cover the damage, so Tim was in a more buoyant mood than he might have been otherwise.

It was getting dark by the time he arrived at the McLeans', and he was grinning and rhythmically nodding to Hank Williams singing his heart out about doing time when he pulled in. He'd found a shop that had hustled to install the eight-track tape machine and speakers in the Healey, and he'd even managed to find a tape of old Hank Williams hits, indulging his new interest in all things Country. He'd also grabbed a new tape featuring the Doors and another of Steppenwolf. He wasn't about to give up that sort of thing. He pulled off the paved road and stopped in front of the big house first.

Lisa must have seen the headlights through a window, for she came rushing outside as he started up the walkway. "Oh, my," she said. "Look at *you*."

He accepted a hug and turned to admire the Healey with her. He was glad he had the top down. The car looked even longer and sleeker that way. It could be seen fairly well in the glow from the nearby security light and that from the house, but he wished that she could see it in the bright daylight. "Like it?"

"Nice," she said, but she only gave it another glance.

"I'd like to say goodbye to your folks. Lance, too, if he's around." It was a Friday, and he hoped that Lance might have come home.

"Are you leaving directly?" Her voice sounded strained.

"Yeah, I'm feeling pretty antsy. I don't think I'd be able to sleep anyway."

He hurriedly thanked her parents for all they'd done, and Lisa followed him back outside and down the walk. Lance hadn't come for the weekend yet, so that would save him some time.

"We were really getting close, weren't we?" she said.

"We really were. We are, actually."

She took two quick steps forward, laid her head on his chest, and put her arms around him. He decently shifted a bit sideways to briefly return her hug then stepped back after a couple seconds.

"I've been thinking of you as the sister I never had," he said. It was the truth. He'd reflected at length on that a number of times during the past few days. He'd thought how safe it was, too. He'd never have to worry about rejection in a relationship like that.

She stepped near again, put the palm of her hand on his chest, and said, "You're not just any old friend to me, Tim, I . . . I do think you might be someone I can trust completely."

"Thanks. It feels weird to . . . you know . . . get pretty close to people and then have to leave so soon." He backed away.

"I don't have anyone like you. I keep thinking you could help me."

"Help?" That bothered him. Of course he'd like to help her, whatever it was she needed, but he was on his way. He just wanted to go.

"He doesn't really love me, Tim!" she blurted.

"Lance? Of course he does." He grinned, thinking how silly she was being. He'd heard about people getting the jitters as the wedding date neared. "Why else would you two be getting married?"

"I think he only wants our farm!"

"Lisa!" He laughed. "He *has* a farm. A huge farm. Bigger than yours!"

"I'm scared, Tim!"

"You'll get over it." He retreated to the side of the Healey. "I'm sure lots of people get jumpy before they marry." He guessed that was so, anyway. It had popped into his mind, and it did seem that he really had heard that before.

He got in and clicked the door shut, saying, "I'll try to swing by again before too long. Around the end of May or the beginning of June."

"Oh, I'm sure we'll meet again," she said. Then she laughed so strangely that he paused as he was about to start the engine and tried to make sense of it.

She straightened and stepped back as he started the engine.

"See ya!" he said in as light a tone as he could manage. The truth was, leaving her was putting a little ache in his heart again. He engaged the gears and drove on down to bid farewell to the others.

* * *

The mysterious headlights appeared in the distance behind him as he slowed and started looking hard for the short jog off Highway 270 onto 283. Once he'd made that turn, he'd head due north across the state line and just keep on going almost straight to central North Dakota. He didn't think much about the lights at first, but his interest in them increased when they followed him off the main highway onto the secondary road.

They were still back there as he jogged north, then west, then got onto 283. He doubted that it was a cop, but he kept his eye on the speedometer and tried to relax and enjoy the music blasting and vibrating out of the speakers right behind the two bucket seats. It was John Kay, singing "Born to be Wild."

My theme song, Tim happily reflected. *For now, that's what it's all about: going down the road, having my adventure.*

The lights were still back there as he crossed the line into Kansas, and he frowned. He doubted that an Oklahoma cop would follow him all the way across the Kansas line. He shook his head. It just had to be a coincidence that some other motorist had taken the same zigzagging route through that lonely country at the same time.

He stopped glancing in the mirrors and settled back in his snug bucket seat to enjoy the music. Now the Doors were singing, "Hello, I Love You." He laughed as he imagined using that line on some stranger somewhere down the line. He'd have to make that part of the adventure. Surely he'd be ready to start dating again soon. What a relief it was to be over Jen! Getting away from LA had been powerful medicine, for sure!

After a while, he pulled into a Texaco station in the typical little wheat-plains town of Englewood. He reminded himself to be sure to have the oil checked. The engine did seem nice and tight, but he didn't want to take any chances. He idly looked in the left mirror to see whether the headlights were still coming down the main drag. They were, and it wasn't a cop. It was just an older, faded Falcon. It pulled right up behind him.

Lisa!

12

DAMSEL IN DISTRESS

Tim scrambled out of the Healey as Lisa's car came to a stop behind him. He wondered whether he'd forgotten something. But that couldn't be, since she could have pulled him over way back on the other side of the state line.

"What in the world's going on?" he anxiously asked.

"I want to ride along with you a little!" she said.

He was flabbergasted. That was bizarre. He dumbly gaped at her, trying to read the intensity of those blue eyes peering into his own.

"I need your advice," she said.

A young attendant hurried toward him. It was one of those full-service stations that were still the norm back then.

"Fill it," Tim said curtly, not realizing how rude he sounded. He was having trouble coping with such a change in someone he'd counted on as being such a smart and stable friend. "Regular."

He irritably turned back to Lisa. "And how would you get back to your car?" he facetiously asked. "Hitchhike?"

"Catch a bus."

"Advice? Why *me*?" Obviously it wasn't something she wanted to discuss with Lance, and he hoped there wasn't some sort of trouble between them. "You've only known me a few weeks, Lisa."

"So we're not such good friends after all? Would you say that if I were a guy?"

Once again, he was speechless.

"I've tried to talk to Ma and Daddy again," she said, "but they won't listen. Once we were engaged, they got into this made-for-each-other mind-set, right along with everyone else. And the best friend who was available? I thought she was, anyhow. I thought she'd be willing to spend some time helping me. I drove down to Norman not long ago and spent a couple hours with her, but she's in love with this new guy and . . . Anyhow, please?"

"Not a good idea." He stepped clear as she opened her door to get out.

"Why not?"

"By the time you got back home, you'd be gone all night. I don't think your folks would be too thrilled. Not to mention Lance."

"I've stayed away for more than one night before!"

"But not like this."

"When you stop for the night, I'll come right on back. Nobody needs to know."

"I'm not planning on stopping."

"That's beside the point. Stop or not, just drop me off at a bus station."

"Well . . . "

"Oh, thank you, Tim!" She lunged forward and threw her arms around his neck, saying, "My Gawain!"

He had no idea what in the world a gawain was, but he let it slide, being much more interested in disengaging from such a passionate hug. He squirmed free and asked, "So where shall we leave your car?"

"Right here? I could just park it over there on the side if they'd let me. I could pay."

The boy called out, "All gassed and ready. Oil's right up there."

Tim turned and went over to him, pulling some bills out of his wallet. "Here. Keep the change."

"Hey, thank you!"

"Would it be okay for my friend to leave her car here overnight?" he asked. He doubted that a bus would be leaving immediately from wherever he dropped her off. For all he knew, it might take her a whole day to get back if she had a very long wait.

"I don't see why not. I could leave a note for the boss and say she'll be in to get it."

"I'd really appreciate it," Tim said. But he began to think that they might not have to leave that little town together after all. "But she'll probably pick it up in an hour or so."

"Whatever she wants. It'll be all right."

Tim turned back to Lisa, gave a big sigh, and thought, *I really don't have to be in that big a hurry.*

"Let's go get some coffee or something," he said, glancing down the street toward an orange neon café sign.

"But you're in a hurry to get up there."

"Not that big a hurry. An hour or so won't make any difference."

"I was in denial for so long!" she said as they drove off together in the Healey.

"About?"

"Lance."

If that meant she was having thoughts about backing out of the engagement, it seemed so wrong. He waited silently for her to go on.

"I sure wish Granny were still with us. Granny Hoelbeck, I mean. She's the only one close to me who ever had any doubts about him. She never said much about it, but she didn't hide how she felt about him. That was quite some time before we started dating. I'd sure like to know now exactly what she was thinking."

Tim sighed again and turned in at the café.

After the waitress took their orders, Lisa said, "There'd been some gossip about him all along, but Granny Hoelbeck was no gossip, and she had a mind of her own. Now I think that it must have been more than gossip. But I've seen the gossips get it so wrong about other people that I chose to disregard all that and believe the good things so many other people had to say about him. And folks do praise him."

Tim nodded, recalling all the excuse-making he'd heard the day Lance had buzzed the church.

She paused as the waitress returned to place a glass of milk before her and a mug of coffee in front of him. As soon as the waitress had left, Lisa said in a hushed and reverent voice, "Tim, I truly believe that the *Holy Spirit* has been warning me."

He groaned, and she eyed him sharply.

"Lisa, all I can say is, I think you'd be making a big mistake if you two didn't get married."

"I can see why you think that. He's something, isn't he? But I'm scared, Tim. I mean really, really scared. I'm so glad you said you'd help."

"Help? I can listen. That's about it. I'm sure I'm not the smartest friend you've ever had."

"You're plenty smart enough. You have no idea how highly I regard you. You really are getting to be my knight in shining armor, you know. My *Gawain*."

"Me?" He laughed. He knew perfectly well that he was no knight in shining armor, which must be what that gawain was. He'd tried to be, however. He'd wanted nothing more in life than to be like his father. *There* was a man who could truly be called a modern knight. Tim was suddenly and painfully conscious that he'd rushed off to war in such high spirits, eager to serve as heroically as his father had served during the Korean War, also to save the world from the Red terror. Oh, he'd had his moments when he'd done a bit above and beyond the call of duty, but he'd never come close to matching his dad's well-documented gallantry.

"You're different," she said. "I saw that right away. When you went down to put your things in the car, I almost came down to ask you to help me then, but all of a sudden I was filled with this terrible dread, and I just started praying. It was like someone right beside me said, 'Do not marry Lance. Leave.' It wasn't audible; it was like me thinking, but I'm sure it wasn't me. They were like my own words but given to me. Then, when you left Johnny and Dave, I saw you turn west."

"Let's get back to Lance," he said. "Don't you think you might just have a bad case of nerves about marriage in general?"

"Now you're sounding like Mama and Daddy. Won't you listen?"

"Sorry. I'm listening."

"Sometimes it *does* seem that the voice is just my imagination. Then I hear it again. And don't mock me, Tim, because you don't really know. You can't experience my experience, as Laing would say."

She paused and gazed into his eyes. He cautioned himself to keep his mouth shut. He didn't know who the heck Laing was, either, and he wouldn't ask. If she thought talking would help, it probably would do just that if he'd just keep quiet and listen. She'd probably even hear for herself how unreasonable she sounded. He was regaining confidence in her, judging that she was too sharp to be confused for long. He was sure she'd be on her way home soon. He simply returned her gaze and admired the crystalline complexity of those blue eyes that seemed to transmit what now looked like minute sunrays slanting concentrically into the depths.

"I hesitate to tell you everything," she said.

He turned his big hands palms-up and slightly shrugged, as though to say, "Whatever you think best."

"I need to get clean out of Oklahoma for a while, Tim, and I don't mean a day or two. More like weeks, maybe months."

"And what did your folks say about that?" he blurted, despite his resolve to only listen.

"I didn't tell them."

"What?"

"I mean not just then. I did leave a note."

"Saying what?"

"I just said I had to get away and think for a while."

"That's it?"

"I didn't have much time if I was going to catch up to you. I saw you turn west, instead of east to head for the Wichita highway when you drove off, so I was pretty sure this was the route you were taking. I had to pack at least a few things, and I had to drive pretty fast to catch up as it was."

"They'll be worried sick!"

"It can't be helped. It isn't like I haven't tried to talk to them about it. Like everybody else, whatever shortcomings Lance might have, they're sure he'll live up to their expectations."

"You need to call them right now."

"There's no hurry. I'd really rather not wake them. They won't see the note until morning. They'll go to my room, wondering—"

"You need to call. You can't do that to them."

"You're right. Why am I arguing about it? Now do you see why I wanted to talk to you?"

"And Lance. What did you tell him?"

"Nothing."

"You need to call him, too."

"I'm scared to death to talk to him. I just can't trust myself to keep my resolve once he gets to talking."

That's a good sign, he thought. *If that's how she feels, she'll get over this.*

"You need to tell him," he said.

"I will eventually. Not now. I'm not going to take a chance on him talking me out of this. He is a charmer."

"Yes, he is."

"That's why everybody . . . Most of us—certainly I was among them—we keep making excuses for him. Going way back. Long before he ever asked me out.

"Like the time he made poor Miz Sellers quit. High school. It was one time I didn't go along with the crowd and find an excuse for what he did. I still don't, not if it happened the way I heard it. But you see? There I go again. I can't be sure that it really did happen that day. I didn't see it firsthand . . . "

Tim caught the waitress's eye, and he held up his cup to signal for a refill. He was sure that he was going to need it. They might be at it for some time, and he had a long drive.

But I'd listen all night if that's what it took, he thought, reconsidering. *Getting up there tomorrow's not all that important. Tomorrow's Saturday. By the time I got up there, I probably wouldn't find anybody at work anyway.*

"Tim?"

He nodded and said, "I'm listening," pretending that he hadn't spaced out.

"You went away for a while there."

"Sorry."

"So, as I was saying, he hadn't handed in some homework. I wasn't there, of course. He's a year ahead of me. But kids in his class talked about how little studying he could do and still get good grades. The way I heard it, he told Miz Sellers that he'd forgotten to bring his homework. And she said out loud in front of the whole class that she'd call his mother and have her check to see. And he said, 'I wouldn't do that if I were you.' "

This is important? Tim wearily wondered. *Lance's high school homework?*

"The girls who were telling about it kept repeating that part, trying to mimic how he must have said it. He can be so dry, so . . . aloof. Anyhow, they said Miz Sellers lit into him with this lecture about him thinking he was better than everyone else and could flout the rules. She supposedly said something about how thankful she was that his ma didn't have two little Levengers like him. And they said that Lance said, 'I'm sure we're all thankful that *you* never had *one.*' "

Tim stifled a yawn and thought, *I may need to sleep a little before North Dakota after all.* He lifted his napkin to pretend he was wiping coffee from his lips and concealed a more insistent yawn.

Lisa was too involved in her story to notice the face he made containing the yawn, and she plunged right on, saying, "They said he said, 'Can you imagine what a grotesque little creature any child of *yours* would have been?' If that's what he really said—anything close to that—it was horribly cruel. She was an old maid, and she . . . well . . . she didn't look very nice. Anyhow, at some point she ran out of that room and she never came back. Some of his classmates begged him to run apologize, but they said he just smirked."

Kids can be heartless, Tim thought. Now and then, some thoughtless thing he'd done came to mind to bother his conscience.

"Can you imagine?" she asked.

"Yeah. Not good." With her looking right at him now, he raised the napkin to conceal another yawn.

"Oh, my. You are tired, aren't you? I don't think you should drive any farther tonight."

"I'll put the top down. That might do the trick."

"Let's just go. I'll drive so you won't have to."

"Oh, Lisa . . . "

"Please?"

"I'd probably fall asleep if you drove. That would defeat your purpose, since you want to talk this thing out."

"This *thing.* What . . . Never mind. Then you drive as long as you can. I do need your advice, and you're getting too sleepy here to do me much good. We'll just do the best we can. We'll have to get my things out of my car."

"You wouldn't be able to turn back until we got to some bigger city with a bus station. I'm not sure how long it would take us."

"The buses stop in smaller places, too. I've seen. I'm sure it's the same as back home."

"Well, I'm not about to drop you off at some gas stop. There's no place to sit and wait. Tell you the truth, I don't feel very comfortable about you riding buses at all. Don't you really think you should go on home now?"

"I know I don't want to sit *here* any longer." She quickly stood and said, "I'll pay."

"No."

"Yes." She got some change out of a pocket in her jeans to leave on the table as a tip and hurried to the cash register.

"So," he said as they drove back to where she'd left her car, "my advice is, go on home and think things through there. I'll get a room and call you in the morning so we can talk some more. It's probably a waste of time for me to try to look for a seat before Monday anyway. How does that sound?"

"Not good. I'll ride with you awhile, or I'll just go on somewhere by myself, but I'm definitely not going home. Not for quite a while."

"Lisa! Didn't you say you wanted my advice?"

"If I weren't a female, would you worry so about my going with you? Or, for that matter, going off by myself?"

"We've already been there. That's different."

"How so?"

"Your parents. They're going to worry about you running off like this. It would be a lot different for them if you were a guy. That's just the way it is."

When he pulled up beside her Falcon, she got out and came around to his side of the car. "Well, thanks for listening." Her voice was husky with emotion.

"You're going home, right?"

She quickly turned, shaking her head in response. But, instead of getting into her car, she leaned against her car door with both arms, and her head slumped down between her shoulders.

Seeing her begin to tremble, Tim knew that she was crying. He turned off the headlights, shut off the ignition, and went to her. He put an arm across her back and pulled her against his side.

After a while, she said, "He deceived me, Tim! He has no real feeling for me!"

"That doesn't make sense. Of course he does."

"He didn't show any interest in me until Billy was gone!"

"Lisa . . . "

She kept talking as she cried, saying, "He and Billy were pretty close, but he never paid any particular attention to me. Billy would just take me along sometimes, since I liked to do the same things if it was outdoors, and Lance would usually have one of the prettier girls from school with him. He put up with me, but it was very clear he wasn't interested in me.

"When he was so very nice to me at the funeral and afterward, I assumed that his own grief made him sensitive to mine. I was grateful. I assumed that it was just natural that, drawn together that way, our comforting each other would blossom into friendship and then love."

Tim nodded approvingly and thought, *Sounds natural and normal to me.*

"He reminded me after the funeral that Billy hadn't died in any final sense of the word, since he was a believer. I did need to hear that. It meant more coming from him than the others because he and Billy had spent so much time together.

"He was a real comfort in lots of ways. He started insisting that I accompany him here and there whenever we were both home from college, and he'd even fly down to OU in that tiny plane he used to have. At first, I was like some wounded coyote, holed up in my den and licking my wounds when I didn't have to be out

172

and about, but he convinced me that it's not Christian to be that sad for someone who's gone to Heaven. That meant so much to me!

"It wasn't long at all before he was telling me that he loved me. Oh, I fell for him, all right! You've seen how he is. But, thanks to the Lord, I think I'm coming to my senses now.

"Tim, do I have to draw a picture? After Billy's accident, I became sole heir to the McLean property."

"Hey!" He immediately withdrew his arm and stepped away. "That's a very serious accusation! Knock it off!"

"I might as well knock it off! Nobody would ever believe it! Not you, not anybody!"

"As I said, he already *has* a farm. And here's what else I think, since my opinion's supposed to be so important. Like you said, it's the most natural thing in the world that your suffering would make him more aware of you. Of course it would. He began to really see you and understand just who you are! He fell in love! End of story! Come on! Why *wouldn't* he love you? Get real!"

"Oh, Lord! How happy I would be if I could be sure that's how it really was!" She peered directly into his eyes once more and asked in a voice full of dread, "Tim, tell me, do we *look* like we're so passionately in love?"

He hesitated, not knowing what to say at first. "Passionate" didn't quite describe what he'd seen. Yet . . .

"Aha! See?"

"No, I've always taken it as . . . How should I . . . as the way decent people should act in public. I've always admired your reserve. It's good *manners*. It makes me —"

"We're that way a lot of the time when we're alone. The truth is, it's confusing. It's like he can turn his affection on and off as easily as I might flip a light switch."

"Well, there must be more to it than you've told me." As soon as he'd said that, he knew that he'd made a lucky guess, for she quickly dropped her eyes.

"And you say you're not smart? There is something more. We . . . well, we . . . Should I be talking this way to you? Okay, so we agreed to save ourselves." She stopped for a moment and peered even more closely at him. "You don't know what that means, do you?"

"Save yourselves?"

"Yes. As Christians. You know."

"Ah." He nodded. "And you just answered your own question. He's probably scared to death he'll get carried away. Don't you see?"

"Oh, you might be right about that, too. That's what *he* said. That's how I feel, too. But this is what I mean, Tim. It helps so much to talk it out."

"Then I'm glad we're doing it."

"But I still have my doubts," she muttered, and she fell silent again.

"Well," he said, "my advice is, go on home. He'll be at school most of the time anyway. I'll call you soon, and we can talk some more on the phone."

"Oh, I'll go, all right. But not home. Not 'til I know for sure whether I'll marry him or not. The truth is," she said, suddenly trembling, "I still have to wonder whether he did everything he could to save Billy!"

"Lisa!" He thought, *She's in way worse shape than I imagined!*

She wept harder than ever.

He began to wonder whether Jeremy's recent death was affecting her mental processes. It could have churned up all sorts of powerful emotions, including anger, about her brother's death. He knew firsthand about that. How could he judge her when he, himself, flipped out so crazily from time to time? For a fleeting moment, he wondered whether Smitty's death could be the cause of his own problem.

He turned her around and held both of her hands, and he

174

tenderly reflected, *She just can't know how irrational she's being right now. Sooner or later she'll be herself again.*

Still holding her hands before him, rubbing them with his fingers as he gave her time to calm down, he became fully aware of her engagement ring. Its ongoing presence buoyed his hope that she'd eventually return to normal.

If she really believed what she just said, she'd tear that thing off and fling it halfway back to Oklahoma!

Little by little, she did settle down. Finally she pulled away, wiping the tears with the heels of both hands, and said, "Well, here I go."

"How're you fixed for gas?" he asked, opening the door for her.

"I'll have that boy fill the tank. Write me a letter whenever you get where you're going."

"Go on home, Lisa."

"On. Not home."

"And just how much money do you have for wandering around like that?"

"Enough." She opened the Falcon's door. "And I can wire for more."

"Stop."

She did, crouching between the open door and the car seat.

Damn! I'll get her turned around yet!

"Come on," he said, tugging gently at the crook of her arm. "You can ride with me a ways."

13
SPRING SEAT

"So, what would you do?" he asked as they left the little cluster of town lights behind and headed into the dark. "I mean if you didn't go back right away?"

"*If*? What do you mean, *if*? *Hellooo.* Anybody home? I will go home eventually, of course, but not soon."

"So you'd get some kind of job?"

"Will, not would. I doubt it. But no job. I'll just write. That's a big part of what's kept me sane after Daddy pulled me out of college. But I'm so thankful that you care. You really do care, don't you?"

"Yes, I do." And, having said that, he felt another one of those incomprehensible surges of emotion for this new friend.

"You're such a sweetie. I knew I could count on you."

She put her soft, slender hand on the back of his, which was resting on the floor-shift knob, and he glanced down and saw by the light of the dashboard glow the reassuring glitter of the flashy engagement ring. He had very strong platonic feelings for her, but he certainly had no desire for it to go beyond that. It didn't occur to him that, despite his intentions, it might.

"How long do you think?" he asked.

"As long as it takes. A week? A couple months? I do have to decide before summer."

"If not 'til summer, you could go back to school." He was only making conversation, not suggesting that she should. "Some really stuffy school for women that wouldn't worry your dad about Commie faculty and hippy war protesters." He affectionately chuckled at his memories of her father's denunciations.

"That's not a bad idea! See? I *knew* you that you could help me figure this out. It's pretty late to get admitted for spring, but summer session's just around the corner."

"Hey, how about calling your folks and telling them *that's* what you're up to. We should have called back there. We'll stop at the next town. Better your folks worry about that than about their daughter running off to have a fling with some crop duster!"

"Good point. I'll do it."

"When your dad told you he wouldn't pay for more school," Tim said, having become much more interested now, "why didn't you just get a job and continue part-time where you were?" He would have kept on himself if things hadn't fallen apart. He might have dropped his business major and concentrated on what had begun to interest him more. He'd sometimes daydreamed that, if he had the brains for it, he might get a bachelor's in philosophy, go on to graduate school, and teach.

"Oh, I wouldn't have had to work" Lisa said. "There's the money Granny Hoelbeck left me, as I told you, and the farm is incorporated, so I have that income, too. It's just that when Daddy got to the point where he'd heard one bit too much news about the problems on so many campuses, he said, 'That's it,' and that was that."

"I don't get it. If you're of age . . . You are 21, aren't you?"

"I may be of age legally, but he's still my spiritual head."

He kept quiet, and she didn't say anything more for a while. The side glow of the Healey's headlights continued to reveal wheat and more wheat, and he wondered whether wheat country ran all the way into Canada. Whether it did or didn't, growing food was a far bigger deal than he'd ever imagined.

So it went as they drove on through the vast plains, conversing about her passion for literature that coincided with his own less formal but habitual reading, about his interest in philosophy, and about her sort of Christian faith, which insisted that knowledge of ultimate value could be gained only by opening oneself to belief and seeing what resulted.

As the glow of Dodge City's lights began to rise out of the darkness ahead, they decided it wouldn't make much difference if she rode on with him to North Platte, Nebraska, and she'd call home when her folks would be getting up.

*   *   *

"Are you sure you don't want me to drive now?" she asked a little later. "I don't feel a bit sleepy yet."

"Me neither. Sitting in that coffee shop made me sleepy, but going down the road is different. I guess I'm pretty wired about getting my spring seat."

"Good idea."

"Huh? Good idea 'wired'?"

"Good idea 'spring seat.' Mess up or the motor quits, activate spring. Spring seat plus parachute."

"Good one!" he said, laughing. And he thought. *If she can make up a joke like that, she's getting over whatever possessed her to start imagining all that stuff about Lance.*

"First it was 'Fort Dodge,' " she said as they left the lighted city behind them and re-entered the night-cloaked farming country.

Tim had commented that he hadn't realized that the famous city was located in Kansas until they'd gotten there. He'd always assumed it was farther west.

"It was built to protect the pioneers from the Cheyenne and maybe others, maybe Pawnees," she continued. "I'm not sure about that. We came up here on Easter vacation when I was in the eighth grade. I did a report on it. But no wonder those Native Americans were upset: White hunters killed *millions* of buffalo around here. Not for the meat, either. Can you imagine how hideous that looked to people who depended on the buffalo for food and winter warmth? For their very survival? The white hunters wanted only the bones and hides to sell. A hunter could earn a hundred dollars a day shooting buffalo. That was a fortune in the 1800s."

"Big money. If a hunter took a day off a week, he'd still make . . . what . . . around twenty-five hundred bucks a month? How long ago was that?"

"Fort Dodge was built in 1865."

"What a memory! That had to be some awesome bucks a hundred years ago. They say the average income *now* is less than a thousand a month, and I'll bet inflation has multiplied the value of that twenty-five hundred bucks back then many, many times. But bones? What good are bones?"

"Fertilizer. They ground them up for fertilizer."

"Really?"

"Really."

"Yeah, they made a pile of money, but they probably had to stay clear of those Cheyenne or whoever. I'll bet it was pretty risky."

"Which reminds me of you and your crop dusting. I hope you really do go back to school. Have you considered the airlines?"

"No, that doesn't interest me. I just need a couple years to get my head back together, and then I'll go back. I started having problems. With my classes and stuff. I don't know why. So I bailed out. But I'll get it together and go back pretty quick."

"You said your major was business?"

"That's right."

"Do you ever think you might have a death wish?"

"Deaf wish?" he kidded. Tim had heard Johnny Crash joking about deaf wishes. Hearing impairment was common among the older crop dusters, who hadn't begun to enjoy the benefit of effective hearing protection until recently. Tim thought of the time he'd been riding along in Dave's pickup between Dave and Johnny Crash when they'd unloaded one of the old standards on him, Dave saying, "Shore are windy," and Johnny replying, "Winsday? I thought it were Thursday," then Dave saying, "Thirsty? Dang right! Let's git us a drink or two!"

"Seriously, Tim," Lisa said. "Is it possible? Some sorrow you're hiding? That's what I sense."

He chuckled and teased again, "Business management definitely was a sorrow for *me*, but it didn't make me suicidal."

"Subconsciously maybe?"

"Nah. No way." Yet she really was making him wonder about the despondency he seemed to be working his way out of. He always tried hard to keep an open mind about everything.

He had to admit that it hadn't originally been a passion for flying that had gotten him interested in crop dusting. It was at least conceivable that his chance encounter with the crop dusters on that ride to the Monterey races had suggested a mortal danger that had somehow appealed to him. Still, it did seem very unlikely. He could recall thinking nothing more than flying that way just looked like a lot of fun. Then he'd met Johnny Crash a little later and had learned what an amazing adventure seasonal crop dusting could be. Johnny had told him about Catfish Kovac's crop-dusting school in Mississippi.

* * *

Lance returned that same evening. He went on by his own home to stop at CR's place. He honked the Corvette's horn, and CR hurried out, wiping his mouth on a sleeve.

"I was eatin'. Then I was goin' on over and check on Mr. Overgrowed Damnyankee and your woman."

"Forget about it tonight. I'll do it." So far, CR had reported just one quick, uneventful visit that Tim had made to Lisa and the two older crop dusters since Will Walker had taken him in. "Here you go." Lance handed CR the crisp, new hundred-dollar bill he'd gotten for him at the bank in Stillwater. "Little treat for you. Why don't you go have some fun?"

"I believe I will. I'm due some relaxation."

"And I'll think up something really special for us to do later on, once that pain-in-the-neck sprayer pilot has left the country."

"It's about that time, what's everybody's sayin'. I'd sure like to kick his ass before he's gone."

"That would mess me up with Lisa. You do that, I'll kick yours. Or worse. You know I would, don't you?"

As tough a scrapper as the feisty little guy was, he glumly nodded.

Lance had CR hand over the binoculars, and he drove on to his own house. He dashed in to give his dad a quick, "Hi, Pop," and paused long enough to give his mother a peck on the cheek before he rushed on, saying over his shoulder, "I'm in a hurry to get over to Lisa's, but I'll bring her over, and we can visit then."

The shortest way to the McLeans' was straight up the paved road that went right past the east sides of both farmsteads, but he took a detour west, north and east so that he could approach the house without being seen from the side where the dining, living and family rooms were. He stopped short of the west end of Ned's airstrip on the little-used east–west road, turned off the headlights, and got ready. He pulled the binoculars out of their case and slipped the strap over his head. Then he picked up the little flashlight he kept in the car for emergencies and got out.

This is probably a big waste of time, he thought as he cupped one hand over the lens in such a way that only a narrow beam would light the way and turned the flashlight on. *I doubt very much that big turd could get anywhere with her. Still, considering the stakes . . .* He left the thought unfinished as he cautiously passed through the shallow ditch beside the road and walked on down the airstrip, which was lower than the built-up roadbed and where the sliver of light showing the way would be less noticeable.

He had called Lisa at noon to say that he'd be late, that there was some family business to take care of as soon as he got home, so she wouldn't be expecting him until morning.

And if they are together? What then? He'd have to think about it. The main thing was to keep cool and stay focused on his goal.

When he got to the base of the airstrip and he could see by the illumination from the security lights, he turned off the flashlight and went up toward the older house. He paused in front of the last T-hangar to take stock of things. He saw the two older pilots' pickups in front of the house where they were staying, but Tim's pile of junk was neither there nor up at the new house. Then he noticed that Lisa's Falcon wasn't in the old detached garage between the two houses where she usually parked it.

Somewhere together? he suspiciously wondered. *Maybe. We'll see what Ned and Amanda have to say.*

He went back for his car, parked right in front of the McLeans' home, and strode up to the entrance.

"Lance!" Ned McLean exclaimed. "Come in, come in! We weren't expecting you! I'll go let Lisa know you're here. Make yourself at home."

"Where's her car?"

"Why, wasn't it in the garage?"

"No, it wasn't."

"Now, that is odd," said Lisa's mom. "I'll go see." Her husband had already started down the hallways toward Lisa's bedroom, and she followed right behind him.

Lance went into the family room to settle onto a couch before a coffee table that had three short stacks of magazines on it. *Women's magazines*, he thought disgustedly, and he shuffled through the nearest stack to see whether there was anything more interesting. He discovered an *Architectural Digest* beneath some of the other magazines. Regaining his confidence that Tim couldn't really be any serious competition, he humorously thought, *Hmm, I wonder what Lisa's been reading lately?*

He was content to leaf through the magazine for a while, for he and Lisa would be building their own home soon, but he began to irritably wonder after a while what could be taking Ned and Amanda so long. Then, when they did enter the parlor at last, both were strangely subdued. Amanda's expression as she stared at him was tender and sad, and Ned looked very somber.

Lance lunged to his feet and rushed to them. By the looks on their faces, they had bad news.

"What's wrong?" he cried.

"She isn't here, Lance," her father said. "She said she needed some time alone."

"Thank God! I thought something terrible happened!"

Amanda handed him Lisa's note.

"Do you think it has anything to do with me?" he said after he'd swiftly read it.

"We're not sure what it's all about, sweetie," she said, letting go and stepping back. "She has seemed very distracted lately."

Run off to be alone with that hired pilot? he had to wonder for a moment. But instead of voicing that fear, he slyly said, "Maybe that Tim has some idea where she is. I'll go down and ask him."

"He's left," Amanda said.

Lance noted her trembling lips as she said that, and he knew that they shared what he had to conclude, himself.

"Well, let's keep each other informed," he said, certain that they wouldn't tell him if they did fear that the two were off somewhere together. "If you hear from her, call me. I'll do the same if she calls me first."

He hurried for the door, thinking, *They are together! They must be!* He looked back and asked before he went out, "When's the last time you saw either one?"

Ned McLean hesitated before he said, "Right after supper."

Lance's first impulse was to take off after them, assuming that they'd use the main interstate north up through Wichita, since Tim had said he'd be moving on to North Dakota. Then he thought it was more likely that they'd be lingering somewhere nearby, maybe Enid.

Maybe those old pilots know. He raced down the slope to the other house.

Johnny Crash answered the doorbell, heartily saying, "Well, Lance! Come right on in!"

"Thank you!" he said, manufacturing a nice big smile. Judging by their open, friendly expressions, he doubted that either pilot was hiding any secrets. "Evening, Dave!" He made sure to give them both another nice, big smile. He needed them to like him well enough to spill the truth if they had any reason not to. "How are you all doing?"

"About as well as can be expected for a couple ol' dogs," Dave said. "Come on in all the way and set down."

"I can't stay. I promised the folks I'd spend some time with them this evening. But I was over to the McLeans', and when they said that Tim had left, I was disappointed. I wanted to know how to keep in touch with him, and they didn't know. Do you all?"

"Nope, I'm afraid not," Johnny said. "Not yet. He said he'd leave word at my sister's in Texas when he found him a seat. Me and Dave are leaving tomorrow, but I could call you. He's interested in coming down to Nicaragua for the winter if a seat opens up down there."

"I'd appreciate it if you would. Well, it's been good knowing you. I do need to get on home now."

He turned to leave then stopped and said as though it was an afterthought, "Lisa didn't happen to mention where she was going this evening, did she?"

"No," Dave said, "she didn't." And Johnny Crash shook his head, too.

They weren't keeping anything from me, he thought as he drove away. *I'll just have to sit tight and see what develops. I really don't think it could be permanent anyway. She'd be an absolute fool to marry some hired pilot. She's smarter than that!*

* * *

"So where will you go, Tim?" Lisa asked. They were still heading west from Dodge. It would be a while until the highway turned northward again. "Same school as before?"

"Yeah, I guess. Back to The Beach. That's what we call it. Long Beach State, actually."

"Where you grew up?"

"Same county. Los Angeles County."

"I'll bet you like the Beach Boys."

He groaned. "What makes you think that?" In the past year or so, they'd begun to sound pretty childish to him.

"Duh! Whut did yuh call yore college?"

"Okay, yeah, The Beach. I can still listen to some of those songs, but the Beach Boys are a long way from being at the top of my chart."

"Did you surf?"

"I sure did. Boy, did I! But I like surfing, not listening to silly songs about it." He began to sing "Surfer Girl" with exaggerated sweetness.

Even though he was making it sound extra-dumb and syrupy, he hoped she'd say something nice about his singing. But all she said was, "Maybe that's where I should go."

"Now, that would be a change of scene for you."

"It sure would. Is it always warm and sunny?"

"No, not always. But pretty much. I like their car songs better." He began to shrilly sing "Little Deuce Coupe."

"Deuce coupe?" she asked, mercilessly cutting him off. "What in the world does that mean?"

"Nineteen thirty-two Ford coupe. Probably the most popular hot rod ever. I had a '41 Ford. It was fast. Nobody knew what *I* had under the hood. Plain Jane with all the original chrome and black factory paint, not chopped and channeled and all that, but still, bored, stroked, ported, three-quarter-race cam, dual Edelbrock carbs, et cetera, et cetera."

"*Whatever* all that means. My humble Falcon should tell you how much I'm into cars. I do like this Austin-Healey, though. Maybe I'll get one like this someday."

"Yes, it is nice." He happily listened to the hum of the tight British engine until she spoke again.

"Are there lots of beaches and palm trees?"

"Yes."

"I'd like that. I've never seen anything like that. Only in pictures. I've never even seen an ocean, except when Daddy flew us down to Houston and Biloxi. If the Gulf can be called an ocean. We vacationed down there a few times. He talked about flying us down to Florida some winter, but we never got around to it. You sure you wouldn't like to fly for the airlines?"

"Nah, that's not my thing."

"I've thought of it. I love flying on instruments and going places."

She fell silent for a while, apparently daydreaming about it, and Tim began thinking again of the further traveling he was eager to do that year.

"Is that college of yours actually on a beach?" she asked.

"Close. Easy walking distance."

"And flowers? All year?"

"Oh, sure." He thought of his mother's passion for gardening. It seemed there'd always been flowers of one kind or another in bloom around the house. But he suddenly remembered a floral fragrance far more alluring than any he'd ever experienced in Southern California, and he said, "I wish I knew the name of this incredible flower they have in Hawaii."

"You've been to Hawaii?"

"Just a few hours to and from Vietnam. Didn't get off the base."

"They probably have a college in Hawaii," she said. "They must. It's a state now. Wouldn't that be something? Some missionary college. For women only. Daddy wouldn't worry about a college like that. I saw the movie. It's beautiful, isn't it?"

"What movie?"

"Why, *Hawaii*, of course. It's beautiful, isn't it?"

"From what I could see. I could see the mountains, and I could see the ocean, but mainly I saw Barber's Point Naval Air—"

A car horn blared behind them. He glanced at the speedometer and saw that he was absentmindedly plugging along five miles an hour under the limit. Cars were approaching from the opposite direction, so the driver behind him couldn't pass. He speeded up.

"I'd love to go sometime," she said, acting as though that horn wasn't still blaring. Now the driver had his lights on high-beam, as well. "There are so many . . ."

The oncoming lane had cleared, and the Plymouth pulled alongside. It just hung there, perhaps a foot away.

Tim forced himself to keep looking straight ahead. *Assess, man. Do not react.* He eased off the accelerator and gently steered to the road's edge.

The Plymouth accelerated and cut right in front of them. Then its taillights suddenly went bright-red.

Tim got on the binders instantly. He reflexively flung out his right arm to keep Lisa from flying forward, and he braced for the expected impact. But the creep ahead of them floored it just in time.

Tim downshifted to a lower gear, mashed down on the accelerator, and took off after him.

"Tim! Stop it!"

He backed off immediately and slowed enough to drop well behind the other car.

"What in tarnation was *that* all about? What's got *into* you?"

Now the Plymouth was pulling onto the shoulder ahead of them. As soon as it stopped, the door flew open, and out came the driver, beckoning for Tim to stop.

Tim took in Lisa's frightened look, and he drove right on by without giving the chunky dude another glance. But he did peer into the rearview mirror in time to see the puke leap back into his car. It slewed onto the pavement with the beams of its lights swinging back and forth as the driver fought to get it under control.

"Faster!" Lisa frantically cried as she looked over her shoulder. "He's coming after us!"

Burning with shame, he drove on as fast as the Healey would go. Finally, however, the lights behind him vanished, and he slowed to just under seventy.

"Sorry," he moaned. "I just blow up sometimes. I don't know why. I wasn't always this way."

"I forgive you," she said. She fell silent for a while.

She broke the silence a couple minutes later by dreamily reciting, "Wild ways in the world our worthy knight rides. For you, we'll change it to 'flies.' Or maybe 'flyeth.' It's from *Sir Gawain and the Green Knight*. So listen, you just had a moral tiff with a dark knight, and you *triumphed*. Your impulse was to do battle, but you chose a higher way. Maybe you've read it?"

"No, I don't think so." He might have, for there had been much mandatory reading that had bored him and which he'd promptly forgotten after the tests. Until his most recent stint in school, he'd been able to memorize whatever was required for a decent grade, then, if it had no obvious lasting value, flush it out of memory.

"I think you're more like him than I first thought."

"He went for hotcakes in a big way, too?" It was a dumb thing to say, but her talk about him being knightly made him very uncomfortable, and he was particularly prone to react foolishly when he felt self-conscious. He was also getting hungry again. "You realize how long it is 'til breakfast?"

"He was very good and very strong. Not just physically. Morally. Few could have withstood the test of the green knight and his wife as did Gawain."

* * *

They were together all the next day, too. They passed through North Platte, Nebraska, after she'd checked in with her folks, deciding that Sioux City, South Dakota, would be as good a place as any for her to turn back. Then, at Sioux City, they decided that it wasn't so much farther to North Dakota, where she might have made up her mind what she was going to do, and he would leave her at some bus station and start knocking on doors.

They took turns driving and dozing, and they chattered more and more about things such as her progress toward an instrument-flying license, the places they'd like to see eventually, their favorite books, and the old dream she'd had before she started dating Lance of going to graduate school and teaching literature and writing at a good university. As they did so, she talked progressively less about her panic over marrying Lance, and Tim was encouraged, taking it to mean that her fear would probably be gone for good before long.

In northern South Dakota, just shy of the state line, he spotted a small airport just off the highway and pulled in to see whether anyone knew of someone needing a pilot a little farther on. Tim found the owner of the operation in the hangar, where the young guy was hanging an engine on a Pawnee. He did, indeed, know of a man across the line who'd been looking for a pilot. He urged Tim to use his phone to call.

"That's not quite as much experience as I wanted," Otto Brunner said. "I suppose we could talk about it face to face, but it's a pretty good drive west from where you are."

"Is now okay?"

"I suppose. It'll be late when you get here. Tell you what, give me a couple references now, and I'll see if I can get ahold of them in the meantime."

So, a couple minutes later, Tim and Lisa were huddled over the road atlas in the Healey, looking for a place where he could drop her off along the way. But there weren't any cities on the quickest route along the state line, and Tim didn't want to arrive late at night. She could just wait in the car while he and Mr. Brunner talked, then he'd drive her up to Dickinson or Bismarck, where she could catch a bus back to Kansas.

14

SITTING PRETTY

That evening, following the directions Brunner had given him, Tim was surprised to be turning off the pavement at a farmstead that included an old barn, a stock pen with cattle in it, an area containing a variety of farming equipment, and a small home. Brunner hadn't said he was a farmer. As Tim got out of the car, a burly, middle-aged man in a long-sleeved denim work shirt, jeans held up by thick black suspenders, and wearing white socks without shoes came onto the front porch.

"You must be Tim," he said.

"Yes. Nice to meet you." The man's hand felt like a scrap of rough-sawn lumber.

"You brought your wife along?" Brunner exclaimed, smiling and motioning for Lisa to come.

"A friend, actually." In unhappy resignation,Tim also beckoned to Lisa.

Brunner's smile vanished. His left cheek began to twitch. Soon, the tic was tugging hard enough to distort his mouth on one side and jerk his round head sideways.

Tim hoped it wasn't Brunner's reaction to him traveling with a female friend, but he had to think it probably was. He had considered that western North Dakota farming country would not be the most liberal place in the world about such things, and he'd almost taken time to find Lisa a room for the night before driving out to the farm. But then he'd thought he could get away with just being honest. Now he wished that he hadn't been so optimistic. As she climbed up the steps, he said, "This is Lisa McLean."

Brunner's eyes bulged as Lisa smiled and shook his hand.

Oh, well, Tim thought, considering it could be expected and understandable that someone might jump to the wrong conclusion and turn him away because of it. *He may not be the best guy to fly for anyway.*

"I was going to take her on up to one of the cities to catch a bus tonight," Tim said.

"Good, good," Brunner said, vigorously nodding. Now the tic was gone. "We—"

"For goodness' sake," a female voice interrupted, and Tim turned to see a short, stout woman standing in the doorway. "Bring them in, Otto!"

They trooped in, and Mrs. Brunner took Lisa by the hand to lead her over to a couch on the far side of the room. "I'm Judith," she said, motioning for Lisa to sit down.

"I'm Lisa."

Mrs. Brunner took a long look at Lisa's engagement ring and said, "It'll be nice to have you here. Otto didn't say we were expecting a couple."

"They're not husband and wife," her husband gruffly stated. "He's taking her up to Dickinson to catch a bus."

"Oh!" Mrs. Brunner's heavy brows knitted together as she gaped at Lisa's big diamond ring.

"Her fiancé and I are close friends," Tim explained. Then he motioned with his hand toward Lisa to say, "And so are we. It was time for me to get on up here to North Dakota, and she had this idea that I could help her figure out some problems if she rode along. So that's what we did." To emphasize the platonic nature of the relationship, he said, "We drove night and day, talking it over."

"That reminds me!" Lisa interjected. "It's late, and I haven't called home! They'll worry unless I call."

Tim solemnly nodded, although he was amused by her apparent ploy to correct any damage her presence might have done to his chances for a job. But he was more doubtful than before that he'd want to fly for this Brunner character anyway. He looked pretty weird with that head-jerking and fits of bug-eyed staring. Besides, Tim wanted to find out how much work the man had done the previous season and what kind of airplanes he was using. He seemed too much the farmer to be much of a crop dusting operator.

Lisa continued, "I'd reverse the charges if you'd kindly let me use your telephone."

"By all means," said Mrs. Brunner. "Come. You can use the one in the kitchen so you don't have us listening to every word." She took Lisa into the kitchen and bustled back into the small living room.

"Have a seat," Otto Brunner said to Tim, waving a hand as overgrown with long blackish hair as Tim's, indicating an easy chair off to one side of the recliner into which he'd begun to settle. He used a lever on the side of his chair to elevate the folding footrest and lay back. He rolled his blocky head of thick, mostly-black hair toward Tim before he spoke again. "Tired," he said. "Been running all around this farm all day.

"I talked to Will Walker," he continued as his wife came back to join them. "He sounds like a real gentleman. Sounds like he runs quite a business. And he says you're as good as gold. Those are his words: 'Good as gold.' " The tic yanked at the side of his face once again, and he explained, "Something's wrong with the nerves on that side."

"I was lucky to fly for a man like that," Tim said, acting as though the tic hadn't bothered him.

"I didn't call anyone else," said Brunner. "That was good enough for me. You'll make some good money here. I pay the usual. I charge a dollar an acre and you get a quarter of it. Same as everybody. You can sit and wait until the weeds sprout, or you can help me farm for a while. The farm work wouldn't pay much, but it would keep you busy."

"What are you flying?" Tim asked.

"Cessna and a Pawnee for backup. Cessna's a couple years old, but it's good as new. I'll guarantee you two thousand minimum. In writing, mind you. But you'll make more than that."

Tim was relieved that he didn't have to ask about the pay. He'd steeled himself to ask, but it would have made him uncomfortable.

"I'm afraid the farm work would have to be minimum wage," Brunner said.

"Tell you the truth," Tim responded, "I'd kind of like to drive around and see the sights. Get up to Canada, over to Montana. See what—"

"Did you reach them, dear?" Mrs. Brunner asked as Lisa came back in.

"Yes, I did. Thank you. I should have called earlier, but we were so worried about being late getting here—"

"I don't want my customers having any reason at all to wonder about my new pilot," Brunner interrupted. "If you don't go on up to Dickinson tonight, it would be best for you to stay at different . . . We've got a motel, and there's a boarding—"

"There's no need for that," interjected Mrs. Brunner. "She'll stay right here tonight, and Tim can make up his mind whichever of those others he prefers. They both need a good night's sleep before they drive another mile."

Her husband gave a start and stared at her for a moment before he relaxed and said, "Of course. That would be fine."

"It'll be fun to have you stay!" Mrs. Brunner said to Lisa, patting the couch beside her. "I'll make something special for breakfast. And you come too, Tim."

* * *

The next morning, Tim awoke in his motel room feeling completely rested and relaxed. It was very nice that he was free to do whatever he wanted until the spraying began.

While he leisurely showered, he wondered how long Lisa would have to wait for a bus heading south. If it was all day, he wouldn't mind at all killing time with her. He was going to miss her. If she left right away, he'd try to find a library that was open on Sunday afternoons. Just in case Johnny didn't call him down to Nicaragua in the fall, he wanted to study up on warm places in the Southern Hemisphere where he could fly when it was winter in the north. He also needed to find out where the best place would be for a stateside summer cotton season.

He slowed when he passed the tiny airport just beyond one corner of the town. He'd glimpsed it in the night, and now he could have a much better look in daylight.

The little town's muny turned out to be nothing more than a single grass strip that butted right up to the main road and had a short row of T-hangars about midway down one side of it. Right next to the furrowed dirt road that led to the hangars was a small warehouse bearing the sign, "Brunner Farm Chemicals." Tim didn't bother to turn off the main road to have a closer look.

Ten minutes later, he arrived at the Brunners' farm, and Lisa came onto the porch to greet him. She was wearing a nice skirt and blouse, and she looked very pretty. "Morning!" she called out.

"Morning. You sure look happy."

"I am. Judith's been making me laugh. She can be very funny. We see eye-to-eye on a lot of things, too."

"That's nice. Pretty dress."

"Thanks. Actually, it bothers me. It doesn't seem quite right for church. A little too casual?"

"I don't think so," he said, opening the door to let her in. "It looks fine."

A few minutes later, Judith Brunner and Lisa had breakfast on the table. They all sat, Brunner mumbled a brief prayer, and they began eating and chatting.

At one point Brunner said, "I'd like you to have a look at the equipment pretty quick, Tim. We'll want to be ready when those mustard weeds pop."

"Sure. I'll get right on it this morning. It wouldn't hurt to start getting used to that Cessna, too."

"You're not going to church with us?" Lisa asked.

"No, I don't think so." To get them thinking about something else, he asked, "Did Lisa mention that she's a pilot?"

"You don't say!" Brunner exclaimed. "A *commercial* pilot?"

"No," Lisa said. "Just a private pilot."

"A very advanced private pilot," said Tim. "She could get a commercial license easy. Just a couple more hours' instruction, and she'll have an instrument rating."

"What's that?"

It surprised Tim that Brunner didn't know. For a moment he wondered whether the man was kidding. But when he saw that he really didn't know, he explained. "It means she can fly when the weather's so bad you can't see the ground or anything else. She can stay right side up and on course in the clouds by watching the instruments."

"Same as a commercial pilot."

Tim had presumed that Brunner flew, but it was clear now that the man knew very little about aviation.

"Actually," Tim said, "she has to be a lot sharper at instrument flying than I had to be for my commercial. It would be easy for her to get a commercial. She has enough flying hours, so I won't be surprised when she does."

"I went up in the Army," said Brunner. "I remember we flew in the clouds. Made me sick. Neighbor friend of mine keeps a plane at the airport, and he tries to get me to go up, but I don't care for it."

"How did you end up with a crop-spraying outfit?" Lisa asked.

Mrs. Brunner answered, saying, "George Harmon was dying. Cancer. He didn't have family who wanted it. His wife made it plain she couldn't wait to get out of here and get back to her big-city life in Fargo. She was just—"

"I bought him out," Otto Brunner hastily interjected. "I was surprised when I started looking into it. There's good money in it. *Good money.*" He stopped speaking for some seconds as his facial tic did its thing, then went on. "Same with the chemicals. I started that up myself. I have some more ideas, too. I'd like to start something up over there in the Red River Valley."

"Oklahoma?" Lisa exclaimed, sparkling blue eyes wide with surprise.

"*Oklahoma?*" Brunner repeated. His shaggy black eyebrows bunched together in a frown. "The Red River Valley is right here in North Dakota."

"Really?" Lisa said, laughing. "We have one, too. Right between Oklahoma and Texas. The one in that old cowboy song."

"No, that song is from here."

"Cowboys here?"

"Of course!"

"I thought Texas because that's where those famous cattle drives began in olden times."

"Well, our Red River Valley is over on the east side of the state. Over by Fargo. It's got lots of irrigated crops, not dryland like around here. We could extend the flying season from a month and a half in the spring here to all summer plus some spring work over there." His eyes bulged at Tim. "I'll need a flier I can trust, somebody who can handle things pretty much on his own. Maybe go partners."

Tim nodded and made a mild, "How interesting," expression.

It sounded as though Brunner was saying that partner might be Tim, but Tim wasn't about to settle down for good anywhere yet.

Lisa spoke up: "I'm going to stay here a couple more days, Tim."

He gave a start and shot her a quizzical look.

"Judith insists I take the car tomorrow and go up to the library in Dickinson. I was telling her how I'd probably just stay in Dickinson or Bismarck a couple days to check on college. The one in Dickinson's closed today, or I'd go there right after church. Maybe I'll go to Bismarck. It's open. But that's a lot farther."

"I can take you," he said. "I'd like to check out a few things, too. How 'bout I pick up some burgers and stuff, and you can meet me at the airport right after church?"

Lisa got up and began to gather dishes and silverware to take to the kitchen. The older woman quickly stood to help, but paused to say, "Won't you come to church with us, Tim?"

"No, thanks. I'd better . . . " Happening to catch sight of Lisa's left hand, his jaw dropped. The engagement ring was gone, leaving a band of paler skin where it had been. "I . . . I'd like to go ahead and start getting used to that Cessna."

"Well, maybe next Sunday," said Mrs. Brunner.

"Here's the keys to the gas pumps," Mr. Brunner.

"Lisa might as well stay with us until she gets her college," Mrs. Brunner said, giving her husband a meaningful look. Then she looked at Lisa and said, "There's no point in leaving before then. You stay as long as you need."

Her husband shrugged and said, "It's fine with me. I just hope you'll be considering the Bisons or the Fighting Sioux. Fargo's bigger if you like city life, but Grand Forks is nice. It's maybe half the size."

Lisa smiled and said, "I'd really prefer to go somewhere that's not so much like home. I'd like to go where it isn't all ranching and farming. Paris would be a dream, but who knows? Maybe New York, Los Angeles."

"Sounds like you won't see your fiancé for some time," said Mr.

Brunner, frowning.

"From what she tells me," his wife commented, "she might just be done with him. We talked."

Tim got up to leave several minutes later, and Lisa followed him onto the porch.

"What's with the ring?" he demanded as soon as he'd shut the door behind them. "You really are giving up on him?"

"Seeing how it feels. I do feel a lot lighter without it."

"You know you could lose him for good delaying like this, don't you?"

"I'll take that chance."

* * *

When they arrived at the Bismarck public library, Lisa headed for the college catalog section, and Tim went to see what he could discover about North Dakota. Standing in a narrow aisle between the high bookshelves, he opened a large coffee-table book and soon discovered that the North Dakota "badlands" were a short drive west. He guessed they might be the long range of buttes he'd noticed when he'd been testing the AGwagon. He'd thought then about driving over there to have a look, but as he read now that it was the Theodore Roosevelt National Park and full of wildlife, he was all the more eager. He liked hiking. He and his old pal Nick had started hiking the Santa Monica Mountains before they'd been in their teens.

He slipped the big book back into its place and went on to gather up a few books on Australia, Africa and South America, and he took them to the table where Lisa had been busy with a heap of college catalogs.

"Hawaya!" she exclaimed.

"Fine, thank ya," he rather sourly replied. He'd heard some fellow surfers doing that routine back home. He was still disgruntled about her going even further to put Lance through what had to be heartbreak.

"Tim, be serious. *That's* where I'll go. They have two universities there. Surely one will accept me."

"You think you can get there in time for spring quarter?"

"Summer session. UH's summer semester begins in May. I'm going to apply right away." She began to jot down the contact information for the University of Hawaii and Chaminade College.

Tim just shook his head. He could see it wouldn't do any good to try reasoning with her at the moment. It would take her a few days to receive the applications and more than a few for the schools to process them and mail them back, so she'd have time to calm down and reconsider.

"Have you seen a pay phone?" Lisa asked. "I've got to tell Judith what I've decided!"

* * *

Brunner popped open the front door before they stepped onto the porch, saying, "Have I got news for you! Both of you! Get on in here!"

On their way into the parlor, Brunner started jabbering, "I wasn't even looking, but I got this call today. Called me on a Sunday because he said it was too good a deal to put off telling me. But it's not just the price. I'd been wondering if we were going to need something like that to keep up, and I do think that's so. Now I think I've got all the more reason!"

Tim wished he'd get to the point. He was getting excited, too, for Brunner had to be talking about buying a bigger airplane.

The portly farmer's head bobbed rapidly up and down, and he went on dancing around the main point, saying, "Yes, sir. Opportunity just keeps on falling in my lap. The timing is perfect. Out of the blue, Bill calls and says he took in a real fine airplane that'll haul twice as much as the Cessna!"

Hey, hey! Tim thought, imagining a Grumman Ag Cat.

"I do trust that man, so if he says it's good, it's good. He's the one who set me up with the Cessna, and that was a good deal," too. Good airplane. No problems. I'm thinking we're going to really take off with some new business this year, and that Snow is exactly what we need!"

"Snow?" Lisa wondered aloud.

"A sprayer!" Brunner explained. The rapid tempo of his speech slowed as he drew out his next words for emphasis: "A *three . . . hundred . . . gallon* sprayer. How's that for a money maker?" He stared bug-eyed at Tim and raised his bushy eyebrows. Then his tic took control, and he averted his face for a few seconds until the twitching stopped.

"That's quite an airplane," Tim said, although he was sorry it wasn't a Cat. During the greenbug run, he'd caught sight of a couple of those new Grumman biplanes honking some very quick turns, and they packed as much as a Snow. Still, he'd heard that Leland Snow's airplanes were very good, too.

Brunner suddenly started laughing. The big belly laughs made his thick midsection quiver. He got to laughing so hard that it made him start snorting, which got Lisa and Mrs. Brunner to giggling, and that cracked Tim up. They all had to wipe away their tears when they got back in control.

"We need to get you over to Fargo to pick it up," Brunner said. "Lisa, can you fly him over tomorrow?"

"Sure. In what?"

Mrs. Brunner, overhearing them from the dining room, protested: "She needs to write to those colleges, Otto!"

"I can write to them tonight and have them in the mail tomorrow. If I could borrow some stationery and stamps, that is."

"That's no problem."

"You'll be using my friend's high-winger," Otto Brunner said. "Remember the one I told you I didn't want to go up in? And that takes us to the other little bit of business I have for *you*." He leaned forward in his easy chair and stared intently at Lisa.

Tim doubted that it could be any more surprising or important than the news about the Snow. After all, in the '60s, a three-hun-dred-gallon sprayer was a big deal.

"Soon as I said I'd buy that Snow, I started thinking how some farmers who stuck with my toughest competitor, Slim, were al-ready getting fed up. And now Slim's drinking is worse than ever. I've known I'll get some of his business this year, but I'm guessing now that I'll get quite a bit more. I got to thinking, with a little extra nudge . . . Then it hit me." He leaned forward in his upright easy chair, continuing to stare at Lisa, bobbing his head.

"We'll put up these posters all over. Ads, too. The Dickinson newspaper . . . maybe even the *North Dakota Farmer*. At the top it'll say, 'Now we're really sitting pretty!' "

He jabbed a thick finger at Lisa and said, "And there'll be this picture of you—"

"*Me?*" Lisa said, and she burst out laughing.

"You! I want you to be my second pilot!"

Brunner's wife gasped and clapped a hand over her mouth.

Tim just shook his head and sighed, thinking, *This is bizarre. He's got to be joking.*

"Whatever Tim can't get to, you'll do. And I'm sure there'll be plenty for both."

Lisa managed to say between peals of laughter, "I . . . don't . . . think so!"

"And why not?"

Tim again shook his head. The man was out of it. For one thing, Lisa had other, better plans. For another, the man obviously knew *nothing* about what it took to become an ag pilot.

"You don't have a good answer for that, do you?" Brunner de-manded. "So! Why not?" But he rushed on before Tim could say a word.

"Now let's be serious. I need another pilot, and Tim says you're a good one. He says you can get the license in no time. With talk going around about the pretty female crop duster to make farm-ers all the more aware of us, we'll pull in all the more business.

It's a cinch. We can range out a little further, too. Goodness knows we'll have people's attention with you in the picture."

No, he's not joking, Tim thought with amusement.

"We're going to be the talk of the county! I believe in it so much, I'll foot the bill for your license. We'll be famous. And you will make some money for summer college."

"All that success because you have a *female* pilot," Lisa said, smirking.

"Sure! Good publicity! *I've* never heard of female crop dusters."

She cocked her head and pensively gazed at the man several seconds before she said, "Okay, I'll do it."

"Lisa!" Tim snickered, thinking that she shouldn't lead Mr. Brunner on that way. It seemed pretty smart-alecky.

Brunner heaved himself off his seat. He rushed over to Lisa and held out his right hand.

As Tim shook his head, thinking she'd taken her little joke too far, Lisa rose, shook hands to act as if she was sealing the deal, and Brunner's facial tic went wild.

"Sounds like fun," she said.

"He's taking you seriously," Tim said. "Knock it off."

"Oh, but I am serious."

"Come on!" Then Tim realized that she might not be kidding after all, and he said, "Get real! You don't go spraying like it's just a little *fling.*"

"Really? Are *you* in it for life now?"

"That's different."

"What? It's man's work?"

"Good grief!"

"Don't worry, Charlie Brown," Brunner said, ducking and grinning as he eyed Tim. His mouth hitched sideways and yanked his head along with it. As soon as it let him go, he said, "You two are going to make a great team!"

"What about *Hawaii*?" Tim moaned.

She turned back to Brunner and said, "Oh-oh. That is a problem. Summer session begins in May."

Brunner sat back down to ponder that. After a few seconds, he said, "We can work around it. What's important is, you spray a good part of the season. I have a man who helps out a little anyway. Semi-retired. Ernie just might have more to do than usual if you leave early."

"You're not that serious anyway, are you, Lisa?" Tim asked.

"Completely serious. I'm going to do it, Tim."

"What about *experience*?" he demanded. He turned to Brunner and said, "She doesn't have any *training*. You can't expect someone to learn by trial and error. Making mistakes is no joke in this business."

"From what Will Walker said, I'm sure you'll make a fine teacher."

"*Me?*"

"Yes, you."

"I don't know about that."

"Well, make up your mind quickly. We don't have much time before the spraying starts. If not you, I'll have to find somebody else to teach her. Ernie'll probably be willing. As much as he wants to stay retired, he does like making a little extra money."

That did it. Tim hated the thought of Lisa playing at ag flying, but if that was what she was determined to do, he didn't want a stranger improvising some slap-dash instruction that could get her in trouble. Besides, he doubted very much that she could work her way through the licensing bureaucracy in time anyway. It wouldn't hurt to play along. "Okay," he said, relaxing, "I'll do it."

"So early tomorrow I want you to bring that Snow back here and get started with whatever you need for her to get that license."

"She's going to need a two-seater with a stick—not a yoke," Tim said. "For the spraying training, at least. Something with a tail wheel, too."

"I don't know stick from yoke, but if the one you're taking to-morrow has that, it's been arranged. If it doesn't, we'll lease whatever we need from someone else. This is going to pay off good! I know it will!"

15

SWEET TALK HAS ITS WAY

They took off very early the following morning. The plan was, they'd fly the Citabria to Fargo for Tim to pick up the Snow, and they'd stop in Dickinson on the way back with both planes so that Lisa could see whether she could line up some quick instruction with an FAA-licensed instructor for her commercial license.

The night before, Lisa had written letters requesting summer-session applications from the two schools in Honolulu, and she had written the University of Oklahoma to send her transcripts. Judith Brunner had eagerly volunteered to mail them special delivery as soon as the post office opened.

"Start teaching her on the way over," Otto Brunner had told Tim. "We don't have much time."

So Tim had Lisa sit in the front seat. He had her skim the bigger wheat and fallow fields that were free of power lines at about ten feet for a while. Then he told her to ease on down to about five feet. A while later, he demonstrated a couple gentle P-shaped turns, and she did a series. However, he didn't want to spend much time deviating from a straight course to Fargo, and he instructed her to fly on, skimming the ground and hopping over obstructions with a conservative safety margin. He did spot one set of power lines with plenty of clearance crossing a field, and, after he'd taken some time to look the wires over carefully, he talked her through a pass beneath them.

And you're supposed to be protecting her! he thought, recalling what he'd said to her dad, knowing that he'd have to teach her to fly beneath much lower wires that left very little room for error.

* * *

On the way from Fargo to Dickinson in the S-2D, which was a bigger, heavier, and more powerful sprayer than the Cessna, he flew a hundred feet higher than the Citabria and a quarter mile off to one side as Lisa went on with her hedge-hopping and made a few more P-shaped turns. Having seen how aggressively she had raced that little farm bike and how she'd flown her dad's six-seater back in Oklahoma, he had severely warned her not to fly under any more wires, shave by any other objects too closely, or tighten up the turns for the time being. "You do anything weird," he warned, "and I'm done with you." He was relieved when they landed at Dickinson, for she had actually complied.

She quickly sweet-talked the owner of the Dickinson flight school into a provisional agreement to speed her through whatever dual instruction she'd need for the commercial.

"But you'll have to rent one of our Cessnas for the instruction," he said. "I've got to make some money on the deal."

"That's fine with me! Let's schedule a couple hours a day. Like today?"

"A half hour. That's the best I can do right now. My instructors are booked, so I'll just have to do it myself."

She plied him with questions about how she might preschedule an FAA check ride, although she knew very well that wasn't the usual way to go about it. She sweetly argued that poor Mr. Brunner would be in quite a jam if she wasn't certified when the season began.

"Well, we'll see how you fly. Maybe I could call some people I know. So let's get started."

"Oh, thank you, Rex!" She gave the dude, a perfect stranger, a quick little hug.

Tim sighed and cynically thought, *I'll bet you make exceptions like that for everybody, don't you, Rexie?* He was sure that if he'd been the one trying to get a prescheduled check ride for a license, he would've had, as Johnny Crash liked to say, " 'bout as much chance as a one-legged man in a butt-kickin' contest."

Later, climbing back up into the cockpit of the big Snow after Lisa had finished her first dual instruction for a commercial license, Tim reflected optimistically, *Well, here's hoping she'll get in too big a hurry and flunk the written.* He knew it wasn't likely, but at least it was a possibility. That would put an end to Brunner's cockamamie plan. If she flunked, the season would be much too far in progress before they'd let her schedule another test, and he wouldn't have to face the possibility of Lisa ending up like Jeremy.

She called her parents and told them she was applying for school in Hawaii and was staying with the Brunners to await an answer. She did not tell them about her flying.

"And call Lance," Tim said.

"I will, I will."

"Or at least tell your folks they can mention to him that you're going to Hawaii. I hate thinking that he might think we . . . you know . . . "

* * *

She still hadn't called Lance several days later when she shouted over her shoulder as they were returning from some simulated spraying in the Citabria, "Tim! We have a visitor!" She halted their low approach for a landing, added power, and climbed the Citabria back up to a couple power lines' height.

Tim was seated behind her, and he pressed his head against the right-side window to try to see what she was talking about as they flew over the grassy runway. However, he couldn't lean far enough to the side to see that far ahead. But when they neared the end of the airport at the highway, Lisa cocked the right wing steeply downward and held the opposite rudder to keep the Citabria flying straight ahead to provide them both a good look out the side window. Plainly revealed for several seconds as they flew by the visitors' tie-down area were Lance Levenger and his AT-6.

He was lounging atop the left wing with his back against the fuselage and his crossed legs stretched out, looking very relaxed at first. But when Lance could see their faces as they flew by, he seemed to angrily swing his legs over the wing's leading edge to slip on down to the ground.

Don't blame him one bit, either, Tim guiltily thought, imagining how he would feel if their roles were reversed. Then he glimpsed CR, who was squatting on the ground a few feet from where Lance now stood. The little guy watched them fly by without any expression at all and with no other movement than the swiveling of his greasy, long-haired head.

"How did he find us?" Lisa cried out over her shoulder, flying straight on to the south.

"Probably asked Mr. Will," Tim replied into his mike. He guessed that the man who ran Brunner's chemical warehouse and pumped gas for flying visitors had told Lance they were out flying and would be back for lunch.

"I guess I have to face him!" Nevertheless, she delayed turning back to the airport for several more minutes.

She also chose to land northward over the electric lines, instead of landing toward the loading area, which she'd been practicing for quick-loading efficiency whether it was into the wind or not. She used up half the runway to land, which was not her usual style, either, and she taxied back toward Lance very slowly.

This could get nasty, Tim thought. He hadn't forgotten Lance's threatening looks when he'd started to misunderstand Tim's relationship with Lisa back in Oklahoma. Their being together now so far from home had to seem many times more incriminating.

I should've known, he painfully reflected. *How did I ever let her talk me into this?*

Lisa stopped the little tandem two-seater directly in front of its T-hangar, obviously to delay the confrontation a bit longer. Normally she would have pulled up to the gas pumps to refuel first. She shut down the engine and sat there without making another move or comment.

It was Tim who opened the plane's side panels, lowering the long, horizontally folding bottom door panel to let it hang by its hinges against the outer side of the fuselage, and swinging the long Plexiglas side window upward to click onto the catch beneath the wing.

Lance rapidly strode up to the point midway along the right wing where the forked struts angled up from the bottom of the fuselage to brace the wing. He ducked and followed the struts in toward the cockpit to stand beside Lisa. "Good morning, Lisa," was all he said at first. He gently smiled and put his hand on her shoulder.

She flinched and tensely replied, "Hello, Lance."

Tim was thankful that she was wearing the thin gloves she'd bought with the motorcycle helmet he'd insisted on that day in Fargo. The situation would be more explosive than it already was if Lance saw that she'd removed her engagement ring.

Now Lance turned toward Tim, and his expression hardened. He leaned into the back of the cockpit to thrust his fine face very close to Tim's. He scathingly muttered under his breath, "You said you don't mess with other people's women!"

"I don't," Tim whispered, struggling without complete success to keep the sound of his own voice soft and free of anger. One of the worst insults was someone questioning his sense of honor. Never—not for a moment once he'd known that Lisa was engaged—had he ever imagined a romantic relationship with her.

He lowered his eyes to contemplate Lance's balled fists. He silently vowed that he would not respond in kind if Lance got violent. He'd just block the blows as best he could. But Lance chose to shift his attention right back to Lisa.

Tim watched him gently touch her shoulder once more. This time she did not flinch. She kept perfectly still.

"We need to talk," Lance murmured, and she nodded. She reached up to undo her helmet's chin strap.

Tim unbuckled his seat belt, raised his knees, and swung his long legs out of the cramped cockpit. Lance's accusation still stung, but he was determined to keep his mouth shut about it and just get away. He used the necessity of bending over as he got out from under the wing to avoid making eye contact with Lance, and he thought, *She'll set him straight soon enough.*

* * *

"I heard what you said to him," Lisa said to Lance when Tim left. "Tim O'Reilly is a man of his word."

"Is he really?" Lance scoffed.

"This was all my idea."

"Are you serious about him, or are you just having a little fun before we settle down?"

She raised her right hand as if she were going to backhand him. But she slowly let it down and said, "That's not amusing, mister. But it does confirm what I've been thinking."

"Oh, I'm sorry, honey. I put that badly. What I was trying to say is, I want you to come home now, and I really *would* forgive—"

"Nothing to forgive, Lance. Have you forgotten what I stand for? And, for your information, I won't be home for some time. Listen to me. Tim was about to leave, and that reminded me how badly *I* needed to get away. I need some time away from you to think. Tim's a good friend, and I wanted . . . Well, the truth is, I've started having some serious doubts about us, Lance."

"Oh, Lisa, honey! Let's talk about it! I just don't know how I could live without you."

"You'll know how it is for sure if you don't treat me with more respect. I will not tolerate your cheap insinuations, Lance Levenger. The fact is, when I caught up with Tim, he tried to make me go home."

"And you're *still* with him," he whined.

"And I'm staying at his boss's home. His wife urged me to stay with them. She prays with me. She's a good friend, and I'm learning to value her input."

"Another new friend . . . another stranger . . . and you're listening to them, instead of your old friends."

"I did think about going to see my very best friend in Colorado— You might remember Julie—but she's dealing with her own problems right now. But here's the essential point: I'm just not sure that we should be married."

He barely reacted. Without a word of protest, he slightly cocked his head and narrowed his stony, expressionless eyes as he peered at her for a few seconds. Then he cautiously inquired, "Is it something I've done?"

"No, not any one big thing. I do question some things, but it's not quite that, either. I think it's *spiritual*, Lance. I fear the Holy Spirit's saying . . . well . . . that we may not be suited for each other."

"Well, thank God you can't be sure about *that*." He formed a sweet, hurt smile and crooned, "*Everybody* says we're made for each other. We're just about as well matched as a couple could be. Think of all the things we have in common. Far more than most. And there's family tradition, too. Our families are very much alike, and who's better equipped to carry on their traditions than the two of us together? We're going to make a fantastic team!"

"Well, there's at least one essential ingredient that does seem to be missing, Lance."

"Missing? What in the world would that be?"

"Passion. There's an absence of passion."

"But we agreed to keep it under control. We wanted to save—"

"I don't mean that way. I mean . . . Oh, I don't know. I'm not at my best right now."

He stroked her thick golden hair, saying, "I think of you and long to be with you constantly. Passionately. Whether it's obvious or not."

And so they continued as she remained buckled into the front seat of the Citabria while he stood beside the parted door and window panels. If the thought did return to Lisa about Lance being much more interested in her family's farm than he was in her, she didn't say so.

* * *

Once he'd gotten clear of the airplane, Tim had plodded dispiritedly over to CR, who remained squatting on the grass just ahead of the T-6's left wing, coolly watching him approach.

"Mr. Clyde Robert!" Tim said, trying to sound cheerful.

"Yep," CR listlessly replied. He didn't bother to stand, and he averted his gaze.

The rude little dude never had been friendly, and Tim had decided back in Oklahoma to not take it personally. He'd thought back then, *It's just his way. He probably doesn't know any better.* So he bent down and held out his hand anyway.

CR reached out to grasp it, but he didn't stand up, and his handshake was completely passive. Tim gave the limp, scaly-palmed thing a couple yanks for form and promptly let it go, thinking, *Might as well shake a dead snake.*

"What's new?" he pressed on.

"Nothin'."

"You can wait in the trailer with me if you want. It's a little warmer in there."

"I'm fine ri'chere."

"Well, that's where I'm going. There's a toilet in there if you need it."

CR looked away without saying anything, and Tim left. He grabbed the paperback book that Lisa had made such a fuss over, *The Politics of Experience*, which he'd left unread in the Healey's glove compartment. She'd found a used copy in a hole-in-the-wall bookstore in Dickinson. Now he wished he'd put something else in the car to read. The several times he'd waited for her during her lessons for the commercial in Dickinson, he'd been satisfied to read *Trade-A-Plane* and the other aviation magazines the flight service had in plentiful supply, or he'd go over to the public library and mainly research cotton-farming areas where he might fly in the summer. He was surprised to discover that cotton farming occupied a broad, southern swath of America from California all the way to Georgia.

Lisa had urgently said about the little *Politics of Experience* book, "At least read the first part. That's the essential part. Consider that each person has only his own experience to judge what other people say about their experience. Laing's no Christian, but my point is, your expectations about what is real could have been drummed into you by those who simply lack the spiritual experience."

He climbed into the trailer with the book and went to sit at the rickety little table in the forward section. There was a larger window there that gave him a view of the sod runway and the Citabria. He could see the lower part of Lance's trousers and his boots, although the rest of him was concealed by the high wing. He'd feared that Lance's meeting with Lisa wouldn't last more than a couple minutes, and he was encouraged by their still beng together.

He sighed and opened the book. He did want to read it to please her, since she thought it was so very important. A half year earlier, he probably would have read it eagerly. He'd been far more interested in epistemology, the analysis of what and how people can know, than he'd been interested in his business classes. He'd taken those classes in order to play the role he so admired when he thought of his father's life. It had gone well his first year in college, but he'd taken the philosophy courses and the class in world religions in response to a despairing need to try to understand life itself. He might have even changed his major to philosophy if he hadn't tried taking a course in symbolic logic. There hadn't been a word of normal language anywhere in the textbook, and he'd dropped the course after attending just one class. However, despite his former interest in such stuff, he was having trouble now rereading just the first paragraph. His vision seemed to ricochet right off the page.

Holding the book open in his lap, he leaned back and started reflecting, as he had repeatedly every day, that it wasn't too late for Lisa to change her mind. How he hoped that Lance would talk her into returning home. He had to agree with everyone else: The two just seemed made for each other, and he liked them both so much.

After a while, movement outside snapped him out of his daydreaming. He hurried outside and tossed the unread Laing book onto the Healey's passenger seat.

"Well!" he said brightly, smiling, determined to act as if Lance had never uttered a harsh word. "Here we are! Together again!" The simple fact that Lance and Lisa had come over together from the Citabria had given him some hope that Lisa had finally conquered her fears. However, that hope began to dissolve when a reciprocal smile failed to appear on her somber face.

"We're going to lunch," Lance said flatly, without any expression to suggest what had transpired between them.

"Yeah, let's do that," Tim said as CR slouched toward them. Tim again consciously formed what he hoped was a winning smile. At the same time, he was trying to glean some hint of what Lisa was thinking.

"We're going to have lunch in a park," Lance said. "Just the two of us."

"Good idea. Beautiful day." In truth, of course, Tim was disappointed. Still, he was glad that the two were going to spend more time together. "Take the Healey. CR and I will be at the café when you're done." He thrust his keys at Lance. "You'll like driving the Healey a lot more than that old truck Mr. Brunner loaned Lisa."

Lance didn't reach for the keys immediately.

"Go on. Take 'em. CR and I can walk. The café's right down the road."

Lance slowly reached out and took the keys, saying, "That car's yours? Nice." He gently took Lisa by the elbow and led her to the passenger door.

Tim watched them get in, Lisa picking up the Laing book and giving him a long look before they drove off. Then he turned to CR and said, "I need to gas that airplane and put it away. Then I'll treat you to lunch."

"I got money. Where's it at?"

"Just down the road that way."

CR set off on his own, leaving Tim to shove the Citabria into its T-hangar alone.

* * *

"Nice little car," Lance said, going through the gears as he drove away from the airport. "That reminds me: What are we going to get *you*? No more Falcons!" He laughed to make sure she understood that he was kidding her.

She finally peeled off the thin leather gloves, and raised the back of her left hand up to where he could see it and keep his eye on the road at the same time.

"Lisa! What does that mean?"

"I took it off to see how it felt. The freedom I feel really makes me wonder whether I'm ready for marriage yet."

"Oh, honey," he moaned. "It would be so hard to wait."

"Well, I'm not going to marry you this summer. I've made up my mind, so let's not go on and on about it."

Lance didn't respond immediately. *She means it*, he thought. *You're going to have to be very careful. Could she be falling for that hired sprayer?* It seemed so unlikely, yet *something* had come between them.

"I respect your decision," he calmly said. She had lowered her hand that had borne the engagement ring to let it rest on her thigh, and he reached out to lightly caress it. "I don't understand it, but I do respect it. My only hope now is that we'll remain engaged. Do you have the ring with you?"

"No. It's at the Brunners'."

He raised her hand to his lips and kissed it. "I love you so much. I . . . I . . . " He thought, *Come on! What?* "Well, I just don't know how I could stand waiting until after summer. But . . . if it's necessary, then wait I will. I'd wait years if I had to!"

"You need to start slowing for that turn. And thank you for saying that. Lance, I'm going to Hawaii for the summer. I may go home after that."

"*Hawaii?*" He groaned. "But not the whole summer, right?"

"All summer. University of Hawaii. At least I hope so. I haven't been accepted yet."

"But you'll come home before you go, won't you?"

"No, I won't."

"Lisa! I'll be tempted to go running after you! But Father expects me to start helping manage the farm right after graduation. It's our busy time. I won't see you for months!"

"You can chalk it up to something I really want to do before I settle down. It should make you happy."

After they got their burgers and Cokes, they went on to the park on the north side of town. As soon as they'd set their lunches on a picnic table, Lance slipped an arm around her. While they were still standing, he drew her up against him and kissed her—lightly at first, then with increasing passion.

Panting heavily after a minute, she shoved him away and said, "Oh, Lance. Let's not do that."

"It's the same with me!" he crooned. "I can tell by your voice. Let's just get married now and stop fighting it."

He leaned toward her again, but she stepped away, picked up her burger, and unwrapped it. She took a bite and chewed slowly, eyeing him.

"Fly back to Oklahoma with me. CR can get a bus. We'll get married and stay in my apartment until I'm out of school. Then—"

"No, Lance."

"You do love me, Lisa. I know you do. Let's get married and just enjoy life. We'll go to Hawaii together."

"I'm going to Hawaii alone. We'll see then just how much we love each other. But we can talk. We'll set up a schedule so I'll be in the dorm or wherever at a set time. But up here, I'd better call you when I can. I'd rather you didn't call the Brunners."

"Will you at least put the ring back on?"

"Yes. It's not right not to wear it and still be engaged. I'll put it back on as soon as I get to the Brunners'."

"Thank you, sweetheart! I love you so much!"

She sat on a bench, and he began to sit down next to her, but she said, "No, you sit on that side."

* * *

CR was noisily slurping coffee when Tim entered the café. He sat down opposite him and said, "Hey," but CR didn't say a word or even glance his way. He just took another noisy slurp, then dumped some more cream into the mug half-filled with liquid that already looked much too pale.

The waitress bustled over with a coffeepot and refilled CR's mug, then took Tim's order of a bacon burger and a vanilla milk shake.

"How was the flight up?" Tim asked, not caring at this point whether he was bugging CR or not.

The young farmhand shrugged.

Neither said anything further, except when the waitress came back with CR's pot roast and potatoes and Tim commented, "That looks good." He didn't bother trying to make more conversation.

After Tim's food came and they'd eaten, the gross sucking sounds CR kept making as he drank his coffee-flavored cream started twanging Tim's nerves so badly that he could barely stay seated. He was about to eject and leave it to CR to relay word to Lance and Lisa that he'd gone back to the airport. Instead, he decided to see whether he had the strength of mind to mentally blank out CR's repulsive proximity.

He asked Molly, the waitress, whether anyone might have left a newspaper, and she got one out from under the counter. There wasn't much of interest to focus on until he got to the big ad on one page with Brunner's corny "Now We're Sitting Pretty" banner. A nice photo of Lisa in the AGwagon was just beneath that, along with a blurb saying that she was the newest pilot. Beneath that was a photo of Tim in the Snow and a bit about him being an "ace" spray pilot and the new Snow S-2D guaranteeing faster service than ever. It got Tim to ruminating so deeply about Lisa that he forgot all about the offensive creature right across the table.

A couple distinctive toots of the Healey's horn released him from his troubled thoughts, and he peered out the window to see his car nose up to the café. They had put the top down, and he wished he had a camera to record the sight of those two fine-looking people in that long, low roadster.

"Well," Lance said evenly, seating Lisa at a table and stonily gazing at Tim, "I'm sure you're wondering." He paused to beckon to Molly, as though she didn't know enough to wait on him. He asked for a cup of coffee and continued. "We won't be married this summer, but she hasn't given up on me completely." He beamed a beautiful smile. "At least we're still engaged.

"Also on the bad-news side of the ledger, she won't be coming home right away. She's off to Hawaii. Anything else, honey?"

She gave him a very odd, prolonged look that Tim couldn't decipher, then slowly shook her head.

She didn't tell him about her spraying, Tim realized. *He would have said something.*

"Lucky thing I've got CR with me to do some of the flying home," Lance said. "I'll be half asleep. This coffee won't help. It's horrible." He made a disgusted face, set the mug Molly had brought on the table, and shoved it away from him. "We left before dawn. I'm going to try to get back to school tonight after I drop him off at home."

"Why don't you just stay overnight?" Tim asked. "I bet there's a vacancy or two where I'm staying."

"I appreciate that, buddy, but I'd hate to flunk a course this late in the game." He slid Tim's keys across the table, saying, "Nice little car."

"No," Tim said, "you and CR go ahead and take it to the airport. That'll save you a few minutes."

"Thanks. What shall I do with the keys?"

"Just put them under the seat."

Lance stood and slid back Lisa's chair as she got up. She gave him a quick hug and a kiss on the cheek.

"The two of us can ride out to the airport," Lance said. "CR can walk while I warm that plane up."

"No, go on," she said. "Take CR with you. I'll call tomorrow evening."

He responded to that by giving her a more prolonged hug and a quick kiss on the lips. He took Tim's hand and warmly smiled. "Thanks for being such a friend, Tim. Lisa told me all about it. You be sure to stay in touch, too.

"Bye," he said to Lisa, dropping Tim's hand. "I love you, honey."

Her eyes grew large, and her lips became so tightly compressed that they'd turned white. She looked as though she was about to cry.

Lance went on toward the door with CR trailing along behind. He tossed some bills beside the cash register as he went by and looked back at Tim and Lisa when he stopped to open the door. He flashed a huge smile, waved, and went out.

* * *

As he waited for CR to get into the Healey, Lance snapped, "Hurry up, will you?" Before CR could draw his lame right leg all the way in, Lance popped the clutch and reversed onto the road.

Meanwhile, Tim and Lisa watched them depart from the café window, and she was beginning to evince much more plainly the heavy stress that Lance's visit had imposed on her. Tim helplessly watched while the first plump tear rolled out of the corner of her eye.

Several minutes later, Lance was strapping himself into his seat in the T-6 when CR, instead of climbing into the rear cockpit, came forward on the wing walk to stand beside him. He said, "Gimme some money fer a room and somethin' to git around in. I'll stay and take keer of it."

Lance swung his head to give him a brief, quizzical look, but turned his attention back to firing up his airplane. He worked the primer, engaged the starter, and the engine chugged to life. Once he'd set the throttle to idle, he gave CR a long, lingering look.

"Keep a eye on 'em," CR explained. "Maybe help that big monkey have a accident or sump'n."

"I doubt you'd see anything. I think it's going to work out, CR. Still . . . "

Why not make sure? he thought.

"Climb in," he said. "I'll drop you off at the next town. I can give you some cash to get by and send more care of general delivery.

And forget about causing that boy any harm. You'd probably wind up in prison, and what would I do without you?"

"I'm smarter than *that*."

"Besides, they might think *I* had something to do with it."

16

POSTER GIRL MAKES GOOD

Much to Tim's disappointment, Lisa did it all without a hitch: She passed the government's written exam, she passed the prescheduled government flight test, and she ended by spraying a few full loads of water one afternoon to Tim's grudging satisfaction. That is, she sprayed the water to his satisfaction as far as giving just the right amount of lead and lag time in turning on and shutting off the spray, she spaced her passes well, and she handled the twelve-hundred-pound load of water without any trouble.

"But knock off them doggone cowboy turns!" he angrily barked when Lisa landed after her last practice spray run, which had ended much too exuberantly. That was exactly what Catfish had yelled at him early in Tim's training. Lisa's first turns had been reasonably cautious, but she'd gotten friskier as the plane's load had lightened.

"*Sorree*." However, she immediately looked ashamed of her smart-mouthed retort and said, "Sorry, Tim. I mean, I really am sorry, sweetie. I'm glad you care."

"Yeah, I care. So get back up there a couple feet and take it easy on those turns!"

Care too damn much, he grimly thought, considering the risk of losing her to a spraying accident. He gave a great sigh and got a little relief by thinking, *Well, she'll be out of here in a few weeks.*

So, the morning after Tim judged that Lisa was ready, she took off with her first real payload, hauling a conservative 105 gallons of watered-down 2,4-D, the common broadleaf-weed killer, to spray a 105-acre field. If she'd had more experience, she would have taken out a full load to spray that field and flown right on to spray the remainder on another field.

Tim took off as soon as he could several minutes later with a full load in the Snow. First he'd do an eighty-acre field not far from where Lisa would be working so that he'd be able to keep an eye on her. Then he'd move on to two more fields with the rest of the load.

As he flew by, she did seem to be taking it easy, but it was hard to tell for sure, since even 105 gallons, which weighs 840 pounds, was heavy enough to keep a beginner from cranking any noticeably tight turns. An ag pilot could be pushing a plane with a fairly heavy load close to the limit without its looking all that edgy. But the heavier the load, the higher the stall speed. Tim was determined to make his own turns very conservatively so that Lisa would see it if she happened to look his way.

He cast a glance back over his shoulder at the Cessna, then focused on his field, a half-mile-long rectangle of gently rolling terrain. He started on the downwind side so that the slight breeze would move any remaining spray mist out of his path by the time he came back for each subsequent pass. The slightly negative g's going over each hillock at a bit over 120 miles an hour reminded him of the roller coaster down at the Pike on the Santa Monica waterfront, and he realized that he was grinning again.

Are you ever going to grow up? he kidded himself. He silently replied, *No, not yet. Give it a couple years. That's the whole point. Just relax and enjoy life.*

He pulled up into a slow, gentle turn at the end of that first pass, using the time to carefully check on Lisa. She still didn't seem to be pushing the AGwagon too hard. If she did start getting wild, he'd be there in a flash and let her know she couldn't get away with it. She'd definitely get the message if he suddenly popped right in beside her.

As he lost sight of Lisa in finishing his turn, he relished the ease with which the Snow was packing its big payload. He hadn't been spraying many days with it before Lisa was ready, and he hadn't pushed it that close to the ragged edge yet, but it was doing very well, considering the weight it was packing. Just as Brunner had said, it was quite a money-maker.

He was earning so much more than he'd expected that he couldn't be as nonchalant about the money as he had been at first. It looked like he'd earn plenty by the time he went on down the road again in about five weeks, and he was having visions of leading a much different sort of life in college than before. There'd be no need for some miserable, boring part-time job or living in a shoddy little room like the one over the pizza shop. He might even be able to improve on the Healey if he could find the right summer seat and make a bunch more.

That made him wonder how Brunner's first summer season in the Red River Valley would turn out. The eager entrepreneur had mentioned a couple times that he'd already found a good non-pilot with lots of farming contacts over there who was already working hard to drum up business. Brunner had said, "I want you over there, Tim."

When Tim had maintained that he was going to fly a cotton season in the South, Brunner warned, "If I have to hire someone else to fly both seasons, I'll have to give him the best airplane and the bulk of the work here next spring."

Truth is, Tim thought, *I wouldn't mind having a good excuse to go somewhere else anyway.* He liked Brunner well enough, and he suspected that he could profit from the man's drive, but he also liked being on the move. If he was lucky, he'd have a bang-up summer season, and he'd probably get a call from Johnny Crash to join him down in Nicaragua soon afterward.

Should Nicaragua not pan out, it would be a great excuse to try flying farther from home than that, perhaps Australia or even Africa.

Preferably South Africa. He'd probably never forget some of the surfing scenes shot there in his all-time-favorite movie, *The Endless Summer.*

He got so involved in daydreaming about surfing that he forgot to check on Lisa in the next turn, but he remembered in the turn after that and each one thereafter, and he was glad to see that she was keeping her flying reasonably conservative even when her plane was nearly empty.

* * *

CR called Lance on the phone and said, "She's done went to work as a sprayer pilot."

Lance laughed and said, "I don't think so!"

"Seen it with my own two eyes."

"Just fiddling around, I'm sure. Heck, *I* want to try flying one of those."

"Sprayin' wheat," CR insisted. "Stuff comin' out the back."

"Unbelievable!" Actually, however, Lance was already beginning to accept the possibility. He laughed harder, thinking, *That's Lisa for you! So that's what she's up to! It isn't that hired pilot, and it isn't me! She just wants to do something exciting before she settles down!* For a moment he was tempted to call her and tell her he was onto her secret, but he wouldn't be able to explain how he'd heard about it.

"I hope you're staying out of sight," he said to CR.

"It's easy with them binoculars you had me buy."

"Good."

"I got me some fine lookout spots," CR said. "Got me a hill by the airport and a tree to git behind."

"Great. But you might as well come on back. We need you down here."

"I done seed 'em huggin' after she lit one time."

"Hugging's no problem." Lance could easily imagine Lisa getting excited about flying and giving Tim a hug. And if she wanted to have a good time with some dunce pilot before she settled down, he didn't really have any objection. The only thing that mattered was their eventual marriage.

"Made me want to git that sunvabitch. I'd like to pour a little water in that gas tank of his."

"Easy does it, Clyde Robert. You come on back now. Sell that little motorcycle you bought, and catch a plane down here. We need you quick. Pop's complaining."

* * *

One night before Tim and Lisa had almost a full morning of spraying to do, they insisted that the Brunners let them treat them to lunch at a nicer restaurant in Dickinson. When the older couple entered the restaurant and approached the two young people, Brunner happily announced, "Lots *more* spraying for you two tomorrow. And here's some mail for you, Lisa." There was a twinkle in the man's warm brown eyes as he handed her a large white packet.

"University of Hawaii!" She ripped it open and rapidly scanned the cover letter. "I'm in!"

They sat and started looking through the menus, with Lisa saying from minute to minute, "Hawaii! I really am going to Hawaii!"

* * *

The weather kept getting warmer, and mustard weeds were soon sprouting everywhere. Now Tim and Lisa were hard at it, working a fast-paced, daylight-to-dark routine every day except Sundays.

"It's working!" Brunner kept saying as he lined them out in the dark each morning. He was referring to his "sitting pretty" scheme. "We're pulling in all kinds of new business! I'll probably have to get Ernie to help out even before Lisa goes."

That day came less than a week later, when there was more work than Tim and Lisa could hope to handle in a timely manner, and Ernie flew over from a nearby town in his little Aeronca 7AC to help out by using Brunner's Pawnee. He arrived before daylight. Although the turf runway wasn't lit, the wizened old pro was able to locate it in the dark and, using his landing light, find his way down while Brunner was still orally giving directions to Tim and Lisa and rapidly making crude sketches of maps to the fields.

"This is getting to be more than I can handle," Brunner muttered several days after that. "It's cutting into my farming. I've got to hire someone to do this for me."

A retired man whose son had taken over running their small farm took the job, and he was able to give the pilots directions every bit as well as Brunner.

The only leisure time Tim and Lisa had together so long as the weather held, which it did much more often than during the previous Oklahoma winter, was during some of the hurried meals they ate together in the little café almost every night. Tim enjoyed being with her so much that he even started going to church with her, although he still avoided getting into any deep discussions about religion. But she was more interested in talking about the flying now anyway.

Ernie didn't join them for those meals at the café, since he flew home every night. His sixty-mile-an-hour Aeronca got him home in a little over three-quarters of an hour.

"I love it!" she kept saying. "I used to wonder whether you all ever got to the point where it was boring, but I don't think I'd ever get tired of it. It really keeps your attention."

Sometimes one or the other had something unusual to report, such as what happened one day after Lisa raised a little dust to check the wind direction before she sprayed next to a farmhouse. Some outfits had begun installing smokers on their sprayers, but neither Tim nor, apparently, Brunner had heard about it. A pilot using a smoker could flip a switch to activate an automobile fuel pump to inject some form oil, which was normally used to allow concrete to release the forms into which it had been poured. The form oil would squirt into the exhaust stack, and out would billow a thick cloud of gray smoke. The pilot would then pull up into a turn and check which way the wind would blow the smoke. In some situations where drifting chemical was critical and an operation hadn't installed smokers, someone on the ground might light an old tire on fire, which would send up highly visible black smoke. Otherwise, pilots did the best they could by observing the motion of leaves or grain or the weather-vaning of the airplane into the wind, but none of that had been an option for Lisa that day.

"The wind was so light," she said, "I couldn't figure it. So I thought I'd just bounce my tires off this dirt road not far from the house. There were power-lines along the road by the house, but none farther south of it. So I did it, and I turned back to check the dust in time to see this huge buck bound out from a culvert under the road. Of all the places I could have chosen, I bounced the wheels on the road right above where this big old boy was taking his afternoon nap! Can you imagine how surprised he was?"

Tim soon had a wildlife tale about a golden eagle. "It was perched on this old wooden fence post," he said. "I kept working closer and closer, pass by pass, and it just kept watching me. Man, those things are huge. I'd never seen one up close before. It got where I was coming almost straight at it, and I thought it would fly. But no, it just ruffled its feathers and glared at me. It looked like it was all set to fight if I got any closer!"

They also talked about Hawaii, of course, and Lisa had a lot of questions about surfing. She was very eager to try it, which didn't surprise Tim at all.

She bugged him only once during that time about renewing

his boyhood faith. "You seem to have had it," she said after she'd pried a few comments about his parents' church out of him. "But like me for so long, whatever the reason, you didn't experience rebirth. I do wish you'd open your mind to the possibility. It isn't something you can think your way to. You need to ask the Lord to show you the reality. You have to experience the experience."

"You know what?" he desperately said, intent on trying to change the subject. "Maybe I could visit you in Hawaii."

"Really?"

"Well . . . " He didn't have any idea where that idea had come from, but he recovered from his surprise and started daydreaming aloud, enjoying the thought of taking a surfing break before summer. "If I found a summer cotton seat right away, I might not have to be sitting there waiting before the season actually started. Nothing much happens in cotton country before July, I hear, and I'm sure I'll be done here by the end of May. I could get a place to stay and hang around a few days to show them I'm for real, then take off for a couple weeks."

The more he considered it, the more feasible it seemed. So they had talked about that quite a bit, too. Also, of course, they had talked about her engagement to Lance.

"I just don't know," she'd say occasionally. "Sometimes I'm so uneasy, especially when I pray. But other times, especially right after I've talked with him on the phone . . . "

* * *

It was Sunday morning on a warm spring day, and Lance taxied the AT-6 from its usual parking place down the farm's private gravel road to the shop, where he called CR away from his work servicing farm equipment to help service and clean the airplane. First they washed the fuselage, using soap, rags, and a power washer.

"I'm going to Hawaii, CR," Lance said as they swirled their

soapy rags over the aluminum skin. "I've got to cut in on that doggone sprayer boy. *He's* talking about going over in June to see Lisa."

"Yep. I told yuh what it looked like. If he ain't yet, he's gonna—"

"Don't say it!" Then, more gently, Lance said, "Just so long as she ends up marrying me. That's what really counts."

"I hate that big, ugly sunvabitch."

"I'm not very fond of him myself. But a man needs to keep cool to get ahead in life, CR. You need to learn to be more practical. You keep an eye on me, and I'll show you how it pays."

Once they'd rinsed all the soap off, they removed the cowling, and CR climbed up a ladder to start cleaning the upper parts of the motor. Lance handed him a can of solvent and a stiff-bristled brush that looked like an over-sized artist's brush to remove any goop that might have collected in the narrow spaces between the exposed cylinders' cooling fins.

"Keep an eye out for cracks in those cylinders," Lance said while he busied himself on the lower cylinders with a second can of solvent and a brush. "I told you about that Johnny Crash blowing the top off a cylinder, didn't I?"

"Nope."

"I didn't? They said if it was this one down here, that would have been big trouble. Look."

CR dutifully bent over and looked as Lance pointed.

"They call this the master-rod cylinder. They said if this one goes, the motor stops. If it's any other, it keeps going. Most of the time anyway."

"Can I look at them manuals for this airplane again?"

"Yes, you can. But don't start thinking I'm going to let you take *this* motor apart."

* * *

Day after day, the flying went smoothly for the three Brunner pilots. Ernie's flying was unspectacular but efficient, Lisa humored Tim by immediately returning to a more conservative pace whenever he saw her getting too frisky, and Tim flew very conservatively whenever there was a chance that Lisa might see him.

They had a few days off because of weather, and Tim and Lisa zoomed around in the Healey, sightseeing. They got over to the Theodore Roosevelt National Park and hiked one sunny but windy day, and they even went on up into Canada another time. They spent most of one day in the Dickinson library, leafing through picture books, quietly talking about places they wanted to see and about Lisa's upcoming trip to Hawaii, and reading or researching one thing or another.

Then, so very soon, Lisa was leaving. Mrs. Brunner was going to drive her to Bismarck to catch the first of her connecting flights, and Tim saw the Brunners' car parked in front of the trailer when he landed for a load. He stopped in front of the trailer and climbed out to say good-bye.

"I'll be back in a few minutes," Mrs. Brunner said when he walked over to them. "I need to check something at the warehouse." She drove away, leaving Tim and Lisa alone.

"Matchmaker," Lisa explained, grinning. "She likes you. She says you're the one I should marry."

They both laughed about it and hugged, but there were tears on Lisa's freckled cheeks when they let each other go. "Oh, my," she said. "I'm going to miss you so. I do hope you come see me."

"I'm pretty sure I will. I'll work hard to get set up somewhere for summer and then get on over and take you surfing."

They stood there talking all about the fun they'd have when he got over there until Mrs. Brunner returned. They hugged again, and then she was gone.

* * *

Several nights later, after Tim had read himself to sleep, the phone rang.

"Hi, sweetie."

"Lisa!" He took her use of the word "sweetie" to be nothing more than the sibling sort of love he had for her. It's a Southern thing. Her mom had used it freely with Lisa, Lance and her husband, so Tim simply appreciated it as an expression of the platonic love they had for each other.

"I'm here, Tim! It's wonderful!"

"I've been wondering."

"Oh, Tim, the beauty! And the fragrance!"

"You haven't been sneaking in any surfing without me, have you?"

"Tim?" she plaintively said, and she paused. "Tim, Lance is coming over. I shouldn't have told him that's what you're hoping to do. I'm sure that's why he's coming. Before I told him you might come, he only wanted to help his daddy manage that farm this summer."

"Well, I wouldn't blame him. I'd do the same if I was in his shoes. About Hawaii, I mean."

* * *

Soon the day came when he and Ernie did not need to fly until dark, and Tim had a chance to start calling around to see whether he could find a cotton seat in south Texas. It would be nice to be able to visit his maternal aunts, an uncle, and a few cousins. He thought the smartest thing to do would be to see whether Dave or Johnny Crash had any leads. He had permanent contact numbers at Johnny Crash's mother's home and Dave's sister's place, although neither vagabond actually lived at those locations. He tried Dave's sister's number first and was surprised to hear Dave himself answer.

"Hello?" His voice was so faint that Tim thought it must be a bad connection.

"Hello, Dave?"

"This is Dave."

"Hey, Dave! I can barely hear you. This is Tim. How are you?" He was anticipating a spry, humorous reply.

"Not so good," Dave uncharacteristically moaned. "Who is this?" His speech sounded a little slurred.

It was strange he didn't recognize Tim's voice. It hadn't been *that* long. "Tim! Tim O'Reilly!"

"Well." There was quite a long pause. "How are you doing?" His voice sounded so brittle and dispirited, and his words definitely were slurring.

It made Tim wonder whether Dave had been drinking. "I are fine," he said, but he wasn't really in much of a mood to clown around with such Southernisms now with Dave sounding so different. "I'm about done up here in North Dakota. Decided to look for a seat in south Texas so I can see my aunt and cousins. Thought you might know some good operators down there. If I do find something, I might be able to see you pretty soon."

"You might *not* want to see. I ain't a very purty sight right now. I done had me a stroke."

"Good grief!"

"You got it, bub. Grief it is."

"How bad?"

"Oh, the doc tells me it wasn't much, but there goes my ticket to fly."

"Wow! I'm so sorry!"

"Well, I've had a good run for lots of years. Say, Tim?" There was a clatter and a pause. It sounded as though Dave had dropped the phone. "I could put in a good word for you in Idyhoe."

Idaho? Although Dave had mentioned that was where he'd been flying summers most recently, Tim had never given any thought to going there. Perhaps that had to do with the indelible picture in his mind of mountains and evergreen forests, instead of open, farmable flatlands.

"Them people have been right good to me, Tim. I'd kindly like to return the favor. Now, Matt might could already have some-body else in mind, but I'd be proud to mention your name. That is, if you think you'd like flying nights. The pay's real good."

Night spraying? *That* sounded like something to spice up his adventure. "You bet I would!"

"It's a short season. You'd be done by September."

"That's fine with me."

"I'll give him a call. You going to be there awhile?"

"I'll be right here."

As soon as he'd hung up to give Dave a chance to place the call, Tim got out his road map. He opened to the front section that had the two-page spread of the entire United States. It already had red lines that he'd marked with a pencil bought specifically for that purpose. One red line led down the highways from LA into the Mississippi Delta, where he'd gotten his commercial ticket and received his training as an agricultural pilot. Another traced his route from the Delta to Oklahoma, and another, the drive to North Dakota.

He had no idea which part of Idaho he might end up going to, so he looked at the highways that led to various parts of that state. It excited him to see that such places as Montana and Wyoming would be on the way, and Washington and Oregon were on Idaho's western border. He imagined vast evergreen forests and lofty mountains throughout the region, with tiny valleys here and there where people farmed. And Yellowstone was more or less on the way, too.

Tim waited on pins and needles for almost a half hour. Then at last the phone rang.

"You got the job, son. Give him a call. Man's name is Matt Henshaw. Here's his number. Got somethin' to write with?"

"Ready!"

When he hung up, Tim flopped backward on the bed and started wagging his head back and forth, muttering out loud, "Unbelievable! Sounds like Dave was reference enough. Let's find out."

He sat back up and dialed.

"This is Matt."

"I'm Tim O'Reilly. Dave says he just talked to you?"

"Oh, sure. Hi, Tim. You're my pilot if you want the seat."

"I do. How soon do you need me?"

"Well, there's no big hurry as far as the flying goes. It'll be a few weeks 'til we get real busy."

Hawaii, Tim thought.

"But you'll have to pass the test for the state pesticide license. So long's you're up on your chemicals and stuff, you'll probably be okay."

Okay, so maybe not Hawaii, Tim thought as his new boss explained and gave him directions to his place in the Snake River Valley. He hadn't needed a state pesticide license in Oklahoma or North Dakota.

"I know what I can do," Matt said. "I'll send you the study material, and you can get started on it before you get here."

It was three hours earlier in Hawaii, and Lisa would be at the university, but Tim called the Fernhurst YWCA and left her a message. When she finally returned the call, he told her all about his newest seat.

"Oh, Tim. I wish you wouldn't."

"Because of the night spraying?"

"Yes. That's just too dangerous."

"Dave's been doing it without any trouble. It's probably a lot easier than it sounds. The main thing I wanted to tell you is, I won't be able to get over there next month. Maybe at the end of August."

"Summer session ends August fifteenth."

"Well, we'll catch up with you somewhere down the road."

"Tim, I'm starting to think I'd just as soon stay and get my degree here."

"I wish you wouldn't. Go home, Lisa."

17

HAWAIIAN ROMANCE

There was nothing for Lance to do but continue with his plans to make the trip after Lisa said that Tim wouldn't be able to visit in June after all. His parents had been all for him making a quick trip to continue wooing their favorite of all the girls Lance had ever dated. His father had said, "The farm can get along just fine without you a while longer. You go on over there." They had said he should spend a couple weeks, and that it would be on them as a little something extra for graduation. However, he had limited himself to a week, wanting to be in on helping run the wheat harvest. He arrived in Honolulu on Monday, May 25.

He easily spotted Lisa waving at him from a throng of students leaving Farrington Hall on the verdant university campus. Her glorious crown of golden hair clearly set her apart from all the others, for most of the throng were dark-haired Asians and Hawaiians. She was wearing white midthigh shorts and a burnt-orange tank top. Unlike so many students who wore flip-flops on their feet, she was wearing immaculate white Keds. He was glad to see once more that she really would make a presentable wife. He pulled the rented red Corvette convertible over to the curb, turned off the engine, and got out to open the passenger's door for her.

As she hurried near, he took the three slender double coils of white leis off the passenger's seat. He placed them onto her shoulders, and he kissed her on the lips.

She apparently didn't even notice the tittering passersby but surrendered completely to the kiss. After some seconds, however, she pushed away, saying, "Oh, Lance. The fragrance of these leis is just heavenly. Do you know what they are?"

"I asked. *Pikake.*"

"Oh, my. And I thought plumeria were fragrant." With the hand that wasn't holding her books, she lifted several of the delicate strands off her breast and held it up where she could see them better. She said, "They're *buds*. They almost look like pretty little seashells." She held the strand to her freckled nose, inhaled, and dreamily closed her eyes.

He held the door open for her and said, "Shall we?"

She laughed and hurried to slide onto the passenger's seat. She said, "I'm the one who should have had a lei for you. You're the visitor. But welcome to Hawaii!"

He got in and said, "It's nice here. I might like it better than the Bahamas."

"Well, just continue straight ahead. I'll get freshened up and put on some nicer clothes."

"And bring your swimsuit. We'll swim and have supper at the hotel. I think you'll be impressed. We can dance there, too. They have everything."

* * *

"Those chandeliers!" she exclaimed when they entered the lobby. The multicolored masses of thousands of small, crystalline pieces certainly did make a spectacular display. She halted to gaze at them.

Lance stood one pace back and studied her, giving a little nod of approval. *No ravishing beauty,* he thought, *but presentable.* She was wearing a pretty yellow print sundress and nice white sandals. *She fits in here as well as most others.*

"Wait till you see my room," he said.

"Alone, please. Just tell me where, and I'll run up and change into my swimsuit."

"Then you'd have to wait for me to go up and change," he protested. "I'll be good. I promise."

"Will you?"

He nodded.

"Really?"

"Yes. You have my word of honor. I do have *some* self-discipline. Surely you know that by now."

She gave him a little hug and a kiss on the cheek, and she said, "Yes, I do. At least, most of the time. Speaking of which, happy graduation again!" She gave him another kiss on the cheek. "I wondered if you were going to forgive me for not being there."

"I'd forgive anything you did. That's what Christians do, but loving you the way I do makes it easy."

"Oh, Lance." She raised her arms to clasp him.

At that moment, the elevator doors opened, and they had to move aside for some people emerging.

They got into the elevator and simply stood side by side while the cab whooshed upward. "I was tempted to get the presidential suite for one night," he said. "Just to see how it felt."

"A preview for when you're in office?" She gently jabbed him with her elbow. "When you move up from your first term as senator?"

"You don't believe I can do it?"

"Yes, I do believe it. I'm sure you can."

The elevator stopped and he motioned for her to precede him.

"But wait until the children are older."

"God willing, of course."

"Of course."

They went down the spotless, pleasantly-scented hallway, and he opened a door and ushered her in.

"Very nice!" She slowly turned about, eying the chic furnishings of the spacious living room. Then she went to briefly peer out the lanai doors at the scene beyond the palm-lined beach that began with the sheltered shallows of the lagoon, waves breaking onto a reef, and, beyond that, the deepening blue of the open ocean. She didn't bother to open the doors to go out on the large lanai. "And huge."

"I thought it would be nice to get a suite so we'd have a quiet, roomy place to sit and visit. This is the smallest they had. It's half the size of the presidential suite. They wanted $150 a night for the presidential.

"But let me get my shorts out of the bedroom. You can change in there, and I'll use the guest bath."

A quarter hour later, beside the oval pool, they removed the white beach robes the hotel provided, and Lance said, "It's slightly heated. After a while, we can go down for a swim in the lagoon. We'll snorkel, but let's just swim here a little where it's warmer and visit first."

"How did you find this place? It certainly is off the beaten path."

"Our travel agent in Dallas. She recommended it. It's much more exclusive out here. And if we do want to run in to Waikiki, it's right over there on the other side of Diamond Head." He gestured toward the renowned landmark rising high a mile or so down the shoreline.

"Do you think presidents really have stayed here?"

"Oh, yes. Dolly said famous people stay here all the time. Royalty, rock stars . . . which reminds me, let's catch Jimi Hendrix Friday night, okay?"

"I know that name. He's staying here?"

"I don't know, but he's going to be playing at this place they call the Waikiki Shell."

* * *

Lisa studied when she could before and between classes, and

they spent every day from midafternoon until nine or so in the evening together. He would drive her back to Fernhurst in lush, fragrant Manoa Valley, and they would chastely kiss good night and part. Of course, that wasn't quite enough excitement for Lance in such a stimulating environment, and he'd go on each night to make solo tours of the nightspots.

On Tuesday and Wednesday afternoons, he hired a limo with a driver to guide them to the island's main attractions, after which they dined at a couple of the Kahala's fine restaurants, and they danced to Danny Kaleikini's Hawaiian music there and spent some time in the suite's living room or on its spacious lanai chatting and necking a little.

On Thursday afternoon, they strolled from one end of Waikiki to the other, then rented surfboards and got some surfing instruction from a beach concession. Lance made sure that Lisa was the first to stand as a small wave carried her toward shore. He was sure that his amusingly competitive fiancée would remember that, and the sole purpose of his trip, after all, was to leave her with such a powerfully memorable time with Lance Levenger that there'd be no doubt whom she'd end up marrying.

"Tim's going to be surprised I already know how!" she said, paddling back out to the first inner break.

"Does he call you often?"

"Every week. He's such a good friend. He said he'd come in early September, but I told him I'll be done at the U a couple weeks before that."

"In time to be married on the date we chose after all."

She didn't say whether she'd consider that or not. She simply dug deeper and faster into the glinting blue water with both hands and paddled as fast as she could away from him and into an incoming wave.

Friday afternoon they snorkeled again along the inner side of the reef in front of the hotel, had an exquisite early supper of wonderfully fresh fish, and took a limo to the Jimi Hendrix Experience at the Waikiki Shell in Kapiolani Park.

They arrived at seven thirty, a half hour early, to avoid having to make their way through a capacity crowd, and they strolled across the large general-admission area where most of the audience would lounge on the grassy ground. There were already hundreds of young people there, many of whom were dressed in typical hippie garb.

"I apologize for the seating," Lance said as they entered the terrace section, where there were regular seats. "It would have been nice to be a little closer, but this was the best I could do at the last moment. I kept asking around the hotel and finally found someone who knew someone who knew a scalper."

"Sounds expensive."

"It was. Almost five times the original price."

"It's that important to you?"

"Jimi Hendrix is a big deal."

"And how much was that?" She sounded genuinely alarmed.

"Fifty dollars."

"*Each?*"

"Each."

"Lance! We probably won't spend that much on the plane rental tomorrow! That would buy three hours in a one seventy-two!"

"But you'll be able to tell our children that you went to a Jimi Hendrix concert in Waikiki."

"You think they'll care? They won't know who that is."

"Well—"

"What's that *odor*?" A few minutes earlier there had been a gentle breeze off the sea that had a fresh, pure scent, but the air was still and pungent now. "I've smelled that before somewhere."

Lance knew perfectly well what it was—marijuana. Yet he didn't want her to be offended by its presence, and he didn't want to reveal that he was familiar with the smell. It was pretty clear to him

248

as well that pot was hardly the most popular drug in use there.

"I'm not sure," he said. "I think maybe they're burning lawn trash in one of those yards over there." He carelessly waved a hand toward the residences just inland from the Shell.

Before Hendrix came onstage, an immense dark orange moon ascended above nearby Diamond Head, and many—perhaps thousands—of stoned onlookers reacted with what sounded to Lance like alarm. He clearly heard one young guy behind him say, "That's a bad sign, man!" And another replied, "It's giving me bad vibes, too."

By the time Hendrix appeared, initiating a great din of mightily amplified acid rock that made Lisa clap her hands over her ears and turn to gaze at Lance in dismay, the crowd's mood was not entirely joyful.

One or more of the stacked amplifiers on either side of Hendrix was humming, and it was obviously disturbing the star and his fans. After a half hour or so and a half dozen songs, he walked off the stage, and it was clear that he was not happy.

"I'm going to the bathroom," Lance said. "Will you be all right here?"

"Go ahead."

"What's wrong?"

"Some of these people . . . I just feel a little . . . I don't know. But it's okay. I'm okay."

"Shall we just leave?" He'd known all along that she wouldn't be thrilled by the music, but he'd thought she'd at least enjoy being present at such a big happening.

"No. Really. I'm fine," she insisted.

So he departed on an errand that had far more to do with ingestion than elimination. He'd seen that people were freely passing pot around, and he wanted some. Surely the speakers would be fixed, and he'd be able to relax and enjoy Hendrix with heightened awareness when he came back onstage. Soon a young woman dressed in something like a Hawaiian muumuu sans floral print and wearing a band of dark beads around her head held a joint toward him and said, "Want a hit, man?"

He did indeed. By the time he returned to Lisa after some further wandering, his perceptions had been very agreeably altered. The lights and the sounds were delightful. Even the monstrous moon, which bothered so many of the others, was a huge upper. He felt very relaxed and content. He felt very superior to the superstitious masses around him.

"Where have you been for so long?" Lisa asked with concern.

"They need more lavatories," he replied.

"It's been an hour and a quarter since it began. It'll probably be over by ten, don't you think?"

Now a slight breeze was coming off the uplands. It felt so good to him. *The only place I've ever been where you can bathe in air.* He didn't even mind that Hendrix hadn't come back on stage yet.

"Lance?"

"Yes?"

"Are you all right? Didn't you hear me?"

"This air is amazing."

Someone audibly bumped a microphone and began apologizing, saying that Jimi felt it wasn't right to subject the audience to any more electronic buzzing. He told them to hang onto their ticket stubs, and they'd be readmitted Sunday night.

A rumble of protest arose, and a blond-haired guy with a crew cut two rows ahead of Lance and Lisa shouted, "Bullshit, man! I got the duty Sunday night!" Other shouts of indignation followed his.

"Let's go!" Lisa said, getting to her feet. "This is getting scary!"

"It'll be okay. We have to wait for the limo anyway."

"Are you alright, Lance?" She bent down to look more closely into his face. "You seem so . . . Are you coming down with something?"

"I'm fine." He giggled. "Just fine."

* * *

Their flight to Maui the next morning in the rented 172 went beautifully. Lance insisted that Lisa do most of the flying. He was sharply aware of the previous night's fiasco, and he was determined to make up for it.

After they'd crossed the ocean channel east of Oahu, Lance had Lisa land at the leper colony on Molokai just to be able to say she'd been to the famous little colony beneath the towering cliffs. Then they proceeded alongside the remainder of the island's awesomely scenic sea cliffs, the highest in the world, turned south, and landed a few minutes later on the asphalt strip at Maui's Kaanapali Beach Resort. They strolled over to one of the restaurants for lunch and lazed around for a while on the beach in the shade of a coco palm. Then they leisurely flew around the rest of the island, climbing up high to have a close look at the summit of Haleakala and descending to nearly sea level for Lisa to shoot a touch-and-go at remote Hana's little airport alongside the tossing windward sea.

When Lisa landed back at Honolulu International, Lance sighed and nodded in perfect contentment, thinking, *Who could ever match what I've shown her this week? It's just a matter of time, and she'll come back to me.*

* * *

After their flight to Maui, as they relaxed on Lance's lanai, he suggested that they dress formally for a sumptuous dinner at the Gourmet in Waikiki that evening. "I read it's excellent," he said.

"I'd be happy with something simpler," she said.

"Perhaps we can tone it down tomorrow. We'll go to that church where they sing in Hawaiian and eat at this great buffet I read about. And let's swim with the hotel's dolphins. But this is

Saturday night, and I want you to enjoy our last real night on the town before I go home. I'll go in and see whether I can make a reservation." He got up from the white wrought-iron chair and went into the living room to make the call. Then he went into the bedroom to get the small gift-wrapped box he'd left on the bureau.

"I found a little something that you can wear tonight if you like," he said, stepping back onto the lanai and handing her the gift.

She held it clumsily, as though she didn't know what to do with it.

"Aren't you going to open it?"

"I'm almost afraid to."

"Go on. It's not like it's diamonds or something."

She hesitantly undid the crimson ribbon, carefully removed the embossed white wrapping paper, and opened the hinged lid of the small, expensive-looking wood box.

"Oh, my," she sighed, withdrawing the lei of small, gleaming, perfectly matched seashells and earrings of gold and much smaller shells. "Oh, Lance." Tears sprang to her eyes, and she held the objects toward him. "I don't think . . . "

He quickly leaned down, kissed her cheek, and placed the manicured tip of a tan forefinger on her lips. "Don't say another word. When I saw these, I just had to get them for you. They're from the island of Niihau, where only native Hawaiians live. The owner of the shop said she has the leis custom-made there, and a Honolulu jeweler does the earrings. That little pamphlet tells about them."

A few hours later, a limo whisked them away to the Gourmet, Lance dressed in a beige tropical-weight suit and Lisa with her hair done up high, wearing a simple black sheath, black pumps, and the Niihau shell lei and earrings.

18

ON THE ROAD AGAIN

Tim was on his way, zigzagging in the night down the farm-road shortcuts revealed by his trusty Rand McNally, heading over to Highway 85. He barreled along with the top down under a starry sky, his leather jacket zipped to his chin. The nights were still a little chilly, but having the top down added some spice to his excitement about being back on the road.

He punched the tape deck's start button and was soon manically trying to mimic John Kay singing about being out on the highway, seeking adventure. It exactly suited his mood, except they could have picked up the beat a bit.

Eighty-five would take him almost straight down to Rapid City. He'd opted for a meandering, rubbernecking route to southern Idaho. Although Hawaii was too far away for a bit of wandering, western South Dakota and a chunk of Wyoming sure weren't.

He figured he'd get down to Rapid City not too long after midnight. Surely he'd be ready to sleep by then. He'd find a motel and sleep in as long as he wanted. Then he'd drive on down to Mount Rushmore. After that, he might spend some time in Yellowstone. It wouldn't be very far from there to his new seat.

The headlights revealed a nice, tight bend in the road ahead. He could clearly see across the fields of low wheat around the bend that there were no oncoming lights. So instead of gradually slowing for the curve, he stayed right on it until the last possible moment. Then, very smoothly, so as to not unbalance the car, he mashed down hard on the brake pedal, gently eased the steering wheel to the right, and carefully initiated a four-wheel drift.

He'd done it more than a few times in his Ford after he and Nick had found a way onto a gated, dirt stock-car track near LA one night, and he had cautiously—*very* cautiously, because it would have been a crime to run that cherry old Ford into the wall— worked his way up from crudely fishtailing around the turns at either end of the track to being able to do less showy but far more precise and efficient four-wheel drifts.

He wasn't about to run a big risk of dinging this Healey, either. He had to be going fast enough to set up the slide, but he was making sure that there'd be very little chance of losing control. He downshifted and added a bit of throttle to keep the Healey pointed exactly where he wanted it to go.

"Oh, yeah!" he shouted. It was exhilarating to be able to steer the sliding sports car with its stiff suspension by small variations in engine power, rather than by steering. "This is what this thing is built for!" Unlike a standard passenger automobile, designed primarily for comfort, the long, low sports car leaned very little and felt perfectly in balance.

Approaching the last part of the turn, he pressed rapidly but smoothly on the gas pedal. Having read a lot about what the pros had to say about it, he wanted to avoid excessive sliding—no matter how much fun that was—and enter the straightaway with optimal traction and acceleration.

He shot out of the bend onto the straight stretch laughing loudly, thinking, *Am I really going to be able to stop living like this? Man, I do love going down the road!*

* * *

Tim spent some of his leisurely travel time to his new seat studying for his Idaho pesticide license, did some sightseeing, and camped along the way. He bought some basic compact camping gear and hiking boots after a night's rest at a motel in Rapid City. Then he had a quick look at Mount Rushmore and stopped at the Devil's Tower monument to sleep in his new bivy beside a stream and hike around the base of the monolith the next morning before he got back on the road again. He spent two nights and took a couple brief hikes at two separate locations in Yellowstone National Park before he continued down through Jackson Hole, Wyoming, to enter southeastern Idaho.

When Tim arrived at his destination in the Snake River Valley, young Matt Henshaw turned out to be every bit as nice and easy-going as Dave had said he was. Tim rented an apartment in a decent building that Matt recommended and went right back out to Matt's inclined strip beside his home on a hillside to get used to flying the 450-horsepower Stearman and to have a look at the various make-do landing sites.

Matt did have a six-hundred-horse Ag-Cat, the one that Dave had talked about flying, but he was apparently being cautious about risking it on a new pilot. That was fine with Tim. At last, he was getting his wish to work a Stearman.

"Take your time getting used to it," Matt said. "There's only one way to land on this home strip of mine, and that's uphill. Land downhill and you'll go right off the end. I don't care how strong the wind may be blowing uphill. If some ridiculous wind sprang up all of a sudden, which does happen sometimes, you could fly on over to the muny and land there. There's a pay phone by the transient parking, and I'd come get you."

After Tim had made a couple landings and takeoffs from the most difficult strip of all, a farmer's narrow dirt road next to a fence of tautly-stretched barbed wire strung on steel posts that lay several feet to the side of the right lower wingtip, he recalled the old saying about Stearman pilots that the guys at ag-flying school had liked to bring up: "There are those who have and those who will"—ground loop, that is, lose control on the ground, which results in the aeronautical equivalent of "spinning out" in a race car.

A slight crosswind had come up, but thanks to Tim's weeks of intense daylight-to-dark stick-and-rudder flying as well as the Stearman flying he'd done in ag school, the Stearman handled as nicely on the ground as any other airplane he'd ever flown. It was just a little harder to see out of once the tail was down with the wide, high-slanting chemical hopper forward of the cockpit blocking the view directly ahead. Leaning his head out the left side of the cockpit the way Catfish had taught him, Tim couldn't see the fence on the right at all, so he just made sure that he kept the Stearman's unseen left wheel very close to the left edge of the packed dirt where it met the soft soil of the adjacent plowed field..

When he was finished with the Stearman, he drove back into town to the apartment, stopping at a grocery store on the way, and studied some more for his pesticide license. The apartment building was a neat, clean one on a little hill at the edge of town, and the apartment had a pleasant view south toward the river and, beyond that, the great sagebrush plains of northern Nevada that stretched far off to where the lines of grayish-blue mountains interrupted the smooth line of the flatlands horizon. Every once in a while he'd look up from his study pamphlets on the small, Formica-topped dining table, lean back, and gaze with great contentment on the placid scene.

When it got so dark that he needed to get up and turn on the lights, he also took time to make some macaroni and cheese and heat a can of string beans for dinner. He read the latest issue of *Time* as he ate. President Nixon was making more noises about pulling out of Vietnam, surging inflation was spooking people, and the U.S. was getting very close to its attempt to put a man on the moon.

Then he studied some more. At last, however, he felt the need for a break.

He didn't have a TV, and he wasn't in any mood to read anything else just then. He set out to have a better look around town, and he impulsively stopped at the Exquisite Spud to get some dessert.

That was when he first set eyes on a wonderful little pixie named Sandy Littlebear, one of the waitresses. She sure was a cute and lively little rascal. He couldn't recall ever seeing anyone cuter. He guessed that she was probably just a little over five feet tall. He kept thinking that she strongly resembled someone he knew, but he couldn't quite recall who that might be.

He wasn't seated in the cutie's section, so he had no conversation with her on that first visit. However, he could enjoy watching her make her rapid rounds, laughing and chatting with her customers. She was so charming that he began wondering whether he might be ready to start dating again.

He wasn't overly eager to do that. He was making progress on getting back to being the original Tim O'Reilly, and he was nervous about taking the risk of going through another breakup.

But you gotta do it sometime, O'Reilly.

He studied the little waitress at a distance and wondered whether she had a boyfriend. He hadn't seen a ring on her finger.

From then on, he started hanging around the Spud, as the locals called it, whenever Sandy was on duty and he wasn't busy doing something else. By the time the season went into full swing, he'd drunk so much coffee as an excuse that the coffee farmers down in Central America must have wondered what in the world was going on up there in *los Estados*. He and Sandy had started chatting some. Yet he still hadn't made up his mind to risk asking her for a date.

She had a knack for getting him to talk about himself in their brief, hurried exchanges, and she revealed all sorts of interesting information in little bits and pieces about herself and her family.

She was Shoshone, born and raised on the Fort Hall reservation farther down the highway. She had come off the reservation to go to college because it was too far for a daily drive, and she'd gotten a part-time job at the restaurant. Then she had decided to stay in town to work full-time during the summer as well. She rented a basement room in a family's nearby home.

Finally convincing himself that he had to take the step if he was ever going to lead a normal life again, he made up his mind to ask her out. He'd just have to make it very clear from the beginning that he wasn't looking for romance but only friendship.

Even though Sandy was exceedingly friendly and outgoing, he asked with considerable trepidation. He was the type who'd prefer dental surgery over date rejection. But when he asked, she just said, "Sure," gave him a big smile, and skipped off to check on other customers before he blurted in a whisper, "Really?"

They went to the drive-in just out of town to see *Barbarella*. Neither had heard anything about it, but it couldn't be bad with a famous star like Jane Fonda in it, could it? Tim was aware of Fonda's anti-war activities, but he'd cooled off a lot about that sort of thing. After all, it seemed to be an apolitical movie, and there was little else to do in that small city.

"So, she's one of your typical California girls?" Sandy kidded him after it was clear that the movie was a dog.

"No way!" he protested. He turned down the volume a little on the speaker that was hooked onto his partially lowered window. "They're way cuter than that!"

"Cute" had been on his mind a lot since he'd first seen Sandy. He'd fallen into the habit of comparing her looks with the celebrities whose pictures he saw in the magazine racks and on TV. He'd bought a very small tabletop set by then to keep from feeling too lonely when he and Sandy couldn't be together. None of those celebrities were as cute as his new friend. Then, finally, he had remembered who it was she reminded him of, but he couldn't remember the name. It was a movie star he'd briefly had a crush on when he was a kid, and now he could picture the pert nose, the delicate, uplifted chin, and the jaunty, shiny ponytail that she had a way of flicking so charmingly with a toss of her head.

Sandy suddenly started singing, "California Girls," trying to mimic the shrill Beach Boys sound. She wasn't a good singer, but she did make it pretty funny. "Tell me," she asked, "what does your steady back there look like?"

"Haven't got one. I take it you don't, either."

"Uh-uh. I don't want to go through that again anytime soon."

"I know what you mean. Me, neither."

They laughed about it and chatted on, completely ignoring what was happening on the distant outdoor screen. "Tell you what I really want to see," he said. "There's this motorcycle movie coming. *Easy Rider*. It was a big deal at the Cannes Film Festival. It's supposed to be out in the US this summer. Let's see it if we can, okay?"

"Sure."

He was very relieved as the evening passed that Sandy didn't make any sign that she expected a little necking. She seemed to be as genuinely content with a casual, nonromantic friendship as he.

She told him how she had a real thing for the outdoors. She said there just wasn't enough time in life to get as much hiking and swimming in as she wanted.

Whenever he could, he tried to help her fill that need. However, those chances became radically fewer as the spraying season heated up and his flying demands increased.

Matt was a serious Mormon, so Tim had every Sunday off, but Sandy had to work the breakfast shift two Sundays a month. Still, they had the two Sunday afternoons, two full Sundays, and the one brief time when it was too windy for him to spray and she didn't have to work.

She had grown up going into the mountains with her older

brothers, and she delighted in cluing him in on how to "read the woods." Her eyes were quick to see the most subtle evidence the elusive animals had left of their passing, and she often spotted the creatures themselves and had to be patient in pointing them out until Tim could see them. The two friends didn't have far to drive to get to such places, for mountain wilderness rises steeply from the north side of the valley.

She showed him how to tell the difference between mule-deer tracks and elk tracks other than by the sheer size of the ones left by the adult elk, and how to differentiate between the scat of a coyote and that of a bear. Once, they came across the awesome prints that an adult cougar had left in a patch of powdery soil. "Look," she'd whispered. "See where it dragged its tail?" She rarely spoke when they were up there and usually whispered whenever she did.

One day, as they approached a meadow in some deep timber, she froze and made a small motion for him to stop. His eyes caught the movement of a cow elk as it slowly grazed out of the shadows. Two more cows appeared. Then Tim felt a puff of wind on the back of his neck, the cows' heads snapped up as they caught the humans' scent, and the lead cow squealed and ran with the others bounding after her. A great bull raced out of the shadows and up the edge of the meadow with his long chin thrust upward and his huge rack of antlers thrown far back onto his haunches.

"Wow!" Tim whispered.

"Yeah," she said in a hushed voice. "It's something, huh? You could probably go on the fall hunt with my brothers if you want."

No, thanks, he thought. Besides, he wouldn't be there in the fall.

As of one mind, they suddenly leaned against one another, but immediately lurched apart.

"We don't want to be *that* friendly," she said in an uncommonly loud voice, laughing.

"No, but I sure am tempted," he said.

"Yeah. Me, too. Maybe some other time. Race you to the car!"

As the weeks passed by and Tim and Sandy maintained their casual friendship, Tim continued to communicate with the far greater platonic love of his life, Lisa. They talked on the phone about once a week and wrote occasional letters. Then one day Lisa told him that she had applied for the fall semester in Hawaii, although she still wasn't perfectly certain that she'd actually end up attending.

* * *

Matt broke his no-Sunday-spraying rule just once. A farmer talked him into agreeing to spray a single load because he had a very nasty infestation. "Do you mind loading it yourself?" Matt had asked, letting Tim do it, since he knew by then that his new pilot avoided church.

"No," Tim replied, "of course not."

So he was all alone that Sunday morning when he cranked up the Stearman and went to mix a load while the motor warmed. The chemical ordered for that job, TEPP, is extremely toxic before it's mixed with lots of water. As with other organophosphates, it isn't toxic only if it's ingested orally but is also rapidly absorbed through the skin and eyes. The label warned that a single drop of TEPP concentrate in the eye was likely to be fatal.

Therefore, although Tim was always careful with the "hotter" chemicals, he was exceptionally cautious in mixing the TEPP. He put on a pair of long-cuffed black rubber gloves, a pair of plastic goggles and one of the respirators that were kept in a cabinet just outside the chemical shed. The only safety equipment that he didn't wear, since he'd be mixing just one load and would make certain that he didn't spill a drop, was a pair of rubber boots and a rubber apron.

As well as having the potential to end his life or make him very sick immediately, organophosphate exposure had a cumulative effect, and the accumulation of too much in his blood could also cost him paychecks. Pilots in Idaho were required to have their blood drawn once a month to monitor their cholinesterase levels. If a pilot's cholinesterase count went over the limit, he would be grounded until it returned to a safe level, and that took time.

Of course those very "hot" chemicals in pure form were only toxic for a short time after they'd been exposed to air. Therefore the countless drops that had been spilled on the loading dock over the years had lost all their toxicity and were no longer a hazard. It was the same out in the fields; after a short while—a very short while for some organophosphates such as TEPP—it was safe for people to enter the fields.

The following afternoon, Matt told Tim, "Field man said you got a perfect kill. Even around the poles and wires. Nice work."

"Thanks."

"The night-flying's coming up pretty quick. I'd like you to make some dry runs tonight and start getting a feel for it."

"All right!"

19

NORTHWEST NIGHTS

One night a little more than a week later, Tim snapped on the Stearman's drive lights as he descended in the dark toward the spot where he'd seen Matt's lights shine out for a landing ahead of him. He thumbed two of the light toggles below the throttle quadrant downward, and the alfalfa field at the low end of the farmer's sloping, private airstrip luminously flared in the intense glare of the Stearman's two forward-pointing wing lights.

The farmer's little dirt strip alongside the power lines was somewhat similar to the strip of rocky soil at Matt's home, running uphill to a large house, a hangar, and some other outbuildings, but it wasn't quite as steep, its rock-free soil and turf were smoother, and it was considerably wider than a wingspan. The farmer's house was bigger than Matt's, but the hangar was smaller, just enough to keep the man's unseen air toy, whatever it was, out of the weather.

Tim was about to do his first paid night spraying, and he was glad that he'd taken plenty of time to practice using the two horizontal rows of thin metal switches solely by feel in the dark. There were eight such toggles, two for each of the plane's four powerful spot lights. Each light could be turned on by flicking its toggle upward or off by moving it downward. Each light also could be raised or lowered by raising or lowering the toggle immediately below its on-off toggle. The panel of toggles was attached to the left side of the cockpit beneath the throttle quadrant and above the spray and emergency-dump handles.

A total of four fully retractable lights were mounted on the bottoms of the lower wings, two on each side. Beneath each lower wing, one light was mounted about halfway out to the wingtip, and another was mounted very near the wingtip. The two midwing lights shined straight ahead when needed. The two wingtip lights were aimed outward at an angle, and they were used independently to shine down at the ground in a turn.

All four lights had to be turned on and off and raised and lowered repeatedly during a single flight, and that had to be done by feel, not by sight. Tim had to keep his eyes on the flagmen's flashing lights and the airplane's proximity to the ground, as well as objects such as bee stations, power poles, occasional guy wires, power lines, fences, barns, trees, and so on. Descending now for this landing on an unlighted airstrip, he was using only the so-called drive lights, the pair that pointed straight ahead.

Matt's Cat was parked just beyond the loader trailer in front of the farmer's hangar. The only light up there in the inky darkness at the moment came from the small bare bulb suspended over the rear of the loading trailer and that which emanated from several windows in the farmhouse fifty yards or so farther up the slope.

Tim leaned out the left side of the Stearman's cockpit to get a better view of a wedge of the airstrip ahead. He was sitting low in the cockpit, just as Catfish had taught all his students. It allowed a pilot to escape some of the buffeting of the prop wash against his helmet. To mitigate that buffeting, Tim also had epoxied a "spoiler," a ridge of surgical tubing, sideways across the top of the helmet to keep it from "flying," since the top of a helmet has the shape of an airfoil and would lift, tugging pretty hard at the chin strap, in strong prop wash.

There was no windshield, since the Stearman was used not only as a sprayer but also as a duster. There was just a short, narrow fiberglass wind deflector that could be raised for spraying or locked down flat on the top of the hopper for dusting. A windshield increases the partial vacuum of an open cockpit, and that causes powdery dust—as powdery as some female's facial powder—to be sucked into the cockpit in heaping quantities.

Just as the last of the strangely-glowing, bushy seed alfalfa was about to disappear behind the leading edge of the lower left wing, Tim eased the throttle handle all the way back, and the tires softly scrunched onto the bare soil. Then he added enough power to raise the tail back up and lower the nose so that he could see straight ahead over the engine's spiky upper cylinders to fast-taxi to the loader truck.

"You go ahead and do that field right across the road," Matt told him. "That half-mile run'll be a good one to get you used to the uglier stuff. But watch out for the hillside. Don't forget it's there. And you can't get under any of the wires, either, so don't even think about it. Take your time. We're not in any great big hurry yet."

Despite Matt's comments, it was just a few minutes later that Tim had the Stearman blasting down the strip with 220 gallons of goop—a watered-down mixture of Systox, Dylox, and sticky Toxaphene. He wasn't straining to be quick, but the typical crop duster's idea of taking it easy when there was work to be done rarely included sitting around with his feet up. Once again, since the tail hadn't come all the way up so that he could see over the nose yet, Tim was leaning out the left side of the cockpit to peer around the back corner of the big, rectangular chemical hopper.

As with a great many other Stearman agricultural conversions across the nation, this one had a thick, spongy, vinyl-covered crash pad on the vertical back of the hopper above the instrument panel. Momentarily glimpsing the pad, Tim grinned as he flashed back on what Catfish had said about them: "If everything has done went to hell, y'all stuff y'all's haids up against that crash pad or at least an instrument panel. Y'all don't want them haids floppin' around loose."

The heavily-laden biplane lumbered into the air near the end of the strip, and Tim backed the manifold pressure off to thirty-two inches and the prop pitch to 2200 rpm. That's quite a bit of power coming from an engine developing 450 horses full on, but 220 gallons weighs nearly a ton, and that's a fairly hefty load on a warm night, considering that a stock Stearman was built to haul two 170-pound pilots.

He planned to leave the setting at 32 inches and 2200 rpm until he got a little altitude and made a 270-degree turn back around and started making his spray passes parallel to the hillside. He would pull back the power to 31 inches and 2100 rpm once he was lined up for the first pass. As much as was prudent, he wanted to avoid making too great a racket near farmhouses in the middle of the night.

He reached down and flicked two of the slender toggles to turn off the drive lights, which were uselessly shining into the sky as he climbed. The glare vanished, and all was black, except for the instruments' faint glow up close and, at a distance, the specks of farm lights scattered across the valley, the mass of city lights off to the east a few miles, and the stars. There wasn't any visible horizon, which is the primary visual reference for normal flight in daylight. There was only the vaguely defined band of black between the farthest farm lights up to the bottom of the dome of stars.

A half minute or so after takeoff, as Tim dipped the right wing to start a shallow turn to come around and line up with the low end of the invisible field of seed alfalfa, cautiously turning into the hill, he felt for the toggle to activate the right-turn light and flipped it up. Unlike the pair of drive lights mounted beneath the lower wings midway to the wingtips and aimed straight ahead, the two turn lights were near the lower wingtips and pointed di-agonally away from the path of flight in level flight but ahead of the path of flight over the ground.

As the biplane banked right, a broad spot of light raced over the alfalfa field adjacent to the one he was going the spray. The primary reason for that disk of light was to clearly show where the ground was, but a pilot could also hold the light steady on one spot, perhaps a large, hazardous object, to study it by varying the plane's bank and manipulating that light's raise-lower switch.

This turning into the hill at the moment was not a violation of Matt's warning. Tim had understood that Matt was talking about making a turn right after a low pull-up from a spray run when the plane would be much closer to the ground and other obstruc-tions than it was at the high point of the turn when it would be necessary to turn back toward the rising ground. This turn into the hillside was being made from a preliminary, extended climb-out to a safe altitude.

Scanning the dark over one shoulder, Tim caught sight of the two flagmen's small blinking lights. Although the flagmen's or-dinary three-cell flashlights would have been very hard to see if they'd been aimed steadily at the airplane, they were highly vis-ible when they were waved from side to side, which produced the blinking effect.

Once Tim lined up on the two flashing lights, he pointed the nose downward, flicked off the Stearman's turn light, turned on the two drive lights, and dove steeply over the set of power lines perpendicular to his flight path. As he pulled back on the control stick with his right hand to level off, his bare left hand shoved the spray-valve handle forward. He wore thin leather gloves for daylight flight, but he wanted to have a better feel for the toggles at night.

The drive lights were very effective, lighting up the bushy, un-cut alfalfa far in advance of the airplane. At first, Tim could see everything he needed to see even as he clipped over the ground at ninety miles an hour or so. However, when he got very near the opposite side of the field, he began to lose sight of the power lines. The lines had glowed nicely from a distance, but the nearer the plane got to them, the higher those wires seemed to rise above the direct beams. So, since he was still getting used to night spraying, he kept the wires glowing with reflected light by nudging the two raise-lower toggles a bit upward as he drew nearer.

He gave the power lines a little more room than normal and pulled up gently. He shut off the spray somewhat sooner than he would have in the daylight, when they didn't use flagmen and used automatic flaggers, instead. He wanted a generous margin of safety for the teenager waving the flashlight on that end of the field. He could make an extra cleanup pass on either side of the field later on.

Clearing the wires, he flicked off the drives and snapped on the downhill wing's turn light. A few seconds later, extinguishing that light and turning on the opposite one, he rolled the wings back over the other way. He brought the Stearman all the way back around, commenced his rollout, flipped off the turn light, and activated the drive lights.

After a couple spray runs across the alfalfa, Tim's vision was blurred by an accumulation of chemical droplets on the plastic bubble shield attached to his helmet. The air was still, and the outward-swirling cloud of the finer, sticky, milk-white droplets of the chemical mixture were settling so slowly that he was flying back through them. He took the shop towel he'd tucked beneath a thigh and wiped the face shield clean. To keep from inhaling those finer spray droplets, he held his breath going across the field and breathed during the turns.

He might have avoided some of the suspended spray if he'd kept hunched down directly behind the small wind deflector, but he kept leaning out one side and the other to keep close track of the bee stations. They looked pretty flimsy from a speeding air-plane, but Matt had taken him on foot into a field in the daylight to show him what a station looked like up close. The bee boards were thick, long planks drilled with numerous narrow holes for the bees to crawl into at night, and they were hung in a row from a stout four-by-four frame deeply anchored in the ground. They were tall enough and thick enough to cause a serious problem if they snagged a wingtip or the landing gear.

Planes just hurdle the pollinator stations with the spray on, and the bees remain perfectly safe in their boards. Since those particular insecticides were designed to lose their toxicity quickly, there would be no danger to the bees when they emerged later.

Although he did feel the need to be very aware, Tim didn't find the spraying of that big, open field a bit spooky. As he worked his way across it pass by pass, he was soon as relaxed as he'd ever been in the daytime, slapping the stick and rudder pedals nearly full travel to initiate a turn one way or another and tugging back on the stick to bring the Stearman to the verge of a stall. The next, smaller field was easy, too, but the third patch of alfalfa was small and pretty-well wired up, and it put him on high alert.

There was a pair of monstrous, steel-towered electric lines that crossed right by the edge of this field at an angle, and there were regular wires at the other end. "You might as well start getting used to it now," Matt said. "We have some doozies around here."

There was an orchard that ended too close beneath the big lines that prevented Tim from flying under them, so he had to dive steeply down over them. To avoid building up too much speed in a dive from such an altitude, Tim slowed the Stearman down very close above the guy wires between the tops of the pylons somewhere around a hundred feet above the ground before he nosed steeply over to get as close as possible to the near end of the field before he opened the money handle. As he seemed to almost hover as he approached the steadying steel cables between the towers, he kept track of them by constantly swiveling the left-turn light downward and leaning out the side of the cockpit. He sprayed the entire field in that one direction, diving steeply over the high towered electric lines, and never risking spraying back in the opposite direction to pull up and over them.

* * *

One Sunday at mid-afternoon, Tim took Sandy to a neighboring town's restaurant that was known for its chicken-fried steaks. It had a spacious dining room, and most of the Sunday lunch crowd had left. Although there was plenty of space elsewhere, two young men entered and sat at the table right beside them. That was the first thing that bothered Tim about the two. Then the pudgy one with a bad complexion, who was facing Tim, started eyeing him and Sandy and smirking.

His problem, man, Tim told himself. *Not yours. Don't you react.*

The porker went on doing his strange thing, and Tim remained perfectly calm. He couldn't even be sure the guy was smirking. Maybe the dude had no control over how he looked. Maybe that smirk was something like Otto Brunner's tic.

They looked pretty much like the sort of young guys anyone would expect to see in a farm town. They wore slightly soiled jeans, T-shirts, and worn, ankle-high lace-up boots. The one facing Tim was wearing a stained green John Deere cap.

"Hi," the smaller guy with his back to Tim pleasantly said to the elderly waitress as she set a couple glasses of water on the table. "I'm gonna have some apple pie and milk, please." He sounded nice enough.

"Same here," the other one said, but his eyes kept flicking toward Tim and Sandy, and those puffy lips definitely were curling.

Tim sighed and forced his own eyes back to Sandy. "Penny for your thoughts," he muttered.

"A penny? Tim, this is 1969. You can't get a thought worth

anything for less than five bucks now."

"Deal," he said. "*Speak* to me." It was worth fifty if Sandy could divert his attention from Piggy Boy.

"Well, for one thing, I'm sure glad you came along to make the time pass quicker till school starts again."

"I'll bet you get asked out all the time."

"Not by the kind of guy I'm comfortable with."

"Hey, thanks. I'm lucky I found a friend like *you*."

Then Tim heard the fat dude say, "She's not bad at all for an Injun." Tim went hot all over and trembled.

He gazed into Sandy's eyes, and she grimly peered into his.

The jerk laughed.

"Take it easy," Sandy quietly said to Tim, apparently sensing his anger. "He can't help being what he is."

The other guy directly to Tim's side didn't seem to be responding, but Porky's tiny eyes were fixed on Sandy now, and he was openly leering. "Maybe she'll give us a little, too. I—"

Tim went up like a rocket. His chair flipped over and landed on its back with a clatter.

Fatso's little eyes widened in fear.

"Tim!" Sandy cried. She was up and rushing toward him. She grabbed him by one arm and said, "Let's just go!"

It didn't register. He took a step closer to the pudge and roughly gestured for him to get up.

"Tim!" She yanked hard on his arm. "Tim!"

His head turned ever so slowly toward her, and his eyes gradually focused on her face. Then he was back in his right mind and fully aware.

"Come on. Let's go." She tugged him toward the cash register.

Tim realized that the embarrassment of a public brawl might be harder on Sandy than if he made the creep pay. "Your lucky day, you pile of puke," he said, and he turned and went on to pay their bill.

"Thank you, Tim," Sandy said as they hurried toward the Healey. She latched onto his near arm and pressed the side of her face against his shoulder. "I'm so glad you let it go."

"He was asking for it. That's for sure." But whatever the dude's problem was, Tim was far more conscious of his own. He was very glad that Sandy had stopped him.

20
NORTHWEST FRIGHTS

One night a couple weeks later, when Tim had time to call Lisa between dusk and the hour the bees would "go to bed" when it got cooler, she had some disappointing news. "Guess what? I'm staying in Hawaii a while longer!"

"You and Lance are finished?"

"I think. Probably."

"Have you told him?"

"Not until I'm perfectly certain."

"And Hawaii's really that great a school?"

"Good enough for my purposes. They have some classes this fall that I'm really going to like. Especially one advanced writing one. The prof thinks I've got potential. Maybe I'll see you in September after all. When you come teach me how to surf."

"Maybe. It'll be a little early for Nicaragua. What does Lancelot have to say about it?"

"*Lancelot?* I like that, Gawain. It never occurred to me."

"How 'bout if you can't remember Tim, you just call me Wayne? Forget the 'Ga.' But tell me, how's he's taking it?"

"He's being very patient. Charming as ever. I think maybe I do love him, Tim. I suppose I always have, really. But still, I go all wobbly with doubt sometimes. I was sorely tempted to just go home right after summer school and marry him. I was about to make up my mind to do that. Then I got really, really scared."

"Well, I sure hope it works out. He's a great guy." He was struggling to avoid saying what he really thought, keeping his tone of voice light and casual. Besides, he had to get back to work. "Gotta go now. See ya."

"He says that if I really do stay to finish up here, he'll come see me again over Christmas vacation. Love you, Wayne."

"And I like you a whole bunch, too, Sis. Or should I call you Lady Bertilak?"

"Oh, no. I'm no Lady Bertilak. But you read it!"

"Took a peek. That green knight business makes a pretty dumb story, Lisa. I'm trying to read that *Experience* thing, too. But I gotta split now. Later."

* * *

"So where's that damnyankee now?" CR asked when Lance told him that Lisa was staying in Hawaii for more college and that Tim was probably planning on seeing her in September. "He's got to be done sprayin' weeds."

"Idaho. She says they spray all night up there."

"Good. Hope he runs into somethin'."

"Now, that isn't very nice, CR. But, to tell you the truth, I wouldn't be terribly sorry myself. Maybe they are just friends, but I do confess he's getting me worried again. I just can't help it sometimes."

"I'm a-gonna git 'im. If the dark don't do it, I will. Soon's harvest's over, I'm on my way down there."

"Well, don't you get *me* involved. I have better things to do with my life than sit around in some prison."

"You ain't got a thing to worry about."

"I was just kidding," Lance hastily added, imagining what he'd be able to truthfully tell a jury and not get tripped up by some lawyer claiming that he'd been a conspirator.

"Well, I ain't. Ain't nobody goin' to mawk me and git away with it."

Lance smiled, thinking how CR let *him* get away with mockery, and he said, "You can't go around *gittin'* people just because they treat you like the fool runt you are." Lance pictured himself sitting in the witness chair, telling the jury how he'd done his best to change his hired man's attitude toward the pilot. The trick was going to be how to encourage CR while leaving evidence that he'd done his best to do the opposite. And why not take advantage of the little guy's hatred? He'd have to mention CR's hatred to his folks and the other hired men just in case he ever did have to testify in court.

"Tell you the truth," Lance went on, "I almost hit him myself one time."

"What'd he do?"

"Called you a crippled little no-good shrimp."

"Say *whaaat*?"

* * *

One day in July, when they were well into the night-and-day spraying routine, Matt asked Tim with his eyes twinkling mischievously, "So! Are you tired of flying that Stearman?"

"Are you kidding?" Tim wondered whether Matt was about to offer to switch planes, now that Tim had proved himself. In the past, Matt had let Dave fly the Cat, and he had flown the Stearman. Matt just sprayed what his hired pilot couldn't get to in time, so he did quite a bit less flying and had time for paperwork, for talking to his farmers, and for all the other tasks involved in running an agricultural flying service. But Dave was an old man, and it had been fitting for him to sit inside an enclosed cockpit out of the buffeting wind. So Tim cheerfully said, "A Stearman's all I've wanted to fly from the beginning!"

"Uh-oh!" Matt said. "Maybe I shouldn't have said I'd take that new Ag Cat!"

"Kidding! Just kidding!"

"Well, if you're real sure you wouldn't mind flying one, I'll borrow a plane and run you over to Yakima to pick it up. By 'new,' I mean new for us, but used by someone else a couple years."

Here we go again! Tim rejoiced. *First a Snow, then a Stearman, and now a Grumman Ag-Cat! How's that for upward mobility?*

* * *

A little after one in the morning some days later, Tim was skimming over a seed field in the newer six-hundred-horsepower biplane when suddenly an incredibly bright light blinded him. It was only his third pass over the field, and he was still packing a ton of payload. He'd been just about ready to ease into a gentle pull-up to clear a line of tall trees at the end of the field.

He jammed prop control and throttle forward and gingerly eased back on the stick. If the load had been lighter, he could have pulled back harder and made a steeper climb to be sure to clear the trees. As it was, he'd have to climb right on the edge of a stall without any visual reference whatsoever. He couldn't dump the load. He was too near the end of the field. One of the flagger boys was down there.

He nursed the stick back until it trembled, signaling an incipient stall. Then, a second later, he heard the sickening sound of the propeller making like a buzz saw.

Even as he shoved the stick forward, knowing that he was in a treetop, he ducked and jammed his brain bucket against the instrument panel. There was no crash pad in the Cat. He swiveled his head and flicked the left-turn light toggle, hoping enough night vision would return in time to give him some idea of whether he was flying or tumbling.

The dazzling afterimage of the blinding light faded. He vaguely glimpsed a large, dark mass sliding over the lower left wing and past the left side of the fuselage. He also saw that the left-turn light had been knocked askew and shone back toward the tail.

The buzz-saw noise had ceased, but the motor was sputtering. Tim raised his head and was able to see the airspeed indicator that registered just under 120 miles an hour, ten miles an hour over its cruise speed, which meant that the Cat was diving. He tugged back on the stick to regain enough altitude to avoid hitting the ground.

The drive lights, which he hadn't thought of clicking off, had been knocked out of commission. He flicked off the useless left-turn light and tried the right one. Just one light canted off to one side of the nose would be some help if he had to put the sputtering Cat down, but it didn't work either.

More altitude would give him more time to make the best of it if the engine quit. He'd also want to be rid of that ton of payload. He immediately turned toward the foothills at the edge of the valley, defined by that vague line between scattered farm lights and the band of unbroken, inky darkness immediately above them. If he had to dump the load, he'd want it to be out where it would cause the least harm. No way would he dump over the populated farming area.

The engine continued to sputter, but it seemed to be putting out about as much power as ever. Oil pressure and oil temperature were normal.

He couldn't imagine what was causing the engine to misfire. Maybe the impact had cracked a jug. But the great news was, since the plane wasn't shaking very badly, he could be pretty confident that he hadn't bent a prop or knocked the engine loose in its mounts. That could cause the engine to vibrate right off.

Once he judged that he was over the foothills, having made sure that he had enough altitude to clear them, he commenced a gentle turn in the general direction of the municipal airport, where he wouldn't have to rely on drive lights for a landing. He could just ease on down between the long, long rows of runway lights until the tires kissed the pavement. He doubted that he'd have to dump the load after all.

Once he was near the airport, Tim began flicking the one operative turn light on and off to get the attention of a control tower operator, and he was very relieved to get an immediate green light to continue. A few minutes later, the tires squeaked onto the asphalt, and a controller in the tower guided Tim over to the transient parking area by shining a spotlight on the taxiways ahead of him.

Tim was looking for the pay phone when he heard the other Cat approaching. Soon Matt landed, taxied up beside Tim's plane, and shut down.

"I'm sure glad you found me!" Tim called out, running back toward his boss.

"One of the flaggers radioed the loading dock. Said he saw you headed this way. Carl's on the way to pick us up. How's the airplane?"

"Running rough. Flew right through a windbreak."

"So I hear. Let's have a look."

In the illumination provided by the airport's security lights, they quickly discovered that all the shadowed spaces among the nine big exposed cylinders were crammed with sappy wood pulp and leaves.

"Look here," Matt said, pointing at one spark plug, then another on the forward face of the big, wheel-like motor. "It tore the leads off some of these plugs on the front of the engine. That's what's making it run rough. The plugs on the back of the cylinders were protected. And look at this."

The prop hub still had faint traces of wood pulp in its shallow declivity. "You hit one of those trees dead on! Boy said he darn near got hit by the treetop when it fell."

"Did he see where that light came from?"

"What light?"

"It was no little flashlight. Got me right in the eyes. Couldn't see a thing."

"Nobody told me anything about a light," Matt said. "I'd better call the sheriff."

* * *

"The damnyankee done had his self a accident," CR said the moment Lance answered his phone.

"And? Spill it!"

"That big beanpole got cat blood in him. Smacked some trees, but he landed on all two feet anyhow."

"Stop beating around the bush!" Lance demanded. "What happened?"

"He was sprayin' in the dark, and somebody done shone a light in his eyes. Hit the trees."

"And?"

"Kep' right on a-flyin'."

Close! Lance thought. *So close!* But he said, just in case, "I sure do hope you didn't have anything to do with that! Get on back here and let him be."

"*Riiight.*"

* * *

Tim called Lisa the day after he hit the tree, but he didn't tell her about it. It would worry her. Instead, he got her to tell him more about her classes, and he asked her whether she was surfing yet.

"Not till you get here," she said. "I don't want to do it alone. I've been doing some things with the teen girls at church."

* * *

On July 21, Matt's wife, Kathy, came dashing out of the house, wildly waving her arms, just after Tim had landed to take on another load. As soon as he got the Cat turned around and had lowered the side window, she shouted, "Neil Armstrong just walked on the moon!"

"Great!" Tim said with feigned enthusiasm, trying to avoid sounding like the uninterested weirdo he had to admit he'd been about all the publicity buildup to a moon landing. Sometimes after 'Nam he felt far, far out of touch with normal people. He just hadn't been able to work up much enthusiasm about the man-on-the-moon thing. "That's just great!"

"Oh, I *guess* great. On the *moon*, for goodness' sake."

Tim had just about enough time before dark to spray another couple loads on some potatoes. If the last load ran into the dark, he had enough night experience now to get by fairly comfortably for a short time using the plane's automatic flagger, instead of flagmen with flashing lights. It was more difficult to get lined up properly without those blinking lights, but he'd already done it before.

"A small step for man, but a giant one for mankind!" Kathy exclaimed. "That's what Neil Armstrong said. *Something* like that."

She kept standing there, expectantly looking up at Tim after Carl had disconnected the loader hose. But all he could think to say in addition was, "We can use all the leaps we can get these days." He saw Matt's plane in the distance. "Here comes Matt. Better get out of his way."

Once she was well clear of the coming prop blast, Tim eased the throttle handle forward to the stop. He latched the side window shut as the Cat accelerated, rocking from side to side and bouncing down the rough strip.

They'd been hard at it both daylight and dark for several weeks now, just catching catnaps whenever they couldn't fly. The alfalfa-seed spraying couldn't be done until the bees "went to bed" when the temperature cooled sufficiently, so there was usually time not only for a relaxed dinner but even a short nap right after sunset.

Leveling off over the valley floor and zipping along toward the distant field at the Cat's normal cruise speed of 110 miles an hour, Tim was guiltily ruminating again about his moon-walk attitude. He had to admit that he was far more excited by the news that the movie, *Easy Rider*, would be showing soon.

But I do have my reasons, he defensively thought. *Big step technologically, but a much bigger step for mankind would be for everybody to just simmer down. What's a walk on the moon if we end up nuking mankind out of existence?*

Only a couple decades had passed since the horrors of Hiroshima and Nagasaki. He was also starkly aware of the millions of deaths brought on by the worldwide expansion of Communism, which threatened worldwide warfare involving weapons far more powerful than the ones dropped in Japan to end World War II. And he still had far more of a mind to resist the spread of Communism than to passively accept it.

No-man's-land, he thought of his isolation from the way American culture seemed to be going. He had some sympathy for the peaceniks who believed that risking the existence of mankind was insane, yet he couldn't imagine Americans peacefully surrendering their freedom to the powers that had made life such hell in Eastern Europe and so much of Asia. What he couldn't figure out was, why weren't the brightest people on earth, such as the scientists and engineers exploring space, able with all that brainpower to reason the world into a lasting peace?

But what about you, Timmy boy? he facetiously thought as he rounded out just above the wheat and shoved the money handle open. *Why aren't you able to reason yourself into some self-control?* He was still ashamed of having lost it so badly when that kid in the restaurant had insulted Sandy. It was one thing to object to such behavior, but he'd gone crazy. There was no other word for it. *Crazy.*

* * *

One windy evening a few days later, Tim was very happy that he didn't have to fly. *Easy Rider* had come to town at last, and Sandy had some time off, too. So, after they'd shared a pizza, off they went to the drive-in theater.

"Can you believe that moon?" Sandy exclaimed. "There must be a forest fire somewhere in the mountains."

The moon was waning but still quite full. On previous nights, Tim had enjoyed spraying in its silvery light; now, however, it was smoky orange.

"It even looks like it's full of smoke," he said.

"Let's put the top up. It's too breezy. Besides, that moon's going to be a distraction."

"From what I've heard about this movie, nothing's going to distract us."

"I don't know," she said, laughing. "That's a pretty romantic moon."

"Even with footprints on it?"

"So long's I don't have to see 'em. Come on. I don't like this wind."

After they'd gotten the top up and were back in their seats, she said, "I'm going to have to be careful about you, Tim O'Reilly."

"Why's that?"

"I really don't want to fall in love again right now."

"Me, neither."

"Maybe next year when you come back we could think about it."

"Maybe we could. Confession: Sometimes I do start thinking the L word about you."

"Me, too."

He reached out for her, but she intercepted his hand with one of hers and pushed it back, saying, "I'm determined, Tim. Sorry. I'm just not going to let it happen right now."

They fell silent, and the movie began a bit later with that Steppenwolf song Tim liked so much, "Born to Be Wild." And here they came, Fonda in his Captain America leathers and Hopper in buckskins and a floppy hat, both riding choppers. However, seeing that the two characters had just made a bunch of money selling cocaine badly detracted from Tim's appreciation of their carefree going down the road.

That, in turn, diverted his attention once again to the uncomfortable fact that he was so out of touch with so many of his generation. Although he had briefly smoked pot in Vietnam, he was against the drugs that so many his age thought were so very cool; and, rather than join their resistance to the war in Vietnam, he'd volunteered, actually hoping for a combat assignment; then, too, a growing number of people would probably think of him as an environmental criminal for his present work; furthermore, men on the moon failed to excite him; and now he had a problem with a movie that critics were predicting would be a great American classic.

When it was over and they had joined all the other cars streaming out of the drive-in, Tim kept trying to figure out why it was receiving such acclaim. *A couple low-life dudes made some bread selling dope, went down the road on bikes to enjoy their big score, and got blown away by some creep. So? What's so great about a story like that?*

So maybe you're just too dumb to see what it was really all about.

"You're awfully quiet, Mr. O'Reilly."

"Yeah. Sorry."

"What's going on?"

"I didn't think it was that great."

"Hey, me neither. It made me feel bad."

"Dairy Queen?"

"Sure. Wait a minute. Now I know. Where were the good guys? Those were all losers. Every one of them."

That made Tim laugh. Knowing more clearly than before that he'd found a kindred spirit in Sandy, he let loose a barrage of thoughts he'd been harboring about what he called "the screwed-up 60s."

"That's what happens when people choose the low life," she said. "Some people think it's so great to rebel against what they call 'the establishment,' but that's how it usually ends. Losers!"

She sounded as though she'd had some experience with it. Tim wondered whether it included the guy who'd made her so leery of falling in love again. She'd never elaborated, and he hadn't wanted to pry.

* * *

It was three days before the big news of the murder of actress Sharon Tate and her four friends that he got sick—so sick that he had plenty of free time to sit around and watch that spectacle develop on TV. He'd grown up not far from Benedict Canyon, the scene of the crime. It was August 6, 1969.

He'd felt increasingly nauseous most of that morning, but he had kept plugging along, hoping that whatever the problem was, it would pass quickly and not leave Matt shorthanded. They were pushing as hard as they could to keep up with the work orders. It would be a very bad time to have to take any time off to have the flu or something.

Just a little touch of food poisoning, he hoped. *Just a passing upset.* He was too careful with the pesticides to have organophosphate poisoning, but some of the stuff in his refrigerator wasn't the freshest. He recalled that some hot dogs he'd eaten had been coated with grease or something. It had seemed unusual, but he'd thought at the time that it must be some new way of keeping dogs fresh. He'd been so hungry and flaky-tired, needing a very quick bite before he hit the sack to wait for bee time, that he'd just wrapped each one in a slice of bread without cooking them, slopped on some mustard and ketchup, and wolfed them down. Maybe the mustard and ketchup had kept him from tasting that they'd gone bad.

Then it happened. He was spreading a load of granular Thimet on a cornfield. It was a light load, so when he started retching, he was able to quickly grab enough altitude that he wouldn't risk running into anything as he bent over and heaved between his legs into the belly of the Cat. There'd been enough warning that he'd thought to hit the trigger on the joystick a couple times to let the automatic flagger drop two tissue streamers in the field so he'd know where to continue later on.

When he could see again, he turned to head for home. Every few minutes, he'd sit upright; then he'd double over and let loose once more. But the heaving stopped before he'd flown half way to Matt's, so he went back to finish the field. Suddenly, he realized that some similar distraction—even a mere sneeze—could have killed Jeremy.

A little later, Matt landed and saw Tim standing on the Cat's wing walk, washing out the plane's belly with the bulky loader hose. The water was draining out the back end of the fuselage.

"What's going on?" Matt asked.

"Ah . . . I just threw up."

"Turn that off and get down here. Carl can do that."

Tim swung the valve handle closed, handed the nozzle to Matt, and climbed down.

Matt stood very near and peered up into his face. "Your eyes," he said. "They're pinpricks, Tim. You're poisoned. Come on. I'm taking you in right now."

He grabbed Tim by the arm and tugged him toward his pickup as he shouted over his shoulder at Carl, "Call the hospital. Tell 'em we're bringing in a man with organophosphate poisoning!"

"I thought it was just a bit of food poisoning," Tim said as they sped away. He wasn't a bit worried about his health because he'd learned in ag-flying school that pilots commonly experienced some minor poisoning, but sometimes they were temporarily grounded for it, which did worry him. "What if they won't let me fly?"

"We'll deal with it. I'll try to find someone to fill in till you can fly again."

"At this time of year?"

"Yeah. Could be tough."

"I know an old guy back in North Dakota. He might be willing to help."

* * *

As it turned out, Tim did have to put up with being grounded. And Matt found a single-plane operator in Washington State's wheat country who was willing to come relieve him for a while. Tim didn't feel awfully bad, but he wouldn't be allowed to fly until his cholinesterase count got down to an acceptable level. He read until he was sick of reading, went for solitary walks in the mountains, spent as much time with Sandy as he could, chatted with Lisa on the phone, and kept up with the news.

He also spent quite a lot of time trying to figure out how he'd been poisoned. As uncomfortable as it was in the summer heat, he'd taken to wearing a respirator since he'd started flying the Cat. He was careful about washing his hands thoroughly with soap and water whenever he had to adjust a malfunctioning spray nozzle, and he seldom handled any of the chemical concentrates, which was Carl's job. He showered at least once a day, and he laundered his work clothes frequently. He didn't use a rag to wipe pesticides off his face shield now that he was in the Cat's enclosed cockpit. He just couldn't imagine how he'd been exposed to enough poison to make him sick.

At first, Tim didn't tell Lisa about the poisoning. He didn't want to worry her with more so soon after the blinding. But the mystery about what had caused the poisoning finally made him mention it.

Then, at noon on August 9, he forgot all about it as his attention was wholly absorbed by news of the mass murder of Sharon Tate, her unborn child, and her friends—another murder so near where he'd grown up. *Dear old Los Angeles!* he thought. *City of angels.* Four of the five victims had been hacked with knives, and "pig" had been scrawled on the front door in blood.

Thoughts of the Watts riots that left more than thirty people dead and RFK's assassination the previous summer flashed through his mind. And now this. He tried to recall such terror in LA before the 60s and couldn't think of a single incident. There had been the normal daily violence, as best he could remember, but nothing like this.

* * *

Tim's cholinesterase readings eventually got back close enough to normal for him to fly again, and he finished the season in good health and high spirits. Except for the two spraying mishaps, hitting the trees and getting sick, it had been a fantastic summer.

Now he'd have a quick look at Seattle, Washington, another at Portland, Oregon, and motor on home through Northern California. Then, after he'd visited with the folks a couple days, he'd be off for Hawaii if Johnny Crash didn't call him down to Nicaragua by then.

21

PARADISE

Long, lunging whitecaps streaked the open ocean a few thousand feet below. Tim imagined how the wind kicking up those whitecaps might be producing some nice shoreline surfing waves, too.

The Boeing 707 had been in a shallow dive for a while now, and the details of the ocean's surface were sharper than they had been for most of the flight, making Tim all the more impatient. He uncomfortably shifted his position in his seat, itching for the moment when he could escape his confinement. He was much too tall to be comfortable in an economy seat. Yet he hadn't wanted to spend so much extra for first class. He hadn't lost sight of his goal of saving enough to carry him the rest of the way through college.

This is taking forever! Five hours!

This flight of only a couple thousand miles over the ocean seemed to be taking almost as long as the ones he'd experienced all the way across the Pacific to and from Vietnam. Nothing— neither the in-flight movie, a *Surfer* magazine he'd bought at the terminal in LA, nor the *Honolulu* magazine in the seat-back pocket before him—had been able to relieve his agony for more than a few minutes at a time.

When will the 747 be ready? he wondered. *It's huge. It can't be this cramped. And if this crate does five hundred, the 747 must do at least five fifty. Maybe I'll get to ride one coming back.*

Soon the jet started to jolt and lurch, setting the overhead baggage bins to rattling, as it passed down through a thin layer of scattered puffy white clouds. He glanced at his watch once more and saw that they were only several minutes shy of their estimated arrival time.

He looked down again and saw that the swells on the sea were slick now, lacking the wind-driven whitecaps that had streaked the open ocean. It was an indication that they must be in the near lee of Oahu, and he sighed with satisfaction. He wished he could see the island. It had to be directly ahead, since all he could glimpse through the windows on either side was the sea.

He tried to visualize the perfect wave, a steep, high, smooth-faced wall of water, rising higher and higher as it swept into the shallows. Then the crest of the blue wall would begin collapsing, breaking snowy-white in one particular spot, and the break would continue across the swell from one side to another, "peeling," in the lingo of some surfers. Or, in some locations, the wave would curl over, forming a tube like that beauty at the beginning of *Hawaii Five-O*. The series had just begun, and he'd made a point of watching.

One place famous for tubular waves was known as the Pipeline, and Tim was eager to get over to the North Shore to have a look at it. However, he wouldn't do that the first day. Instead, he wanted to start shopping immediately for some kind of cheap used car to knock around in for a couple weeks or so.

He'd rent a car until he found one to buy, but he hated the thought of paying rental-car fees for more than a couple days. If he could get a deal on a vehicle that would suffice to get him to the surf, it wouldn't matter if he didn't break even when he sold it. He'd still be money ahead. He'd have to buy a local paper and check the ads. He might have time for a look at a couple used-car lots, too. Thanks to Lisa's cluing him in, he already had an inexpensive room reserved at the YMCA near Waikiki. But whatever he did, he didn't want to be late meeting her.

Hydraulic motors began to whine, driving down the wide flaps from the trailing edges of the long, flexing wings, adding to the shuddering caused by the turbulence. Tim pressed the side of his head against the small double-paned side window to try to see the island. Soon the famous southeastern promontory, Diamond Head, edged into view five to ten miles away. There, too, slowly appeared the long white beach and numerous tall hotels of Waikiki. Waves were making thin white lines at Waikiki, and he wondered whether they were big enough to be worth riding.

As the plane drew still nearer and the view of the island broadened, he began to see a small part of the jagged and luminescent green mountains not far inland. They rose steeply and were deeply and invitingly cut with shadowed emerald valleys, and Tim wondered how it would be to hike into them.

The jet continued its rough descent, jinking around in the turbulent air, and he observed the woman sitting next to him fearfully grasp the armrests. She was clenching them so tightly that the backs of her pudgy hands had turned much whiter than her chubby alabaster forearms.

"It's the wind that makes it so rough," he said, hoping his casual tone might relieve her anxiety. "It breaks over the mountains and rolls. Like ocean waves."

She did not reply, and her hands did not relax. She continued to rigidly stare at the high back of the seat ahead of her.

The sea below turned chalky-green and murky, and the huge plane descended very close above it. Then a beach of sun-bleached coral rubble suddenly slanted up out of the milky water. The smooth dark gray end of a tarmac runway displaced the coral, and the whistling roar of the jet's engines ceased. The wheels slammed roughly onto the asphalt.

Tim grinned and thought, *Wake up, Mr. Pilot! Time to do some flying!* He humorously imagined how the guy must have been idly lounging for five hours with the autopilot doing all the work until he'd finally had to sit up and take the controls.

The pilot shifted the engines into reverse thrust and added power, causing the jet to decelerate so swiftly that it pitched the passengers forward against their seatbelts. Tim grinned wider and wider, anticipating his escape from the cloying confinement of his cramped seat.

Then a look of utter amazement suddenly displaced the grin, and his head whipped hard right.

Ya gotta be kidding!

He had only a few seconds to glimpse the two parked Stearmans out his small window, but it was long enough for him to be sure that they were dusters. Then the big airliner was turning onto a taxiway to proceed in the opposite direction.

Pineapple spraying, he guessed.

* * *

His thoughts kept flashing back to those two biplanes as he signed the car-rental papers, got into the vehicle, and followed the signs leading him toward the highway to Honolulu. However, when he saw that the road was taking him past the north end of the runway where he'd seen the two dusters, he couldn't resist taking a little detour, turning right instead of left toward the highway. He parked in front of a big metal building bearing a sign reading, "Aloha Dusters," and went in.

"Hello!" said an attractive Oriental woman in a nice flower-print dress. She smiled and rose from her chair at one of the desks behind a counter. "How may I help you?"

"I saw those Stearmans when we landed. There's crop dusting in Hawaii?"

"Oh, yes. We'd be fertilizing right now if it weren't so windy."

"I had no idea. I'm a crop duster myself. Okay if I drop by when I get settled?"

"Why don't you talk to our manager now? I'm sure he'd like to see you."

He liked the sweet, musical quality of her voice. It was a lot like the voice of the darker woman who had rented him the Chevy. "Well . . . " He did want to get on his way. Yet he really was eager to know more. "Sure!" he said. "Why not? For just a minute."

She went into a private smaller office at the rear of the large front office, and a stooped, thin young man in a loud aloha shirt—bright yellow background and deep blue palm trees—came rushing out. He yanked a big cigar out of his mouth as he approached and gave Tim an exuberant, "Hey, there!"

Tim beamed at the sight of him. The man looked very much like Groucho Marx, and he was so obviously happy.

The man rapidly strode up to the counter and stuck out a thin, deeply tanned hand for a shake. "Solly Greenberg!"

"Tim O'Reilly."

"Aloha! Come on back!" Greenberg quickly moved a few steps and yanked open a low swinging door in an opening through the counter, motioning with his free hand for Tim to enter. Tim had to hurry to keep up with him as they went to the cubicle. Solly Greenberg was half a foot shorter than Tim and much skinnier. His skin was so dark that it made Tim wonder whether he surfed.

Greenberg flung a hand at one of the two upholstered chairs before his desk and hustled around to his own swivel chair, flopping down. "So, how much time do you have?" he asked.

"Just a few minutes. I need—"

The man rocked back in his chair and burst out laughing. Then, with a wide grin spread beneath his dark mustache, he rocked forward and said, "*Flying* time. *Ag*-flying time. She told me you're a duster driver."

"Well, I've only—"

The man threw up one bony hand like a traffic cop signaling "stop!" Before Tim could say any more, Greenberg said, "We require five hundred hours ag time." His hand was still up, and Tim started thinking he was a pretty strange character.

Greenberg madly puffed on his stogie for a few moments, then took it out and tapped the ash into a very large glass or crystal ashtray. "Keeps our insurance rates down," he explained. He finally lowered the hand that had signaled "stop," but he kept his dark eyes locked intently on Tim's.

"I've got—" Tim started to say, but Greenberg jabbed "stop" at him again. Tim sharply exhaled in exasperation. He'd been about to say that he'd logged 634 hours of ag time so far.

"Let's go for a ride!" Greenberg heaved himself out of his chair.

"A ride?"

"In the two-holer. Come on!" He was already heading out the door.

Tim beamed again. A little tour in a light plane would give him a lot better picture of the island than all the reading and photo gazing he'd been doing lately. He glanced at his watch.

"I don't have much time," he said. "I have to meet somebody."

"We'll make it fast. Maybe a half hour."

This is fantastic, Tim thought as he hurried to keep up. *This dude is strange, but he sure is nice. I wonder if we'll get over to the North Shore.*

"Hey, Ola!" Greenberg shouted as they entered the adjacent hangar. There were several dark-skinned men applying fabric to a couple partially covered wings resting on big worktables. The largest one looked up. "Come give us a hand with the two-holer."

They shoved the unmodified two-seat biplane onto the concrete hangar apron outside and got the little 220-horsepower motor started.

"You fly," Greenberg said. "I'll sit up front and handle the radio."

Soon they were stopped beside the nearest taxiway onto the nearest of two parallel runways, waiting as two long lines of distantly spaced airplanes landed. Greenberg was still puffing on his cigar. There were military transports and fighters, big and small airliners, and private planes. But at last a control-tower operator said, "Stearman five seven Victor cleared for takeoff on four right. Expedite. Oil burner on short final."

At an altitude of 400 feet, Greenberg wagged his hand a couple times to the left, and Tim banked away from the rising hillside as he continued climbing through the rough, jarring air. Greenberg couldn't speak to Tim over the radio, since they were still necessarily tuned in to the tower frequency.

Once Tim had completed a ninety-degree turn to the west, still climbing, he could see some large medium-green fields on the slopes above a subdivision off to the right a mile or so away. The wind was rippling the fields, making it look like they were full of some kind of very tall grass.

Below and to the left lay several great lochs that fanned out from one inlet on the seacoast, and some were ringed with docks and many gray ships. *Pearl Harbor,* Tim thought, but he didn't have time to reflect on it, and he got even busier monitoring all the air traffic around him. There were more aircraft far out to sea, up and down the coast and almost directly below him now. The ones below were landing and taking off from an airport on a small island within Pearl Harbor. Then he began to see that many square miles of lowlands to the west and northwest were green with great fields that had the same look as the first few at the edge of the city.

After Tim had flown on for a while, Greenberg began jabbing a finger downward. Tim strained to see what he might be pointing at. There just wasn't much out there, other than whatever that tall, grassy-looking stuff was. Greenberg turned his head around as far as it would go, as if he was asking Tim what the problem was. He jabbed the finger downward again. He made quite a sight up there, his cigar jutting out of his brown goggled face and the sleeve of his loud blue-and-yellow aloha shirt flapping in the slipstream as he made his hand an airplane and gestured for Tim to descend.

Tim eased the stick forward, heading on down close to the grassy-looking, wind-whipped ground cover. The wind gusts rolled across it like waves in the sea. Then Tim noticed a low crop of something not much farther inland. The individual plants were more obviously laid out in rows, and lines of reddish earth showed vividly between them. But that was too distant to be what Greenberg had been pointing to. Finally, however, Tim discerned what he was supposed to see.

It was a short, narrow airstrip. The main reason Tim recognized it was that what otherwise would have looked like a narrow road that ended abruptly without seeming to get anywhere in particular. The far end "T"d into a long public road, but the near end terminated where there was nothing more than that same tall grass, which also pressed up against the sides of the strip.

Greenberg kept jabbing a finger at it as Tim flew by. When Tim still hadn't caught on, Greenberg made a plane with the palm of his hand and a landing motion.

You land it! Tim thought. He waggled the stick to communicate the thought. That wind was pretty stiff, and it was blowing almost directly across the strip. He wasn't about to take a chance on pranging the guy's airplane. But Greenberg hitched around in his seat and insistently jabbed a forefinger directly at him.

Maybe he's never landed on an ag strip, Tim thought. *Pilot, but not an ag pilot. Hey, what if he's airsick?*

Now he did want to land very much—crosswind or not—and quickly. He imagined the guy tossing his cookies and the prop blast blowing it back over the rear cockpit. He whipped a tight turn back toward the strip. He shaved the power lines that ran along the roadside, cut power, and eased back on the stick to let the plane sink flatly toward the ground.

Then they were in the trough between the tall, whipping grass on either side and bouncing around, much as the airliner had. The critical difference was, that tall grassy vegetation was only several feet from either set of wingtips. It was much taller than he'd thought. It was taller than the Stearman.

Seeing now that he had a fair length of airstrip left ahead, Tim eased the throttle forward to have more control with a power-on landing. He eased the stick to the right to get the right wings cocked down into the gusting wind, but he counteracted the biplane's tendency to turn in that direction by applying left rudder.

He felt the right tire touch, and he slowly reduced power, ready to shove the throttle forward again should a strong gust threaten to blow the tail around. However, he was able to counteract the wind with rudder alone, and when the tail wheel touched the ground, he pulled the stick all the way back, and there was no longer any danger of the landing going haywire. At the end of the strip, he discovered that he had very little room and had to lock up one brake and blow a bunch of prop blast back at the rudder to turn around.

Greenberg unbuckled and flung his seat belt and shoulder harness straps over the sides of his cockpit. He turned around until he was kneeling in his seat, facing Tim, and he pulled off the canvas-and-rubber flying helmet that contained the earphones. He removed the stogie from his mouth and said, "You didn't switch frequencies?"

Tim shook his head. If they were outside the airport control zone now, it wasn't by a mile or more.

Greenberg shrugged and, giving Tim a big, nonchalant smile, said, "Okay. That landing was good. Time to time, we have a pilot come all the way over here and find out he can't handle what we got. Sometimes we do fertilize in a pretty good wind. Now I want you to simulate a few runs across the cane."

"Cane?"

"Sugarcane. You didn't know that's what this is?"

Tim shook his head and asked, "And what's that up the slope a ways? Pineapple?"

"Yeah, but our big deal is cane. Anyhow, make like you're working. Stay up at power-line height like you're fertilizing." He turned around and started buckling himself in.

What the heck is this? Tim wondered. *An audition?*

Recovering from his surprise, Tim was about to ask the question out loud, but Greenberg had already slipped his old-fashioned cloth helmet with the big black rubber earphone mounts over his head. He was swinging his hairy brown arm cavalry-charge style again.

This dude thinks I want to fly for him!

Tim started the takeoff roll toward the road, thinking, *I wonder if it's just to have my name on file or if they need a guy now?* He wasn't really all that eager to go back to work so soon. He'd come mainly to surf.

Still, a crop-dusting job in Hawaii! Some other time, maybe?

He made a few mock fertilizer passes and tight, vertical, P-shaped dusting turns over the cane. Then, before he remembered to switch his radio to intercom, he followed Greenberg's hand signals toward wherever they were going next.

"You need to get some altitude," Greenberg said, his voice coming in now. "We're going to be crossing over that Army airfield up there."

They ascended the higher slopes, and Greenberg soon radioed to request permission to cross through the Army's airspace that occupied the pass between the near ends of Oahu's two long, forested mountain spines. Then, crossing over the crest of the pass, they headed downhill with the sea in the distance ahead and miles of sugarcane in between. Greenberg directed Tim to a landing site that looked a lot trickier than the crosswind strip he'd landed on earlier.

This strip was cut directly into a very steep hillside with a high bulldozed cutbank along one side, a steep dropoff into a gully on the other, and tall trees on the uphill end. The jungle-filled ravine passed along the edge of the one side then curved around to run down toward the sea in line with the strip. That low end of the strip also dropped sharply into the ravine. Tim felt very relieved when Greenberg had him only circle it a couple times, then proceed diagonally down the steep and rugged hillside of cane. All of the sugar fields were irregularly shaped on the higher, steeper, more rugged slopes, their borders simply conforming to the narrow, wooded gulches and ravines that snaked down toward the sea.

Tim guessed that he had passed his flight test and that Greenberg was now showing him some of the strips he thought Tim would be using. It was so tempting a thought that he didn't just pick up his mike and ask, for fear that Greenberg might not want to hire him after all.

He considered the possibilities, thinking, *Maybe one of those guys he said couldn't hack it just went down the road. Left them in the lurch. If so, maybe I could just fill in a week or two until they get somebody.*

They angled on down the rugged cane slopes toward the shore off to the left. It looked desolate past the cane in that direction, but back to the right stretched the North Shore of worldwide surfing fame. Tim had studied a map of the island well enough to know that the one little town on the shore over to the right must be Haleiwa. He'd heard some surfers mention it back home, and he'd located it on his map.

In the direction they were headed, a large, deserted airfield without buildings or airplanes came into view. There were wide paved rectangles among the trees where there must have been base facilities at some time in the past. The cane fields ended close by the airfield, and its single long runway lay between a sharply rising, forested mountainside near the inland side and a narrow, sandy beach near the other, but the waves were no good and empty of surfers.

A few minutes later, having rounded a sharp point that jutted out from the steep mountainsides, Tim finally did get to see some surfers ahead. He aimed the plane lower. Greenberg didn't seem to care as Tim took it down to about power-line height above the swells. As they bypassed the rocky point on the near side of the bay where the waves began to unzip, Tim could see that the surfers were getting some very nice rides. He flew about a hundred yards seaward of the surfers, and some of those sitting astraddle their boards, waiting their turns, waggled that same weird sign with their thumbs and pinkies that some of the surfers back home had started making.

The shoreline continued to run very near the unpopulated mountainsides, and there were small communities of small, simple homes nestled in diminutive valley after valley. Then a large and active airport came into view, Greenberg pointed at one of his earphones with one hand and made a dial-twisting motion with the other. Then he called on the radio, which identified the airport to Tim as Barbers Point Naval Air Station, for permission to pass through their control zone. That's where Tim had spent a night on the way home from Vietnam.

A quarter hour later, when they parked on the apron in front of the hangar at Honolulu International and shut off the motor, Greenberg said, "Let's go fill out the paperwork. I think you're the one we're looking for."

"I might not be able to stay. I might have to go to Nicaragua."

"Might? That'll work. You'll be helping us out of a jam either way. You can turn that rental back in and use the spare pickup. We'll . . . "

* * *

Tim sat in the lobby of the YWCA and waited for Lisa to come down from her room. The Fernhurst Y was a very nice building located a couple miles inland from Waikiki in a mixed-housing neighborhood of lush lawns and widely spreading shade trees. Lisa had said it was an easy stroll of just a few minutes from the university. However, although he did appreciate how nice and convenient it was, he kept grinning over the news he had for her.

A strong surge of emotion unexpectedly filled him when she appeared, and he thought anew how strange it was that he had such affection for her. Lisa's sweet, round face radiated her delight at seeing him, too, and they hurried to each other. She tipped her head forward against his chest, and he lowered his face into her thick and fragrant hair for just a moment.

"It's so good to have you here," she said, laughing and quickly stepping back. How her blue eyes sparkled when she said that!

"I missed you," he said, trusting that she knew without his saying more how very much he cared for her.

"You look different somehow," she said, eyeing him. "I know. You've put on some weight."

"Yeah, I have." He grinned. He had an appetite again. He'd let his belt out two notches since North Dakota, but it wasn't that he was getting fat. He was simply able to enjoy life once more, despite his one relapse into rage in Idaho.

"Shall we?" She took his hand and led him outside.

He almost told her about his new seat right then, but he changed his mind. He just wanted to stroll along with her for a minute and enjoy a few quiet moments in that luxurious atmosphere so powerfully charged with floral fragrance, lush greenery, and mutual affection.

With Lisa happily chattering away, they went on down the sidewalk past a couple cars until they got to the battered company pickup that Greenberg had loaned him. There were dark rust spots on it where the green paint had chipped, and a couple-hundred-gallon gas tank with a hand pump rose out of the bed just behind the cab. A circular sign bearing a picture of a banking Stearman duster and the words "Aloha Dusters" covered most of the door panel below the side window. Tim stopped beside it, opened the door, and waved her in.

She halted and looked up at him with her mouth hanging open. Then she said, "What in the dickens is *this*?"

"Is that incredible or what?" he said, laughing. "How's that for a coincidence?"

"What is going *on*?"

"I got another seat is what. Come on. I'll tell you on the way."

She suggested that he drop his things at the YMCA on Atkinson, where he'd reserved a room for two weeks, and then they could get some sandwich makings for an impromptu picnic at the beach.

"And I'll get a newspaper," he said. "I'd like to check the ads for a car. Boss says I can use this backup truck as long as I want, but I want to have a look anyway."

When they arrived at the Y where he'd be staying, he was delighted to see that it was not only a very decent-looking place for such a low rate but was across the street from a beach park. Immediately to the west sprawled a huge, two-story mall, where there would be restaurants and, surely, a bookstore. He wanted to keep reading up on the island to be sure he didn't miss something important.

Lisa saw several coin-operated newsstands on the sidewalk and bought a *Honolulu Advertiser* while Tim went inside to register and drop off his suitcase. When he returned, she directed him to a small market in the mall, where they bought some food and drinks. Then she had him drive right around the corner into the Waikiki district and on past all the hotels into a coastal residential area and onto Diamond Head Beach Road, a little spur that ended just below the narrow main road that went around Diamond Head. They climbed down the low bluff to a small strip of sand with the extinct volcano rising steeply behind them, and Tim was pleased that there were very few other people present.

It was a quiet place, for the breaking of the small waves in the lagoon pleasantly muted the sounds of the cars passing along the main road above them. If the two other couples sitting some distance away were talking, Tim couldn't hear them.

Like the several other couples there, he and Lisa sat side by side, facing the sea. Wavelets lapped up to a couple yards of their bare feet, his huge, boney white things with their gross black hair and her shapely, lightly tanned ones. He removed the classified-ads section of the paper and handed the rest to her. There was so little wind in the lee of the high volcanic cone immediately behind them that the free corners of the opposing pages barely moved.

"So?" she asked after a while.

"Cars aren't cheap here, are they?"

"I never noticed."

"Well, I just need something reliable for a short time. I don't care what it looks like. I told the boss I'd probably be moving on to Nicaragua pretty soon. But I'd still kind of like to have my own car here if possible."

"Will you really do that, Tim?"

"Nicaragua? Yeah, Johnny Crash says they try to hire the nationals down there, but they have a tough time getting good, experienced ones. He says one of the operators will probably get tired of beginners wrecking planes and be ready before long for another American."

"Are you hungry yet?"

"Sure. I'm ready if you are."

She began setting things out, sandwich makings for him, just brown bread and some salami, which was all he'd wanted, a "bento box" for her, and a couple cold cans of Hawaiian guava juice.

"Not to ruin your appetite, but I still think that looks pretty weird," he said, eyeing her small box with the clear-plastic top. "What's that black stuff?"

"Black? Dark green, actually. See?" She unsnapped the lid and lifted one of the small cylinders so he could see it clearly, and he jerked his head away. "Silly," she said, "It's just seaweed. It's a kind of sushi. It's delicious, and it's very healthful. You must have a taste."

"No way!"

"Tim! There's so much tasty variety here in the islands! You're really going to miss out on some wonderful experiences if you don't at least try things."

"I want to try that salami and good old American bread."

"Here, I'll make it for you."

"I can do it."

"No, let me. You aren't afraid the recipe will confuse me, are you? I mean, just salami and bread? What kind of sandwich is that?"

"My kind. A good-enough kind for somebody like me."

She laid the thin slices on a piece of bread, then covered them with another slice. She leaned against him and tendered the sandwich toward his mouth, saying, "Here, I'll feed you. Come on now. Open your little mouthie."

"You're crazy."

"I know. Crazy happy. I'm so glad you're here. My old friend *Wayne*. Come on. Take a bite."

He gave in, bit, and chewed as he shook his head at her.

"Here's another."

"Give me that thing!" He snatched the sandwich away from her. "Just feed yourself! And don't expect me to look while you're doing it!"

They fell silent as they ate. A dove gently cooed somewhere in the strip of brush and scrubby trees behind them. Wavelets softly lapped at the pale sand.

"Do you smell the gardenias?" she asked after a while.

"I smell something fantastic."

"Gardenia. I'm learning all about them. Gardenia, plumeria, *mokihana* . . . That's a Hawaiian name."

"Yeah, the sea smells good, too. The smells here are amazing."

"Fragrances. Not smells, not odors." She giggled.

"Yeah, yeah. Whatever."

"I'm so glad you were able to come."

"Yeah. This is incredible."

22

A NEW RIDE, A KISS, AND A SCHEME

S o," Tim said. "Ready for brunch?" They had agreed that they'd sleep in a little, and he'd call her at the appointed time. He suddenly felt very hungry. "Half an hour?"

"Tim! I'm still in my jammies! An hour!"

"What?" He smiled as he pictured her in jammies. For some unknown reason, he imagined long-sleeved, long-legged blue-and-white-striped flannel PJs. Cute and maybe practical, too, since the nights would be cooler up where she was at Fernhurst. His vision of her included her wonderful, thick golden hair gathered into two puffy bunches, one on either side, which was how he'd glimpsed her once at home in Oklahoma. "Flannel jammies? I think I have ESP. Stripes?"

"None of your business. An hour, okay?"

"Okay," he said, chuckling. An hour really was okay with him. He could use the time to look at some cars on his own. They had planned to have breakfast somewhere, shop for his car together, and do a little sightseeing. "I'll be there in an hour."

It was 8:30 on his second Saturday morning in Hawaii, and he had the whole weekend off. That's the way it usually went, according to Solly, his boss. The plantations provided two flagmen per pilot and strictly limited the flagmen's overtime. Tim had never heard of a forty-hour workweek in ag flying before. In Hawaii, work began at seven o'clock, there was a half-hour lunch break, and quitting time was three thirty, Monday through Friday. There was one other pilot on that island, Oahu, and a few others on the other sugar-growing islands, and they all usually followed the same schedule.

At first Tim had thought about buying something like the ratty old Dodge he'd driven from California to Mississippi and then on to Oklahoma, something he could dump in a hurry without losing much money. But now he was thinking of making another effort to try dating. He'd met his senior loader man's cousin, an entrancing young lady named Lei, at a luau, and Punchy had told him she'd probably go out with him if he asked. He definitely did need to start dating someone again some time, but he wouldn't take a girl on a date in a heap anything like the old Dog. He never gave a thought to running Lisa around in Aloha's ratty old spare truck, but she wasn't really a date.

The Atkinson Street YMCA had a little restaurant downstairs, and he got a cup of coffee there after he'd grabbed an *Advertiser*. He rapidly scanned the latest car ads but still didn't find anything very interesting. So he hurried off in the pickup to drive by a couple nearby car lots that he'd noticed before.

As he drove, he tried to picture Lei's face, but he couldn't get a clear enough image to satisfy him. He had no trouble recalling what she'd been wearing—the shape of it anyway, if not the exact pattern. It was a clinging sort of sheath that made him think *sarong*, and a print of some kind of delicate greenery on a pale background. He visualized her sinuous hula dance on Punchy's lawn in the flickering firelight. Some of the people had brought their ukes and acoustic guitars, and the entire crowd had sung, mostly in the Hawaiian language.

He'd have to be very careful if he dated anyone like that. He could easily imagine himself falling in love for all the wrong reasons at this point. Jen, the one great true love in his life, had been perfect. They'd fallen for each other after a few casual encounters on campus had established that she had a lot more going for her than her looks, although she certainly was one foxy-looking lady, too. Jen was every bit as attractive as Lei, but their love for each other had gone far beyond mere physical attraction. Physical attraction, however, when it came to Lei, was the accelerant that had started Tim's present fire in his innards. How that slender but curvaceous young Hawaiian had moved!

Punchy had made a big bonfire in the earthen pit where he had baked a whole pig earlier, and Lei's movements in her clinging sheath—her supple twisting and turning, rising and falling—seemed one with the movements of the leaping flames in the pit. He'd never in his life seen anyone move like that. It was downright magical.

"Why you no ax her out?" Punchy had asked the following Monday at work. They'd been standing side by side at an airstrip, waiting for the Stearman to warm up. "She no mo' boyfren' ri' now. She looked like she enjoy talking to you." Punchy had then jabbed Tim with a thick brown elbow and kidded, "Maybe us could be cousin-in-law or somet'ing!"

Asking Lei out sure would be a lot easier than trying to get to know some complete stranger. He had made a couple attempts to chat with some ringless clerks at Ala Moana Center so far, and he'd actually been relieved when they hadn't shown any interest. They were nice, and they were reasonably attractive, but he'd just been going through the motions, trying with mind alone to make more progress in resuming normal life. He wasn't only going through the motions in his attraction to Lei, and it would be a good idea to have a fairly presentable car if he did end up dating her. Renting a car for a date seemed such a waste.

He suddenly hit the brakes and craned his neck. He'd been more or less absently gazing at a line of used cars he'd been passing. Now, focusing on one old blue station wagon that had caught his eye, he was a hundred percent back in the here and now. He hurried around the block and pulled in between the sales office and the row of cars facing Kalakaua Avenue.

A slim, nicely dressed guy with dark, glistening skin hurried out to greet him. "Hi!" he said. "I'm Ben Polacol." He reached out, and they shook hands. "How can I help you?"

"That station wagon," Tim said. "I'd like to take a closer look."

"The '56 Chevy? Nice car."

They went over to it. The interior was in excellent shape, and Tim considered how impervious to salt-water-wet surfing shorts the plastic seats would be.

"Shall we take it for a spin?" Ben suggested.

"I have to pick someone up pretty quick. But I would like to hear what the engine sounds like."

Ben went to get the key, and Tim slowly walked all the way around the wagon, noting that there was still plenty of tread on all four tires. He noted some small rusty spots where minor dings had exposed the metal to the elements, but it was just light surface rust.

"Here we are!" Ben said, returning with the key. He started the engine and popped the hood release.

Tim propped up the hood and leaned over the motor. It was just a straight-line six, but that was okay with him. All he wanted was something reliable that looked okay. This wagon would actually look quite a bit more than okay with a surfboard atop its long, flat roof.

"Sounds good, doesn't it?" asked Ben.

"Yeah, it does. I'll be back in a few minutes."

* * *

"There!" Tim said to Lisa as they approached the car lot. "See it?" It wasn't one of those classic California-surfer woodies, but now that he was seeing it a second time, he was sure it was what he wanted so long as it ran okay.

"You're back!" Ben said, hurrying over to them. He held up the keys and, smiling, jangled them with a humorous look in his dark eyes.

Tim liked the guy's style. He wasn't a bit pushy, and he seemed genuinely friendly.

"Nice, huh?" Tim said to Lisa a couple minutes later, cruising up Kalakaua. She was sitting beside him, and Ben was in the back seat.

Several times, Tim glanced into the rearview mirror, and he was amused to see Ben casually relaxing with one dark bare arm draped along the seat back and the other on the bottom of the open window, smiling and apparently just enjoying the perfect air burbling in through the four open windows and rippling his dressy dark-blue aloha shirt. He was about Tim's age. He saw Tim glance back at him a couple times, and he smiled as if he was just joyriding with friends and wasn't focused on making a sale.

Tim stopped at a red light, and when it turned green, he accelerated faster than he normally would have. He also held the wagon in first and second gear longer than normal to put some added stress on the engine. It revealed nothing more than a reasonable howl of protest from the six-cylinder engine.

"Why don't you take it out on the highway?" Ben suggested. "Runs well, doesn't it?"

"It does," Tim agreed. "I just need something reliable that'll get me to work and out to the North Shore."

"It will do that. You live on the North Shore?"

"No, at the Atkinson Y. I like to surf on the north side."

"Hey, so do I. What do you do?"

"I'm a crop duster."

"What's that?"

"I use an airplane to fertilize sugarcane."

"Oh. I never knew about that. I saw the sign on the truck, and I wondered what it meant. Fertilizer from the sky?"

"From the sky." Tim looked back in the rearview and grinned. "About thirty feet up in the sky. A couple feet up in the sky when we spray weeds."

"There's so much I don't know about. But I'm something like a pilot. Not like you, though. I've usually got my head *way* up in the clouds. I'm taking a break from the university to earn some money. One of my dad's friends is the sales manager, so . . . " He let the rest go unsaid.

"I'm on a break from school, too," Tim said. "What's your major?"

"Philosophy. Actually, I already have a BA in philosophy. I plan to go on to grad school."

"Philosophy? No kidding? I was a business major, but I got way more interested in philosophy electives than business."

"We've got a lot in common. Whether you buy a car or not, drop around anytime. We'll talk philosophy. Or surfing. Maybe we could go catch a wave or two."

"Lisa's at UH. She's majoring in English."

Tim turned onto the freeway as Lisa and Ben made small talk about UH. He punched the station wagon up to sixty, listening intently for the least indication of anything wrong with the engine or tranny, but he couldn't sense a thing amiss with either one. He rocked the steering wheel back and forth, and he stood on the brakes a couple times, but the suspension was tight, and the brakes were sound.

"I'll take it," he said as he slowed to get off the freeway.

"Good choice! How much are you offering?"

"What you said. Four twenty. This thing's in great shape."

"I think so, too. We'll give you a warranty, of course, just in case. So how about three seventy-five?"

"Why not?" Tim replied, and he laughed, looking back in the rearview. He thought the guy was joking.

"Deal," said Ben. "We'll make a decent profit, and you'll get your money's worth."

"Are you serious?"

"I take it you think it's a fair price."

"Of course!"

"Three eighty-five then."

"You said three seventy-five!"

"You drive a hard bargain. Done."

They did the paperwork, and Tim and Ben escorted Lisa back to the wagon. She'd drive it to the airport, where Tim would drop off the pickup. "Hey, thanks again, Ben," he said. "I really do appreciate everything."

"No *pilikia*. Come back anytime. If I'm not selling a car, we'll get our heads *way* up there. Drop by."

"I'll do that," Tim said. "See ya."

Ben headed back toward the office, and Tim opened the wagon's door for Lisa, saying, "What a guy, huh?" He laughed again at Ben's weird deal.

"Yes. Nice. So many people here are that way."

A half hour later as he and Lisa returned to the city from the airport after dropping off the pickup, Lisa asked, "Have you been out the coast past Diamond Head?"

"Not yet. I'd like to."

So they drove through downtown Honolulu, past the university district and out through Kaimuki. The seashore came back into view after a while, but Tim didn't find it very interesting. The reef was far across a murky lagoon, and the waves that broke onto the reef were not noteworthy.

The highway crossed over a hill of reddish cinders and took them onto a narrow ledge cut into a high sea cliff. A small cliffside viewing area appeared, and Tim pulled over. They got out of the station wagon and stepped up to a low masonry wall.

It was a dramatic view. To their immediate right, a high promontory that seemed to be a single gargantuan stone jutted away from them into rough deep-blue water. Great blue swells smashed spectacularly into the part of the cliff that faced them directly, exploding into soaring white shards. Directly below them, a crescent-shaped sand beach curved outward toward a low rocky point to the left.

The same parallel lines of glinting deep-blue ocean swells topped by whitecaps that swept in from the open sea to smash into the cliff also broke in the shallows fronting the sandy beach and out in front of the flat, low lava point just beyond the sand. The first swimmers that Tim spotted were getting short rides in the brutal-looking, overcurling break right in front of the sand. Some had swim fins on their feet, and some of those with fins were riding short boogie boards.

"Body surfing," Tim commented disdainfully, watching most of the people in the sandy shallows get knocked around by the crashing waves. He shook his head with a typical board surfer's sense of superiority.

Then he noticed that a few, some of those with boogie boards and some without, were getting fairly decent short rides by cutting sharply across the face of the shore break as it curled over them. Still, it looked like very poor sport compared with the much longer rides on a regular surfboard that he was used to. But that impression came before Tim noticed a few swimmers beyond the far end of the beach and out in front of a low shelf of lava that, combined with the high black seacliff, formed the cove in which lay the crescent of white sand. What had drawn his attention to that small group was their flailing rush to deeper water and safety from an approaching set of much bigger swells.

The first of the series broke in one spot far out in front of the lava shelf, and one of the swimmers, who was precisely where it first began to break, turned to speed shoreward on it. He kept right at the edge of the progressively breaking white water, angling away from the low, rocky shelf and toward the sandy beach. He was getting a much longer ride on that gradually breaking wave than the body surfers right in front of the sand.

Seeing how that one surfer's body bounced along just within the edge of that white turbulence, Tim knew the guy had to be experiencing quite a rush. Tim had fooled around in some of the shore breaks near home when he'd been a boy, but that had been nothing like what he was witnessing now. He'd heard that there were similar body-surfing conditions at a couple places back home, but he'd never been curious enough about it to go have a look.

"I gotta do that!" he exclaimed, now that he'd seen that there might be a bit more to some body surfing than he'd presumed.

"Me, too!"

Tim swung his head toward Lisa, and he opened his mouth to say, "No way!" On second thought, he shut it. She had no idea what power there was in waves such as those. Yet there was no reason she couldn't start surfing the shore break on a calmer day.

A calmer day for both of us, he thought. He knew very well from his board-surfing experience back home how foolish it was for strangers to jump right into rough water without cautiously testing the local conditions.

"Well, let's see what else we can see," he said, turning away from the scene. He let her back into the station wagon and thought with profound contentment, *Man, what a place to be a five-day-a-week ag pilot! What more could a guy ask for?*

* * *

That evening Tim parked on the little side street next to Fernhurst and began to walk Lisa to the entrance in front. She reached out to tug at his hand and halted.

"Tim." Her voice was strangely husky. She quickly stepped up before him when he turned. There was enough illumination from the streetlights and the light falling out of the windows of the rooms that he could faintly see her looking at him very oddly. She reached up to the back of his neck. She pulled his head forward as she rose to her toes and kissed him on the mouth.

He found himself responding. They both staggered a little, and their lips parted long enough for them to catch their breath. Then they kissed again, and their hands flew over each other.

Time passed, and their embrace got more intense.

"Come!" he said. He tugged her toward the station wagon. They climbed in and immediately reached for each other again. The shadowed sidewalks were vacant. No cars passed by, except for an occasional one out on the main road.

"Tell me you love me!" she said.

That did it. It was over. He did love her, but not that way. He felt like a creep for going as far as he had.

* * *

"Way to go, CR!"

The young farmhand was in the front seat, and Lance was in the back, shouting into his mike. CR had just softly touched the T-6's main wheels on the muny's blacktop runway, and he was adding power to complete the touch-and-go landing with Lance's coaching.

"Now take us on home and we'll call it a day. I'll do the landing there if you don't mind." Lance wasn't about to ruin CR's latest flight by having him try to land on the narrow home strip. He was consciously going all out to maximize CR's sense of loyalty.

After Lance had landed, he taxied the plane down the private farm road from the strip to the shop. After they'd climbed out of their separate cockpits and down to the ground, Lance complimented CR again. "Let me shake that grimy paw of yours!" He whacked the little guy on the shoulder as they shook hands and said, "You may be an ugly little mess, but you sure are quick to catch on to some things." He laughed to make doubly sure that CR knew he was kidding him. "Now, let's get this airplane cleaned up."

They went into the shop for a few minutes and came back out, CR dragging a high-pressure washer on wheels and Lance carrying some rags and a couple screwdrivers.

"We'll wash the whole plane first, then wash the motor," Lance said.

A little later, having pulled the cowling, Lance was blasting the bugs out of the little gaps between all the cooling fins on the motor's wheel-like circle of nine spiky cylinders, and he was telling CR that Tim was flying Stearmans that had engines very similar to this one. "I sure hope his luck holds out," Lance said. "Those nine-eighty-five duster motors have had a lot of hard use, and the jugs do blow now and then. Remember I told you that other pilot had one let go? There are other ways it could happen, too."

CR's eyebrows bunched as he frowned and peered up into his idol's face.

Lance told him all over again how lucky Johnny Crash was that it hadn't been the number-five cylinder. "That one," he said, aiming the stream of highly pressurized water at the bottom right-hand jug. "I hate to think what would happen to me if some half-asleep mechanic set a torque wrench wrong when he checked to see whether the bolts holding that cylinder down were tight enough. Strip the threads on a few of those bolts, and off she'd come!"

When they were finished, he let CR taxi the T-6 back to its parking spot at the strip, where he said, "I've got another little surprise for you." He reached into the left front pocket of his jeans and withdrew a thick green wad as CR's eyes greedily widened. "This is an investment in your future on this farm, boy. Now that planting's over, I want you to take this and go enjoy another one of your vacations. I mean, have some real fun."

CR grabbed the wad, opened it, and counted the hundred-dollar bills. He was so surprised he couldn't speak. He could only hold the money out toward Lance and dumbly gaze at him in gratitude.

"You might enjoy someplace tropical for your scuba this time. Forget the Gulf. I wish I could go with you, but I can't miss that much college. Come on. I'll drive you . . . No, come to think of it, you've tickled me so the past few days, *you* drive."

CR's head jutted forward, and his thin, bearded jaw dropped as he stared in wonder.

They got into the Corvette, CR at the wheel, and Lance casually said, "There are lots of places you could go to enjoy your diving. The Bahamas are nice, and Cozumel down in Mexico is okay. Hawaii would be great, but you'd spend all your time trying to get back at your favorite damned Yankee, instead of just enjoying that nice, warm sea."

CR's head was cocked toward Lance as he listened, and it tipped slightly one way and another, much as some pet tries to catch every nuance of its adored master's words. He'd been frowning, concentrating, but a couple seconds after Lance stopped talking, the frown vanished, and he grinned his brown baccy-chewing grin and nodded. He inserted the key in the Corvette's ignition, turned it, and seemed to nearly swoon at the sweet sound of the tuned exhaust.

23

LOTS OF LUCK

Tim and his loader men were crossing over the pass between Oahu's two mountain ranges. They were on their way to the one-way duster strip that had looked so spooky on Tim's test flight with Solly. It was the uphill-downhill strip cut into a very rugged hillside. It was about halfway up the ravine-furrowed slope between the famous North Shore and the US Army's Schofield Barracks.

Back then, in those days before the collapse of the great Hawaiian sugar industry, much of that slope along the north side of the island was covered with cane fields. They rose from nearly sea level to a little over a thousand feet in elevation several miles inland.

Since it was so time-consuming and financially inefficient to coax heavily loaded dusters up those steep hillsides, many of the plantation airstrips throughout the islands were situated at higher elevations. Most of the strips were short and narrow to avoid taking up more than the necessary amount of cane-growing ground. Some were one-way, uphill-downhill strips, since downhill takeoffs require less length. The strip that Tim and his crew were headed for that morning was the one that had been bulldozed into a scrap of hillside that was too steep for cultivation and lay at the edge of a crook in a rugged wooded ravine.

They had worked there the previous day and had left the

Stearman there overnight. Tim and the senior Oahu Island pilot, Les, usually left their planes on the plantations if they'd be returning to the same strip for more work the next day. They would ride to and from Honolulu International with their loader men, which reduced the aircraft fuel cost considerably over the long run.

Tim thought of this airstrip several miles inland from Haleiwa as "the Slot," for it had been partially dug into the hillside, with a wall of packed reddish earth that crowded the strip on one side, a sharp drop into a ravine on the other, and some tall trees at the inland end. The low end of the strip terminated abruptly at the very brink of the ravine that snaked from one side of the strip to right in front of it. There was only one way into and out of the Slot, no matter which way the wind blew, and that was from the downhill end. Even without a load in it, a duster could not outclimb the trees and hillside above the strip, and it would be very difficult to come in over the trees and lose enough altitude to get stopped before the dropoff at the low end.

At first, when he was nervously getting used to it, Tim had imagined that landing in the Slot had to be a lot like landing on an aircraft carrier, except that the steep terrain and trees, forward and to the sides, precluded a go-around for another try if he botched an approach. Although the strip didn't bounce around on waves like an aircraft carrier, tailwinds gusting up the rugged slopes sometimes made the plane bounce around on downwind landings, which had a similar effect. But now that he was used to it, Tim seldom gave landing there a thought anymore.

As they proceeded along the highway with the sun ascending above the Koolau range to their right, Tim was only vaguely aware from time to time of the loader men's chatter. Mainly he kept thinking about Lisa, wondering when she was going to talk to him again. He sympathized with her embarrassment over their stupid little fit of passion that night, and he wished that she'd give him a chance to tell her much more convincingly that it was perfectly understandable.

Punchy was driving, and Kaleo, his nephew, was sitting in the center of the bench seat. The two husky loader men were talking about a fistfight that had left Kaleo with a so-called "black" eye. In fact, that gross swelling was various shades of red, purple, and even yellow. The puffy flesh left only a narrow slit between the lids of the younger man's bruised left eye.

Gazing absently out the pickup's side window, Tim made a sour face as he recalled how Lisa had hung up on him the two times he'd tried calling. He was confident that she'd get over her embarrassment after a while, but she sure was taking a lot of time getting there.

He hadn't been able to spend more than a couple evenings with Lei to compensate for Lisa's absence, and he was feeling a little lonely. Lei had the swing shift out at the industrial park on the west side, and she was living with her mother way out in Nanakuli, which was an hour's drive or more from Honolulu, depending on the traffic. However, if he'd been able to be with Lei the Sunday morning after the incident with Lisa, he probably wouldn't have called Ben, which had been a very good move.

After the rejection Sunday morning after he'd unsuccessfully tried to fix things with Lisa, he'd been about to leave for the North Shore to surf when he thought of the friendly car salesman. He doubted that Ben would mind a pretty early Sunday-morning call if he was as eager a surfer as he'd seemed to be.

He looked up the last name, scanning first under P-A-L-A . . . but eventually found it listed as, "Polacol, JBN." Hoping that the number was Ben's, he went ahead and dialed.

"Sure!" Ben said with all the enthusiasm that Tim had hoped for. "After we go to mass. Why don't you come over for lunch? Bring your lady. What's her name again?"

"Lisa. Not my lady, actually. Just a friend. She's busy today."

"Well, we were all going to the beach anyway. Let's have lunch, and we'll go."

So Tim ended up at the Polacol home in Kaimuki and joined Ben, his wife, Naomi, their little son, Joey, and Ben's dad, Joe, for lunch. Joe was a widower, and Ben and his young family lived with him in one of the modest houses a couple blocks off the main drag.

Tim and three-year-old Joey hit it off right away. Before Tim could take his seat in one of the living room chairs after lunch, the little fellow brought him a thin, illustrated children's book about the scary *manananggal* of traditional Filipino lore and begged Tim to read to him.

The moment Tim was seated, Joey climbed right up onto his lap and settled in for what obviously would be a rereading of the story, for the little guy was quick to correct Tim's mispronunciations. He said several times, "Say it like this, like Grampa," and he would slowly pronounce it, *"Mah-nah-nahn-gahl,"* until Tim could pronounce it correctly.

Tim learned that *manananggal* could be warded off by chili peppers, and when he'd finished reading the story, Joey asked him whether he had any chilis at his home. When Tim said he didn't, Joey urgently said, "Ask my mom for some! You'd better take some home with you!"

"You're right!" Tim replied. "I'd better do that."

After a while, Ben strapped his board onto the Chevy wagon's new roof rack beside Tim's, and Joe lashed a Hawaiian-sling, three-pronged spear to it and placed a pair of fins, a mask, and a fish stringer and float in the back. Then Ben was back again to add a small ice chest with soft drinks and some leftovers that they could eat later. They left, laughing and chatting, Tim and Joe in the front seat and Ben, Naomi and Joey in the back. They could have fit just as well in Ben's big four-door Mercury, but Tim had insisted on using his car and gasoline, since they'd treated him to lunch.

It surprised Tim when they got to the turnoff to the North Shore and Ben told him to drive straight on, saying, "Let's give Makaha a try. One of Dad's favorite places to spear fish is near there, and there should be some waves."

A bit later, Ben said about Tim and Lisa, "I thought you two were probably married. That's what it looked like to me."

"Lisa and I are pretty close, all right, but I'm dating someone else. This Hawaiian girl. She lives not far from here."

"You should have asked her if she wanted to join us."

"I didn't realize we'd be coming here. Besides, she has the night shift right now. I'm sure she's still sleeping."

Although the waves weren't great at Makaha that day, some fairly nice ones did sweep in from time to time. Nevertheless, as it turned out, the two young men did enjoy the long intervals between the better waves. Judging by his new friend's intensity and bursts of delighted laughter, Tim gathered that Ben enjoyed their philosophy-religion yakking as much as the surfing.

"I haven't adopted any of the formal philosophical systems as my own," Ben said. "All I can say about my personal orientation is, I've been strongly influenced by Gabriel Marcel."

"I don't think I've ever heard of him."

"He spoke of God as not being some phenomenon to be proved by normal use of the intellect but as a person to be encountered."

That's pretty much what Lisa says, Tim thought.

"I try very hard to be rational," Ben went on, "but in my attempts to do that, I still believe that I have encountered God. What about you?"

"Basically, I'm a skeptic. I believed those Bible stories when I was a kid, but I started doubting as a teenager. In my first year of college, I did Descartes' belief testing, as any good philosophy student should, but I've never found my way back to certainty about much of anything. His way back seemed phony to me. I'm sure you understand that I mean *absolute* certainty."

"I do understand. I've entertained similar thoughts, of course, since philosophy's what I want to do for a living. But I also believe that I've encountered God. That experience has more power than my dutiful philosophical questioning."

"Me?" said Tim. "I'm so skeptical I'm skeptical about being skeptical."

A series of nice steep swells bobbed them up and down as they went on talking, and they ignored them.

"It was Sartre who kept me from getting too badly bogged down," Tim said. "I read his *Defense of Existentialism*, and that was it for me. I saw that I didn't have to be paralyzed by doubt. I started making an effort to shape the person I want to become, trying to keep an open mind and be rational at the same time. It's pretty goofy, I guess. I'm a hodgepodge of all sorts of systems: a skeptic, a pragmatist . . . "

"And a solipsist to boot!" Ben grinned and shook his head. "You're quite a wreck, all right!"

"For sure. But I'm glad you understand my interest in such stuff. Most people think it's weird."

"I know. It's cool to be dumb now. Most folks don't realize that this good life we Americans enjoy—we Westerners, actually—derives from philosophers' woolgathering. John Locke, for example. Such a profound influence on the good old American plenty and security that we enjoy. Of course some Western thought has led to that other outcome, that abomination people have to bear in some countries."

"So would you condemn me for doing my part to stop them in Vietnam? I volunteered."

"If I were single, I'd probably volunteer, too. But, hey, maybe we should keep a better eye out for waves. We'll have to get together again. And be sure to bring your friend. Either one, actually. Maybe both? But why do I think the latter wouldn't be a good idea?"

Tim's daydreaming was suddenly interrupted by Punchy's raised voice saying, "No way, Kaleo! You gotta get rid dose revenge-kine thoughts! You gotta learn how fo' fo'geeve!"

Tim was still learning the local lingo, but he felt good that he'd gotten the meaning of Punchy's insistence that Kaleo had to forgive someone.

"How I can fo'geeve two guys go lump me up for not'ing?"

"Dat's jus' how it is. You gotta learn how fo' aloha even you enemy. Even if dey punch you out fo' not'ing."

"Da Bible tell one eye fo' one eye."

Tim got that, too, and he grinned and shook his head.

"Dat's da *'Ol Testamen'*!" Punchy countered. "Dat one was fo' da Jews! Da way of da *New Testamen'*, da Jesus one, only aloha. Get t'ree main t'ings: hope, fait' an' love, but da bes' is love. It is written, 'God is love.' When you get His love, you going *aloha* people supahnatrilly."

Everywhere I go, Tim thought. *Aloha this, aloha that. And everybody's a Christian, too.* The latter sure seemed to be true to his personal experience, but he'd read that there were also many Buddhists among Hawaii's Asians.

As the two Hawaiian loader men argued on about the conflicting demands to forgive and to get revenge, Tim thought how that one Hawaiian word, *aloha*, was used by locals to say hello and goodbye, but Punchy was obviously using it to mean something more.

"So," Tim said as soon as the two second cousins paused, "aloha also means love?"

"Also?" said Punchy. "Only. When I use one of da real Hawaiian greeting, like, 'Aloha *kakou*,' he mean, 'Let's love one anaddah.' Deed you evah t'ink about my las' name, Kealoha? Mean da love."

"So when two guys say aloha . . . "

"Don' get no ideas! Get diffren' kine aloha: da man-lady kine, da Jesus kine, an' da 'Howzit?' kine. You heard dat saying, 'aloha spirit,' right?"

"No, I haven't."

"What? Dat's a big deal, man. We take pride how we treat one anaddah. Basically, we t'ink of Hawaii as the land of aloha."

Tim thought of the way Lei had softly breathed, "Aloha, Tim," when he'd picked her up for that first date. The words had floated out to him on her sweet breath as she had leaned forward to touch her soft creamy-brown cheek to his for just a moment. The way she had seemed to breathe that word had been so wonderfully exotic.

He couldn't help recalling how beautifully and simply done up Lei had been for the date. She had worn a black sheathlike evening dress and skimpy black high-heeled shoes—sandals, really, except for the high heels—that emphasized how tall and shapely she was. She wore a single thick coil of her gleaming dark hair draped forward over one shoulder. He literally hadn't been able to think straight right after he'd picked her up, and he'd made a number of blunders about getting back onto the highway and aimed in the right direction for Honolulu. Not even Jen had gotten to him that badly at first.

On the other hand, Lei wasn't nearly as interesting to talk to as Jen—not at first, anyway. There were so many painful silences before they even got as far as Barbers Point that he turned on the radio. Then and all through dinner, they mainly filled the silences with stilted, typical questions and answers about their lives.

His first question, of course, uttered once she had gotten him turned around and onto the highway in the right direction, was, "Do you surf?" After all, she'd grown up right there a couple blocks from the beach. But she had said, "No, not now. I went a little when I was young."

Quite a change came over her, however, as they strolled from the restaurant toward the old Moana Hotel, where she liked to slow-dance to Hawaiian music under the great banyan trees, with Waikiki Beach just beyond the big patio's dance floor. It was the place from which the famous *Hawaii Calls* radio program was broadcast across the nation. Along the way from where they'd parked, they happened upon a free outdoor hula show, and she began pouring forth detailed and very articulate explanations about the words of the Hawaiian songs and the swaying dancers' movements and gestures.

He recalled how they had slow-danced later in the hotel court-yard. She began to softly sing along to one English-language song, "Waikiki." The swaying of her sinuous body, the mellow sound of her voice, the fantastic fragrance of the yellow plumeria lei he'd bought her to wear, and her occasional high-pitched laughter, ap-parently over nothing more than the joy of dancing, had made him giddy.

His renewed daydream abruptly ended a second time as Punchy stopped the pickup in the Slot's loading area. Tim climbed up into the Stearman's cockpit, and Kaleo went around to the front of the plane and started pulling the prop through to clear and prime the cylinders. Meanwhile, Tim stood on the seat and stretched an arm over the center section of the upper wings to reach the fuel-tank cap and twist it off. He would have had to somehow hoist himself onto the upper wing's center section to visually check to make sure the tank was full, so he just stuck his index finger into the filler neck. His fingertip immediately touched the gasoline, signifying that the tank was full, and Tim screwed the cap back on. Then, while he sat in the seat to handle the throttle, Kaleo swung down hard on one prop blade, and the nine-eighty-five coughed and chugged to life.

The two Hawaiian swampers unhooked the two-wheeled buck-et loader from the back of the pickup and reattached it to the trail-er hitch on the front of the truck's custom-made bumper. While the biplane's motor warmed up and the two swampers stood on the flatbed trailer and began slitting open and dumping the hundred-pound paper sacks of fertilizer into the loader bucket, Tim, who was dressed in nothing more than a T-shirt, shorts, and flip-flops, did his morning calisthenics. Encouraged by what the frequent surfing had already done for him physically, he'd made up his mind that he was going to get back in top physical shape.

Several minutes before seven, Tim climbed aboard, hung his go-aheads on the wire hook that he'd fastened to a longeron beside his seat, and pressed the front pads of his bare feet on the upper rims of the rudder pedals so that Kaleo could remove the rock that was acting as a chock in front of one wheel. Aloha's Stearmans were not encumbered with such useless-extra-weight items as parking brakes, electrical systems, full windshields, or compasses. The dusting essentials were oil pressure, oil temperature, manifold pressure, and tachometer. Tim's Stearman did have an airspeed indicator, but it wasn't working. It didn't matter. No ag pilot who had to look at a gauge to know how fast or slow he was going would be sharp enough to handle the islands' steep and rugged hillsides.

Tim taxied the Stearman into position so that Punchy could maneuver the A-frame loading rig between the right-hand wings and tail to bring the hydraulically hoisted bucket over the plane's hopper. Kaleo scrambled onto the base of the left bottom wing and raised the hopper's hinged lid. As Tim tugged on a dangling rope loop that opened the loader gate and let the fertilizer rapidly spill down the short chute into the hopper just in front of the cockpit, the muscular young Hawaiian standing on the wing crammed the swiftly rising pile of white fertilizer crystals forward with the palm of his right hand. In less than a minute, the hopper was stuffed full of ammonium sulfate, and the young swamper slammed the lid down, leaped off the back of the wing, and dashed out of the way while Punchy backed the loading rig clear of the tail.

Pressing his bare feet hard on the forepart of the combined brake-and-rudder pedals, Tim ran the engine up to seventeen hundred rpm. He checked the right and left magnetos by switching the ignition, cycled the prop, then suddenly cocked his plastic-helmeted head to listen more attentively to the revving engine.

Huh? Had he heard something subtly amiss? He ran it up to two thousand rpm. *No,* he decided, *I guess not.*

He shoved the throttle forward to the stop. The plane lumbered forward, and he leaned out the left side of the cockpit to get a better view of the strip's narrow shoulder that fell off into the gulch. Seconds later, very near the airstrip's end, which also dropped into the gulch that snaked around in front of it, the blocky biplane got airborne.

Pop!

It wasn't a very loud sound. The Stearman had been making its usual rasping roar, but after that little *pop,* it became nearly silent. The only sounds were the guy wires between the upper and lower wing panels whistling through the air and a strange fluttering noise.

Instantly, Tim hunched forward to flip the gate-stop bar out of the way. Then he rammed the money handle all the way forward to jettison the load.

He was still directly over the gulch. He tried to angle over toward the canefield to the left as the load lightened. That steep edge to the left was a little lower than the one on the right. But the load was slow in coming out even with the gate wide-open, and the plane, initially packing a three-quarter-ton payload, was still far too heavy to be much of a glider. If he tried to reach the cane on either side, he'd surely hit the trees growing along the edges of the ravine. So, as the Stearman sank deeper into that ragged gash in the slope, Tim leveled the wings, eased the stick slightly back, and jammed his helmet hard against the crash pad.

* * *

The next thing he knew, all was quiet and still. All he could see was a very dark haze. Yet he was sure that his eyes were open.

He had no memory of what had happened after he'd got his head down. He even forgot that he was wearing a crash helmet, and he raised a hand and tried to rub his eyes to clear his vision. His hand slid across a hot, slick object, and he realized that it was the plastic bubble shield attached to his helmet.

That's a lot of blood, man. You've had it.

He had no fear of what was about to happen. Sometimes, when he'd been a boy, lying in bed at night, waiting for sleep, he would fearfully think, *I'll go out hanging onto the bedsheets,* and there had been times in 'Nam when he'd been absolutely terrified, but there was no such fearful clinging to life now. Here it was at last, what every man and woman on Earth was born to. He'd had other close calls, but he'd never felt this close to it. Here it was, and that was that. He was just glad that he wasn't going out the way Smitty had. He wasn't in the least bit of pain.

It's okay, he thought. *It's okay. It's okay.*

More time passed, maybe seconds, maybe minutes. It surprised him that he was still conscious.

All of a sudden he desperately needed to *see.* He raised both hands. They felt amazingly light. He yanked at the leather tabs on either side of the smeared face shield. The right side popped loose after a struggle, but the clenched thumb and finger of his slippery right hand kept sliding off.

He pried more energetically with a thumbnail to unsnap the right fastener, and the whole bubble shield finally came free. He watched it fall away into a world of deeply shadowed green and black.

He saw that he was hanging upside down, strapped tightly into the seat by the tough, original military seat belt and shoulder harness of the former trainer. Twenty yards farther down the steep side of the ravine oozed a stream of black water through a rocky little channel among a great jumble of mossy rocks, tropical undergrowth, and slender trees.

He brought the warm, gooey palm of his hand up before his

face, expecting to see crimson. It was brown. Momentarily baffled, he gaped at it.

Then he understood: *Engine oil!* He sniffed it. Sure enough, it really was nothing but hot motor oil.

He started sizing up the distance to the ground, and he took careful note of the kind of ground it was. The plants rising out of cracks among big sharp-edged chunks of rock wouldn't provide much cushion if he fell. The inverted cockpit was about a man's height above the ground.

He was glad that he hadn't reflexively yanked the seat belt release before he'd been able to see. He probably would have broken his neck.

The mangled right upper wing was swept back toward the tail at a sharp angle and crunched into the bank of the ravine. The left upper wing was precariously propped twenty feet up the trunk of one of the scrubby trees growing nearer the edge of the stream. The trailing edge of the wing near the tip was partially bent around the trunk, indicating that the plane had plowed backward through the jungle after it had flipped.

He cautiously moved his head from side to side, twisted his body a little each way, and moved his legs to see just how badly injured he might be. There didn't seem to be a thing wrong with him.

"Ho!" a distant voice yelled. "'Ey, Tim! We coming!"

"I'm alive! Come on!"

Some minutes later, there they were, unsteadily balancing on moss-covered rocks, staring up into his face with very big, coffee-colored eyes.

"Okay, we go lif' um down," Kaleo said.

"No way! We no can move um. Maybe he get broke bones o' somet'ing. Go use da radio one mo' time an' tell da boss he stay conscious. I going check um mo' good."

"I'm okay. I don't think—"

"Bettah safe dan—"

"I'm okay! I know I am! Look!" Tim moved his head vigorously from side to side and waggled his dangling arms. "Just help me down!"

* * *

"Lucky you," Teddy ironically commented while he and Tim stood side by side, gazing down into the gulch. The chief mechanic turned to eye Tim and slowly shook his head. "Sounds to me like you probably blew number five. Nine to choose from, and you pick the master-rod cylinder."

"*Now* you tell me," Tim kidded in turn. He hadn't gotten a scratch, and he was feeling *great* about his luck. "I'll pick a better jug next time!"

They didn't have a very good view of the upended Stearman from where they stood fifty yards above it on the unpaved field road. There was a lot of vegetation obscuring their view of it. Teddy hadn't bothered to climb down to get a closer look.

"Let's go," Teddy said. "I'd better get back and get everything organized. We'll pull the wings off and just drag everything up with the winch. I'd better buy a chain saw, too. We've never had to use one of those before. We'll have to clear some of those trees out of the way."

They climbed into the pickup, and Teddy continued. "It's a long drive back to the airport, and you wouldn't have much of a work-day left by the time you flew back out here. But the spare is ready when you are. If it was me, I'd call it a day, have a couple beers, and come back tomorrow."

Tim had a good view of Haleiwa straight ahead in the distance as they descended the field road. He could see that the surf was up. He was tempted to use the crunch as an excuse to go surf-ing, but he didn't. He returned with the spare and worked until the wind got so strong that it started breaking up the fertilizer pattern.

* * *

"Don't hang up on me," he said urgently as soon as Lisa answered later that afternoon. "Okay?"

She didn't say anything, but at least there was no click followed by a dial tone this time.

"I really could use some company for dinner," he said. "Have you eaten?"

She didn't reply.

He hesitated about using the crash to manipulate her emotions, but he plunged on: "I bent an airplane today, and you'd probably get a kick hearing about it."

"Are you hurt?"

"No, just hyper. I got blown out early and caught a few waves at Ala Moana. That helped, but I still can't relax."

"Bad one?"

"Yeah, there's another for the boneyard. It's totaled."

"Did you see a doctor?"

"Nah, I feel fine. They say I'll probably be sore later on, but I didn't get a scratch. So dinner?"

"I'm really ashamed of myself, Tim. I don't think I can face you."

"Come on, Lisa. So we got a little carried away. Big deal. We can handle that."

"*I* got carried away. Not *we. Gawain.*"

"Oh, Lisa."

"Sir knight. Ever true, so very strong."

"It takes two, Lisa. It wasn't just you. Let's forget about it."

"Sure. Just like that."

"Anyway, dinner. I'll take you to that place you like so much in Kaimuki. Okay?"

"Oh, I suppose."

* * *

"So," she said after they'd ridden along in silence for a minute or so. "What happened?"

"Master-rod cylinder. Popped loose at the base on takeoff. Went right into a ravine! Nothing but rocks and jungle."

She didn't say a word for a while after that, and she didn't react in any other observable way. She just turned her face and stared out the open window on her side of the station wagon, as if there were something other than the same old line of middle-class homes out there.

"Greenberg kept implying it was my fault," he went on after a while. "Talked like I'd never flown a radial before. Told me how I shouldn't use more than thirty inches of manifold pressure for two thousand rpms, thirty-one inches max for twenty-one hundred, and so on. Kept repeating it. Then he went through the whole flying-in-the-hills lecture like he did when I first started. As if I'd been using full throttle to get up the hill the day before and put too much stress on that engine. As if nobody at Aloha has ever blown a jug before."

* * *

They both decided to try the Japanese-American-style veal cutlets, once again ignoring the offering of sea-turtle cutlets, and he ordered his first margarita. Lisa cocked an eye at him, but she didn't protest. It was when he ordered a third that she did so.

"What are you *doing*?" she sharply asked.

The waitress hesitated, looking back and forth from her to Tim and back again.

"I need something to calm me down. I'm so wired." He saw the waitress hesitating. "One more," he said.

"I'll drive you home if you just have to do that. I'll drive you home and catch a bus to Fernhurst."

"Okay, okay." He waved off the waitress, saying, "Never mind." He didn't care that much. The main thing was, he had his sis back.

He shut up about the accident and simply sat there, admiring her, thinking how much he loved her.

"What are you grinning at?" she demanded.

"Just happy, I guess."

"It's creepy. Stop looking at me that way."

So he tried to look very serious, and they stared with profound gravity into each other's eyes. It was obviously no struggle for her, but he finally had to put his hand over his mouth, turn away, and fake-cough to hide the laughter that was surging up.

"Tim, don't you realize how close you came to dying today?"

"Yes, I do. Maybe that's why I'm so darned happy. It sure isn't the margaritas. They haven't had any effect at all."

"Tim . . . " She had to pause. She was finally starting to get choked up with emotion. "Didn't you wonder whether you were going to heaven?"

He didn't want to go off on that tangent right now. He only said, "I didn't have time to think about it. The guys got there pretty quick."

"Oh!" she exclaimed. "I almost forgot! Your accident has me so distracted!"

"What's up?"

"They're all coming out this Christmas vacation. Lance and his folks and mine, too."

"Too bad I won't get to see them. If I'm not in Nicaragua by then, it'll be Australia or maybe even Africa."

"And I'll have to make up my mind about Lance," she said. "I do need to tell him I will or won't this time."

"I hope you will."

Instead of making some comment about that, she angrily said, "You need to make a decision, too!"

"Really? Like what?"

"Like getting back into school. Tim, have you stopped to consider that you've been a crop duster less than a year, and you've already had a major accident?"

"Shore nuff?" he teased in what he'd started thinking of as Southernese. *And*, he thought, remembering the Idaho incident, *another you don't know about.* "Like good ol' Hank Williams says, I've done had me lots of luck, 'cept it's all been bad!" He knew that wasn't quite how it went, but it was close enough. He laughed again. It was good to be alive.

24

SPIRIT OF ALOHA

It was a windy no-fly day when Tim was forced to doubt that he'd made any progress at all with his temper. He'd begun to think that he'd licked that problem and only had to feel comfortable dating again to be back to being the original Tim O'Reilly.

He had started the day enjoyably enough by having a leisurely late breakfast over a copy of *The Honolulu Advertiser* at the food court in Ala Moana Center. However, it wasn't so enjoyable to see that Jack Kerouac had died. *Forty-seven years old*, he thought. *Pretty short road.* The news swung him back into one of his reflective moods as he once again pondered the puzzle of existence, which stayed with him all the way out to Makapuu.

He was going to give bodysurfing a try. As he parked in one of the vacant spaces fronting the long, low lava shelf to the cliffless side of the sandy beach, he could see that a few expert surfers were getting very nice long rides by catching some big waves directly in front of the sharp-edged lava, and his ruminations about the mystery of existence quickly faded away. That low rock shelf formed the opposite side of the wide, sandy cove from the high cliffs. It was directly below Sea Life Park, Hawaii's version of the old Marineland that Tim had once enjoyed visiting as a boy back home.

He was alone. It was a weekday, and Lisa was doing her thing at the university. Lei was sleeping in after her night shift. Although Aloha's other Oahu pilot, Les, didn't have to fly, either, he was no surfer. Ben might have been interested, even though he didn't care much for bodysurfing, but he was at work.

Most of the couple dozen people enjoying that bright, sparkling morning at the beach were either relaxing on the sand or dealing, according to their various levels of expertise, with the brutal shore break directly in front of the sand. Although the long, slanting rides the guys were getting out in front of the rocks didn't involve getting pounded by the over-curling surf in the shallows, Tim knew that it was wise to approach a new spot with caution when the surf was high. So at first he rode only the smaller, yet violent, waves that broke just in front of the sandy beach. When the bigger ones rolled in, he'd dive beneath each rising swell before it broke and swim out beyond the break to wait. Whenever he dove beneath the biggest swells just before they broke, he'd feel the force mightily tugging at him, threatening to draw him backward into the boiling, churning chaos as he finned beneath the surface into deeper water.

Once he swam too far seaward and inadvertently discovered the powerful rip current that runs parallel to the beach when the surf is up. He noticed it when he happened to glance shoreward after a monstrous set and saw that he'd drifted far down the beach toward its terminus beneath the towering cliffs. For a few moments, as he futilely attempted to swim against the current, the sharp little teeth of fear started nibbling at his innards. He fought down the panic and began trying to figure a way out of his predicament.

He considered riding one of the big combers all the way in while there was still a bit of sand in front of him. However, there weren't any other surfers nearby, and he had to wonder why. Perhaps the shallows nearer the cliffs were studded with rocks or coral.

Another option was to just let the current take him around the cliffs and on toward another beach a mile or so down the coast where he'd also seen people bodysurfing.

Then he reasoned that, if the high surf was creating the current, he might get out of the current by getting farther away from the surf. After all, the surfers far out in front of the lava on the opposite side of the cove didn't seem to be bothered by the rip. So he tried swimming directly out to sea. It worked. The swift current was confined to a surprisingly narrow band of water, beyond which Tim had no trouble getting back in front of where the other shore-break surfers and sunbathers were gathered.

He finned shoreward to where the waves were breaking and began trying to "shoot the curl," as he'd heard one of the locals happily yell at a friend. After a few tries, he succeeded. It was a pretty good rush to zip into one of those mightily thundering tubes and have it finally collapse on him.

He did that a couple more times, then headed out toward the small group catching the better waves in front of the low, rocky point—better because the break would begin there and progress a long way across the face of the onrushing swell toward the beach, leaving a wide mass of heaving white water behind. Only when the swell neared the wide crescent of bare sand would the entire breadth of it flip forward to briefly form a tunnel and then collapse with a mighty *whump* and flying spume.

The break out there in front of the lava that day began with a slick swell steeply peaking six or so feet high and spilling the first white water in just one spot only a foot or two wide. That was where each surfer tried to be, but the exact location of the first break varied. Once a surfer out in front of the lava shelf had been snatched up by one of those zippers, he stayed right at the leading edge of the white water, keeping pace with the gradually-collapsing forward part. Usually the one surfer who was in the right spot at the right time had the wave all to himself—or herself, as he would soon see. Ahead of the break, the swell usually wasn't steep enough for another surfer to catch it, and back where it had already broken, it was a great, chaotic mass of unsurfable, boiling white water.

Tim swam up to the cluster of surfers who were seaward of the rocks and, for a while, simply observed. A few clutched short boogie boards, which were not stable enough to stand on, and others did not. All wore stubby green Churchill swim fins.

He noticed now that the jagged shelf of lava directly shoreward of the first break wasn't the only hazard out there. As the swirling foam and suspended sand from one set of riotous waves were settling, he noticed for the first time one of the massive coral heads that studded the sand beneath the surface. There hadn't been any of those where he'd been catching the shore break in front of the sandy beach. The rounded, yellowish-green heads reminded him of gigantic, widely-spaced molars. The first one he'd only been able to hazily see, since he wasn't wearing goggles or a mask, hadn't been more than a yard or so beneath the tips of his fins. He could see how one of the waves out there might tumble some novice such as he down through them before it spat his gnawed remnant onto the rocks.

Once he was ready to give it a try, he began to eagerly jockey for position to try to ride one of the medium-size waves. None were too small to ride that day, but some were even too large for the experts.

"Outside! Outside!" one of the surfers would start shouting from time to time when he'd see an unusually large swell developing far out toward the horizon. Everyone would swim like crazy to get out to where they judged it would break. If it was too big, they'd dive beneath it and fin seaward. If it was surfable, whoever had correctly divined the location of the initial break would give a few kicks of his fins to accelerate shoreward, then just let the momentum of the wave pick him up and fling him along.

After Tim had made one frenzied swim and dive seaward, he was just about to dive under a closely following and rapidly rising wall of blue when a slight, brown-skinned girl with long dark hair braided into a single pigtail darted past him. The wave went nearly vertical just behind her and spilled a small patch of white. She casually turned, gave an expert little kick, and shot away above him, leaning left to stay at the edge of the cascading white water that was beginning its race across the remainder of the great swell. Just as he was about to flip fins up and head down, he saw her calmly glance down at him as she ripped by.

He dove hard for the bottom, thinking, *What a cutie!* The lovely little female on that huge, perfect wave left an indelible imprint in his mind even as he struggled down deep against the tug of the thundering wave rolling shoreward. The *whump* behind him reminded him of an artillery round even as the image of that pretty face lingered. The girl had so distracted him, he'd been late in diving beneath the break, and he had to fin with all his might to make up for it.

He shot to the surface just as another great wave loomed high. Once again he found himself in almost the perfect spot to catch it. At first he intended to dive under it. Then, at the last possible moment, he impulsively changed his mind.

The rising, steepening swell hoisted him sharply upward, and a bit of white water began to break just above and to one side of him. He turned and kicked. A second later his prone body went skipping like a smooth stone hurled across the surface of a placid pond. Halfway up the left side of his jolting, speeding body, the white water was tumbling from the wave's peak like a roaring waterfall; yet his head and the upper part of his torso projected from the smooth, unbroken, forward part of the wave. His right side and his right arm jutted almost directly above the wave's base a dozen or more feet below. He held his position there at the edge of the break just as he would on a surfboard, making minor adjustments left and right by leaning in either direction. Soon he was out in front of the sandy beach and clear of the rocky point.

He caught another glimpse of the girl. She was standing on the beach, and she had her eyes on him. He grinned and gave her a wave with his shoreward hand. But he didn't have time to watch for her reaction, since the entire, long remainder of the huge swell was about ready to roll over and crash.

For a moment, he was tempted to drive forward with his fins to try to surf all the way in to the girl's feet. However, he instantly came to his senses. He ducked his head and let the force of the wave toss him into an underwater somersault just before it collapsed, just as he'd seen a few others do. He sensibly waited outside the rest of the waves of that set to pass by until he could swim in without getting pounded. He stood in knee-deep water and saw that the girl had turned her back and was walking toward the parking lot.

Tim hurried after her. She was just starting up the slope of lava-studded sand, and the tailgate of her little pale green bikini twitched in an exceedingly beguiling way. His legs were much longer, and they ate up ground more quickly than hers. Furthermore, he was still stoked with the adrenaline rush of his wild ride. Very soon he was only several yards behind her. He began trying to think of something to say. He was determined to ask her out.

Just then she dropped her rolled-up straw beach mat. He was there before she could complete her graceful turn and very feminine bending of the knees to pick it up. He scooped up the mat and held it out, and she straightened to stand facing him. He was taken with a rush even stronger than the one he'd gotten riding the wave, and it robotically moved him a step nearer.

"Thank you," she said in a small voice. A delicate brown hand reached out to grasp the mat. The skin of her slender arm looked so incredibly smooth, and how it still glistened in the intense sunlight! "You got a nice ride."

"Nice," he stupidly echoed.

She gave him a sweet smile and gently pulled the rolled mat free of his tense grasp.

"Do you like the Beatles?" he blurted. He couldn't believe he'd uttered such a lame-sounding line, but there it was. And here came another big rush from having dared to say it as he waited with misgiving for her reply.

She laughed, and it somehow reminded him of delicate chimes stirred by a sudden breeze. There was no hint of the mocking tone he'd expected when she said, "Is that an example of non sequitur?"

"You just reminded me of the Beatles . . . " He paused, unsure now that he could go on, but he plunged ahead, blurting, "Hello, I love you, so won't you please tell me your name?"

Her mouth made a surprised "O." Then her dark eyes snapped mischievously, and she said what might have been, "Mickey," but she pronounced it *Meekee*, so maybe it was some Hawaiian name.

"Tim. Tim O'Reilly."

"You're funny. That's not exactly how that song goes."

"Would you like to go to lunch?" He felt like he might start hyperventilating.

"I have to go somewhere," she said. "On principle, I should just say no way. I mean, if you don't even know it's the Doors, not the Beatles . . . "

"Oh, *man*. What made me *do* that?"

Her eyes glinted, making him think that she knew perfectly well that it was she that had him so helplessly befuddled.

"Do you come here often?" he asked.

"Sometimes. I don't remember seeing you here."

"I'll make a point of changing that." She had such an unusually round face.

"Well, I gotta hurry," she said.

"How about—"

"Gotta go. Sorry. I'll probably see you again out here."

She trotted away, taking the trail to the right, heading up to the parking lot, and Tim turned to trudge up the trail to the left toward the outdoor shower. But he did see her stop at the edge of the parking lot to look back and wave before she disappeared beyond the rise.

The showers were located at the base of the steep flight of steps leading up to the public lavatories in a small clearing among some tall, succulent beach plants. Four showerheads pointed in different directions from a cluster of high, goose-necked galvanized pipes. The clearing was maybe a dozen feet square, and it was vacant at the moment.

Tim stood before one of the showerheads and, daydreaming about the girl, opened the valve, held the waistband of his shorts out as he turned about, and let the single heavy stream of cold water wash away the sand. *I'll be back for sure*, he mused, thinking of Mickey.

"'Ey!" a rough voice barked behind him.

He turned to see that three dark-skinned local guys had just come up from the beach.

"Dat *wahine* you was boddering, her my fren' girlfren'," the nearest one said. "Who da fahk you t'ink you, coming ovah here and boddah our *wahines*?"

Tim kept his mouth shut and avoided eye contact. *Don't react!* he frantically thought. He was trembling, a buildup to rage that he'd experienced before. Sudden, unexpected threat was always what triggered it. He forced an innocent shrug and peaceably said without really feeling any peace, "I just told her she dropped her mat."

Tim thought the blowhard might move on if he kept his cool. He turned his face, looked down at the skinny little dude, shrugged again, and made himself form a friendly smile.

The guy stepped closer. His hand shot out to give Tim a rough, flat-palmed shove on the chest. "'Ey, what da fahk you *laughing*?" he shrilled.

Despite his own intentions, Tim knocked the hand away with a sideward flick of his left forearm. His right fist drove diagonally upward and caught the dude at the edge of his jawbone. It sent him down hard on his skinny butt in the sandy, pooling shower water.

Here came his pals now, fists up, grimacing. They started swinging.

Tim did his best to duck and weave to escape their blows, but his boxing training in junior high with his pal Nick had been nothing more than one of their many passing interests, and he was taking more punches than he could avoid. Their fists thudded solidly here and there. Yet he felt no pain. He'd experienced that a couple times before when he'd been forced into teenaged scraps. The two drove him backward until his back was pressing into the bushes.

He gritted his teeth and took the offensive, swinging hard and plowing forward. One of the locals' blows glanced off the side of his head and made him stagger, but he quickly got in a driving right. Bright blood bloomed on the dude's mouth. Then Tim hooked a follow-up left cross to the other guy's head. That one connected, too. Now he had both of them backing away, but the third was lurching to his feet.

Out of the corner of his eye, Tim saw a muscular, deeply-tanned white guy come up from the beach and stop where the path led between the bushes into the shower area. He calmly watched with his bristle-haired blond head cocked to the side and his bulging arms crossed on his thick chest.

Meanwhile, the three locals had regrouped, standing shoulder-to-shoulder, and one of them screamed, "We go put dis *haole* down!" Side by side, crouching, they moved forward.

Tim shouted, "Come and get it, bitches!"

With that, the three furiously rushed him.

The bystander stepped in. Tim, from the edge of his field of view as he braced for the attack, noticed that the other *haole* guy was laughing.

Just as the three locals got to Tim, the *haole* stranger shouted, "Surprise!" His bronze fist drove into the side of one local's face. Then Tim got too busy to see what else his helper was up to. He was aware only that one of the locals was down—flat on his back and not moving.

Very quickly thereafter, another went down, and Tim knew it hadn't been from one of his own punches. He was left with only one attacker, and that one scuttled back against the bushes.

The *haole* stranger was standing with his muscular arms once more crossed on his thick chest, smiling in bemusement. He nodded when he saw Tim looking at him and calmly said, "Let's go. I don't think these *bitches* . . . " He paused to throw back his head and laugh. "I don't think they'll give us any more shit." He laughed again and turned to go up the stairs to the restrooms.

They mounted the steps, the stranger leading the way with Tim below and behind, marveling at the guy's hugely bulging calves. When they had gained the sidewalk between the driveway and the lavatories, they stopped and faced each other. Tim noticed that he was probably a half foot taller than the other guy. He reached out a hand and said, "Thanks. I . . . Ouch!"

The guy chuckled and said, "You prob'ly won't want to shake hands for a few days. You could toughen up those knuckles, you know." He laughed again, but this time he enjoyed a good, long, rollicking one. A large tattoo of an anchor with the letters "USN" overlaying it adorned one bulging bicep. On the opposite shoulder was tattooed a crossed pair of swim fins and a diving mask.

"I'm Tim O'Reilly. Thanks for stepping in."

"Chuck. Chuck Harmon." He glanced up toward the sun and said, "Chow time. All same beer o'clock. Join me?"

"Sure."

"Which way you headed? Pearl or Kaneohe?"

"Pearl. Honolulu, actually."

"Me, too. How 'bout stopping at Kuliouou?"

"I don't know where that is. I'll follow you."

"Let's do it." He turned and jogged over to a battered old ragtop Willys jeep.

A short time later, they sat at an open-air table on a restaurant patio facing the calm lagoon, and Chuck chortled. "*Bitches*? 'Come and get it, *bitches*'?" He laughed so hard that it brought tears to his eyes. People were looking. "I'll have to tell the team about that!"

Tim nodded and gave him a thin smile. He was a little embarrassed by the commotion.

"What branch're you in?" Chuck asked.

"Branch? I'm out. I'm a civilian."

"You're from this rock?"

"California."

"Hey, me, too! Oceanside. You?"

"Santa Monica."

"What're ya doing out here?"

"Crop dusting."

"No shit? Crop dusting? Like in *North by Northwest*? Here?"

"Sugar cane. I gotta see that movie. People keep talking about it. But there really wasn't much crop dusting in it, I hear."

"No, not much. You get hazardous-duty pay?"

"Nah, we get paid by how much we get done. You still in the navy?"

"Yeah. I'm in for 20. Hell, maybe 30 if the old bod can stand it that long. You say you served?"

"Yeah."

"What? Army, Navy?"

"Marines."

The waitress took their order. They both asked for cheeseburgers, fries, and Buds.

"'Nam?" Chuck asked when she left.

"Yeah."

"You're a talkative son of a gun."

Tim grinned. "I know. I guess it's that demonstration of the good old aloha spirit's got me so wound up. I just can't stop talking when I get that way."

"You got a short fuse. That or you just like a three-on-one challenge."

"Short fuse. Not proud of it, either. I wasn't always that way."

"Come and get it, bitches!" Chuck said it in a quieter voice, but he laughed pretty loudly again, and people glanced their way once more. "You ever consider UDT?"

"You're a frogman?"

"That's my thing."

"Talk about hazardous duty . . . But lucky me! UDT to the rescue! They would've had my ass if you didn't show up."

"Maybe not." Chuck laughed again, and Tim noticed that he had a few gold fillings. On him, they looked good. They almost matched his golden tan. "Attitude counts! Come and get it, bitches! Plus, you had a lot of reach on them shaky shitbirds. You were kicking some ass."

"Not proud of it. Sometimes I just freak."

"After 'Nam?"

"Don't start thinking battle fatigue. I'm not exactly a puss."

"No, you're not a puss." But Tim could tell from the way the dude was studying him, he was wondering if combat had pushed him over the edge.

25

WEIRDLY WENDS THE WAY

It was November now, and Tim was beginning to wonder whether Johnny Crash was ever going to call. He was thinking that maybe he should just go ahead and contact some operators in the southern part of the world. He might try Africa first. If he didn't have any luck there, Australia. Both had great surf. But the early winter surf was building so very nicely right where he was, and it was hard to get in a hurry about leaving, so he procrastinated.

Life was very good for other reasons as well. He and Lisa were getting to know his fellow duster pilot, Les, and his wife, Malia, better, and they'd become even tighter with the Polacols. Also, he and Lei still dated occasionally and got along well. Lei had finally confided that she was going out now and then with an ex-con and was keeping that relationship more or less casual until she could be confident that he'd learned his lesson. Tim wasn't extremely disappointed. He still had his hangups engendered by the ghost of the fabled O'Reilly Way that continued to be in powerful conflict with other considerations. If Lei was that serious about another guy, there was no pressure on him to get too close. He especially enjoyed dancing with her and hearing her fascinating explanations of Hawaiian culture, as well as simply delighting in her appearance, and he couldn't help but be tempted to try to take it farther; yet his adherence to honorable family tradition, however much of it might have been exaggerated, kept him free. It might not have, of course, if he'd fallen for her the way he had for Jen, the one great true love of his life, back in California.

He hadn't seen Mickey again, although he had gone back to Makapuu a number of times. He hadn't seen the clowns he'd started calling "the *locos*" instead of "the locals" there, either.

He had called Chuck Harmon once to see whether he wanted to do the double date he'd suggested, but Chuck had the duty. Soon afterward, Chuck's ship had left Pearl on another tour of Vietnam.

Now, on a fine, sunny work day, as he followed the Aloha Dusters pickup down the north-slope highway in his station wagon, he was stoked to see some really nice big surf breaking again, as it had the day before, in the distance at Haleiwa. Since he'd still have at least another day's work off the same airfield the following day, he'd driven over separately from the flagmen so he could stay to surf after quitting time.

Not long after they got down near the coast, Punchy turned left onto the coastal road to proceed to the abandoned military airfield at Mokuleia, where they'd left the Stearman overnight. They were using a taxiway at midfield as an airstrip.

Unfortunately, while a new duster was being assembled from Aloha's stash of military-surplus two-holers to replace the Stearman Tim had crashed, he had to fly the rat that Aloha kept as a spare. However, happily, most of the fields he had to do near the old airport were on the relatively flat coastal plain, where staggering through the air in such a piece of junk wouldn't be as difficult.

When he made his first takeoff, he cautiously bent slightly right once he barely cleared the jumble of thorn trees on the inland side of the airfield and proceeded several seconds later to make a beeline for the nearby cane field where he'd left off the previous day. He had the money handle open less than a minute after takeoff, and he merrily chanted while he held it open, "Dollar, dollar, dollar." He was really into stacking up his savings now for his eventual return to college.

The engine sputtered while he was putting out the third load of the day. His head automatically snapped upward so that he could see the gas gauge on the underside of the center section between the two upper wings. The pointer was now on E. He glanced at his wristwatch.

He should have had plenty of fuel. As always, he'd stuck a finger into the gas tank to make sure it was full, and he had also checked his watch just before his first takeoff of the morning. The rule for a working 985 Stearman was, "One hour of flight and gas up." But the sputtering and the very sudden change in the fuel gauge reading didn't leave any doubt what the problem was.

His head rapidly swiveled left and right as he sought a place to set the Stearman down. The fields all around him were thick with mature cane that leaned into the narrow field roads.

He tried jamming the stick back and forth to see whether he could slosh any remnant of gas into the fuel line. It worked. The engine resumed its smooth firing.

He was very close to the entangled band of big trees along the south side of the runway now, angling in toward them. If he was going to put it down in the cane without ending up in the trees, it had to be done in the next few seconds.

The motor sputtered again. Once more he rocked the plane. And once again the motor ran smoothly.

It would take only a second to clear the trees. Tim went for it.

The engine sputtered again, and he rocked the stick back and forth. The motor quit completely this time. Too late to even turn aside from the onrushing line of trees, Tim heard once again what he'd started calling Stearman gliding after the '64 hit song, "the sound of silence."

He dumped the load and tried to spot two tree trunks that he could fly between to simultaneously wipe out all four wing pan-els, which would absorb much of the energy of the crash. But he couldn't clearly make out any such pair of trunks amid such a tan-gle of branches and leaves. Then, as his entire field of vision filled with looming vegetation, he jammed his head against the crash pad on the vertical back of the hopper and hoped for the best.

* * *

As in his crash into the ravine, he came to his senses with no recollection of the airplane plowing into the trees. This time he found himself sitting upright. He wasn't sure whether he'd been unconscious for a while or not. If he had been, it couldn't have been for long.

A cloud of pale dust still swirled all around him from the impact, and dusty beams of sunlight shone down through the breaks in the leafy canopy to make the swirling motes glow. He sat perfectly still for a while, astounded once again that he was not only alive but pain-free and apparently uninjured. Then he looked about to see that the right-hand wing panels were swept back at slightly different angles, and were twisted and wrinkled. Apparently those wingtips had hit the thick base of one tree first, and that had spun the plane around so that the tail had then slammed into another tree on the left hard enough to put a very visible kink in the fuselage.

Again Tim peered at the fuel gauge. The needle was on E, al-right. Even though he'd learned to rely on his wristwatch to gauge fuel consumption, he was sure that he'd glanced habitually at the gauge from time to time, too, and he was sure it had read normal-ly for much of the two-thirds of an hour since he'd started work. It occurred to him that his watch might have quit, and he quickly checked, but the seconds hand was still making one of its circuits of the dial. He really had started work less than two-thirds of an hour earlier. He should have been able to put out that load and another before another refueling.

He released the seatbelt lever and tested for broken bones by cautiously moving his arms and legs. He took the time to lift his go-aheads off their hook, climbed over the side, and was about to ease down off the base of the crumpled wing when he got an eyeful of the long thorns that projected from the dried twigs and branches. He let himself down very carefully and began to slowly pick his way through the tangle. Those thick thorns were more than long enough to go right through the go-aheads' thin soles.

It wasn't far to the taxiway, and Punchy and Kaleo came roaring up with the pickup in reverse and the bucket loader still hooked onto the front bumper.

"Not again, Tim!"

"Really!" Tim said. "It is getting old, isn't it? Hey, Punchy, do me a favor, since you got boots on."

"Shua. Whatevah you like."

"How 'bout going in there and checking that airplane for me. Clean off one of those bare sticks and poke it in the gas tank. See if it comes up wet. Then see if you can get any gas out of the drain."

Punchy ducked under a thorny branch immediately to go check, and Tim asked Kaleo, "Did you see me take off the gas cap and check this morning?"

"No, I wasn't paying no attention."

"I'm sure I did, though."

* * *

"I don't know why I don't send your sorry butt down the road!" Greenberg shouted when Tim entered his office. "I really don't! We're used to losing airplanes, but not at *this* rate. Now you've gone and torn the damn *spare* all to pieces."

"That damn spare almost tore *me* to pieces," Tim dully replied.

"Just admit you didn't check for gas before you started!"

Here we go again, Tim thought, but he responded more carefully this time. "Like I said on the CB, I stuck a finger in the gas tank before we cranked up. I definitely touched gas." Surely he had. It was so much a part of the morning routine that he couldn't have forgotten.

"Bullshit! You hadn't even flown an hour!"

"That thing either sprang a leak, or it started gulping an obscene bunch of gas. Don't ask *me* why."

Greenberg was pacing back and forth behind his desk, and Tim was standing in front of it. The wiry boss abruptly whirled, grabbed the big ashtray off his desk, and hurled it through the view window of the airport, shattering the pane. "Son of a bitch!" he shouted. He whirled back and stared wild-eyed at Tim with his Groucho hair going every which way.

Tim started laughing. He couldn't help it. He didn't care what Greenberg might think about it. At that point he'd go down the road gladly. He hadn't been there three months, and Aloha Dusters' airplanes had put him down twice. Maybe he'd go over to the one other dusting operation in the islands and see if they had safer equipment. He laughed again at Greenberg's bizarre antics.

Greenberg turned back to gape in shock at the shattered window, then turned back to stare at Tim. Then *he* started laughing.

Midge, his secretary, cautiously peeked in through the doorway. Her dark almond-shaped eyes were huge and worried. She quickly ducked back out of sight, leaving both men to their lunacy.

Having seen that, the two men laughed even harder.

"Let's go get a drink!" Greenberg said. "*I've* had enough work for one day. And you don't have an airplane to fly until the boys can finish building the new one. Come to think of it, we'd better start building up another for when you break that one, too."

They went toward the front door, and Greenberg called out to Midge, "Call Les's people. Tell them to tell him we'll be at the Outrigger if he wants to call it a day and have a drink with this one-man wrecking crew and me."

As they went down the steps toward their cars, the boss said, "I'll give you one more chance to come clean. Did you really stick a finger in a full tank of gas?"

"I did."

"I believe you. You crash airplanes, but you're no liar."

"Nah, I was kidding. I ran out of gas on purpose."

They both cracked up all over again.

* * *

Tim remained stone-cold sober even though he'd guzzled several more margaritas than the previous time, and that amazed him. It made him wonder whether he was in shock. It was very odd.

After Solly dropped him at the Y a few hours later, he rapidly walked the several blocks to the dealership where his friend Ben worked. He could have phoned, he could have driven, since his wagon was at the Y, and he felt perfectly sober, but Tim also had an insistent urge to walk after sitting around at the Outrigger for so long. He was hoping that Ben had brought his surfboard to work, which he sometimes did, and they might catch a few waves before he headed home for dinner.

Ben was strolling across the lot toward the office with an older couple, and he hurried over to say, "I'm busy right now, but I should be free in a half hour."

"Broke another airplane this morning. Don't have anything to fly, so I'm off early and heading for the beach. Join me when you're off?"

"Again?" Ben groaned, frowning deeply. "We need to talk about that, my friend, and never mind catching waves. I wish you could come over for the evening, but we have plans. How about tomorrow? Come for dinner. Bring one of your friends if you like. We do need time to talk."

"I'll bring Lisa if she isn't busy. I'll bring some Chinese food. My turn to treat."

* * *

Tim spent some time the following morning bugging the mechanics. He wanted to know how that airplane started gulping gas so much faster all of a sudden. They were willing enough to talk to him, but only as they hurriedly went about building a new duster out of one of the few original war-surplus sets of fuselages and wings they still had in storage. They had hung new fabric on the four wing panels, on the fuselage, and on the tail components, but the front cockpit had to be removed to make room for a big fiberglass tank, and a motor needed to be mounted.

"Could be the impeller," Teddy said. "That's what I'm thinking. But we need to get this plane ready for you before I start tearing that engine down."

"Or how about a leak?" Tim asked.

"We checked everything easy to get to. We can check more later when we have time."

Tim went into the fenced boneyard on one side of the building to have a look for himself. He carefully examined the hoses and other parts of the fuel line, and he closely inspected the underside of the center section that contained the fuel tank between the upper wings, looking for any small stains that leaking red aviation gas might have left there. No matter how carefully he looked, he couldn't see anything amiss. He tried pouring a gallon of gas into the tank, getting a precise fuel-level reading by marking a stick he poked into the tank, and checking again a quarter hour later to see whether the level had changed, but that didn't indicate any leakage either. He gave up and returned to the Y to try to read until lunchtime, when Lisa would be finished studying and they could have lunch and surf a couple hours at Waikiki.

At dinner that evening, Ben said, "You say none of the other pilots are having trouble with their planes, but you've had two breakdowns in a very short time. Don't you think that's strange?"

"Just the way the ball bounced," Tim said, grinning, but everybody else just solemnly stared at him. Even little Joey did so, copying his elders.

"Maybe you should do something else for a living," Ben said. "Why don't you consider it?"

"It's not like I—"

"You should, Tim," Lisa urged, and the others nodded again. "Better yet, go back to school. Do it now. Don't put it off."

Tim laughed out loud and said, "Look at it this way: I've probably used up my lifetime allotment of prangs, so I don't have to worry about them anymore."

"I just had another thought," Ben pressed on. "Have you gotten anybody upset with you? Upset enough to sabotage your planes?"

"No. Of course not." There'd been that scrap with the locals, of course, but that didn't mean anything. (He hadn't told anyone except Les about that. He'd made excuses to avoid Lisa and the Polacols until the reddish lump over one cheekbone had subsided and a couple other bruises had faded.)

"Are you sure?" Ben probed, and Tim nodded with exasperation now and was no longer smiling.

After they'd eaten in silence for a couple minutes, Ben said, "Maybe somebody at work has it in for you."

"Nah. No way."

"Those guys at your helper's luau? The ones you said were giving you the *haole* treatment?"

"Not likely at all. It wasn't that big a deal."

"Things can get pretty strange when it's local boys versus haoles. Some lowlifes are constantly looking for excuses."

"What's this?" Lisa asked.

"You know. I told you." Tim had already told her that he'd gone out a few times with a Hawaiian girl, and he told her now how the two locals had given him a hard time the first time he'd talked to Lei. "But nobody did anything to those Stearmans. Stuff just breaks sometimes. The mechanics will figure out what happened."

"Maybe," Ben scoffed. *"Maybe* when they get around to it. Can we go see that airplane ourselves after church tomorrow?"

"What's the point? What would you see that we didn't?"

"I doubt you're as picky as I am. Not with that careless attitude. And you're far too willing to believe in coincidences. Besides, what harm would it do? Also I've never seen one of those dust croppers."

Tim eyed him and realized Ben hadn't been making a joke of the name, so he just said, "If you insist. It's not like I'd rather just relax and have some fun. Like go surfing."

So the following afternoon, Ben, Lisa, and Tim drove out to Aloha Dusters while Joe took Naomi and Joey to a Disney movie at Kaimuki Theater. Tim used the one key he had to get into the hangar and went to the key rack to get the one that opened the boneyard gate. The boneyard, a paved area to one side of the hangar, was enclosed by a high security fence, and littered with bits and pieces of Stearmans and old fertilizer loaders, from which the mechanics occasionally salvaged parts.

Ben, Tim, and Lisa stood beside the rat's bent fuselage as Tim pointed up toward the elevated center section and told the other two how he'd checked the entire fuel system for leaks. The crooked, wingless fuselage was still on its wheels, slanting steeply upward from tail to nose. The lower wings had been detached from their mounts at the bottom of the fuselage, and the two upper wings had been detached from the elevated center section so that everything could be neatly fitted onto the flatbed truck and hauled to the airport. He told them the gas tank was inside the center section to which the two upper wings had formerly been bolted. He pointed out the gas gauge that was screwed into the underside of the center section.

"Did you look inside?" Ben asked.

"Inside?" Tim asked, having no idea at first what Ben was talking about. "You mean the gas tank?"

Ben nodded.

"No, you can't actually see inside. You stand in the seat to insert the gas nozzle, and it's a long reach up. But you don't have to look in. You just dip your finger—"

"I know. That's what you said. I mean afterward. After you crashed."

"Of course not. Why would I?"

"I want to have a look. It's possible if I climb up there, right?"

"Possible, but tricky. Unless you used a ladder. But it can't have anything to do with the inside of the tank."

"Can we get one? A ladder?"

"*Ben* . . . " Tim was about to say again that it wouldn't do any good, but he shut his mouth, nodded, and went into the shop to get a folding aluminum ladder. If he helped Ben satisfy his curiosity quickly, they might get in the water yet before the day was over. He saw a flashlight on one of the mechanic's tool chests and grabbed that, too.

Ben took the flashlight and promptly climbed the ladder. He shined the light into the fuel tank. "What's that lumpy stuff in there?" he asked almost immediately.

"Lumpy stuff?"

"Like pebbles. They *are* pebbles. What are pebbles doing in there?"

"Let me see!" As soon as Ben was out of the way, Tim scrambled up to have a look. Sure enough, the bottom of the gas tank was covered with what appeared to be dark-gray pebbles, the sort worn smooth by rushing water. Many of them. The hair went up on the back of his neck.

"Coincidence?" Ben said. "Accident? Pebbles in your gas tank, and the motor happens to stop?"

At first, Tim couldn't figure out how in the world pebbles would make an engine quit, much less why there'd be pebbles in there in the first place. His mind raced, struggling to make sense of it.

"I got it!" he said. "Displacement!" He rapidly thought it through again, it was so hard to believe. But then he said, "No accident. Definitely not."

He heard sobbing. He hurriedly climbed down and went to hold Lisa.

"Don't worry," he said. "Probably just some kid . . . " But he'd said that before, back in Idaho that night when he and Matt had been wondering who had blinded him. The realization silenced him. He shook his head, thinking, *No, there can't be a connection. We've just been asking for it around here, leaving these planes out where nobody can keep an eye on them.*

The abandoned airfield at which he'd left the Stearman overnight was a very isolated place. There were no homes in the vicinity. There was a short row of little cabins along the beach that the military used for rest and recreation, but Tim hadn't noticed any activity there. However, he had seen the black tire marks where someone—teenagers, he imagined—had been using the one long runway as a drag strip, and a solitary parked airplane might have attracted their attention.

And it's gotta be a coincidence about Idaho. I'd have to be paranoid to believe someone's followed me all the way out here.

"Displacement?" Ben asked.

"With those pebbles in there," Tim said, "the gauge would have registered full even if the tank wasn't full of gas. I touched gasoline right up at the top when I stuck my finger in there. The tank was full, all right. It just wasn't exclusively full of gasoline."

There was no getting around the evidence now that someone had made him crash. Whoever had come up with the idea had quite an imagination. Tim doubted he would have been able to dream up such a trick. But he didn't see how anyone could have caused a jug to break loose to cause the first crash. And the landing strip where that plane had been parked the night before had been miles up a perfect maze of cane roads from any public road.

For a moment, he wondered whether this Stearman's incessant

noise the day before the crash had made some soldier staying in one of the military beach cabins come unglued. It wasn't easy to imagine someone getting so upset that he'd risk killing a pilot, but the worst of Tim's own rages made it seem at least a possibility. There were probably plenty of pebbles along that beachfront of mixed sand and rocky outcroppings.

"Is that the first one over there?" Ben asked, gesturing toward the earlier wreck.

Tim nodded, took Lisa by the hand, and followed Ben over to that wingless Stearman.

The gap in the upright ring of what had been nine large cylinders bolted to the exterior of the central crankcase was plainly visible, and Ben stepped close and squatted to silently gaze at the bare flange and exposed piston of the missing cylinder. "Any guess how someone could make this happen?" he asked.

"*If* anyone did. But I wouldn't have a clue. I just don't see how it would be possible."

Down on his haunches, Ben waddled closer beneath the engine and reached up to run an index finger all the way around the cylinder-base flange, pensively tapping each place where a cylinder hold-down stud had given way.

Tim, meanwhile, was thinking that the guys he'd fought at Makapuu would have reason to sabotage his planes. But that first crash had happened *before* the fight, so even if there was a way to make a jug blow, nobody would have had reason to do it. Furthermore, those pukes at Makapuu had no way of knowing what he did for a living, much less where he might have left his airplane from one job to another. The rough-talking locals who'd been at Punchy's luau might know where he worked, and they probably could have found out from Punchy or Kaleo where he'd left the Stearman the night before the crash, but they just didn't seem to have sufficient reason to do such a thing.

The fact remained that *someone* had sabotaged the *one* airplane.

And the punks at Makapuu might have tracked him down some-how. Then, too, it really could have been just another prank. Kids didn't always give a lot of thought about consequences when they came up with some of their brainstorms. Tim had been there of-ten enough himself to know that.

So, he thought, chalk the blown jug up to the same old metal fatigue that had popped so many others. With the stress on those cylinders of so very many full-power takeoffs each day, year after year, along with the sustained high power settings to haul such heavy loads, it had to happen. That still seemed far more likely than someone being able to figure out how to make it happen. As much as Ben resisted the idea, reality did include coincidences.

"I need to call the boss," Tim said, turning to go.

"And the police!" Lisa said, once again bursting into tears.

26

HIDING PLACES

The boss arrived before the cops did. He jammed the flashlight into a pocket of his khaki trousers and climbed up to have a look into the gas tank for himself.

He took a look, grimly cast a glance at Tim, and climbed down. He went right over to Ben and said, "I can't thank you enough. I can't believe everybody overlooked that."

"It's understandable. Who would expect such a thing?"

"Well, *you* sure seem to have some sixth sense. We're gonna have to be careful where we leave those planes from now on. Where the hell are the cops, anyway?"

"Maybe that's them," said Lisa, pointing toward an ordinary blue Ford sedan coming down the lightly traveled road.

The car slowed, and they all hurried over to meet the police at the chain-link gate into the boneyard. The driver was a chubby, balding *haole* with pinkish skin. The other was a younger, dark-skinned local of indeterminate race, who carried a clipboard and had a camera hanging by a thin strap around his neck. They were both wearing nice-looking slacks, loafers, and aloha shirts.

"Which one da pilot?" the white guy roughly demanded in a heavy local accent. And when Tim waved a hand, the man officiously demanded, "Timothy O'Leary?"

"O'Reilly," Tim absently replied.

"I am Detective Ludwing. Dis is Officer Namaka." He paused to reach into a hip pocket and pull out a handkerchief to wipe away the perspiration that beaded his high, sunburned forehead. "We need one preliminary statement."

Tim quickly told them about the crash and about Ben finding the pebbles in the tank as Officer Namaka jotted notes.

"So rocks plug da gas hole," Ludwing said.

"No, the pebbles made the gas gauge give a false reading. I ran out of gas."

"How did rocks made you ran out of gas?"

Tim was still so lightly concerned about it all that he was able to wonder before he answered whether the white detective's fractured English was natural or an effort to fit in as one of the locals. He explained in more detail, but he didn't see anything that indicated comprehension in the cop's pink face. He wondered whether the guy might be temporarily distracted by some other matter. Surely HPD wouldn't make a bottom-rung-dumb kind of cop a detective.

"We will observe da rocks," said Detective Ludwing. "Now what airplane get da rocks?"

"That one," Tim said, pointing. "The gas tank's up there in the center section. You'll have to climb up that ladder."

"He had another wreck that's very suspicious, too," Ben said.

Ludwing swung his rosy face toward Ben and sharply said, "If you don't mind, sir! We are interviewing Mr. O'Leary at dis time."

"*O'Reilly*," Ben indignantly shot back.

"O'Reilly," Officer Namaka gently confirmed.

"Is dis true?" Ludwing asked, peering at Tim. "Dey was one mo' time?"

"Well, another engine did quit on me. Cylinder blew. Probably just metal fatigue. It happens."

"You can show us dat one later."

Ludwing climbed up to have a look at the gas tank. After he

descended, Namaka then went up and, using the flash, tried to get photos of the pebbles through the filler neck.

Tim reluctantly showed the police the other wreck. He told them that it wasn't uncommon for such engines to blow jugs, and that it was just a coincidence that this one happened to be the master-rod cylinder. But Namaka got some photos of it anyway. The gap where the master cylinder had been part of a ring of nine large exposed cylinders was very noticeable.

"But how someone can make dis one happen anyway?" Ludwing asked, stroking his dimpled chin.

"Yeah, doesn't seem likely," Greenberg commented.

Ludwing gave Greenberg a hard look and turned to say to Tim, "We need to speak mo' private."

"My office," Greenberg curtly said, returning the hard look. "This way."

While the two detectives continued interviewing Tim in Greenberg's office, the others waited in the larger outer office at the vacant desks of the secretary and the accountant.

Ludwing asked Tim whether he knew of anyone who might have a reason to harm him, and Tim told them first about the fight at Makapuu and did his best to describe the three locals. Then he told them about the two locals at Punchy's luau. He ended by stating why he doubted that it could be either group. He suggested they contact the Army and see whether any of their people had been staying in the beach cabins.

When Ludwing pressed Tim to try to recall anyone else he knew who might want to harm him, Tim said he'd been trying hard to think of such a person but couldn't imagine anyone else.

"Mr. O . . . " Ludwing paused, looking flustered, apparently still unsure of Tim's name. He turned to the younger detective.

"O'Reilly," Namaka said.

"I don' know why dat ahddah name stay stuck in my head."

"It's on the news," Namaka said. "That LSD guy."

"So," Ludwing said, "fooling around ahddah people's girlfriend could explain this. We will find dis people and interview dem." He stood and handed Tim a card, saying, "Call us if you can t'ink of anyt'ing else."

At that moment, as Ludwing reached for the doorknob, it suddenly dawned on Tim: *Overtorque the studs! Just put a wrench on a few studs and tighten them close to the breaking point.* Oddly, he hadn't even been thinking about the blown jug at that moment. The thought had just flashed on him out of nothing. *Still*, he stubbornly thought, *could is a far cry from did.* He dismissed an impulse to mention it. But he would mention the idea to Teddy, the chief mechanic, to see what he thought about the possibility of someone causing a cylinder to separate from a crankcase.

The detectives left the building. Tim, Ben, Lisa, and Greenberg remained in the outer office, all but Tim animatedly speculating aloud about the crime. Tim was conscious of what they were saying, but he was too occupied mulling over ideas about the blown jug to join in. Then he changed his mind.

"Maybe I figured out how someone could make a jug blow, too," he muttered.

"And how's that?" Greenberg said, sounding doubtful.

So Tim told him about his theory, expanding it as he imagined how a torque wrench would measure how much tightening would break the threads that anchored a hold-down bolt to the crankcase. Some or all of the other studs could be tightened to a reading just shy of the breaking point, leaving it to a full-power takeoff to put enough internal pressure on the cylinder to complete the deed.

"We'd better move you," Greenberg said after the long silence that followed Tim's speculation. "Just in case. Get you out of that Y and someplace else real quick on the QT."

"Good idea," Ben said as Lisa nervously clutched at Tim's arm.

"Could be some nutcase," Greenberg said. "Noisy planes flying low do attract attention. May seem like a threat to some wacko."

"Interesting thought," Ben said.

"Give me a couple hours to set something up," Greenberg told Tim. "Where will you be? Not the Y."

"At my place," Ben said. "We'll have dinner there and see whether we can make any more sense of all this."

* * *

As they drove back to Kaimuki, Ben and Lisa plied Tim with questions about what had transpired between him and the detectives in the privacy of Greenberg's office. Probably assuming that he'd told them about his blown-jug idea, they didn't ask about that. Mainly, they were trying to get a satisfactory take on what the police were planning to do.

"I'm glad you're moving," Ben said. "You shouldn't go to work for a while, either."

Lisa had said little. Tim guessed that she was having a silent conversation with God. She was sitting between them on the front seat, and she clung to Tim's arm and leaned her head against his shoulder all the way to Ben's place.

* * *

As they were going through it all one more time with Ben's dad while Naomi took little Joey over to the neighbors so he wouldn't hear it, Greenberg called. After the call, Tim told the others that Greenberg had reserved a hotel room in person, and was going to drop off the key at the Polacols'. "I won't even have to go to the front desk" he said. "He's using his name and credit card. He says he wants me completely out of sight for a couple days."

"Great," Ben said. "Good thinking."

"He's coming over to the hotel first thing in the morning so we can give it some more thought together. He's going to bring me food and stuff. I'll give you my room number in case you want to call or come over, too."

"No, we won't," Ben said. "Not even us. Don't give your location to anybody. Only your boss."

"That's pretty extreme."

"Someone has gone to extreme lengths to kill you."

Lisa was crying again. Naomi, who'd just returned from the neighbors', got up from her chair and went around the table to stroke her back and comfort her.

"If someone did cause both crashes, he's known exactly where to find your airplanes," Ben continued. "The most obvious person would be one of your mechanics. One of them would have the expertise, too. Have you noticed any one of them acting unusual in any way?"

"No. We get along fine. You're going to make me paranoid."

"Paranoia is an unreasonable fear. You have plenty of reason to fear this."

"And maybe not. Some teenage prankster dumped some pebbles in my fuel tank. And a tired old jug finally did what so many do and parted company with the rest of the engine."

"Why don't you go on into the dining room?" Naomi said. "It'll be just a few minutes, and dinner will be ready."

"I'm worried sick those police just aren't up to it," Lisa moaned as they stood. "Maybe the FAA can figure it out. They need to know everything. But it's so hard to believe someone would intentionally try to hurt you!"

"The noise might do it," Tim said. "I made some pretty loud takeoffs by some beach cabins all day the day before. It wouldn't take full-on mental illness to come unglued over that noise. Some dude back from Vietnam with combat fatigue. Trying to get some peaceful R and R."

"That makes sense," Ben said. "But whatever the case, he just might be crazy enough to keep trying."

"Leave!" Lisa exclaimed. "Just leave! Go home. Better yet, go on to Nicaragua now. It doesn't matter whether there's a seat for you there or not. Or go look for that winter work you wanted in Africa or Australia. Get as far away as you can."

Tim laughed and said, "Maybe I will if you keep spooking me like this."

But what if the cops never do solve it? he wondered while the others rehashed everything. *Hide out forever? No way! No more than a dying man would want to sleep away his last days!*

"Uh-oh!" Lisa said, and they all looked at her. "It just struck me: Could it be connected to your poisoning?" She was staring at Tim, her eyes going wide with that possibility.

"What's this?" Ben asked.

So Tim told the Polacols about getting sick. "But I'm sure it happened the usual way."

"Which is?"

"Like touching something contaminated—a windshield, whatever—and gnawing on a fingernail afterward. Whatever. There's lots of ways it could happen."

"Any trouble with anyone there?"

Tim shook his head, but the back of his neck prickled despite his strong doubt that the poisoning had been intentional. There was no denying that both the poisoning and the light in his eyes *could* have been intentional, but that was extremely unlikely. As the others kept trying to wring more possibilities out of all they knew about Tim's mishaps now, he silently thought of other ways he could have been poisoned on purpose. His gloves and maybe even his helmet could have been doused with some chemical. *Like pour Thimet crystals into my gloves, then dump 'em out to leave just the powder. That would do it.* He'd never bothered to take his gloves or helmet home with him when he'd flown in Idaho. Since the planes were kept right by Matt's house, he hadn't needed to worry about them being swiped by some stranger passing by. He'd simply left them on the airplane's seat.

There was a knock at the Polacols' front door. It was Greenberg. Tim left with him, and he decided on the way to tell him about the two incidents in Idaho.

"Eerie," Greenberg said. "I don't know what to think about that, except that it can't have anything to do with your problem here. But listen. I've got a plan to get you off this island in a couple days. Instead of having Roger over on Maui do some pasture fertilizing on Molokai before he goes on vacation, I'll put you on it. Then you can fill in for him there on Maui while he's gone. There's probably other neighbor-island work I can send you off for, too. It'll all be hush-hush, so nobody here will know what's going on. How does that sound?"

"Sounds like fun. I'll just sit tight at my new pad until I hear from you. I wonder what we should do about my car?"

"Yeah, we need to do something. How about I hide it in my garage? Give me your keys, and the wife can give me a hand moving it."

Greenberg drove toward one of the smaller, plainer hotels in Waikiki, far back from the beach.

"What about Les?" Tim asked. "A nut would be out to down any duster, not just mine."

"Yeah, I thought about that and talked it over with Les." Greenberg stopped the car a couple streets away from the hotel. "Les suggested we hire a good retired cop to keep an eye out wherever he's flying. But hide you in case it's personal. That's what we'll do.

"Take that sack on the backseat," he said. "I got you a toothbrush and razor and other things, plus a little food. Make a list of whatever else you need. I'll see you tomorrow."

After Tim put the milk, fruit, and luncheon meat in the small refrigerator, he used the hotel's complimentary notepaper and pen to start making a list of things for Greenberg to pick up, and the first items he noted were a detailed map and a good guidebook for all the islands. He had both at the Y, but it would be best if Greenberg didn't go inside to get them. The less anybody he knew was seen around there, the better. It wasn't likely, but somebody could be keeping an eye on the place.

He tried to just relax and watch television, but his thoughts kept grinding over and over through the question of whether the gas-tank trick really had been the only intentional cause among his mishaps. The only broadcast on the tube that grabbed his full attention was a replay of OJ Simpson's famous 64-yard touchdown run in the '67 USC–UCLA game, but that lasted only a matter of seconds. They were airing it to build interest in the upcoming Rose Bowl.

That guy has it all, Tim mused, hitting the channel changer again a few times. But there was nothing more that he wanted to watch.

He leaped to his feet and started doing deep-knee bends. He could toughen up in case someone tried something physical. After three sets, he dropped to the carpet to do some push-ups, thinking, *If some puke really is after me, I'd love to put the hurt on him!*

After he'd done three sets each of deep-knee bends, push-ups, jumping jacks and sit-ups and was dripping with sweat, he had an urge to go for a run. *It's not like people are prowling every street in the city looking for you*, he reasoned. *Assuming anybody's looking for you in the first place. You look like just another Waikiki tourist haole.* But he immediately realized that wasn't quite true. He was too darned tall. And in addition to that, the tourists he'd seen so far hadn't been into jogging.

He wondered whether the detectives had found the locals he'd told them about yet.

* * *

Molokai was a kick. Tim shared a bunkhouse in the high country with three Hawaiian ranch hands who, unlike the other cowboys who lived in regular houses on the ranch, were single.

The three served as Tim's loader men. They spent most evenings drinking beer, singing, and learning from one another what life was like on that tiny island and in Los Angeles. They also spent an evening fishing with handlines for what the Hawaiians called *ulua,* which Tim recognized as big jack trevally.

Tim enjoyed Molokai so much that sometimes hours went by without his thinking about the sabotaged duster. Those Molokai Hawaiians were the happiest, most carefree people he had ever known, and he was very reluctant to return to Honolulu to go back into hiding. But he did and tried to make the best of his dull hermit's life. Greenberg was still anchored in his better-safe-than-sorry frame of mind and wouldn't let him fly anywhere on Oahu. Tim resumed his calisthenics routine. As he exercised, using the TV to supplement his antiboredom effort, he started thinking that if he got too itchy, he'd sneak over to the public library. But the news about the My Lai massacre held his attention in his cramped room for a while. He also managed to get a call returned from Officer Namaka, and he asked the detective whether they'd discovered anything of interest.

"We've finished checking out those people you mentioned," the detective said. "We're sure they don't have anything to do with your accidents."

"Accidents," Tim said.

"Sorry. Poor choice of words. We know for sure the last . . . *incident* . . . wasn't an accident, so we'll keep working on it. But we don't have much left to go on."

By alternating exercise, channel-switching on a hunt for more My Lai news, some absent-minded attempts to read in his old favorite, *History of Western Philosophy,* as well as impatiently leafing through the surfing and news magazines, Tim was able to hang in there in his stuffy little room each day until it was time for Lisa to get back to the YWCA from the university, and he'd call her to chat for a while.

"We're getting awfully close to the Christmas visit," she said.

"December thirteenth is right around the corner. I'm really not sure I'm ready. But how are you doing?"

"I'm fine. Just bored is all. Is Lance really going to be that big a strain for you?"

"He sure is. I just don't know what to do. My heart gets all fluttery when I think about it. But I'm relieved, too. Just a few weeks from now, it will be decided one way or another, and that will be that. I must decide!"

"He's an amazing guy, Lisa."

"Do you think you'll still be here when they come? How likely is Nicaragua, really?"

"Johnny Crash said it was pretty likely."

"*You'd* be happy enough to see Lance."

"I would. I've been thinking how much I like them all. Lance and I could buzz around in the two-holer if he had time, and—"

"There's nothing new from the police?"

"No."

"I'm praying for you, Tim."

"Keep it up. I'd just as soon not check out while I'm young enough to surf."

"You don't sound concerned at all!"

"I'm not. I'm sure it was a one-time thing." He thought again of Idaho, but he wasn't about to mention that to her. It just had to be coincidence. "What's really getting to me is being holed up in this room. I got a fresh taste of freedom on Molokai and—"

"Molokai? I didn't know you went there."

"It's all supposed to be a secret. Remember? Anyway, it was great, and I can tell you because I'm not there anymore. Those people are fantastic." He told her all about it.

Tim also called Ben and Lei. He told Ben about Molokai, and he told Lei only that he'd been unusually busy working. After all, he wasn't sure that those two dudes who'd bothered him about her weren't involved.

He called Lance, too. Lisa had told Lance about the crashes, of course, and Lance kept probing about the investigation of the latest one. Tim told him a few details, but kept switching the conversation back to the Christmas trip, telling him all the things they might do together but also acknowledging that Lance would probably want to spend lots of time with Lisa, too.

"Sometimes I do have to wonder about what you really think, old buddy," Lance said. "Are you really all that eager for us to be married?"

"Same as always, Lance. Actually, I've been going out with a Hawaiian girl. Maybe we could double-date. That is, if I'm still around when you get here."

* * *

"I can't believe I let you talk me into this," Solly said when he picked Tim up at the hotel for the pre-dawn takeoff for Maui. He pointed upward toward the roof of his Buick.

"Nobody's going to notice. It's just another surfboard. They're everywhere."

Solly had removed the board and rack from Tim's station wagon and had put them on the roof of his very nice, late-model sedan.

"Well, you'd better tie the damn thing down good. If it flies off, it could tear the tail off. I'm tired of you breaking our airplanes."

Tim knew Solly was kidding him, and he mildly said, "I figured it out, and it's foolproof. We'll pass one rope around the front of the skeg, all the way around the fuselage and across the back of the cockpit. Another around the nose just ahead of the lower wings will snug it down so it won't go anywhere."

"Well, just try not to pretzel this airplane. Okay?"

"I'll give it some thought."

Tim was sure the surfboard would stay put, and he wasn't worried about drawing strangers' attention to it on Maui. He wouldn't be landing at the main airport in Kahului. He'd be using the main duster strip in an obscure cane field.

* * *

Maui was a much lonelier experience than Molokai. Manuel, the local Portuguese loader man, was polite but very reserved. He pronounced his name the local way, *Man'-el*, putting the emphasis on the first syllable. Tim tried to draw him out during their half-hour lunch breaks, but the older man never did loosen up and do anything more than minimally answer Tim's questions, which were intended to be conversation starters.

Tim saw other surfers when he went to try one break or another after work, but he never got into prolonged conversations with them. They'd exchange a few words about the surf and re-focus on what they'd come to do.

Tim's stay there was much longer than the one on Molokai, so Greenberg had provided a rental car, as well as a hotel room in the little port city of Kahului. Tim spent some of his spare time there preparing for a SCUBA-diving certificate. He also drove around the island, including a Saturday drive out the tortuous road to Hana, and he made the requisite drive up the twisting road to the summit of Haleakala and viewed a spectacular sunset. In the evenings, he studied for his diving test, read the magazines and books about Hawaii that he'd bought, watched some television, and called his closest friends and the boss in Honolulu. He'd given Johnny Crash the number at Aloha Dusters, so he was covered as far as that went, too.

Oahu could still hold some danger for him, but he didn't think that was likely, and he was eager to return and get back to work there. Once again, he chose to believe that some of those kids who did their drag-racing at Dillingham must have put the pebbles in the gas tank. It had been an impulsive, one-time mistake, and that was the end of it.

27

CHRISTMAS SPIRIT

Tim spent more time than usual gazing at the TV the evening of December 9 and a few nights afterward as monstrous storm surf battered not only the islands but distant California. He was still on Maui. Except for one Hawaii surfer who rode a gigantic wave and made the news, nobody else dared to surf those waves. There was a report that some were fifty feet high. Tim also spent some time gazing at the awesome spectacle in the daylight from a couple locations along Maui's north shore not far from his hotel.

He was still on Maui as the storm surf abated and the Levengers and McLeans arrived in Honolulu. He called them at the Waikiki Hilton their first evening on Oahu to tell them how eager he was to see them.

The evening he returned, he hustled over to their hotel for dinner with the family. He'd flown on Maui until midafternoon the day before, forced himself to get into bed and turn the lights out early, and impatiently waited for sleep so that he'd be up early enough to get over to the airport in Honolulu by six in the morning, when nobody else would be there, to meet Greenberg and submit to another secret ride back to his hotel.

Later that morning, he had a cab take him to a ritzy men's clothing store and bought the most expensive outfit he'd ever owned in his life: a pair of luxuriously soft brown loafers, fine beige slacks, a silky long-sleeved casual shirt of dark brown, and an exquisite light-chocolate sport coat. Having arranged for some quick tailoring once he'd made his selections, he waited in the store for the slacks to be hemmed and the jacket to be let out a little for his broad shoulders.

The coat and trousers were just off-the-rack clothing only a few cuts above average, but he'd become so devoted to saving money that even that bit of a splurge on mere clothing made him uneasy. However, he planned to spend as freely on the McLeans and Levengers as they'd permit. He was very much into the Christmas spirit about doing whatever he could for them.

Later, he called for another taxi to take him to the Hilton. With his long legs and his improved physical condition, he probably could have walked it in ten minutes, but he didn't want to perspire. The Hawaii winter evenings had been getting cooler, but it wasn't all that cool, and it was humid.

Arriving at the hotel entrance, he saw Lance, who looked like some movie star as he stood waiting in the glittering lobby, and Lance spotted him before the cab stopped. Lance rushed across the lobby with his incredibly handsome face all lit up with a huge smile. He was making heads turn, and Tim was even happier now that he'd gone all out on his new clothing. The young farmer wore casual beige shorts, gleaming penny loafers without socks, and a fantastic aloha shirt with gold specks in the filmy brown fabric that precisely matched the color of his gleaming, carefully styled hair. Lance looked so elegant in his casual clothes that Tim didn't feel one bit overdressed.

"Hey, buddy!" Lance called out, clapping him on the back and shaking his hand.

"Hey, there! Aloha!"

"Come on. Let's go on up. They should be just about ready. I'll put on some nicer clothes for dinner, too. Don't want you looking better than me with Lisa around."

Tim grimaced, shaking his head in mock exasperation, and they turned and strolled across the lobby toward the elevator. Tim couldn't help but note the admiring glances they were getting. Lance was much handsomer, but Tim knew he looked pretty cool in his new outfit as well. He did have his height and physique going for him.

"I keep thinking about your trouble with that airplane," Lance said. "I'd sure like to get my hands on whoever did that to you!"

"I'd enjoy doing that, myself. If they're real bad guys, that is. I keep thinking it was more likely just kids who didn't stop to think they might hurt somebody."

"Some prank!"

"Yeah. But let's forget about it. Let's talk about what you want to do while you're here."

"Well, surf, of course. June was phenomenal."

"Just let me know if you want me to come along. Surfing's my thing. But I know you need time alone with Lisa."

"I'll do both, buddy."

"We could go SCUBA diving, too, if you want. And I think you'd enjoy making a run around the island in the company's two-holer Stearman."

They got into the elevator, and Lance asked, "Two-holer? You mean two-seater?"

"That's right."

"Maybe we can do that tomorrow while Lisa's in class. Speaking of which, how's *your* love life these days? Still dating that Hawaiian?"

"She's a knockout, Lance, but we're not really getting that close. She's kind of waiting to see how this other guy works out. I have been looking for this one cutie I met at the beach, but I haven't been able to find her again."

"Here we are." They got out of the elevator, and Lance said as they walked down the hallway, "It's pretty reassuring to think you're spending some of your time with babes other than Lisa. Do you think that Hawaiian lady of yours would like to go dancing? I'd like to get a look at her."

"We usually go dancing. Actually, I'd call what I do shuffling. She likes this great hotel on the other side of Waikiki where you dance under a couple huge banyan trees."

Lance stopped, unlocked a door, and ushered Tim into a suite as he called out, "Look who's here!"

"Tim!" Lance's dad cheerfully called out, and Lisa's father shouted, "Hey there, Tim!" Both older men scrambled to their feet and hurried over. Judging by the cards and chips, they'd been playing poker.

"How are you, son?" Levenger asked, pumping Tim's hand.

"Fine, fine. Good to see you. You all look well."

"We are," McLean said. "Everybody is, even Mrs. Levenger. I hope you can spend some time with us."

"Some. I don't want to get in the way." He was going to let them take the initiative about how much they wanted him around.

"Lisa says you have a right good job here."

"I do. Sometimes I'm tempted to stay."

"Why don't you?" Mr. Levenger asked.

"It's not his life's work," McLean said. "He's saving up for college. Is that still so, Tim?"

"Exactly," Tim said, feeling pleased that the man had cared enough to listen and remember.

"Well, come on over and let's sit," Levenger said. "It's getting dark, but there's still a little view left. The ladies will be ready in a few minutes."

They went to sit in a semicircle of easy chairs and a couch facing a large window beside sliding doors that led onto the balcony, and they started pumping Tim about his problem. Tim politely told them the basics, then turned their focus off him and his trouble by asking how the harvest had turned out. It had been a good one.

"You boys killed them bugs good!" Lisa's dad said. He was about to say more when a door to one of the bedrooms opened and Mrs. Levenger entered.

"Tim!"

He got up and went over to her. She looked so lovely in a blue, rather formal dress and silver sandals. She held out her slender hand, and Tim carefully grasped it.

"Oh, give me a hug," she said, putting her other hand behind him and giving him a squeeze. "It's so nice to see you again!"

She let him go, and he straightened, thinking that she'd been very friendly the few times he'd seen her in Oklahoma but never that demonstrative. She did look unusually well. She had looked so ill when he'd seen her before that he was surprised.

Then there was a knock at the main door, and Lance let Lisa and her mother in. Mrs. McLean gave him a hug, too. Mother and daughter made a lovely pair in their floral-print dresses, sandals, and great crowns of wonderful golden hair.

"Shall we?" said Mr. Levenger, and they filed out of the room to go to dinner.

Lance came alongside and put his arm around Tim's shoulder, saying, "Man, it's good to see you again, buddy!"

* * *

Here we go! Tim merrily thought as the two-holer lifted off the runway and made a low turn to cross the lagoon. Lance was at the controls in the front "hole," handling the controls, and Tim was strapped into the rear cockpit, thinking, *Payback time!* He was delighted to have the opportunity to return the hospitality that Lance had shown him in Oklahoma.

Lance gained four hundred feet as they crossed over the milky green shallows off the eastern edge of the airport and held that altitude to fly over the clearer blue shallows in front of Honolulu. Luckily, since it was wintertime, which can be very rainy, it was another bright, warm, beautiful morning. There was just the right amount of small white cumuli scattered about to ornament the pure sky. As usual, the little clouds had gathered more densely over the steep green mountains just behind the city, and wherever the sun struck among the dappling of the clouds' shadows, the brilliant vegetation seemed to be lit from within as well as by those golden rays. It was such a splendid scene from their vantage point free of ground clutter, and it thrilled Tim to be providing his friend an eyeful of paradise that few tourists ever see.

He wanted very much to do the same for the others. As they passed seaward of Waikiki and approached Diamond Head, Tim reflected again on the suggestion he'd made the night before, that the entire group rent a couple four-seaters for a lengthier tour to one or more of the other islands. They could fly past Molokai's spectacular sea cliffs, which were the highest in the world, on a luncheon flight to Maui or even to the Big Island. But Kauai, in the opposite direction, was said to present spectacular scenery, too. Since there were four licensed pilots among them, two could fly over and the remaining two fly back.

Lance flew on around Diamond Head. As planned ahead of time, they switched from the control-tower frequency to the intercom frequency once they were clear of the control zone. They passed red Koko Head, crystalline Hanauma Bay, and Sandy Beach with its small shore break and ever-present bodysurfers, then hugged massive basalt cliffs as they rounded Makapuu Point. On the opposite point of low rocks beyond the wide crescent of white sand, a half dozen bodysurfers were catching some good waves.

Tim thought immediately of Mickey and told Lance he was taking control to see whether he could spot her. He cut the power, banked steeply, and tightly spiraled the Stearman down close to the water. Flying toward the cluster of surfers in front of the rocky point, Tim held the nose high in slow flight and used only enough power to remain safely airborne. His plan was to shout her name if he did see her, and he grinned at the thought. She wouldn't be able to recognize him in his leather helmet and goggles, and she'd wonder who it could be. After the first pass, he was pretty sure that she wasn't down there, but he made another to be sure.

Instead of having Lance resume the flight along the coast, Tim retained control to cut diagonally along the eastern mountain range's spine that ran inland from the Makapuu cliffs. His intention now was to give Lance a close view of the fantastically scenic inland cliffs of Nuuanu Pali. He flew a little below the fluffy white clouds and out from the cliffs a couple hundred yards, knowing that no view of the *pali* from the ground could have as great an impact on the senses as this one.

As they approached the cliffs, which is what *pali* means, Tim started telling Lance about the Hawaiian warriors who leaped from the cliffs rather than surrender to Kamehameha's conquering army. They had just passed the place, and Tim was about to tell Lance to take control and fly on when he caught sight of movement on a ridgetop. Edging nearer, he saw that it was a small band of wild goats. "Look," he said into his mike. "Off to the left." But Lance still hadn't seen them by the time they had flown by, so Tim turned back to get closer.

The biplane passed near enough to them this time that it made the shiny, dark creatures mill about nervously on the narrow ridgetop. There were big ones and little ones, a shaggy, bearded billy with very long, slightly curved horns, smaller billies, nannies, and two kids. Each of two nannies had one small kid close beside her.

"I see them," Lance said. "Let me have it." He wobbled his stick a couple times, and Tim let go.

Lance turned the biplane back toward the goats and dove toward them, which started them running along the incredibly narrow crest of the ridge. It was one of those downward-slanting ridges that jutted out toward the coast like ribs from the mountain's knobby spine. One side of this particular ridge fell vertically to the forest far below, and the other side slanted downward very steeply, indeed, but not vertically. Lance turned back for another pass.

Tim grinned, wondering whether his friend would ever grow up completely either. They had so much in common. But Tim had made up his mind that this would be the last pass by the goats. They'd already caused the poor animals more than enough panic.

This time Lance flew straight toward the goats, which had stopped where the downward-slanting ridge went vertical. The two-holer was getting much too close to the creatures, now milling at the brink in greater agitation.

Tim reached for the stick, but he was too late. He saw one nanny suddenly spring away, launching off the far vertical side of the ridge into space. Her tiny kid immediately leaped after her.

Lance pulled up, missing the top of the ridge at the last second by ten or twenty feet, sending the other goats bounding back up the ridge toward the mountain. He made a very rapid, steep turn seaward to look back and watch nanny and kid sail down toward the forest below. Their forelegs were perfectly still and thrust forward, and their hind legs were perfectly still and thrust back. They held their heads high, and it looked as if they were doing nothing more than routinely leaping from one crag to another.

Lance's head rapidly bobbed. He hitched around in his seat, and Tim saw that he was grinning like crazy. His eyes were hidden behind his darkly-tinted aviator glasses, which by contrast emphasized the brightness of his joyous smile. "Splat!" he shouted loudly enough without his mike that Tim could hear.

Tim angrily shook his head and shouted in turn, "That's sick!" He grabbed the stick and gave it a vicious yank, taking control.

He could not comprehend the guy's delight in having done such a thing. It made him so angry that his hands and arms were shaking.

He had the Stearman in a shallow power dive now, aiming for a distant low point of land down the seacoast. He was suddenly in a great hurry to get back to the airport and put some distance between himself and Lance Levenger.

A puffy little cumulus cloud floated in the way, and he angrily snap-rolled right through it. Struggle as he might to soften his reaction to Lance's cruelty, he was still so angry that he didn't give a damn about initiating that wild gyration exceeding normal cruise speed. There was something deeply satisfying in the resulting violence of the maneuver. However, as he flew around the island's northernmost cape, he kept trying to bring his reaction under control and be more reasonable.

The goats had certainly been killed instantly on impact and had not suffered. He thought how he'd never felt the impact of his two crashes, and he doubted that the goats had been aware of theirs. Once they'd leaped, they hadn't seemed to be afraid. Surely their legs would have involuntarily scrambled if they had been full of terror. They had been so still they'd seemed like inanimate forms cut from black construction paper as they had fallen, fallen . . . Besides, back where Lance came from, few animals were kept for cuddling. Most were nothing more than useful objects—horses for herding, cats for rodent control, dogs for warning about strangers or bird hunting. Cattle were food. Coyotes deserved killing because they had a taste for newborn calves.

And hadn't he read that alien goats were decimating rare and precious native-Hawaiian vegetation that grew nowhere else in the world? So, really, what was so horrible about Lance getting rid of a couple?

Tim began to climb, returning to his original plan to have Lance try some aerobatics in the Stearman. They climbed on past Waimea Bay, and Lance pointed excitedly at the surf.

Tim nodded, thinking they could go back down for a closer look at some board surfing later.

As soon as the altimeter indicated three thousand feet, Tim shook the controls and, when Lance looked back, made an inverted-airplane motion with one hand. So Lance went through his usual sport pilot's repertoire, and Tim did a few stunts before he spun down closer to the water and proceeded around Kaena Point. Off Makaha, where they could see board surfers getting some good rides, Tim took it down lower and flew about fifty yards seaward of the surfers who were farthest out from shore.

Lance shook the controls, and Tim turned them over to him once again. The young farmer made a low 180-degree turn to recross the bay. He wasn't lining up directly on the surfers, which eased Tim's concern that Lance might want to buzz them.

The wind was light so near the water's surface in the lee of the steep mountainside nearby, and the sea close in was slick, although the swells from the open ocean rose up to form very nice breakers beside the rocky western point. One of the surfers, a dark-skinned local guy, shot away on a beauty, stood, and went out of sight on the shoreward side of the wave.

Tim was still relishing the memory of that sight when suddenly his awareness of flight sprang back to mind. His toes, which he'd absently been resting on the rudder pedals, began to flutter. He realized immediately that Lance was waterskiing the crest of the following swell. The rudder pedals were trembling just as they had whenever he'd felt a sprayer's wheels ticking over the wheat.

So! he thought, recalling what Lance had said when he'd gotten CR to try skiing the motorcycle across the stock pond. *He wasn't kidding!*

28

MORE MAKAPUU MAYHEM

Lance, Lisa, Tim, and Lei went on their double date the following night, and the three went bodysurfing without Lei the day after that. Lei had to work, but Lisa's fall-semester classes were over, and she was free to schedule her activities around five final exams or papers for a few more days before she was finished for the semester.

She had been diligently preparing for her eventual finals since the beginning of the term, and she didn't seem to be concerned about not spending as much time studying now. Her main worry, instead of finals testing, seemed to be that Tim was so nonchalant about letting his guard down to go out in public. She had tried to convince him to stay completely hidden, but he'd laughed it off.

He was just as nonchalant about taking them to Makapuu. His plan, should he see "the three wise guys" there, was to simply leave, rather than running a risk of Lance and Lisa having to witness anything ugly. He might even see Mickey. He might even get her to come to the Polacols' with him. But they wouldn't stay at the beach more than an hour because Ben and Naomi had insisted that Tim bring everyone to Joey's birthday party, which was going to be more than a simple gathering of children. Tim had carefully shown the elder Levengers and McLeans where the Polacols' house was on a map, and the plan was to meet them there.

Once they arrived in the parking lot at Makapuu, Tim did quickly scan the area for "the three wise guys," as he'd started to think of them because it was so near Christmas. He was pretty confident they wouldn't be a threat, since the cops said they'd been warned about it during their questioning, but he'd leave anyway.

He was much more intent about trying to catch sight of Mickey. He hoped that he'd have lots of reason to be much closer to Mickey than he was to Lei, as pleasant and loneliness-lifting as Lei's company was. He was overdue. Jen had dumped him nearly a year and a half earlier. Surely he had to be ready for some real romance now. In retrospect, it seemed weird that he hadn't gotten closer to Sandy back in Idaho. They'd gotten along so well that, if he'd made a determined effort to find out, she might have made him forget all about Jen.

Lisa and Lance had bought Churchill fins, which didn't get torn off by rough surf as easily as the snorkeling type. As they sat on the sand, pulling the fins onto their feet, Tim said, "You've got to be really careful you don't go over headfirst. Seriously. You could break your neck. And don't just stand in front of a breaking wave if it's a big one. They'll knock you around pretty bad. Dive under and head for deeper water."

So Lance and Lisa began by trying to ride the smaller waves, and Tim refrained from catching any waves himself as he began coaching them. However, they were doing so well after a while that he did leave them long enough twice to catch a couple of the bigger ones.

"You lucky dog!" Lance said later on as they drove away, heading for the birthday party. "I'd give anything to live here! Well, everything except the farm, of course. But *you're* not really going to leave all this, are you?"

"It'll be hard," Tim said, ignoring the fact that he, not being one of the landed gentry, being free to settle anywhere, could have felt slighted by Lance's comment. "I'll just have to take full advantage of being here in the time I have left. And I'll definitely be coming right back here in the morning to do that. We're supposed to start getting some really nice easterly swells tonight."

"You mean you'd miss church to surf?" Lance teased.

"That'll be hard, too, but I'll try not to feel too bad about it."

"You should join us for church in the morning," Lisa said, "and we'll come with you after lunch."

"Uh, probably not a good idea." They were good swimmers and were catching on to bodysurfing quickly, but Makapuu on a really big day required more than a few minutes of experience. "You have no idea how brutal it can get."

"We can just watch," Lance said. "We'll go to church with the folks to make them happy, then come out here with you. And if it turns out not to be so bad after all, we'll surf, too. We did pretty well today, didn't we?"

"You did." In fact, they had caught on far more quickly than he'd anticipated.

"If it's that bad," Lance said, "we'll just watch. Should be interesting."

* * *

They made it to the birthday party by a quarter to five. Naomi saw them coming and rushed outside to greet them.

"Welcome!" she called out. "I've been watching for you!" Before Tim could introduce her, she said, "I'm Naomi, the birthday boy's mom!"

Tim introduced the Levengers and Lisa's parents, and Naomi led them around the side of the house into a wood-fenced backyard. Ben saw them and left his post beside his father at a pair of charcoal grills, striding past several groups of men and women, young and old, of various races, who were seated at two picnic tables under a wide-spreading shade tree. A man and a woman were playing ukuleles, and most of the adults were singing as the little children screamed and chased one another around the lawn. Two white-haired, dark-skinned women sat conversing intently at a third picnic table in the shade of the neat, shed-type roof of corrugated aluminum that had been attached to the back of the house to shelter a patio.

"Here comes Ben," Naomi said. "I'll leave you in his care and get back to work."

"Aloha!" Ben called out. "Come over and sit under the tree. Beer?" He looked from one to another.

The McLeans and Levengers declined, but Tim said he'd like a beer, so Ben ushered them to the picnic tables and got people seated, then led Tim toward a big old-fashioned galvanized-tin tub filled with ice and beer. Tim picked up a bottle of Budweiser.

"I'll have one of those, too," Lance said, showing up beside him. "I don't want to be obvious about it. The folks wouldn't make a big fuss, but they do discourage it."

"Let's go visit over there on the patio then," Ben replied, quickly stooping to get a Bud for him. "Tim's mentioned you quite a few times. It's great to finally meet you."

Ben introduced Tim and Lance to the two older women, then motioned for the two young men to join him at the next table. "Tim told me you're a farmer," he said.

"*Did* he? We think more in terms of *agribusiness* these days. I'm an officer of the corporation, and I'll be involved in its management when I get out of grad school."

"Tim did say it was big," Ben stiffly commented.

Tim was cringing and trying to think of something to say that would make Ben forget Lance's little lecture, but Lance apparently read the looks on their faces and tried to make up for it himself. He laughed as though he'd been joking, and he said with a hillbilly accent, "Yes, sirree, we gittin' up there in *high* society. Ag-ri-*biz*-niss. As if our cows don't poop and . . . "

Ben had been watching Lance's lame performance with his head cocked inquisitively to one side, and when Lance was finished, he said in a flat tone of voice, "Tim told me you raise quite a lot of wheat."

"True. It's really more about wheat than cattle."

"It must be absolutely fascinating work," Ben dryly commented.

Uh-oh, Tim thought. *Ben's pissed.* It might not have been evident to Lance, but Tim knew Ben well enough to know he wouldn't have put it quite that way if he'd been sincere.

"Well, if not fascinating, lucrative."

Tim interrupted, saying to Ben, "You should have seen what we did out by Makaha the other day!" He went on to tell about waterskiing the Stearman.

"Sounds risky," Ben commented in a disgusted tone of voice, frowning.

"Oh, water's hard when you hit it at speed," Lance said. "You can bounce right off."

"Well," Ben said, getting up, "here come the ladies with the rest of the food. I'd better get back and help Dad with the chicken."

A couple hours later, Tim was standing apart from the others with Ben, thanking him as he was about to leave, and Ben said, "Your friend's an interesting guy."

"He sure is!"

"I didn't mean it as a compliment."

"I know. That agribusiness thing sounded pretty snooty."

"It's more than that, Tim. I can see why Lisa's having second thoughts about that guy."

"Ben, you don't even know him. He's amazing."

"He gives me the willies. Do you really think he's normal?"

"Normal? He sure isn't that. He's way over average, I'm sure."

"Well, I see we're not on the same wavelength. I didn't mean normal that way. What does the Bible say about eyes?"

Tim groaned and said, "Come on, Ben. You two just got off on the wrong foot."

"Ah, now I remember. It isn't in the Bible. It's an old French saying. 'The eyes are the windows of the soul.' Tim, haven't you ever wondered about those scary eyes of his?"

"Scary?" Ben was no dummy, but Tim was certain that he was being far short of rational about this. "Come on!" To the best of his memory, Lance's eyes were ordinary brown eyes.

"They're flat, Tim. Something's missing. That guy's trouble."

Tim laughed and said, "Well, thanks for having us. I'll call soon." He turned and walked away, shaking his head and wondering what was wrong with Ben that all of a sudden he could turn so vehemently against someone for acting a little snobby. And he couldn't figure what had moved Lance to behave that way, either.

Just guy stuff, he decided. *Sometimes humans aren't any better that way than animals.* He put it out of mind with a shrug and hurried to catch up with the Levengers and McLeans.

* * *

Lance's phone rang later that night. He shared a suite with his parents, but the phone in his room was on a separate line. It was CR, as he'd thought it might be. Lance was irritated. He wanted their phone contact to be minimal.

"Lonely?" Lance sneered.

"Naw, just checkin' in. It's been a while. She goin' to marry you or not?"

"She's playing hard to get. But we've been having a nice time. Hopefully we'll set a date before we go home."

Lance was sharply conscious of his unplanned use of that word "hopefully." It was hard to believe that Lisa was still avoiding commitment to a specific date.

He went on talking as he wondered what could be done about the problem. "Went for an airplane ride and out to some beach called Mackapoo," he said, pronouncing it the mainlanders' way instead of sounding each separate u. "Out by Sea Life Park. Do you have any idea where that is?"

"Yep, I done rode a bus all the way around this island. I done went and seen them dolphins."

"We're going back tomorrow after church. He wants to surf. Supposed to be some big waves. He's going to try surfing in front of the rocks by the parking lot. Sure hope he knows what he's doing."

"I ain't tried that surfin', myself. Maybe it's time."

"Who else knows you're here, CR?"

"I ain't told nobody. Only you."

"So only the airline and wherever you're staying has your name, right?"

"Nope. Paid cash and told 'em my name's Charley Rogers. Remember—"

"Never mind that. I'd watch out for that big surf if you're thinking of trying it yourself tomorrow."

"I'll surely to do that. I'll give that a *lot* of thought."

* * *

The following afternoon, the surf at Makapuu was booming. Literally booming. And cracking, too. Sometimes, when just the peak of a swell far out from the rocks broke, it cracked like a rifle shot, but it boomed when it curled over and collapsed nearly all at once in front of the sandy beach.

"Oh, Tim," Lisa moaned. "I don't want you to go out there!"

The lava shelf in the foreground was completely awash with flying white water. Yet a sun-blackened young local, perhaps in his early teens, stood casually on the higher rocks just beyond the reach of the waves with his green swim fins on, waiting to make a dash for the water in the lull that would come between wave sets. The wind was strong, and it whipped his long, slightly sun-bleached brown hair out in front of his face. As soon as the foaming sea went flat, he bounded across the draining lava in the knee-pumping, flat-footed way that kept a runner with fins from tripping. He belly-flopped into the rushing white back-surge and swam rapidly with it toward deeper water.

"You see?" Tim said reassuringly. "Even kids do it. Experienced kids, mind you, but kids. I'll be fine."

"Don't, Tim," she said. "I have a very bad feeling about this."

Tim laughed and climbed out of the back of Lance's rented two-door Mustang convertible instead of waiting for Lisa to open the front door. He headed on down the slope toward the wide crescent of sand, saying to Lance and Lisa, who trailed along after him, "I'm not used to running in fins like that kid. I'll get in the same place as yesterday."

Once they'd reached the sandy beach and another lull ensued, Tim dashed into the water, belly-flopped, got onto his back to quickly pull on his fins. Then he started swimming hard to escape the shallows before the next set of huge combers arrived. When he was near the half dozen or so other surfers far out in front of the rocks, he hopefully scanned to see whether Mickey was among them, but she wasn't.

"I don't like this, Lance," Lisa said. "Pray with me."

So Lance began, "Heavenly Father, we ask you in the name of your holy son, Jesus, to bless and protect our friend, Tim . . . " He went on for a few minutes, gradually shifting the prayer to asking God to bless him and Lisa in their thoughts about marriage.

Meanwhile, as before, Tim started having trouble being in just the right place at the right time to catch the breaks of the somewhat smaller waves that preceded the very big ones. It was obvious that he still had a lot to learn about Makapuu. One local in particular had the knack for judging far in advance where a wave would break. He was a pudgy guy who didn't look like much of an athlete, but he seemed to have a sixth sense about the waves, and he turned out to be an extremely powerful swimmer. He'd usually beat everyone to the first good wave of a set and go zipping away while Tim and the others dove deeply beneath it to fin as strongly as they could seaward, struggling against the shoreward rush.

Tim still hadn't caught a wave when he momentarily lost interest in the surf. His attention was consumed by the appearance of a new surfer swimming out to join the group.

"Hey! Mickey!"

"Beatle man! How *are* you?"

"Fine!" How he loved that sweet, heart-shaped face!

"Watch behind you." She wiggled her dark eyebrows and jutted her little chin in that funny way some locals had of signaling where to look. Then she swam very rapidly past him.

It was a monster. Having been distracted by Mickey, Tim was the last swimmer to get out to where it was about to break.

He just happened to be in position to catch it, and he crazily considered doing so. It rose steeply before him, hissing menacingly, streaks of froth stirred up by its fierce energy sweeping up its steep, dark face. *Crack!* went the crest high above him, and Tim chickened out and turned fins-up, diving for the bottom. It was deep enough that far out to make his ears ache before he pinched his nostrils and blew some air into them to equalize the pressure. The wave broke all the way down to the sandy bottom behind him, thundering with such tremendous force that it bounced him up and down and reminded him of an impacting artillery round. It amazed him that he wasn't sucked right back into the clouds of roiled sand that he could see only a few yards behind his madly-pumping fins. He'd figured that, if others could negotiate that surf, he could, but he wasn't so sure about that now.

He stayed down so long that, when he broke the surface, another great swell was about to crash over him. He had just enough time to hastily suck in another lungful of air and head for the bottom again. And so it went until the lull that followed the monstrous set.

The other surfers were unusually noisy now. They were gleefully shouting at one another: "Far out!" and, "'Ey, Kale! Why you no ride dose ones?" and, "No can believe dakine wave!"

"Beatle man," a sweet voice called. "I was worried about you." Here she came, swimming hard. "You were pretty late ducking that one," she said when she got right up to him and stopped.

"I wonder why I was distracted?" he asked, laughing. He was about to ask her whether she'd like to do a double date that evening, but she spoke before he could.

"Well, pay attention. Here we go again. Be *careful*."

Watching over her shoulder, she swam a few strokes shoreward, let the first, smaller wave go by, and flew away on the second, larger one.

Tim lucked out and got into the right spot for the third. As small as it was, compared with some others that day, it was the biggest wave he'd attempted to bodysurf so far. It shot him toward the rocky shore like a rocket. It was a wildly jarring ride, and it made him shout with joy as he tacked away from the rocks and toward the beach. However, he was careful to make a very conservative exit from the wave before the moment when it rolled over and exploded in the shallows. Instead of waiting to do a fancy tumble forward just as the wave completely collapsed, as he would have done on a smaller one, he simply cut more sharply to the left and let the peaking crest pass beneath him. The wind-lashed spray of the overcurling wave blew back so hard that it stung his face.

As he swam back toward the starting point, he caught a glimpse of the girl and swam hard to try to catch up. Before he could reach her, he heard the other surfers shouting and pointing seaward. Another huge set was rising out to sea. Everyone, including Mickey, started swimming like crazy to get way out into deep water to avoid the break.

Tim's rapid flailing was doubly motivated, for he was in a great hurry to get out there with Mickey. He imagined how the unbroken set would smoothly pass by beneath them, providing a perfect interlude for him to ask her for the date.

He was still twenty or thirty yards short of reaching the others when he was yanked under. He felt no pain. That was how the surfers back home used to guess it would be. The keen, serrated teeth would slice so smoothly through soft flesh that the only sensation would be the terrible force yanking at you.

He struggled with his hands and arms and one free leg to swim back to the surface. There'd been no time to take a breath. He wondered whether he would drown before he died from loss of blood or worse. With his eyes blearily fixed upward on the tossing, shining surface, he fluttered away with his one free leg and clawed water with his hands, but he made no progress. He looked down, expecting to see the broad gray head of a great shark.

He saw a blurry glint of silvery metal. And the pale shape of a man.

Tim futilely tried to yank his trapped leg free. Then he desperately bent over and groped for the hoses leading to the diver's mouthpiece. His hand passed through wisps of long hair.

The guy was ready for it. He batted Tim's hand aside.

Tim reached down again. If he could get a hand on an air hose or, better yet, the mouthpiece . . . But the diver was head-down and swimming hard toward the sandy bottom in the direction of the open sea. He kept the crook of one arm locked around Tim's calf.

Tim was in a great panic now, far greater a panic than when he'd thought he was caught in the maw of a shark, reacting now to the imminent threat of inhaling water. He feared that he wouldn't be able to hold his breath much longer. He kicked at the diver, but his other leg was in the way.

He doubled over and flung out his hand again. Again the diver batted his hand away. Tim instantly did it again, making what he knew would be his final effort. The palm of his hand hit the man's face mask. He strained to reach the mouthpiece as the guy ducked. Tim blindly clawed at the ducking face and felt the mask tear free.

He hazily saw it slowly fall away just as he heard the first mighty wave break directly overhead. A second later, the tremendous force of it slammed down on them.

It flipped Tim over backward. And over again. And again. Over and over he went, straining mightily to resist the need to inhale.

He tumbled past a coral head. He felt his right leg barely brush it. Another foot or so and he would have smacked right into it.

Somehow he came to the surface alive. He voraciously sucked air. And roiling water with it. He started having coughing fits. He was very near the deadly ledge of foam-drooling lava, but the great wave's powerful backwash was sweeping him seaward now. He started kicking hard, driving seaward, coughing and heaving as he went. The puny flapping of one finless foot was maddening. It was a crucial loss in seas so powerful.

Meanwhile, another wave had broken, and a billowy white wall of water came leaping and skipping toward him. He dove beneath it and single-finned as hard as he could against its fearsome force, knowing that he was being dragged backward anyway. Yet, when he surfaced, the backwash helped him gain some progress toward deeper, safer water.

Another wave broke, and he struggled through another chaotic onrush of exploding white water. Again he knew he was being tugged backward. Yet, again, he advanced.

He doggedly kept struggling until the final wave of the set had passed, and he was left in a surging but relatively calm expanse of thick foam. He turned onto his back and kept single-finning as hard as he could toward the open sea, sharply darting looks all about him for the diver.

Once he was safely beyond the breaks, Tim turned parallel to the shore and rode the rip current, still occasionally puking a gritty mixture of sand and salt water and frenziedly coughing as he went. He wanted to get in front of the sandy shore before the next set of waves rose up. He made it just in time to catch the first and smallest wave, taking it straight in toward the beach. Kicking as hard as he could, he managed to keep his body horizontal, and the wave flung him shoreward at the forefront of its boiling mass of white water.

"Tim!" Lisa screamed.

Here she came, dashing madly into the water. And there was Lance behind her. They thrashed into knee-deep water to grab him.

He lurched to his feet, but he was thrown off balance by the backwash and fell.

"We've got you!" Lance said. "Come on!"

A larger wave broke, rushed in, and knocked all three sprawling, but Lance and Lisa hung onto him. They washed ashore like chunks of flotsam, but they were safe now. Once they'd crawled up to the hot, dry sand beyond the reach of the waves, Tim was happy enough to remain on his hands and knees, coughing, trying to clear the last of the inhaled sandy water.

"Come on!" Lance said. "We've got to get this taken care of."

Tim noticed that Lance was applying a lot of pressure to the side of his right calf. He looked back to see the backs of Lance's hands covered with a bright red network and realized for the first time that the coral head had done some damage after all.

"You're cut pretty badly, buddy."

A lanky Hawaiian guy came running down the sloping sand toward them. He tore off his T-shirt, ripped it up, and went right to work, applying a couple folded pads of it to the wound and tightly winding a strip of it all the way around the leg. "You gotta get that sewn up," he said. "Friend of mine's already gone to call an ambulance."

Tim got control of his coughing and said, "Somebody better call the cops, too! Somebody tried to drown me!" He saw the Hawaiian look fiercely out toward the surfers. "Not a surfer," Tim said. "Diver—" He coughed up another dollop of sandy saliva and said as soon as he could, "SCUBA."

"I'll take care of it!" The guy bounded away, and shouted back over his shoulder, "You two get him up to the parking lot!"

Lance and Lisa each got one of his arms over their shoulders, each wrapped one arm around his torso, and they began walking him up the sandy bank toward the parking lot.

"Keep an eye out for a white guy out there," Tim told them, halting and peering down toward the surf crashing into the lava shelf. "Small white guy, I think. He had SCUBA gear, but he might have dumped it. Not that boy with the blond hair. This guy had dark hair. Long, dark hair."

"Let's keep moving, sweetie!"

"Keep watch in the foam. We might be looking for a body. Or maybe the rip took him down by the cliffs." He halted again to look back and search the cove's surface toward the cliffs, where the combers smacked the vertical base with tremendous force and cast up white wind-blown curtains of spray.

As soon as they had climbed all the way up to the parking lot, Tim could see quite some distance down the low coastline in the opposite direction from the great cliffs, and he carefully swept his gaze back and forth and farther and farther. There were no boats out there. Since no boat was in sight, he thought it was likely that the diver had entered the water at some calm, protected niche in the low, rocky coast to the north. If he had survived, there was a chance that he might have made it back to wherever he'd gotten in.

* * *

Tim caught sight of Mickey watching from the throng that had gathered around the police car and the ambulance with the flashing emergency lights. She saw that he'd seen her, and she mouthed, *You okay?* She pointed at him and made the *shaka* sign to make sure he understood.

He nodded vigorously and returned the *shaka* sign, clenching the middle three fingers on one hand and extending his thumb and pinkie, signaling that everything was cool.

She looked at him tenderly and slowly shook her head.

"Sir, I need your full attention," the police officer said. "If someone attacked you . . . "

A helicopter flew by as Tim and the cop continued through the necessary questions and answers. At first Tim reflexively thought the approaching chopper was coming for him, as if he was still in Vietnam. It flew down the coast for a couple miles, turned, and flew back toward the cliffs a little farther out to sea this time. He guessed that it was searching for the diver.

* * *

The police didn't find Tim's assailant, but a one-ton flatbed truck that had been reported stolen, along with SCUBA gear from its garage, was located off the highway just down the lower part of the coast from Makapuu. There was one set of clothing on the seat that might have been left by someone entering the small patch of relatively calm water behind a small natural breakwater of lava. When Officer Namaka interviewed him in his room a few hours after Tim's trip to the hospital, where his wound had been stitched shut, he said that the only evidence found in and around the truck had been a pair of brown cotton gardening gloves, a pair of jeans, a pair of lace-up shoes, and white socks, along with a white T-shirt.

Namaka's interest in the case, of course, was the fact that it was the second known, undeniable attempt to kill Tim. He said that he'd heard what was going on over the police radio and hadn't been able to contact Officer Ludwing. He said that the truck's owner had reported it stolen that very morning from the street in front of his home in Kailua, along with a SCUBA rig and other gear that had been lying in plain view in the open garage.

"Not even the truck's keys were found," Namaka said. "The guy must have hung on to them. Same with his license and whatever, unless he put them under some rock out there. The clothing does match the approximate size of the person you described."

And who in the hell could that be? Tim agonized after Namaka had left. He searched his memory for some small white guy—or maybe a paler local—with long hair. Thousands of people on the island had 60s-style long hair. He couldn't think of anyone of any relevance who looked like that.

* * *

Tim hid far more willingly after that second unmistakable attempt on his life. The boss signed for a room for him at another small hotel, just in case someone had found out about the earlier one, and provided him with bandages and ointment for his leg, as well as food to stock the room's small kitchenette.

Tim didn't step outside the room for two days. He made a couple telephone calls to Lisa and to the Polacols, making them quick and highly veiled for fear of someone at the front desk eavesdropping. And Greenberg called a couple times a day to briefly ask him how he was and whether he needed anything.

Tim was hyper-acutely aware of what he could hear and see going on around him. Occasional voices in the hallway made him flinch with alarm, and he'd peek through the peephole. The blare of a horn in the street below made him jerk with alarm. He slept fitfully and suffered bizarre dreams that were not about 'Nam but about being hammered by gigantic waves and someone repeatedly pulling him under, and he'd awaken kicking and waving his arms and sweating.

He couldn't concentrate well enough to read away the dragging time. Television and radio made a meaningless racket, except updated newscasts that gave some new and different slant on the pair of attempted murders of the crop-duster pilot. But his luck held in not having any photos or film of him printed or broadcast. Tim had seen a woman coming with a camera as he was being loaded into the ambulance at Makapuu, but the paramedics had slammed the doors shut, and they'd driven away in time.

Of course there was a good chance that the diver was on the bottom of the sea somewhere, held down by the diving weights but sufficiently buoyant to be tugged here or there by the currents. If that was so, it would probably take days for him to float. And when he did—if he did—it might be miles out to sea. Or the edible, buoyant parts might make a feast for the fish and never float.

Tim spent most of his isolation racking his mind for all the people he could remember interacting with since he'd come home from Vietnam. He made a small list of heated encounters, mostly with strangers, and a much longer list of casual and even happy interactions, including the ones with waitresses, clerks, fellow employees, and so on.

The guy who'd tried to get him was probably someone from Oahu, but Tim was in no frame of mind to put such a limit on his speculations now. Nevertheless, no matter how carefully he pondered each recalled contact, nothing clicked.

He sure as hell wasn't that big Idaho boy. Makes me all the more convinced there was no connection. Not unless that kid hired somebody . . . Hey, come to think of it, that pig might look like some poor farm worker's kid, but who knows, really? Truth is, he could be as rich as Lance Levenger. He could have hired somebody. Okay, so don't be too quick to dismiss any possibility.

After two days' isolation and a call to Lisa, Tim decided to run the small risk of a furtive cab ride to the Hilton for Christmas Eve. He doubted that anyone would think of looking for him there. The Levengers arranged to have Christmas dinner brought to their suite to minimize Tim's exposure. They'd also had a large Christmas tree brought in and lavishly decorated.

After dinner, they opened presents, and Tim was embarrassed when Mrs. McLean handed him one from all of them. Someone had gone to all the trouble of finding a card that portrayed Santa

Claus in a biplane, which was tucked beneath the ribbon around the soft and flexible gift wrapping. He felt a scary surge of emotion that threatened to set tears to flowing when he unfolded the card and read, "We love you, Tim," signed by them all and including a disclaimer by Lance, who had written, "Well, maybe not love but *like* for sure. Your buddy, Lance."

"Ma found it," Lisa said when Tim held the card up and shot her a questioning look. Then she quickly looked away, also apparently overcome with emotion.

"Open the present, boy!" Ned bellowed.

It was a new pair of surfer trunks with a pattern featuring a bony-kneed, big-footed, comic figure riding a board. Tim nodded speechlessly, thinking, *Cool! Very, very cool!*

"We noticed how ragged your others were getting," Lance said.

"Thank you," Tim was finally able to say. "Thank you so much!"

"To be used *after* they find that crazy man," Lisa's mother warned.

The party got merrier as the others opened their presents, and Tim noticed that Lance was noisier and apparently happier than he'd ever seen him. He discovered at least one reason why when Lance subtly beckoned him into his private room, which was located across the living-and-dining area from his parents' bedroom. He closed the door and poured two heavy crystal tumblers full from a bottle of Jack Daniel's Black Label.

"Here's to luck, buddy!" Lance said, clinking his thick tumbler against Tim's. "Here's hoping you've seen the last of that murderous son of a gun!"

404

29

FIRE IN THE SKY

A couple mornings later, Greenberg called Tim with a new disappearing-act assignment, first asking, "How's that leg? Can you fly?"

"I sure can!"

"Then I'm sending you to the Big Island. Two birds, one stone. They're behind schedule, and you should be safe over there for a few days. Just you and me and the Hilo guys will know where you are, and I've told them to keep it quiet or else. We'll see you at the crack of dawn."

"I'll be there."

"But Tim? When you get back? Why don't you just can Hawaii? For the time being. Come back when it's safe."

"Let's give it a few days. Weights or not, that puke should float. Bloat 'n float, I always say."

"You're nuts. If he survived . . . You know he could shoot next time."

"Yeah, I know. I'm keeping my eyes open."

After Greenberg hung up, Tim started hobbling back and forth, unconsciously favoring his damaged leg, so lost in thought that he wasn't aware of the slightest pain, crossing his small room from the closed sixth-floor balcony doors past the bed to the main door and back, again and again. He was still pretty sure the diver had been a white guy. He hadn't had the slightest disagreement with any *haole* on the island. Somebody must have put him up to it, and that just had to be the Idaho piggy boy.

But if so, why not just use a rifle and get it done? Or maybe that would be too easy on me for payback. Too quick. Maybe terrorizing me gives him more satisfaction.

Tim halted in the middle of the room, opened the drapes to let in some light, and absently gazed into the dazzling brilliance beyond the patio doors as he tried to process everything. After a few minutes, he realized with a start that people in the condos across the way could see right into his room. He could be in the crosshairs of a rifle scope that very moment. He quickly drew the drapes.

Ha! I'll bet that's it! That hog hired himself a hit man! And if he didn't drown, he's not about to give up. Not after all the trouble he's gone to already.

He tried to stop thinking about it. *Give your brain some rest.* He wadded some notebook paper into four small balls, sat on the edge of the bed, and started tossing them toward the wastebasket. The first round, he sank only two.

"Come on! Tighten up!" That was what his drill sergeant used to shout in boot camp, except that he'd add the one expletive about the recruits' mothers that Tim detested above all others.

He tossed the four wads again and sank three. "Yeah! Way to go!" He gathered up the wads to see whether he could get four for four. How he wished now to be on a real court, wearing off some of this nervous energy. He tossed the wads instead, and tried to imagine what kind of person that hired assassin must be.

He thought about calling the cops and telling them about the Idaho incident, but that incident in the restaurant seemed such a pitifully small reason for someone to go to all that trouble. And even if that kid had somehow found a local haole to do that, it didn't seem likely that Ludwing would see the possibility. Tim hated talking to that man. He was the main cop on the case, and he was slow. It probably would seem too far out for Namaka, as well.

"I wish I could get to a library." The sound of his own voice speaking so loudly startled him. Then he gave a cynical snort and said, again aloud, "You're talking to yourself, Timmy boy. Not good. And what are you thinking? Gonna take a do-it-yourself short course in criminal psychology?"

Tomorrow, man. Patience. You'll be out of here tomorrow.

* * *

Bill Osborne's Stearman was idling outside the hangar at the Hilo airport when Tim landed and taxied in. The chunky, middle-aged pilot rushed out to wave Tim over to the gas pumps. He reached up to grab the athletic bag of spare clothes that Tim pulled out of the hopper and the compacted life raft that Tim had been using as a seat cushion to cross the wide channels between islands. Then Bill handed up a gas nozzle. Having pulled his regular seat cushion out of the hopper and set it on the seat pan, Tim took the nozzle, stood on the cushion, and inserted the nozzle in the filler neck.

Bill ran Tim's things into the hangar, and he quickly returned to wait for Tim to hand the nozzle down and said, "If it's clear up at the volcano, we'll go straight on over. I'll show you the one that's been erupting lately. Hopefully it's fountaining again today. But we'll have to take the long way around the coast if the clouds are on the ground up there."

Not far out of Hilo, Tim was surprised by how undeveloped the island was. There were small, scattered communities among the cane fields in the lower part of the country. Beyond that, mazes of rough-looking roadways had been cleared to lead back into dense tropical forests, but there were few houses away from the paved, two-lane highway they'd been keeping in sight.

Soon, Bill led him farther away from the highway over road-less forest, which began to be broken by bleak fields of congealed black lava. Smoke rose from the forest perimeter of one field of new, swirly, fudgelike lava, and more smoke wafted out of a rath-er small pit not far uphill from it. Bill rocked his wings and circled the pit once, pointing out of his open cockpit at it, surely indicat-ing that this was the one that had been acting up.

The two pilots weren't the only observers. A few cars were parked on the only road in sight, and some tourists had followed a walkway of boards on the inland side of the crater to a viewing platform at the very brink of the pit.

Flying on, the two Stearmans emerged from beneath the clouds that hung over the Hilo side of the hump, and Tim's breath caught at the sudden appearance of the stupendous, soaring mountain to his right. In the foreground and for some distance upward and inland, the vast slope was thick with beautiful sunlit forest that had a much less somber appearance than the one beneath the clouds back toward Hilo. Way up high on the great mountain, the forest ended, and an immense bluish dome of barren lava stretched into the wonderfully pure, pale sky. He'd heard that the Big Island had some high mountains, the highest two being close to fourteen thousand feet, but it was one thing to read about them and quite another to see one up close like this.

I gotta come back and have a better look at this place! he thought. Although the attempts on his life had been occupying his thoughts far more than anything else since he'd departed Honolulu, he completely forgot about all that now. The view everywhere around him, not just the mountain but small volcanic craters and primitive forest full of gigantic ferns, was simply too spectacular to leave room for any other thoughts.

They flew past a huge crater a quarter mile or so to the downslope side of the main two-lane road they now followed over the hump, and it was nearly as awesome a sight in its glistening vast sprawl as the mountain. Then, after a several-mile stretch of much rougher, chunkier lava stretching away from the highway toward the invisible sea, lush green pastures and a few small cane fields began to appear upslope. Some minutes later, the ocean and dark green rectangles of what he guessed must be macadamia-nut orchards came into view far ahead in the lowlands.

Bill led him in a low dive past a duster strip in a notch between a high windbreak of tall, closely planted trees of some unknown kind on the seaward side and the short dark-green trees all around the strip that Tim took to be the macadamias. The loader men were waiting for them on the airstrip's uphill end beside a long flatbed trailer stacked with large fertilizer sacks.

As each pilot began to work independently on separate sections of orchard, Tim caught glimpses of Bill's extremely aggressive style of flying. He'd never seen anyone crank turns so quickly, and he'd never seen anyone power-dive at an airstrip to save time landing, then, at the last moment near the end of the strip, drastically kill off excess airspeed by abruptly swinging the fuselage radically sideways in a severe, wings-level, low-altitude sideslip.

Solly had told Tim that Bill was a charger. He'd proudly said that Bill had broken the old record at the big macadamia orchard near Hilo Airport one day by spreading 150,000 pounds of fertilizer in the orchard's eight-hour workday, making 100 takeoffs with 1,500 pounds of fertilizer aboard each time. "That's a takeoff and landing less than every five minutes," Greenberg had said. "You believe that? And that includes gassing up every hour and getting the stuff into the plane! That's the sort of efficiency that makes our competition look like amateurs. You can't argue with numbers."

Bill had told Tim that the only thing Tim needed to be careful about as they worked their separate fields was to avoid getting into a race with him. "I've been flying here 14 years," he said, "so I know these planes and conditions pretty damn good. We had this one new guy . . . But never mind that. I'll just say, You fly weird, and I'll go on back to town and leave you on your own. Okay?" He'd waited for eye contact and a nod of agreement from Tim before he'd turned away.

So Tim comfortably flew at his own pace. However, he, too, cautiously started making those dives and broadside skids to landings. He was sure that Bill would be able to tell by the smoothness of his maneuvers that he was staying in perfect control. After a couple hours, he found himself flipping with ease through the quickest turns he'd ever made. It was so stimulating to fly with Bill that he felt as though the tough-looking little guy had somehow psychically transmitted telekinetic power over an airplane to him.

They were dumping 400 pounds of fertilizer per acre, so they were landing and taking off in less than ten minutes on average, since most of the fields were not especially close to the airstrip. Their landings were usually more or less evenly spaced, so the loader men had enough time, though barely enough, to rapidly slice open the sacks and dump the fertilizer into the bucket and be ready to load a plane immediately after it landed.

There were three loader men, two dark-skinned, apparently mixed-race locals and one pale-skinned guy whom Tim had heard kidding the others, saying they'd better not be hung over if they wanted to keep up with what he called "one purebreed Po'tagee." The Po'tagee and one of the others who was about his age had to rapidly heft, cut, and dump fifteen 100-pound sacks of fertilizer into the lowered steel loader bucket for each planeload as the driver waited at the wheel to pneumatically hoist the bucket and zoom it in over the hopper as soon as one of the Stearmans sped in, whipped the tail around, and stopped.

There was some uphill-downhill flying, but the slopes weren't very steep in that lower swale not far from the sea. They had a light downslope wind off the mountain at first. The cold air from the vicinity of the frigid summit was still sinking, flowing downslope and out to sea, countering the usual northeast trade wind. As the sun warmed the mountain and the air along its flanks, a calm displaced the outflowing air and prevailed for a while. But not long after midmorning, the strong trade wind that accelerated around the eastern bend in the coastline began to blow in over the land, and Tim could see a dense mass of whitecaps, signifying much stronger wind, gradually approaching from far out to sea. The Portuguese swamper called the whitecaps, "Po'tagee sailboats." He told Tim, "You no going believe what kind wind Ka'u get. When those Po'tagee sailboats reach over here, going get crazy."

Crazy, indeed. When the wind finally did arrive in full force shortly before noon, the flying got very wild. Tim had made many rough-air landings since he'd come to Hawaii, but none to match what he was doing now, and Bill hadn't given any indication that they were about to stop flying.

At lunch, while Tim shared some extra sandwiches made by Bill's wife at Greenberg's request the night before, the older pilot told Tim that the combination of the heavier "orchard mix" fertilizer and its release at a somewhat lower "orchard height" would keep the strong wind from blowing the material off-target. He also asked Tim whether he'd ever made "reverse-P" downwind turns." Tim had never heard of such a thing.

"They work real good. Even uphill. Instead of starting your turn right after you pull up, you just keep going straight ahead for a few seconds. Go ahead and grab a little altitude. When you turn back, the wind's blown you far enough away that you've got room to hook back in and line up."

As the wind viciously hammered at his airplane, Tim experimented with the reverse-P. Once he got the hang of it, he found that it made a very surprising difference. Soon he was making downwind-uphill turns so rapidly that the flagman would barely have the next swath paced off before Tim would be back at the edge of the orchard with the money handle open.

Those gusting winds knocked Tim around far more violently than he'd ever experienced in flight. It used to irritate him in Idaho when, flying the Ag Cat, he'd hit some hot, rough summer air, and the jolt would rap his helmet against roll cage, so he was glad there wasn't one like that on this Stearman. Some gusts shook the plane so hard that it disrupted the fuel flow, causing the engine to sputter, and that had never happened to him before. It didn't alarm him, though, since Bill had to be experiencing the same thing and continued to work. In fact, Tim began to enjoy the wildness of it all so much that he started laughing. Once again, Superpilot notions nibbled at the edges of his mind, just as they had back in Oklahoma and a few other times since.

When they finished for the day, he and Bill had to fly back to Hilo because there was no room in the pickup's cab for any more than the three loader men. The volcano was socked in now, a frequent occurrence late in the day after the usual cumuli drifted in from the sea to stack against the windward slopes, so they cut around the lower slopes of congealed rivers of old lava that descended from beneath the jutting shelf of gray cloud.

Aloha had rented a car for Tim, and he used it to get to the small hotel on the edge of the bay where the company had made a reservation. He got cleaned up and walked around the corner to a drive-in he'd just seen, preferring to eat at an outdoor table after being confined to his lonely room in Honolulu. It was pretty early for dinner, but it had been a long, hard day, and maybe he'd be able to sleep a couple hours earlier than usual.

He took along a book that Greenberg had given him. It was Bob Hoover's memoir. That guy had led such an exciting flying life that his tales could occasionally make Tim forget his trouble.

After he'd consumed a couple local-style gravy burgers and a milkshake and had read a chapter, Tim closed the book and just did some people-watching. All the customers were locals, and he enjoyed listening to their pidgin English. The Hilo locals seemed to use it more than the ones in Honolulu. It was nice not to have to worry about the possibility that one of them might be looking for him. However, as he thought about that, the mystery began eating at him again.

The more he pondered it, the less certain he was that that Idaho guy had been behind it. He really hadn't looked like someone who'd have the brains and the money to find someone so far away to do such a thing.

It struck him that a similar attack on an airplane or pilot might have occurred on Oahu before—long enough ago that the cops had forgotten about it. It might be on record.

He returned to the hotel, got a map of Hilo from a stand in the lobby, and asked the desk clerk to point out where the public library was. He drove right over.

He asked a librarian about local newspaper files, and she directed him to the microfiche area. He spent an hour searching in vain. He was walking toward the exit when he passed the card catalogs, and he hesitated.

But what could you possibly learn from a book that'd be any use? Criminal psychology? Not likely. But maybe. What else is there to do?

It was a very long shot, but it was better than just helplessly wondering. He was pretty good at rapid scanning. It would be a lot better than lying awake in bed wondering.

Soon he came across a card for a book entitled *The Psychopath, an Essay on the Criminal Mind*. He immediately pictured the shower scene in *Psycho* and shook his head. Obviously, all criminals weren't like *that*. Not even most killers. Yet what did he really know? The second part of the title, "*the Criminal Mind*," looked more to the point, so he turned to get one of the stubby pencils and one of the small rectangles of notepaper left for the patrons and jotted down the information he needed to locate the book in the stacks.

It turned out to be a little paperback that wasn't even a half inch thick. That was fine with him. He didn't really feel up to slogging through some thick, exhaustive volume of dense scholarly language.

He soon discovered in the preface that the word "psychopath" did not mean to a psychologist or a sociologist what he'd thought it meant. After a few minutes, he was trying to make sense of a comment about Billy the Kid, who was said to be psychopathic, according to the defense in his case, but not insane. *But not insane?* Tim tried to make sense of the distinction as he stumbled on. Most of what he knew about psychology was no more than what he'd retained from an introductory course during his first year at the Beach, and he couldn't recall having ever read anything at all about psychopathy.

By the eighth page, he was totally absorbed and completely unaware of his surroundings. He ceased his hurried scanning. He was fascinated. However, by the twenty-fifth page, he still couldn't connect anyone he knew to what was being described. He did make a mental note of repeated references to case studies by someone named Cleckley, who'd written a book with the intriguing title, *The Mask of Sanity.* Nevertheless, despite his interest, he was yawning so hard by the time he finished page 41 that tears stung his eyes.

As he drove back toward the little hotel, he thought he'd have to read more about psychopathy someday. It was clear from what he'd read that a psychopath was not necessarily a killer or even a major criminal. What he'd learned had been very interesting, but he didn't think he'd learned a single thing to help him figure out the identity of his enemy.

* * *

The following day, Tim flew back to Ka'u alone. Bill had been dispatched to a pressing, last-minute job on a sugarcane plantation, and Tim had been told he'd be finished on the Big Island whenever he completed the orchard work.

It went much the same way that it had the previous day, except that the loader men weren't so hard-pressed to keep up. Making use of his improved speed-flying skills, he finished the job almost an hour before the orchard's regular quitting time.

I can make it back to Honolulu before dark easy, he thought as he flew straight up the slope for Hilo. Since the Stearman didn't have navigation lights, he couldn't leave for Honolulu in the dark of the following morning and be hidden away in his room soon after daylight anyway. He thought how Lance and Lisa might be able pick him up, and the three of them could sneak off to some obscure spot for a fairly safe visit over dinner. Then they could drop him off at his hotel. It was silly to go on keeping where he was staying a secret from them.

Suddenly his eager musing turned to fury. He gritted his teeth as he thought how sick he was of having to act like some low-life fugitive. Until that moment, he'd taken the two recent attempts to kill him much as he had taken what the enemy had tried to do to him in 'Nam. It was just the same old typical human craziness. The older he became, the more irrational behavior there seemed to be out there. He never had been able to sustain flashes of anger for long. In 'Nam, he'd mainly just done his duty, his bit to keep the unthinkable from happening to a clearly superior nation to anything the Commies ever bloodily brought into existence.

He was blind now to the magnificent Hawaiian forest rising close beside him, its dense canopy sprinkled with pale-yellow *ohia lehua* pompoms. His mind only seethed with thoughts of how he'd like to get his hands on whoever was after him.

Minutes later, he had to pay much keener attention to his flying, for clouds were thickly hovering close above the volcano, and he might have to turn downhill and detour around the seacoast. He hoped not. Remembering that he was in a hurry, he wanted to try calling Lisa and Lance as soon as possible on the chance that they hadn't already made plans for dinner.

As he approached the edge of the first crater, the big one that had been inactive for a while, he flew by a little roadside campground alongside the highway. There were some taller trees of a different type from those in the surrounding forest, and he noted that the foggy bases of the clouds were in the tops of those trees as he tore by. He wasn't much higher than the power lines, but he could still see a pretty good distance down the highway.

He did need to stay close to the road to Hilo in those conditions, since the duster was not equipped with a compass, much less a turn-and-bank indicator if he lost sight of the ground in the fog. So long as he kept the road in sight, he'd be okay.

He also knew that he was either at or very near the road's highest elevation and probably could fly right down the nearing slope toward Hilo and out from under the clouds after just a few more miles. He flew past a golf course and didn't see any golfers on it, which made him think that he could also make a quick turn back and land there if the clouds happened to settle around him, sealing him off from flying back the other way. But not even those crucial thoughts freed him from the return of his aching need to figure out the mystery of how he'd made such a deadly enemy.

Come on, O'Reilly! he thought. *Who? Who in the world would want to snuff your dumb ass?*

Now he was actually passing through lower wisps of fog. He wasn't sure how much time had gone by since he'd left the golf course behind. A minute? Two?

He could be several miles beyond it now, heading down lower, where he might get free of the clouds at any moment. But the airspeed indicator didn't register dive speed, and the fog sank lower. It was definitely time to turn back.

He made a gentle right turn. He didn't want to turn too steeply, since his view of the forest close below was getting so hazy. He stood a chance of losing sight of the ground completely, and he'd want to be close to having the wings level if that happened. But he was confident that he'd be glimpsing the highway again in a few seconds.

He'd have to remember to stay a little to the left of the road. Those tall trees at the roadside campground might be very difficult to see if the blanket of cloud had settled lower there, too. All he had to do was pass the campground, and the road would begin pitching downward. Then, it would be a simple matter to skirt the clouds hugging the slopes and take the longer coastal route to Hilo.

Seconds later, Tim knew he was in serious trouble. The highway still hadn't come back into view, and the fog was thicker than ever. He had to descend very close to the treetops. If one of the higher ones rose up directly in his path, he might not be able to turn away from it in time. Finally, he was so low that he had to bring the wings back to nearly level.

He wasn't sure how much of the turn back to the highway he'd actually made. He guessed he'd turned close to 180 degrees, which should take him almost straight back in the opposite direction, but there had been no visual reference by which he could be assured. The good news was, since he had not crossed the highway, he was not headed uphill; he had to be heading downhill toward the sea, however obliquely and gradually. Surely he couldn't have missed seeing the highway flit by in the fog.

So long as he could stay out of the tops of the trees, he had to break out of the clouds eventually. He might even end up at the biggest crater, and he'd be able to dive down into it, and if there were clouds on the far rim, he'd be able to land on the paved road he'd seen on its flat, naked floor.

An occasional tree did loom higher than he was forced to fly now, and he'd reflexively jink around it, mainly by skidding so that the wings would remain nearly level. He wasn't about to risk flying over any of those trees, for the fog was so low that he'd definitely lose sight of the ground. Each time he'd go around a tree, he'd try to get back in his original line of flight. He didn't want to lose a general sense of which way he hoped was more or less downhill.

He wished the slope was steep enough there that a big increase in airspeed would make a dive downhill obvious. To inadvertently get turned uphill, where the clouds would press against the slope all the more tightly, would be disastrous.

The forest looked all the same in the haze. A dense undergrowth of large deep-green tree ferns was spiked with thousands of silvery dead trees, as well as living trees. There were no distinctive features, such as roads or meadows.

Put it down! Tim thought. *Now!* Those gigantic lacy fronds made the woods look almost soft and inviting, except that they were studded so thickly with trees. He didn't know what the stall speed of a Stearman duster was, since he'd never looked at the instruments when he'd been at the edge of a stall flying so close to the ground, but he guessed that it was probably less than forty miles an hour with the power on. That wasn't very fast. Once he got it slowed down, he could chop the throttle just above the scattered treetops and settle in nose-high. He knew from experience that a Stearman was a fantastically strong crasher. The odds seemed excellent that he'd live through still another prang.

Better a controlled crash than . . . But if you got hurt . . . If you couldn't walk . . . His mind raced through replays of earlier clear views of that thick, trackless forest just north of the craters. If he couldn't walk, there was no telling how long it would take someone to find him—if ever. With that thick, unbroken canopy of giant ferns . . . And the truth was, it was exceedingly improbable that he could escape still another crash unhurt.

You've used up your share of luck, dumb ass.

He was right on the treetops now, and the filmy shape of one taller tree popped out of the fog dead ahead. He made a panic skid left, then back to the right as he concentrated on maintaining his dubious course seaward.

Another filmy tree shape loomed just ahead. He skid-banked away in a great panic.

Shit! You've had it!

His left hand was already easing the throttle back. His right hand was gently tugging the stick back. He had to get the plane slowed down before he went in.

He thought of Lisa. He imagined her grief when she was told. And that, finally, triggered some emotion.

"God!" he shouted. "Help me!"

A reddish glow suddenly colored the fog off the Stearman's nose to the right.

The volcano!

Tim forced himself to make a cautious, gradual flat turn toward the filmy apparition. Then, so very quickly, he was making a panic turn to avoid flying right into a fiery fountain of red and orange shards of molten lava.

As he jinked left to go around the spouting lava, he noted several tourists who were on the boardwalk that led to the viewing platform just below him. They ducked as he whipped by close above.

Now he was absolutely certain which way led downhill to safety. Recalling his flight over it with Bill the day before, he knew the way to safety was straight across the pit in line with that boardwalk. He shot a glance back past the tail to make sure he was flying directly away from the spouting volcano.

Only a minute or so later, the slope pitched much more steeply downward, and he could see the ocean. He turned sharply northward to skirt the intersection of cloud and forest to get back to Hilo just as quickly as he could.

"I love her!"

The thought rocked him.

"I really do!" It wasn't platonic love he had in mind now.

"I'm going to marry that girl!" he shouted into the buffeting slipstream.

It began to dawn on him, too, that he was made of considerably better stuff than he'd ever thought. He'd been way down on himself about college and his crazy rages as he harbored dismal thoughts of inferiority to his dad, but there had to be something pretty decent about his worry about another person when he'd seemed so near death.

And Lance? He's a friend, but he'll just have to take his bad luck. If Lisa just couldn't wait to marry him, that would be different. And who knows? Maybe she's already started to love me.

He landed the duster right on the end of the runway and cut across the grass instead of taking the first paved taxiway. He had to get to a phone *now*. He had to tell her! Since she was on vacation, he had reason to hope that she'd be at the hotel with her family.

It occurred to him as he piled out of the plane and hurried into the hangar that Lance would be with her.

Tough! I doubt she'd ever marry him anyway.

Nobody answered. He got the same lack of response from all lines in both suites. When she didn't answer her phone at the Y, he leaped into the car he'd rented and went back to the hotel to throw his things into his bag and try calling again.

This time Lisa's mom answered.

"Hi, Mrs. McLean. Is Lisa there?"

"Hello, Tim. She is. You sure do sound excited."

"It's been quite a day! I'm out of town right now, but I'll be heading over pretty quick."

"Well, come see us. We've had quite a day, too. Here's Lisa."

"Hi, Tim."

"Hi!" He hesitated, thinking that it might be better to tell her he loved her face-to-face. "Lisa . . . " At least he could tell her about the volcano.

"What is it, Tim? What's wrong? I *knew* something was wrong. I've been praying for you."

"Not wrong. Right. I got into some fog coming back to Hilo, and—"

"Oh, Tim! I'm so sick of hearing things like this!" She sounded angry. "You—"

"Just listen! I was about to stall into the forest. I called out to God, and the volcano erupted and showed the way!"

"Oh, Tim!"

"Lisa, something else . . . I . . . " He choked up and couldn't go on for several seconds, but she didn't say a word. He decided to tell it all.

"Lisa, I thought I might die, and I thought of you. I mean . . . " He paused, then plunged on: "Lisa, I love you!"

She gave a shrill cry, and it did not sound like a cry of joy. It was followed by silence. Then he heard her snuffling and knew she was weeping.

"I have to go!" she sputtered. "Sorry!"

"Can we go to dinner tonight?"

"No, Tim."

She hung up without saying another word.

Profoundly shaken for the second time in an hour, he called Greenberg to tell him he'd finished the job and would time it to get there after working hours, a little after five, when fewer people would notice. He'd need a ride to his hotel. Greenberg told him he'd pick him up at the Waipio strip in the boonies just past Pearl Harbor, where there was no chance that anybody at all would see him land.

* * *

Tim entered the deserted lobby of his small hotel thinking, *I know she doesn't love him. I'm not giving up now!*

He called the McLeans again. Ned answered this time, and Tim asked whether they had plans for dinner, all of them and not just Lisa. He said he wanted very badly to treat.

"No," Ned said. "We'll pay. But get yourself on over here. We have some good news for you."

"About the guy who tried to get me?" He thought there might have been something in the news that afternoon. He hadn't looked at a newspaper or a TV since the night before.

"Never you mind. You'll know when you get here."

Tim speculated that it was probably some much less exciting news about one or both of the two families. Maybe they were going to extend their stay in the islands.

Not much later, Lance opened the door to the Levenger suite, saying, "Hey, there, buddy!"

The parents were standing with Lisa behind Lance with "we've got a secret" expressions on every beaming face except Lisa's. Her expression was strangely somber.

Lance reached out to tug Tim into the room, saying, "We're getting married! We're going home!"

30

SO LONG, SIXTIES

im trudged across the car lot toward the office building while Ben frowned and shook his head, holding the showroom door open for him. "What are you looking so worried about?" Tim asked.

"About you not worrying enough. Get in here. You said you'd get a taxi."

"Changed my mind," Tim said. "I need the exercise."

"You do enjoy taking chances."

"I used the back streets. What're the odds I'd be seen?"

"To someone looking really hard? Who knows? I'll tell the boss I'm leaving, and we'll get out of here. I can't believe he kept this place open all day New Year's Eve." He began to hurry away but stopped and looked back, saying, "I can't tell you how sorry I am about Lisa, Tim."

"Thanks."

"It doesn't make sense. We thought it would end up being you. How could she love *that* guy? Anyway, I'll be back in a minute."

It was Wednesday, December 31, 1969. Tim was risking a night out of his latest room for an end-of-the-decade costume party at the Polacols'. Just in case the news media might reveal Tim's identity before Tim's assailant was apprehended, Ben had instituted a rule for the party to keep his name secret. He'd told everyone they'd have to use only their masquerade names or bear some penalty all the others would dream up and enforce.

At the moment, Tim was wearing blue casual shorts, a plain white T-shirt, and go-aheads. He carried a small sports duffel, which held his costume. If he'd worn what was in the bag on his way to the dealership, being as tall as he was, he would have attracted far too much attention. He'd thought of using charcoal or shoe polish to turn himself into Wilt Chamberlain, but he'd had second thoughts about possibly offending someone, so he just had a jersey with Jerry West's number on it and a pair of matching shorts that he'd sneaked over to Ala Moana Center to buy, along with some white sneakers.

"Okay, let's go," Ben said a couple minutes later, reappearing to lead him to a side door.

"You think that eruption could have been a miracle, Ben?" They had talked briefly about his volcano adventure the day after it happened, and Tim had told Ben that Lisa had been praying for him at the time.

Ben halted and turned to give Tim a pitying look. "Well, I do know for sure that you're lucky. You certainly are. It's phenomenal."

"But think about the odds. You're into that. She was praying, and that fire started gushing up into the fog the minute I needed it."

"It's *been* erupting, Tim. On one day, off the next. You know that. It's been in the news constantly." Ben motioned for him to go on through the door ahead of him. "It probably erupted again before you even got there. If it was that foggy, you just didn't see it."

They went to Ben's car and got in.

"I don't mean to be contentious, Tim, but it's not a good thing when people say something's a miracle when all they mean is, someone had some good luck. The Roman Catholic Church goes to a lot of trouble to verify whether something truly miraculous has occurred. We believe that the habit of calling every stroke of good luck a miracle seriously detracts from the wonder of God's actual interventions."

"Killjoy," Tim glumly kidded.

"I'm sure you could call the Geological Survey over there, and they'd tell you to the second what time it erupted. Did you note the exact time?"

Tim groaned and muttered, "Right. I was dodging trees in the fog and thought I'd better take time out to see what time it was."

"Well, what's most important is, you are opening yourself up to the possibility of God." Ben reached out and squeezed Tim's shoulder.

If it had been a few months earlier, Tim might have flinched. This time, he just sighed, and it wasn't because some guy was getting too chummy for comfort. Tim wasn't aware of it, but he'd become much less touchier than he had been some months earlier.

Ben said, "I just hope you stay open to the possibility of God until you know."

"Well, nobody hardly ever said I'm not skeptical, and that holds for being skeptical of atheism, too."

"I'm so sorry about Lisa," Ben repeated.

"Win some, lose some," Tim said, trying to sound as though it really wasn't that big a deal. "Great timing, huh?"

"Hey, it's New Year's Eve—time to look ahead. We'll pray that things go much better for you in the future." Ben slowly wagged his head from side to side with a gentle look on his face. "But from the little I saw of them together, she didn't seem all that excited about Lance. We were so sure that she was in love with *you*, and you couldn't admit that you loved *her*."

"I'm sure she did love me. Just not that way. I was thinking I'd probably have to figure out how to cultivate that. I'm sure you know the Sunday school words: *Agape, phileo*, and man-lady kine."

"Huh?"

Certain that his intellectual Christian friend would know all about the various kinds of love cited in the original Greek New Testament, Tim told him with a smile about his senior loader man's conversion of those words to Hawaiian and pidgin English. Although Tim had been painfully rejected once again, he had retained a better sense of humor this time. He was in much better shape than he had been a year earlier.

* * *

A banner over the Polacols' front porch proclaimed in big red letters, "So long, 60s!" Someone, probably Naomi, Tim guessed, had painted glittery blue, yellow, and green party hats, horns and ribbons around the letters, which gave a strong impression that here was a household glad to be done with a bizarrely radical decade.

Tim entered through the kitchen door in the carport and found himself gawking at a very blonde, very pretty young lady who looked vaguely like Ben's wife. She was at the sink, running water into a big pot of uncooked rice and stirring it with one hand to clean it of any foreign matter. Her shimmering blouse of silver sequins on white, along with the white leather boots that came up to just below her knees and the white short-shorts, contrasted beautifully with her gleaming golden-brown skin.

She quickly dried her hands and rushed over to give him a lingering, tight hug, saying, "I can't believe she's marrying him. It seems so wrong. We both thought you two . . . But never mind all that now, I guess.

"I'm Nancy, by the way." She winked as she stepped back and held out a slender hand. "And you are . . . ?"

"Still Tim O'Reilly," he said. "But that's about to change. You're going to see a new me very soon." Then, as Ben entered, "And this is Ben Polacol. He lives here."

"Pleased to meet you both! The others should be here shortly."

"Let's go change," Ben said to Tim. "You can use Joey's room.

We sent him off to the neighbor's for the night."

As Tim changed, a firecracker, probably a cherry bomb, burst right across the street, and he didn't flinch much at all. He flashed back on the recent times when he'd reacted to every little sound outside his hotel-room hiding place and earlier, when he'd still been jumpy courtesy of Vietnam. *Not bad, Timmy boy*, he thought, pulling on his jersey. *Sometimes you do seem to be making progress.*

He went back to the kitchen and smiled at the sight of Ben's dad, who had appeared, wearing a woman's long, wavy brunette wig that hung down to his shoulders. He also wore a bushy brown fake mustache and beard. Several thick carnation leis of red and white were bulkily piled on his shoulders.

When Joe saw Tim, he steepled the palms of his hands together at his chest. Then, smiling sweetly, he called out in a goofy approximation of an Indian accent, "Happiness blooms like toadstools in cow poo!"

"Your Holiness!" Tim said, catching on. He pressed the palms of his own hands together and, bowing deeply, asked, "How are your friends the Beatles getting along these days?"

"They seek transcendence by dubious means," the guru intoned, sadly shaking his head. "And who might you be, young man?"

"I'm Jerry West, Holiness."

"Ah, yes! Putting the ball in the basket! This I see on the TV!"

So the evening goofily went as the sound of fireworks steadily intensified.

The next person to arrive was the maharishi's girlfriend, Joan Baez, packing an acoustic guitar and a bottle of red wine. Then down the hallway clumped the famous moon-walking Filipino astronaut Neil Armstrong in a silvery costume-rental space suit. He and the maharishi went through a silly, "Kneel, Armstrong," routine that made Tim think the holy man had gotten a head start on the beer or wine.

The first of Ben's close friends to show up was a chubby young Oriental guy with a comical, engaging smile, who came striding across the lawn toward them. He was barefoot and wore long khaki pants, along with what looked like an old surplus khaki army shirt buttoned to the throat and a khaki military hat with a big red construction-paper star pinned to it.

Meanwhile, others were arriving. By the jocular comments they were making to each other, Tim could quickly gather that they were very bright people, and Tim kept wishing he could ask what they did for a living or what they were studying if, as he suspected, some were doing graduate work at UH. They were very warm to him, and they drew him into a humorous discussion about the 60s. Tim got to laughing and debating so enthusiastically that, once again, he forgot all about having been some killer's target so recently.

Mao Tse-Tung, who constantly made foolish, Mao-mocking comments, had brought Lady Mao, who joined them after checking in with Miss Sinatra. She was dressed in a stunning golden cheongsam with crimson trim. A stubby, dark-skinned Fred Flintstone showed up with his date, a tall, lithe Cher. Lyndon and Lady Bird Johnson came, and so did Richard and Pat Nixon, all primarily revealing their identities through the well-known accents, gestures, and favorite phrases. John Lennon and Yoko Ono, testifying that they had become ultra-conservative Republicans, made a very unbelievable appearance.

They all sat on beach mats on the back lawn by a bonfire and sang 60s songs, led first by Ms. Baez, who began with a professional-sounding rendition of, "Diamonds and Rust." As they sang on, an exceptionally powerful explosion sounded from the yard behind Ben's, making Tim jerk with surprise. But instead of flopping down to get out of the way of flying shrapnel, he threw back his head and laughed about it.

After a potluck dinner of local food (*pancit*, chicken *luau*, macaroni salad, *pipi* stew, *kau yuke*, rice, of course, and so on) Nancy Sinatra finished her busywork and joined Ms. Baez in singing "These Boots Are Made for Walking," then did a passable solo rendition of "Something Stupid." Lennon led them through some Beatles hits; then he, Cher, and Ms. Baez led them in "Don't Think Twice, It's All right"; "Let It Be"; "Where Have All the Flowers Gone"; "If I Were a Carpenter"; "Kumbaya"; and so on. They ended with "Danny Boy," "Cry Me a River," and "We Shall Overcome."

I shall! Tim vowed, raising his frosty can of Bud in a silent toast to the last song. He nodded emphatically as fleeting thoughts of Lisa, plane crashes, and Makapuu flashed through his mind, and he drank deeply.

Neil Armstrong stood and said, "Almost midnight, everybody! Let's get the fireworks!" Until then, nobody at Ben's had set off a single explosive device.

The astronaut hurried into the house to get his, and the other men went to get the sacks of fireworks they'd set on the patio. It hadn't occurred to Tim that he might bring fireworks, so he went over to the cooler and got another beer instead.

He watched Ben and his old friends set up a tall ladder beneath a big tree limb to hang one long string of firecrackers. If it wasn't ten feet long, it was close to it.

"Happy New Year!" Ben shouted after a while. As if by his command, right after he lit the one long string of closely packed firecrackers, that entire side of the island seemed to explode all at once. Tim had never witnessed anything like it in civilian life. The previous New Year's Eve back in Painter Creek, Mississippi, the Fourth of July in Idaho, and the fireworks he'd experienced most of his life in the Los Angeles area had been a paltry puttering compared with this riot. Soon veils of smoke drifted through air pungent with the odor of burned explosives.

"And so long, 60s!" someone shouted. Others took up the cry, soon turning it into an enthusiastic group chant, "So long 60s, yeah!"

* * *

With a half dozen pairs of *pikake* and *maile* leis hanging from his left forearm, he resolutely hurried through the terminal toward the McLeans and Levengers. He'd almost bought *plumeria* leis instead of the *pikake* before he thought better of it. He'd realized just in time that Lisa might think there was a message in it.

"Hey, Tim!" Ned McLean called out.

"Hey!" Tim shouted back, putting on a big, fake smile. "I don't know why you're rushing off like this! Was it something I said? Sure you don't want to stay awhile longer?"

"Man, I wish we could. It's nice here."

The others—all except Lisa, that is—smiled and bobbed their heads in assent. Lisa just reached out to clutch Lance's hand and dropped her gaze to the floor.

"Here you go!" Tim said, turning to Mrs. Levenger. She was still looking quite well, considering her illness, and that made him happier. With his right hand, he removed the paired strand of *maile* and the delicate, fragrant *pikake* lei from his left forearm, and she helped him drape them over her shoulders. He pressed his cheek to hers and said, as Punchy had taught him, *"A hui hou aku,"* and repeated in English so she'd know what it meant, "Until we meet again." Next he placed one on Mrs. McLean's shoulders, and she kissed him on the cheek and gave him a strong hug.

He turned to Lisa. Without looking directly at him, she hurriedly took the two leis out of his hands and set them on her own shoulders. She quickly bounced her cheek against his and turned away, looking off to one side of the crowded concourse as if there were something important happening over there. He was too flustered to say anything at all.

Had he seen the glistening of a tear as she'd turned? Fiery

little pricks of emotional fallout skittered around his insides. Nevertheless, he stoutly soldiered on, turning to Lance's dad, who was nearest.

He gave him what he judged must be a very sickly grin, no matter how carefree he tried to make it. "Mind if I don't give you the traditional kiss with this?" he feebly kidded.

Mr. Levenger chuckled and held out his hands to receive the leis. Then Lisa's dad did the same, saying, "No smooch for me, either, if you can stand it."

"Are you going to make it to the wedding?" Lance asked, once Tim had given him his leis. "We'll be getting married pretty quick. We'll call when we set an exact date."

"I sure *hope* I can make it," Tim hedged.

"We're not taking time to plan anything big," Lance said. "The folks want something a little fancier, but Lisa and I want to get it done in a couple weeks."

"Well, I'll try to be there."

The two young men turned and moved back with the others, who began telling Tim to be careful about the danger that he faced. Soon, however, they were making small talk as they anxiously glanced at their watches. Then it was time for them to leave.

They filed past the boarding gate. Each turned back to give Tim a big smile and a wave good-bye, except, once more, for Lisa. She turned to give him a lingering, unsmiling, and completely unreadable look before she fled out of sight.

31

REVELATION

Solly phoned Tim before he left home for the office. He told Tim to just sit tight in his room for a few days.

A couple hours later, tired of being cooped up and tired of trying to figure out why Lisa had acted so strangely and hadn't wanted to speak to him, believing the risk would be slight, Tim called a taxi to take him to the downtown branch of the public library. All he could imagine was, now that Lisa was so close to marriage, she might be embarrassed all over again about their kissing each other so passionately that one night. Settling on that as the probable explanation for her sudden reserve, he started daydreaming in the back seat of the cab about going to the wedding. After all, Lance was becoming a very close friend, and so was Lisa, whether she wanted to act that way right now or not.

He'd make every effort to attend. Greenberg wanted him out of Hawaii for a while anyway. The only thing that could keep him from the wedding now would be a call from Johnny Crash to get down to Nicaragua right away.

As soon as he entered the library, he searched out the psychology section. He wanted to see whether they had that Cleckley book he'd read about in Hilo. It wasn't that he had any great confidence he'd find out anything that would enable him to identify his enemy, but giving the book a quick look would help pass some time. And there it was: *The Mask of Sanity.*

He began scanning. Once again he read that psychopaths were not necessarily violent people but did lack a conscience. He impatiently flipped pages, reading bits of the first paragraphs but slowing to read more carefully from time to time. There were numerous case studies, and he did not find them interesting. So many were accounts of relatively harmless men or women whose behavior got them in minor trouble and merely embarrassed their families.

Becoming bored but doggedly scanning on, he began thinking that he'd like to read up on ancient Hawaiian surfing while he was there. Surely something had been written about it. He'd noticed before that there were many books about old Hawaii in the local bookstores and libraries, including the Hawaiiana collection at the university, where he'd waited for Lisa several times. However, he made an effort to stay focused on Cleckley just a bit longer, even though it seemed clearer by the minute that his would-be killer was not a psychopath or, to use the new term that Cleckley suggested, a "sociopath."

I'm probably looking for someone who's a real mental case, he thought. *Just like Solly said. A real wacko. Not psychopathic but psychotic. Completely out of touch with reality. Forget that Idaho kid.*

If that was so, he didn't see how it could be anyone he'd ever been around very much. If he remembered correctly from his one psychology class as a freshman, serious mental illnesses—psychoses, as they were known at the time—did involve being bizarrely out of touch with reality. He'd never been aware of knowing any such person. On the other hand, he seemed to recall that severe mental illness sometimes took years to reveal itself.

Absent-mindedly scanning on, glancing more and more often at his watch and thinking about Chinatown and lunch as his stomach growled, Tim began to realize that one of the more interesting traits among Cleckley's psychopaths was that so many came from prominent families. He guessed that it only seemed there were more psychopaths from that class because such families were the kind who could afford to send a son or a daughter to a psychiatrist or to a private hospital for evaluation, which was the sort of place where Cleckley practiced.

Something else that eventually seemed odd after Cleckley had mentioned it in case after case was that so many psychopaths could be unusually exciting and fun. Cleckley admitted that he, despite all his experience with their deceitful ways, couldn't help enjoying them.

Then Tim happened to spot something about a relatively late onset of psychopathic behavior in one case, and that got him to thinking. He ceased reading for a while to ponder more seriously the possibility that maybe someone he had known to be fairly normal as a teen had subsequently gone over the edge into psychotic delusions and had become fixated on him. But he'd seen so few of his high school classmates in the last few years that he had no idea who that might be.

About to give up for good on the notion that his enemy was a psychopath, notwithstanding what he'd read about a strong link between psychopathy and criminality, Tim flipped back to the table of contents for a final check before he went to search the card catalog for something on ancient surfing, and his interest faintly flickered over a chapter entitled, "The Psychopath as Businessman." That suggested that at least some of Cleckley's psychopaths weren't like the ne'er-do-well characters that took up such a big part of the book. There was a slight chance that one of those would bring someone he knew to mind.

Tim sighed, told himself to be patient just a few minutes longer, and turned to that section. He hurriedly read enough to see that some psychopaths, unlike the ones he'd read about at first, were able to stay sufficiently focused to be highly successful. As Cleckley had done with other psychopaths, he made these out to be exceedingly charming and persuasive, too. With reawakened interest, Tim riffled through the next chapter and came across Cleckley's comments that psychopaths had an uncommon sway over women.

Now, that's extremely interesting, Tim thought. *How does that work? I'd sure like to read this more carefully someday.*

There was also a chapter entitled, "The Psychopath as Scientist," which particularly interested Tim because the scientist, too, like the successful businessman, was so unlike the first cases in the book, the losers who couldn't stay focused on long-term goals. The nut who'd been after Tim sure had been able to stay focused on his murderous intent. *My dark knight,* he thought, remembering Lisa's kidding that Gawain needed an adversary to test him and thereby give him a truly classical adventure. He nodded emphatically, thinking, *Congratulations! You're now enjoying a real-life classic! Lucky you!*

He got up and went to the lavatory. A few minutes later, as he proceeded back toward his table with his mind still on Cleckley, Tim imagined what it must have been like for that psychiatrist as he tried to comprehend the mental processes of one especially charming psychopath he'd known. Clearly, the psychiatrist had liked that patient very much. Then, suddenly, Tim realized how similar that psychopath's behavior was to Lance's.

Lance?

For a moment, the glimmer of suspicion seemed preposterous. Yet he thought again, *Lance?*

It seemed ridiculous, but it did seem to fit: Lance's wildly impulsive behavior, his tall tales, his lack of empathy in watching those goats . . .

But murder?

It was preposterous. Nevertheless, Tim couldn't help remembering Lisa's fear that Lance only wanted to add the farm she'd inherit to the one he'd be inheriting from his own parents. And that memory was followed by the one of that time they'd been flying in the T-6 when Lance had said that the immense tract of land belonging to his family all around them looked so small from aloft. So there was a motive, too.

Unbelievable!

Tim was hyperventilating now. As much as he strained to dismiss his suspicion of his friend, it stubbornly clung to him. He abruptly lurched to his feet, bumping back his chair, causing it to loudly screech over the floor tiles.

And what did Lisa say about CR? He was recalling the hazy underwater sight of a small and pale diver with long dark hair. *He'd do anything for Lance? "Anything!"*

As a frowning local woman watched from an adjacent table, Tim slowly shook his head as he stood there and, as the truth overwhelmed him, muttered like some madman, "He *is* the one. Lance used him!" Yet, seconds later, doubt—his old habitual doubt—set back in.

Greatly alarmed to be thinking such a thing of someone he'd considered such a good friend, he muttered, "You'd better think twice about an accusation like that!" He collapsed into his seat, noisily scooted it forward, and propped his elbows on the table. He bowed his head, holding it in his big hands. He was totally unaware of his surroundings, and he wasn't in any condition to notice the nearby woman casting nervous glances at him.

No matter what excuses he could make for Lance, memories of the young heir's outrageous cruelty to animals and showboating and exaggerations and risk-taking flooded his mind. *No, not exaggerations*, Tim thought. *Lies! Lance is a compulsive liar, and Cleckley had a lot to say about that, too!*

Now he was certain that Lisa really had intuited the truth when she'd come to suspect it was the McLean farm that Lance loved.

And she wants to be his wife anyway? Does that make any sense?

Still, Lance did have a motive, and he had the means, knowing airplanes and being as bright as he is. And, yes, CR's handy with a wrench and a SCUBA rig.

"Bingo!" he loudly exclaimed. "Incredible!"

Another chair loudly scraped on the floor, and Tim, startled by the sound, turned to watch as the young woman who'd been seated nearby rushed away. She glanced back at him as she turned toward the area near the entrance, where there were more people, and went on out. Tim still hadn't quite enough presence of mind to make some sort of apologetic gesture before she scurried out of sight.

He left his table and, with his injured leg still bothering him, hurriedly limped toward the pay phones to call for a taxi.

If he'd kill me for the McLeans' land . . . It was obvious to Tim that Lance might try to speed his inheritance of the McLeans' property by getting rid of *them.*

"You've got to warn them!" He wasn't even aware that, despite people passing by, he'd spoken out loud again.

But would they believe it? Even Lisa?

And what about those Oklahoma cops? Would they believe the town's favorite character capable of such a thing? And the Honolulu cops. What would they think with no hard evidence?

Everybody would think of Lance pretty much as Tim had once thought: Why would Lance take such a risk to get some land when he already had so very much of it already? But Tim had a pretty good idea why that was now: Lance Levenger must have a gargantuan ego, and no amount of wealth would ever satisfy it. And, if he really was a psychopath, which he certainly was, he had no more feeling for another human being than he had for the two goats whose deaths had so amused him.

Come on! Face it! He really is the brains behind your trouble!

Fury overcame Tim, and he thought as he trembled, *So give that sick ass some of his own medicine!*

The taxi arrived, and he got in, still trembling with fury.

Nobody would believe you, he thought right after he'd given the driver the name of the hotel. *Nobody. Once he's married and a legal heir to the McLeans, they're next! So just do him.*

What's so different from 'Nam? Or would you just sit by and let him snuff the McLeans? Hell, if he's that out of it, maybe he'd even get rid of his own people! Do him!

In his rage, Tim fantasized about ways he could dream up to sabotage Lance's T-6 and make it look like an accident. He imagined the control stick suddenly going slack in the creep's hand. *Give him a taste of his own medicine!* For a moment, furious at such deception from a counterfeit friend, Tim wished that Lance did his stunts at a much higher altitude, way up there where he'd have lots and lots of time to contemplate a tumble out of control back to earth.

Arriving at his hotel, he entered his room and flopped onto the bed, thinking now that he should pass on what he'd figured out to the cops and let them handle it. Moments later he sat back up, swung his feet over the edge, and reached for the telephone. Then his hand on the phone relaxed, and he withdrew it. Namaka seemed pretty competent, but he couldn't say the same for the lead detective, that Ludwing dunce.

Lives hung in the balance—no longer his own but very possibly the McLeans' and maybe even the Levengers'. He needed a little more time to think it through. He wondered whether the Hawaii police might be able to trace CR's movements. His name would be on the passenger list of the flight he'd taken to Hawaii. Maybe it would, that is. But what if he'd used another name and paid in cash? People like CR didn't have credit cards—not in the 60s.

He began to call the Honolulu Police Department. It would make more sense to them than it would to police in Lance's hometown. Ludwing might be able to see enough possibility to approve some investigation of CR. He and Namaka, more probably Namaka, might be able to find some hard evidence to place CR in Honolulu. On the other hand, that would take a lot of time and might not yield anything at all. And, as days passed, the risk to the McLeans would mount. The surest way to protect them was for Tim to eliminate the threat himself. Immediately. He'd get a confession, of course. Somehow. There had to be a way.

He phoned Greenberg to say he was going to take his advice and leave Hawaii for a while. Then he dialed Pan American World Airways and made a reservation for a flight to LA. He made another for the following day from LA to Oklahoma City, where he'd rent a car. Finally he called Ben to let him know he was leaving. The only reason he gave them was, "I've decided to play it extra safe." And that was the truth. Safe for the McLeans anyway.

* * *

Whether he sat or paced the aisles of the 707, he was far too agitated to do anything but think about Lance and the threat he posed. Tim would be absolutely certain one minute and full of doubt the next, switching back and forth over and over all the way across the Eastern Pacific. All that time, he also kept wondering whether he really would be able to kill Lance.

He had killed before. He'd never hesitated in combat. Never except for failing to end Smitty's suffering. He'd been convinced that the war was a noble cause, that he was risking his own life to save his fellow Americans and other lovers of freedom from the Red terror, and he had the approval of the US government. So, too, was eliminating Lance a just cause.

Lance, Tim reasoned, was every bit as much society's enemy as any VC. He was a murderer, whether he did the work with his own hands or not. So was CR the enemy, of course, although Tim doubted that nasty little thing—provided he was still alive— would continue to bother him without Lance's encouragement.

So what about the apparent fact that a psychopath can't help being psychopathic? Tim kept telling himself that it didn't matter. The *only* thing that really mattered was to keep innocent people alive.

He could simply lie in wait for Lance somewhere. Buy a good folding knife with a five- or six-inch blade—a lockable blade so it wouldn't fold if it hit bone. And waylay Lance where? If Lance was in college, he'd have to check the layout there. If he was at home, would the wheat out where he parked the T-6 offer enough concealment? It seemed so. If that wheat hadn't been harvested by now.

Tim once again considered jimmying the controls on Lance's airplane instead. He could remove a nut from an elevator-cable bolt or something and set the bolt so that it would work its way out some time after takeoff. But what if Lance took along a passenger? Like Lisa?

As Tim rode home from Los Angeles International with his parents, he struggled to respond normally to their happy chatter and simultaneously think of a way to eliminate the threat to the McLeans. Later, after dinner and an hour's conversation, he had to give it up and get away to be alone and figure out what to do. He excused himself and restlessly drove down past the beach in the Healey, wishing at that point that he could take Lance for a payback ride in some open-cockpit airplane. He could probably rent an aerobatic plane at OKC. There had to be some way he could make Lance's seatbelt buckle pop loose during a negative-g stunt. He'd need an open-cockpit plane, of course. An outside loop would do it. Way up high so that Lance would have plenty of time to appreciate his chuteless free-fall. That idea appealed to Tim very much.

Would you really? He had to wonder. He'd thought he was done with killing.

He'd need that confession first, of course. He'd need to be doubly certain that it had really had been Lance and CR. A few stunts and disclosure to Lance that his seatbelt had been set to break loose might do the trick.

Woops! What a terrible accident!

But why do him if you get a confession? Why not just tell the police about it?

Because it would be his word against mine. Lance Levenger versus some nobody crop duster.

Besides, even if you did get a confession and the cops did take it seriously, think what that would do to Lisa. To her folks, too. Think of the shame. And what about the Levengers? They're good people. A lifetime of shame. Think of their suffering if you were too chickenshit to do what you should. Again. Like Smitty.

Once again, he could hear Smitty's screams. His periodic screams, "Jesus! Jesus!"

He absent-mindedly ended up taking his habitual route to Jen's mom's house, and he felt like a fool when he came to his senses and noticed where he was. Jen was probably married to "Mr. America" now, "Mr. America Golden Boy Engineer," and the absence of her car from its usual spot on the street in front of the little cottage seemed to confirm it.

Again, he had a powerful urge to call the McLeans to warn them. Yet if Ned didn't believe him and his warning somehow got to Lance . . .

Suddenly, he realized that there was something he could do to test his suspicion of Lance and CR. He could call to say hi and, after a while, casually ask how CR was getting along. If nobody had seen him for a while, he'd be more certain; if CR had remained on the farm fall and winter or had demonstrably been in some other location than Hawaii, Tim would know definitely that he'd been on the wrong track.

He found a service station that had a pay-phone booth outside and pulled in. He inserted a dime in the phone's slot, dialed the operator, and using the phone-charge card he'd obtained before he'd left Idaho, placed a call to the Levengers.

"Hi, Mr. Levenger. It's Tim . . . Fine, thank you. Is Lance there, or is he back in college?"

When Tim learned that Lance wasn't in college or at home at the moment and after Mr. Levenger had told his wife to pick up the phone where she was, Tim engaged them in a three-way conversation about the wedding plans, about how the two families wished it was as warm in Oklahoma as it was in Hawaii, and about the Honolulu police investigation having failed to turn up any leads. Then, when the pace of the conversation slowed, Tim asked, "How's CR doing? Is he still racing that motorcycle?"

He listened to Mr. Levenger's reply and said, "Oh, you haven't? Wonder where he's gone off to?"

Mr. Levenger replied that CR had left in the early fall, and they hadn't heard from him since then.

Get on up there and just do him! he told himself as he drove on. Once again, he was visualizing Lance being ejected from an open cockpit. *Hell, you could buy yourself something aerobatic for that! You've got way more than enough saved. Tell Lance you're just dinking around the country for the winter, that you'd come up for the wedding early. Take him for a little spin.*

He drove out to the airport. The flight service whose instructors he'd used for his private pilot's license would be open if someone was getting some night-flying instruction. They'd have the latest *Trade-A-Plane*, and he could look through it to see if he could find what he needed.

He began to wonder how he could make it look like an accident. He'd been visualizing how he could gum up a military-style combination seat belt and shoulder harness release in such a way that it wouldn't latch securely, but that might be difficult to bring off. Now he thought of a slightly different plan.

All I'd have to do is undo one bolt, substitute a bit of thin wire, like that flimsy hardware-store copper wire . . . He imagined how he could land on some road out of sight of farmhouses immediately afterward. He'd simply get rid of whatever might be left of the copper wire and re-attach the bolt and nut. It would seem to anyone investigating the accident that Lance had failed to completely latch the belt.

But whether you'd actually do it or not, you could at least take him up and threaten to dump him out. Have him reach down and feel that bit of wire. Tell him you'd settle for a confession, that you'd report it to the police instead of just dumping him.

At the familiar old flight service, he found a *Trade-A-Plane* ad announcing the sale of a 450-horse, two-holer Stearman in Scottsdale, Arizona.

"I need radios front and back," Tim said over the phone.

"It's got. Plus two sunburst-painted military helmets with earphones and boom mikes. It's a sweet airplane, but I'm switching to a Pitts. Teaming up with a couple guys to do a formation act."

"Well, let me make a couple calls, and I'll call you right back. I might want to pick it up tomorrow. Assuming you're available . . . "

"I'll make myself available. Sounds like you're in a hurry."

First thing in the morning, he'd get a cashier's check for the asking price. He was too intent on his objective to consider haggling over the cost. He made two more calls, one to book a flight to Phoenix and one to cancel his reservation from LA to OKC.

He drove away from the airport wondering, *Now what?* He was too hyper to go home and go to bed. His old pal Nick wouldn't mind if he called so late in the evening. He'd keep an eye out for a pay phone. Or maybe he'd take a chance and call Jen's mom. Her place was much nearer than Nick's. In the earlier days of his relationship with Jen, he and Stella had some pretty good conversations. She'd been pretty testy with him toward the end, but maybe she'd gotten over it. He spotted a phone booth by a Shell station and turned in.

"Tim!" Stella exclaimed. "For goodness' sake!"

"Hi. I know it's getting late, but I was wondering if you'd mind if I dropped by."

"Sure you can! You know we're not the early-to-bed type."

We? he wondered as he drove. At first, he'd assumed she was just using the word the way people do a lot of the time when they're speaking of themselves as individuals. Or maybe she'd married the creep she'd started going out with. He wouldn't enjoy sitting around for long with *that* dude. If he was there, he'd cut it short.

He saw Jen's car parked out front, and he panicked. He speeded up and drove on by.

And what? he wondered. *Call and say what? That would be pretty obvious.*

He turned around, drove back, and parked. He'd get some quick small talk done and get the hell gone if Jen was there.

"Tim!" Jen said, opening the door and beaming him a warm smile.

"Hey. I didn't expect to see *you* here."

"Never left. It didn't work out. Home for good?"

"I gotta leave tomorrow."

Stella appeared beside her and said with a chuckle, "Aren't you going to let him in?"

Jen quickly stepped aside, saying, "Come in! Come in!"

"Can I get you something?" Stella inquired, crossing the tiny living room. "I've got coffee on. We have chocolate cake."

"No, thanks. I'm fine."

"Well, I'll fix a little something for myself." She left the room.

"Nice to see you," Jen said quietly, keeping her distance.

"Really? We're still friends?"

"Really. Friends."

They just stood there for a few seconds, gazing at each other.

"Well!" Tim finally managed to say.

"So it didn't work out," she said.

"Oh, that's . . . I was sure . . . "

"You can come over again before you leave if you like," she said after a few more moments of silence.

"I won't have time. I'll call when I get back."

"Can I join you for a few moments?" Stella asked, re-entering the room. "I'd like to hear what you've been up to since we saw you last. I wasn't very nice to you the last time we talked. You know how I got when I was dating that guy. Jen told me you had it figured out. But I'm clean now. Clean and sober going on four months!"

So he gave them a quick rundown of his travels, except for his trouble, and he told them he'd be going to Oklahoma for a wedding. Jen's mother was acting like the normal, reasonable Stella he'd known when he and Jen had first started dating, and Jen was treating him as a long-lost friend. That felt pretty good, but he couldn't enjoy it fully.

As they chatted, he kept thinking about what might happen within the next few days. It made him edgy, and he couldn't sit still any longer after a while. He got to his feet, saying, "Well, I have to be up early tomorrow."

"Nice to see you," Stella said. She gave him a hug. "See you when you get back from the wedding."

"He was a cheater," Jen said after her mother had left. "I caught him. I think he was playing around all along."

"It hurts to hear that." It really did. Jen had caused him a lot of pain when she'd jilted him, but he wouldn't have wished her that outcome. She was far too decent a person to deserve that.

"I'm so glad I found out before we were married. Can you imagine what it would have been like after?"

He nodded.

"It was one of the things that got me to missing you." She suddenly straightened and looked alarmed. She touched him on the forearm and blurted as an obvious afterthought, "Don't read too much into that, okay?" Then she went on. "But, like, it hit me after I knew for sure about him that you would never do anything like that."

"Thanks," he said. "Anyway, I'm glad I called. I almost . . . Anyway, I'd better go."

"Be sure to call when you get back."

"I will."

I sure hope I'll be back, he thought as he went to his Healey.

* * *

He called the Levengers again in the morning.

"Hey, buddy!" Lance said. "I was just going to call *you*. Is January sixteenth going to work for you?"

"It sure will," Tim said. "Actually, I've been thinking of swinging up there sooner than that. I know you and Lisa will be busy, but I'd kind of like to hang around and visit a little with Will Walker and the others. Just enjoy some rest and relaxation for a change. Plus I've got a little something I want to show you."

"What is it?"

"It's a surprise."

"Come on. What?"

"You'll see. I think you'll be impressed."

Lance nervously laughed and said, "Can't you give me a hint?"

"Why not? What has four wings and buzzes a heck of a lot louder than some bug?"

"I've got it! Tell me exactly! A Pitts? I remember you talking about them."

"You'll see. I might even let you take it for a spin if you promise to be good."

32

RETRIBUTION

I've just got to report it, Tim thought, arguing again with himself as he drew near his destination. He was hunched down low, trying to avoid the icy blasts of slipstream that burbled around the stock windshield into the rear open cockpit. *Make 'em understand the only person with a motive is Lance Levenger. Once they talked to the Honolulu cops, they'd have to take it seriously.*

But then what? With no evidence . . . Even if I got him to confess to me, he'd deny it to them. So would he dare to try something with the McLeans after the cops heard my accusation? He might. He is sure of himself. What if he believed that he could stage it so that nobody could think it could be anything but an accident, accusation or not?

Can you take that chance? We're talking about the McLeans' lives, man.

Tim was so lost in thought now that he wasn't even aware that he was shivering. The seller of the Stearman had driven him by a store that catered to men who worked outdoors, and he'd bought some wool long johns, but they'd turned out to be less than the perfect protection against the Northern Oklahoma mid-winter air in an open-cockpit airplane.

One necessary delay would give him a little more time to think things through. Before he flew on to the Levengers' and tried to get a confession, he would need to make another stop for gas, and he headed for the airport where Will Walker's operation was headquartered. His former employer wasn't in the gas-peddling business, but Tim was sure he'd gladly sell him some.

The spare brain bucket and a small rollup canvas toolkit took up enough room in the baggage compartment that there was no room left for the sports duffel that contained a few extra clothes and his toiletries kit. So he'd passed the thick, wide seat belt in the front cockpit through the bag's handles and cinched it down to the seat. The wired-on seat-belt anchor on the right-hand side was strong enough to hold the bag down so long as he avoided any violent negative-g maneuvers. It would also hold just fine when Lance strapped himself in and snugged it down. Tim had carefully experimented to see how few loops of the thin copper wire would part with a snugging down of the latched seatbelt. Then, he'd added just a couple more loops. He was sure that the flimsy new seatbelt anchor would snap if he subjected his passenger to a few negative g's.

Although he might not really go that far, he could use the jimmied seatbelt as a threat to wrest a confession. He was absolutely certain that Lance and CR had been in cahoots and had dreamed up most of his troubles, possibly beginning in Idaho, and if he only made an accusation and made sure it was publicized, that would have to make Lance leery of trying to get rid of the McLeans. Still, the downside remained: The McLeans and the Levengers would have to bear the shame of any such publicity. That alone was a point for simply eliminating Lance.

Soon the municipal airport where Mr. Will based his operation came into view, and Tim landed. He taxied over to the gas pumps and parked beside them.

"Well, look who's here!" shouted one of the mechanics, emerging from the hangar. "Fancy airplane!"

"Yeah, thanks!"

It was a beauty, alright. It was sparkling white and bright red. It had a cherry-red sunburst pattern over white on the top of the upper wings and the bottom of the lower wings. Its bulky, round engine was enclosed by a bright red cowl, and a red stripe ran all the way back to the tail on either side of the fuselage. The entire biplane had been kept thickly waxed and buffed to make the strongest possible impression on the air-show crowds. If Lance wasn't too suspicious, he wouldn't be able to resist flying such a machine.

"How you doing, Arnold?" Tim asked.

"Cain't complain. Looks like you might want to bum some gas."

"I'd sure like to buy some. Is Mr. Will in?"

"Nope. He went to OKC. I'll top you off, and you go ahead on in and get yourself a cup of coffee. It's too cold to be flyin' one of these things right now, Tim!"

"Yeah, tell me about it," Tim said, turning to head for the hangar. "Can I use the phone?"

"Help yourself. Go on. Get out of this cold."

"Welcome back to God's country!" a much older man called out as Tim entered the hangar.

"Thank you, Ike."

"Coffee's thataway!" The old gent gave him a snaggle-toothed grin and pointed a thick, gnarly finger toward the office door.

"Thanks."

The office was vacant. Tim eyed the nearest phone, the one on the boss's desk, as he went in. He began to turn toward it, thinking he should call the McLeans first and try to convince them of the truth. After all, if they got Lisa to call off the marriage for good, they wouldn't be in any danger. But he doubted very strongly that they would believe.

No, he decided. *You need that confession. You take care of that first. Then you can tell that to Ned!*

He turned to the table supporting the coffee paraphernalia. He felt an urgent need to very carefully think it all through one more time and be sure he wasn't making some big mistake. He poured a cup and went over to lean on the countertop and enjoy some warmth. He kept eyeing the phone.

Are you absolutely sure it is Lance? he asked himself. *Absolutely? Well, pretty close,* he mutely answered. *Way beyond "a reasonable doubt," as they say.*

The door between the hangar and the office popped open, and the old man came in and asked, "What in tarnation brings you back here in the dead of winter, Tim?"

"Came up for Lance Levenger's and Lisa McLean's wedding."

"I've heard about that boy. He's a real cutup."

The door opened again, and Arnold entered as well, saying, "I'm due for a cup, myself."

Tim tried to manifest a friendly smile, but he was hardly in the mood for chitchat. "How much for the gas?" he asked.

"Nothin'. Mr. Will wouldn't let you pay if he was here his self."

Tim visited a few minutes longer, bringing the two men up to date on his travels since they'd seen him last but trying to think of anything he might have overlooked before he took Lance for his spin. Then, just as soon as the two men went back to work, he called the Levengers to make sure that Lance was home and said he'd be out in a few minutes.

He went on out to the Stearman and climbed aboard, thinking, *Okay, I'll try to wring a confession out of that puke and tell the McLeans what I've learned, confession or not. Then I'll just turn it over to the cops however it works out. That's it. That's my final decision.*

Not much later, he was within sight of the Levengers' place. Farther north, the McLeans' farmstead was barely visible. Soon he could see Lance's parked AT-6.

He'd originally thought about buzzing the house, but he had Mrs. Levenger's illness to consider. Also, the horses were on the east side of the house, and he didn't want to spook them, either. He eased the prop pitch up to twenty-one hundred rpms so the horses and the people in the house would hear him coming and be prepared. He angled to the right of his original course straight toward the house and flew off to one side instead, beginning to circle the house and keeping a couple hundred yards' distance.

At the beginning of the second orbit, Tim watched four people rush out the front door, and Tim recognized them as Lance, his parents, and Millie, the maid. He rocked his wings at them, increased power, and climbed very steeply to a thousand feet above the ground.

He got the plane into position so that he'd fly straight past the front of the house about fifty yards away from it, out where the lawn met the wheat, then eased the nose steeply downward. The air shrieked through the flying wires between the upper and lower wings as the airspeed neared the red line. He activated a switch and got a strong whiff of the pale oil smoke that came billowing forth. Once he passed over the entrance to the farmstead, he commenced a sustained series of barrel rolls. He was careful to maintain positive g's to keep his duffel bag pressed firmly to the front seat and avoid snapping the one wire seatbelt anchor.

Then, completing the third roll, having flown on past the house, he stood the smoke-streaming Stearman on its tail and zoomed straight upward. He eased the prop control and throttle all the way forward so that the Stearman was putting out maximum power. He kept the nose pointed straight up until the airplane was about to slide back down through the perfectly perpendicular column of white smoke behind it, then kicked rudder. The big round red engine cowl fell to the right and sliced straight back down through the smoke-obscured horizon.

Tim recovered several hundred feet above the ground and flew straight back alongside the corkscrew swirls of smoke he'd left from the previous pass. The blocky biplane bucked a little as it encountered some of its own lingering wake turbulence. When he was very near the house again, he yanked the stick all the way back and hard over to the left and kicked the left rudder pedal all the way forward. He gritted his teeth and held the controls in those extreme positions as the Stearman violently rotated through two snap rolls. That, too, was a positive-g maneuver, avoiding any risk that centrifugal force on the duffel would snap the thin wire that flimsily secured the right seat-belt strap. He nodded with satisfaction, confident that the stunt had produced the distinctive, nasty rapping sound that airplanes made when they were snap-rolling. It was just the sort of sight and sound that would make Lance ache to come join in the fun.

You'll have your chance in just a bit, Lancie boy!

Recovering from the snap roll, Tim simply made a wide, shallow turn to make a final pass in front of the house. He had considered landing on the driveway, just as he had the day Jeremy had saved that woman from the pickup fire, but he would have had to waste time talking to them all. So he landed on Lance's airstrip.

Shortly after Tim taxied up beside the T-6 and climbed out, Lance's Corvette came tearing down the farm road. Tim unsnapped the front seatbelt and lifted the duffel out of the front cockpit and set it off to one side of the plane. He was pulling the spare helmet with the sparkling red-and-white sunburst paint job that matched his own helmet out of the small baggage compartment behind the rear cockpit as the 'Vette skidded to a stop and Lance leaped out of it. Tim strode forward to meet him.

"Surprise!" Tim said, forcing a smile and waving a gloved hand at the Stearman.

"I guess surprise!" Lance said.

He nodded, laughed with such a convincing show of delight, and seemed so wonderfully wholesome that Tim had to doubt all over again that Lance was capable of murder. If Tim hadn't happened to start reading about deceptive psychopathic charm, it would have been extremely difficult to continue believing that Lance was not what he seemed.

"Yours?" Lance asked.

"Sure is! I had to show it to you!"

As Tim spoke, he studied Lance's eyes. He'd read a number of references to the "flat" look in psychopaths' eyes. And Ben had said something about Lance's eyes. But the first thing he noticed was, the pupils of Lance's eyes were squeezed down to two minute dots. Two tiny black pits in two lusterless brown orbs. He'd read about that long before he'd learned about psychopaths. Those tiny pupils did not match Lance's toothy, welcoming smile at all.

He handed Lance the spare helmet and said, "You're going to love this!"

"I came prepared!" Lance said, fingering one sleeve of his heavy mackinaw coat. He donned the helmet and pulled a pair of fur-lined leather gloves out of a pocket. "Let's do it!"

Lance climbed onto the base of the left lower wing, and Tim called after him, "It's got an inverted system, Lance. It'll do anything you ever dreamed of."

Still standing on the ground, Tim stuffed the small duffel into the space left in the baggage compartment by the removal of the spare helmet. The duffel fit so tightly that it pressed the small roll of tools to the floor of the compartment and would keep them from flying around in there if Tim had to take the Stearman slightly negative to scare Lance into a confession. He'd have to be sure that it wasn't too heavily negative, though, or the wire would snap, dumping Lance out of his seat.

Lance was climbing into the front cockpit now, and Tim worried that he'd look down over the right side of the seat and see the thin, shiny loops of copper wire that had replaced the bolt and nut. He knew it was extremely unlikely, but he couldn't help worrying about it. "Be sure to hook that helmet to the radio," he said.

Now Tim climbed onto the wing and on into the rear cockpit. He buckled in, connected a phone jack to his own helmet and turned on the rear-cockpit radio. "Do you copy, Lance?"

"Loud and clear."

"Ready to rock and roll?"

"Ready!"

"Let me do a few, and then you, okay?"

"Just hurry. I'm itching to feel how this compares to mine."

Tim fed in the power, got the Stearman free of the ground, and made a maximum-efficiency climb straight ahead to get up to altitude as soon as possible.

"Here we go," he said, once he'd climbed to three thousand feet.

Tim pulled the throttle handle and stick all the way back. When the plane lost flying speed, he did exactly what he'd done earlier to initiate the snap rolls, except it was at power-off stall speed. With the engine at idle and the plane slowly mushing through the air, the nose flipped around and downward, and the plane began a loose, nose-swinging spin toward the earth.

Tim's plan was to start up high with very conservative positive-g maneuvers and work his way steadily up the gradient of difficulty until he was nudging just a slight touch of negative g if necessary, coaxing Lance to confess or die a horrible death.

He let the spin continue past the customary turn or so, wanting to make Lance a little nervous. He was pretty sure it was possible to make a psychopath fear for his own life. He was no expert, but he doubted that a psychopath's lack of concern for others was matched by a lack of concern for himself.

"Hey, are you still awake?" Lance coolly asked the third time the Stearman's nose had swung around the same spot below.

Tim answered by initiating a recovery but let the nose stay pointed steeply downward to allow the airspeed needle to sweep on up to the bottom of the red line. Then he tugged back on the stick to send the Stearman shooting straight up. As soon as its fuselage was perfectly vertical to the horizon, he did a climbing slow roll and fell into a hammerhead reversal straight back downward.

"I have some other surprises for you, Lance," he said, pulling out of the dive.

"Uh-oh!" Lance replied, laughing. "Sure it's not my turn yet?"

"Not yet. You can fly in a minute. Feel up to some negative g's?"

"Especially when you give me the chance to do them."

"First I'd like you to reach down on the right side of your seat. Take off your glove first." Tim waited a couple seconds before he asked, "Is your glove off?"

"No, it isn't off. What are you getting at?"

"Take it off. Then run the palm of your hand all the way down that right-hand seat belt strap."

He saw Lance's helmet tip to the right, and Tim asked, "Feel anything strange?"

"No. Nothing."

"Try harder. You should feel some twisted wire. Real thin stuff. Feel it?"

"Yes! What the heck is this?"

"Careful. I wouldn't want you to prick yourself. But why does that word make me think so fondly of *you*?"

"Hey! What are you up to?"

"I'm sure you know by now, *buddy*."

"What are you up to?" This time Lance's voice trembled.

Tim grimly nodded and said, "Remember my 'accidents,' good buddy?"

"What does that have to do with *me*?"

"I just hate to hog all the fun is all. I know you appreciate a little shot of adrenaline now and then yourself."

Tim suddenly jammed stick and rudder to the extremes once again, still positive. The plane immediately whipped into a double snap roll.

"Woops!" Tim said. "Those were positive g's. We need some *negative*. We need to see how much strain—"

"What do you *want*?"

"I want you to know that enough negative g's will snap that

wire and dump your sick ass right out of this airplane. That—"

"What in God's name is going on?"

"Lance, Lance. You're usually such a rational guy. Surely you know such pretense will get you nowhere now."

"What do you *want*?"

"You're repeating yourself. One thing I want is to put a little more distance between us and your family. I'd hate for them to hear you when you do your first flight without airplane. It would be cool if you used your hands like ailerons and—"

"Oh, God! Are you insane?"

"No more than you." Then a new thought sprang to Tim's mind: He might talk Lance into a confession more easily if he lied and assured him he could always plead insanity. He knew very well it would be a lie, since his reading had made it clear that psychopaths were not insane. They usually did have knowledge of right and wrong; they just didn't usually have a conscience to make them comply with moral knowledge.

"Here's something I might settle for," Tim continued. "I want you to confess. The truth is, I want very badly to dump you out of this airplane with or without a confession. I hate you so much I'm shaking like crazy back here. But here's the deal. You confess your part in all that shit CR pulled, and I'll think about setting you back down on earth more gently than I planned."

"I have nothing to confess!"

"Bullshit!"

Tim rolled the Stearman upside down and started a very lazy split-S recovery, holding just enough back pressure to press Lance's butt into the seat but as little as possible, making it clear to Lance how easily he could pop him right out of that open cockpit if Tim shoved the stick forward. As the nose of the inverted airplane slowly arced downward, Tim calmly said, "Say *baaa*, Lance. Remember the goats? Come on. I'm serious. A little *baaa*, please."

Tim guessed it would take three or four negative g's to pop the wire. He nudged the stick just a hair forward for a moment to make Lance go about one g light in his seat.

"*Baaa*! Oh, God! Please!"

"Good boy!" The nose was coming up toward the horizon, and Tim made it ascend a little faster, adding power and going for the completion of the positive-g loop from the top. "Now you're catching on. Shall we do one inverted next time around?"

"Please! I'll do anything!"

"Great! Speak to me! Confession, please."

"I can make you rich!"

Tim rolled upright at the top of the loop and very gently nosed the plane over. He felt his own butt gradually get light in the seat.

"Listen carefully," he quickly said. "I checked it out, Lance. You're psychopathic. See if this strikes a chord: You're very impulsive, you take lots of chances, and . . . *ta-dah*, the biggie . . . you have no feeling for other people. Or for animals. Plus a few other things like your compulsive lying. You've got all the signs, Lance." Tim gave a little nudge of forward pressure on the stick.

"But the good news is, since you are clearly psychopathic, you could plead insanity. What do you think?"

"We can work this out! I can start with maybe ten thousand cash and the Corvette. Today!"

"No deal, Lance, but suit yourself. Here we go. If this doesn't snap that wire, we can try a Lomcevak. Oh, and go ahead and fight me for control of this airplane if you want. I really don't give a shit if I die neutralizing your sick ass."

"Tim, I beg you! Anything!"

"I named it! Admit or die!" He eased the stick farther forward. "Now!"

"It was CR! He sucked me in!"

"Keep talking. Look. I'm turning back. But I'm still tempted—"

"He shone that light in your eyes. He told me. But I had nothing to do with it. I only wanted him to keep an eye on you."

"And Hawaii?" Tim began to circle.

"His idea!"

"Lance, Lance. I want to hear about *your* part in it." Tim leveled the wings and nosed the Stearman into a slightly-negative-g dive. However, Lance remained silent.

"Lance? The master cylinder? The fuel problem?" Tim eased the stick a bit farther forward, being very careful to avoid putting too much stress on the wire that anchored Lance's seat belt.

"CR!"

"He must know a lot about airplane engines!" Tim shouted into his mike. "Good-bye, you piece of shit! I'm done waiting for you to admit it!"

Tim was bluffing, but he was tempted anew to actually do it. Hand all atremble, he eased in more forward stick.

"My idea!"

Tim backed off.

"Let's go land somewhere private!" Lance said. "Not the farm! We need to talk!"

"We need to talk for sure," Tim said. "We're both going to switch frequencies to the Enid control tower, and we're going to tell them they need to have the police waiting for us. You're going to tell them why."

For emphasis, Tim rolled the Stearman upside-down and started making a series of gentle climbs and dives, going slightly positive one moment and slightly negative the next. "Okay, Lancie," he said, "Do you remember Enid tower's frequency?"

Tim was sure he did, and he switched frequencies on his own radio in the rear cockpit. "Enid Tower," he said, "this is—"

His control stick, linked to the one in front, violently jerked back. Before he could think, Tim reacted by ramming it forward.

Away Lance went. For a moment, his flailing form filled Tim's field of vision, and then it was gone.

Wildly shaking from head to toe, Tim made a split-S, letting the Stearman's nose swing downward as he tried to catch sight of Lance. Blurring tears complicated the task. Lance was nowhere to be seen in the fields of dark green wheat far below. Tim spiraled lower, searching and searching.

He was about to call the tower again to tell them what had happened when he became conscious of the banging of the loose end of the buckled seat belt on the outside of the cockpit. If he didn't do something about that, *he'd* be up for murder.

He spotted a clear stretch of dirt road. The nearest house was several miles away. Nobody could possibly see him putting the jimmied seatbelt back in order.

As he let down for the landing, he made the call: "Ahhh . . . Enid tower . . . " His voice was quavering badly. "I . . . " He choked up. He couldn't go on for a couple seconds. "Ahh . . . I lost a passenger."

The control-tower operator asked him to repeat, and Tim said, "We were doing aerobatics. He grabbed the stick. Ahh . . . " He had to pause again. "We went negative. Oh, God! He fell out!"

The operator asked him his location, and he gave them an estimate.

"I'm looking for him," Tim said. "I'll circle until someone gets out here."

Instead of circling immediately, he snapped off the radio and landed. First he'd reattach the belt to its mount with the nut and bolt. He'd have to hurry, too, just in case there happened to be a law enforcement officer somewhere nearby already.

He decided that he would tell the police only that Lance had taken the controls and had begun a negative-g maneuver. He reattached the right seatbelt end, and he unfastened the military latch that had held the two straps together, making it seem that Lance hadn't snapped the latch all the way closed.

That deceit wasn't solely for his own benefit. He still had the McLeans and Levengers to worry about. Now that the threat to their lives no longer existed, there was no need for them to bear the shame of anyone knowing about Lance's actions. As he struggled to refine the lie, Tim kept doubling over and groaning in agony.

33

A NEW DILEMMA

"Tim!" Ben exclaimed. "What's new, friend?"

"I'm freaking out. Got to talk to somebody who's not a cop."

"Hold on. I need a second. I'll be right back on."

Tim turned his back to an icy gust of wind. He was using the pay phone in front of a facility at the opposite end of the single runway from Mr. Will's operation. He'd tied down his Stearman in the transient aircraft parking area there, and the sheriff and a deputy had just finished interviewing him.

"What *now*?" Ben demanded, coming back on the phone.

Leaving out how he'd jimmied the seat belt, Tim quickly told him that they'd been doing aerobatics, and Lance had fallen out.

"That's terrible! How's Lisa taking it?"

"I don't know. I haven't talked to her. Actually, there's more."

"Which is . . . "

"Well, I need to tell somebody. So I guess you're it."

"Say it."

"I was threatening him. I trust you'll keep this to yourself."

"Of course. Threatening?"

"Yeah. I figured it out. *He* was the one trying to do me. He and this clown who worked for him. The punk who worked for him was a SCUBA diver. I took him up—Lance, that is— and tried to scare him into admitting it."

"Did he?"

"Admit it?" Tim was stalling. He knew he could trust Ben, but having a second person know what had really happened was making him nervous. "Yeah," he said at last.

The phone was silent for a few seconds before Ben said, "Because of you and Lisa."

"He wanted Lisa because she'd be inheriting a few miles of prime land right next to what he'd be inheriting."

"It's not hard for me to believe that. So I'm sure you told the police. That'll—"

"Actually, not. It would be nothing but my word, and he's got way too much respect around here. I just said we went upside-down and he fell out. Something was wrong with his seatbelt.

"But the main thing is, everyone's safe with him gone now. I'm pretty sure his little helper's gone, too. And even if he isn't, he's got no reason to fool with me anymore."

Tim went on to tell Ben in detail how Lance had yanked on the stick and how he'd reacted. However, just as he'd kept the rest of it from the sheriff and his deputy, he did not tell Ben that he'd jimmied the seat belt. He wished he could, but he wasn't about to. He wouldn't go that far.

When they hung up some time later, Tim took a few deep breaths, dropped another coin into the slot, and dialed the McLeans' number. He'd made up his mind that he'd ask for Ned if Lisa or her mom answered, and if they hadn't heard about the accident yet, he'd tell Ned only that they'd been doing aerobatics when Lance's seat belt came unlatched.

So that was what he did after Mrs. McLean answered. She wanted to engage him in small talk. It hadn't been much more than an hour since Lance had died, and they obviously hadn't heard about it yet. But Tim said he was pushed for time and needed to speak to Mr. McLean right away. Her husband accepted the news quietly, solemnly thanked him, and hung up without attempting any further conversation.

Tim called for a cab, and as soon as he got a motel room, he just sat on the edge of the bed for quite some time, completely lost in thought. Eventually he realized that it had become very dark. The only illumination in the room came from the dim glow of lights outside that entered through a narrow part in the drapes. He had no inclination to turn on the TV, not even if there might be news about Lance. It didn't occur to him that he hadn't eaten. He eventually lay down atop the bedspread, fully clothed and shod, and his mind raced on, replaying the horror over and over, blaming himself for causing an unnecessary death.

He phoned the Levengers the following morning. After a couple minutes' agonized conversation with Lance's dad, Tim impulsively said that he'd be staying for the funeral and just as quickly afterward, wished he hadn't. Now he had mixed feelings about staying: On the one hand, he felt very uneasy about remaining at the scene of a death for which he, however accidentally, was responsible; on the other hand, he yearned to be near Lisa.

His second was to Lisa's dad and lasted somewhat longer. Tim told him a bit more about his new plane and doing aerobatics with Lance. When he was done telling his doctored version of the accident, he refrained from asking to speak to the women, and Ned seemed to share his reluctance by saying without prompting that it would be best if Tim waited another day or so to talk to his wife and Lisa.

Then he phoned his mother. He told her that he had to remain in Oklahoma for a funeral, but he didn't tell her about Lance. However, she had news for *him*: Johnny Crash had called. He'd told her that Tim needed to get back to him as soon as possible. If he didn't answer, Tim was to call a Mr. Garcia at a second number.

At first, Tim wasn't interested. Far too much had just happened for him to be thinking about work. Besides, he felt a need to be with Lisa for a while, to be available to do whatever he could to comfort her. But then he began to wonder, *Would she let me get that close? She sure wasn't friendly at the last in Hawaii!*

Then, too, it wouldn't be easy to hang around for days so near the scene of what had not been purely accidental. Tim couldn't imagine how anyone could ever know for sure about that seatbelt latch, but he felt nervous anyway. He thought how some pilot, constantly reminded of the incident by the sight of that gleaming Stearman parked at the airport, might start spreading the word that a partly-latched seatbelt didn't sound likely at all. And it would be even harder to believe that an experienced pilot such as Lance would just forget to latch it, especially for aerobatics. However slight a chance as there might be, the sheriff might want to have a few more words with him about that.

Now he wanted nothing more than to get away from there. Then, having gone that far in his thoughts, he decided that he didn't want to let the crasher down, either.

Johnny answered, and he said, "Get on down here, Tim. The new boy tore up another airplane."

Tim struggled with a few seconds of reawakened doubt about his decision, but he then said, "I'm in Oklahoma. It might take me a few days." He wasn't going to say a word about the accident. There'd be plenty of time for that later. "Is that okay?"

"We can get by. Just get here quick as you can."

He called for a cab to take him back to the airport, cranked up his Stearman, and took off for California.

* * *

He called the McLeans again from a pay phone right after he landed at the airport in Santa Monica the following afternoon. He had procrastinated too long about calling from a motel along the way the night before. Mrs. McLean answered, and Tim told her about his obligation to answer Johnny Crash's call to Nicaragua, apologizing for not being able to attend the funeral and asking

466

that they tell the Levengers so.

"We understand, Tim. We do appreciate your concern. Let me get Lisa."

A minute later, Lisa quietly said without any evident emotion, "Hi, Tim."

"Hi. Just want you to know I'm thinking of you all." (He'd rehearsed that so that he wouldn't forget the word "all." It wouldn't be appropriate to be more personal so soon, especially since he still didn't know why she'd kept him at such a distance toward the end of her time in Hawaii.)

"Thanks, Tim."

"Johnny Crash needs me right away down in Nicaragua. I wanted to stay for the funeral, but . . . "

"I understand."

Neither said anything more for some moments, but Tim finally ventured, "I'd like to visit you all when I'm back stateside in the spring."

"We'd like that. Ma and Daddy would, even if I weren't here. I need to get away for a while."

He wanted to ask why, but it seemed much too soon to engage her in that sort of conversation. He only asked, "So where now?"

"Nigeria, probably."

"Nigeria?"

"Our church has a mission there. Our conference, actually. Maybe I can do something useful. But mainly I just need to get away."

He couldn't help saying, "Again."

"Yes, again. But I'd better go now. We're going over to the Levengers'. We can stay in touch through my folks."

After she hung up, Tim pondered what she'd said about staying in touch. For a moment, hope flickered that she was suggesting more than friendship at some time in the future. However, on second thought, that didn't seem to make any sense. Lisa McLean wasn't the sort who'd be in love with someone one moment and in love with someone else—or even considering the possibility—a moment later. She had to have been saying nothing more than she was still a friend.

For some reason he didn't pause to wonder about, he had a strong urge to call Ben again. Ben would be at work, but he could probably talk if he wasn't with a customer. Tim would call his mother first so that she could pick him up, then check in with his friend.

When Ben picked up the phone, Tim said, "I'm on my way to Nicaragua tonight."

"Hey, I'm glad you called!

"Thanks. I—"

"Tim! I think I know what she did. I've been thinking."

"Who?"

"Lisa! She did it for *you*."

"What are you talking about?"

"Why she married that creep. She's smart. She had to know he was bad news."

Tim couldn't imagine what his friend was babbling about. His own thought was, *Bad news some ways, but irresistible other ways.*

"It was you she loved," Ben went on, "not that weirdo. She married him to keep you safe. She—"

"Wait! You're saying she did it to keep him from doing me?"

"Exactly."

Tim went all hollow inside. As unlikely as it seemed at first, Tim weighed the possibility. *Considering what she thought before . . .*

He began to weep. He struggled to keep the noises contained and private.

Ben kept silent until Tim's distress subsided. Then he said, "She was ahead of us all. I wonder when she caught on that it was him and that other?"

When you found those pebbles in the gas tank, Tim thought. *Started to, anyway. Even with her other suspicions, it would have been so hard to believe.*

Just as hard as . . . Swiping at a fresh flood of tears, he pondered her passing suspicion—surely it had been temporary—that Lance could have saved her drowning brother. But Lance's charm, that mysterious sociopathic charm, had won her back. At least for a while.

"You still there, Tim?"

"I'm here. What's that line in the Bible? No greater love?"

"I know the one. I can't quote it, but I can paraphrase it: Nobody can have any greater love than to lay down his life—let's say *her* life—for friends."

"Yeah. Something like . . . " He choked up again and couldn't go on.

"You've got it right," Ben said. "A *living* sacrifice."

Some time passed until Tim was able to say, "I doubt she'd admit it."

"Why not?"

"I don't know. I'm not sure what's going on. She hasn't been very communicative."

"Don't let her go, Tim."

* * *

"Lisa?"

"Yes, Tim?" She definitely did not sound happy that he'd called again. Also, she definitely did not sound as sad as Tim would normally expect of someone whose cherished husband had just died.

"Ben says he thinks you knew that Lance might have had something to do with, you know, my problems."

"Tim? I'm in prayer right now. Okay? You can write, and if I'm not here, they'll send it on."

Since she didn't deny it, Tim had to conclude that she had, indeed, married Lance to save him. And she wasn't going to talk about it. Not now, anyway. Stunned, he pressed her no further.

There wasn't much time before his flight would be departing LAX, so he made a quick call to his old friend Nick to tell him that he'd be sure to see him after he returned from Nicaragua, then called Jen.

"Just when I'd started to appreciate the thought of having you around a while again," Jen said in a mock-peevish tone. "Fine friend you are."

"Sorry. I'll be done down there in a couple months and be back. I'll see you then."

"Tim?"

He waited for her to go on.

"Why don't you write?"

"I'll do that."

"I don't suppose you'd change your mind at this point, like stay right here and come up with something safer to do."

"I will pretty soon. I do want to give school another shot."

"That's wonderful!"

"Anyway, gotta run. Mom's putting dinner on the table, and then we need to go. I will write."

* * *

If I hadn't promised, I think I would just can this trip, he reflected as the jet rumbled toward Houston. (There'd be a brief layover there before he continued on to Managua, and another layover before he took a connecting flight to León.) *So much to think about. If Lisa wouldn't have me, could I fall in love with Jen again? Could she fall in love with me? It's weird to even think that way!*

Good thing I'm getting out of here. Way too complicated.

Just make sure your head's fixed real good when the time does come for love again. I wonder if there's shrinks in León? Probably. But good ones? Still, it sure wouldn't hurt to talk to somebody. It just helps to talk it out sometimes. I'd never tell anyone about jimmying that seat belt, but there's so much more to try to get untangled. Not that I'll—

"Can I get you anything?"

The voice startled him. He flinched and stupidly asked, "What?"

"Sorry to disturb you. Can I get you anything? A drink?"

"No. Thanks."

He forgot the intrusion immediately.

It's not like the shrinks are bowling everybody over with success stories. That's what everybody says. Still, it always has clarified things when I've talked things out with anybody.

He smiled faintly and thought, *Good old Nick. Smitty, too. They sure used to get an earful. A lot of times it did make things clear.*

For some reason, his thoughts suddenly flipped back to Lisa: *I wonder if I was in love with her all along? "Man-lady kine," I mean. Just couldn't admit it, trying to be a big hero. Huh, Gawain?*

The fasten-seatbelt alert softly dinged, and the captain announced they were letting down for Houston.

* * *

He snacked on a burger as he waited for the connecting flight to Managua and revisited his thoughts about being in love with Lisa. *Yeah, you just couldn't admit it. Definitely not the O'Reilly way to fall in love with another man's woman.*

He was still ruminating about it after his connecting flight had departed Houston. He kept thinking about that brief flash of passion between him and Lisa back in Honolulu.

So what was that? Was she in love with you? What if she was in love with me all along?

Could she love me even now?

If so, why run off? Decency? Wait a decent length of time?

Wouldn't that be something!

On and on the questioning went as the jet flew southward. He even began to wonder if it would be a good time after Nicaragua to stop flying and get back into school. Lisa would like that. He definitely was in better shape than when he dropped out. He was pretty confident that he was as capable of concentrating on school work now as he had been before 'Nam. If he found a good shrink, he could probably get a much better take on that, too.

That's it! he thought in a burst of great optimism. *I'll do it! No spring flying for me!*

I'll do Nicaragua, but then I'm going to take a few courses, and I will see a shrink. Not anywhere near LA, either! Too confusing! What would I do about Jen? But where? Hawaii? I don't know about that. I mean . . .

The answer didn't occur to him until he was getting off the flight in Managua: *South Africa! They gotta have decent shrinks there. And colleges. And surf and pristine scuba diving!*

For just a few months. And after that? Who knows?

Nigeria? Wonder what they got in Nigeria?

The End

Author receives written comments from readers through Allswell
Publishing Company, AllswellPub@gmail.com.

www.ingramcontent.com/pod-product-compliance
Lightning Source LLC
Chambersburg PA
CBHW030847030726
47495CB00005B/1416